VAMPIRE ARMADA

The Immortal Knight Chronicles Book 7

Richard of Ashbury
and the Spanish Armada
1568 - 1603

DAN DAVIS

Vampire Armada

Copyright © 2019 by Dan Davis

All rights reserved. No part of this book may be used or reproduced in any manner whatsoever without written permission except in the case of brief quotations embodied in critical articles or reviews.

This book is a work of fiction. Names, characters, businesses, organizations, places, events and incidents either are the product of the author's imagination or are used fictitiously. Any resemblance to actual persons, living or dead, events, or locales is entirely coincidental.

For information contact:
dandaviswrites@outlook.com

ISBN: 9781711018430

First Edition: Nov 2019

1

Assassin

1568

THE IMMORTAL was almost in London. I had been tracking him for three days, all the way from Dartmouth on the south coast of England where he had disembarked from a Spanish ship. I did not know it yet but he had come for a single purpose.

To murder Queen Elizabeth.

A few weeks earlier, one of Eva's men had blundered and caused an immortal we were tracking in London to flee. He got away but we found a note hidden in his rooms at an inn. That note said a new agent was coming to England by ship at the end of the month but not where he would land nor where he would go once he arrived. Walter had ridden to Dover, Eva to Tilbury, while Stephen had watched the ports of London.

My duty was to watch Portsmouth for the arrival of the agent. A Spanish ship had come into the harbour and when the dark figure climbed from the ship's boat onto the dock I judged by his gait, his clothing, and his behaviour that he was both an immortal and a killer.

"There's the bastard," I said to Philip beside me at the window.

We had taken a room down at the waterfront with a view of the busy port. The inn was overflowing with raucous mariners, day and night and my men kept trying to slip downstairs for a beer or three. Philip had been my valet for decades and was a dutiful man but the other two were younger and had been soldiers before I turned them and welcomed them into the Order of the White Dagger.

"That one there dressed in black?" Philip asked, pointing a hand out of the open window.

I slapped his hand down. "Move back, Philip. Yes, that one there. Who else? See how he covers himself?"

He was a tall man, walking stooped beneath his black hood with a cloak around him, blinking and wincing at the late summer sun.

"Sure you don't want to nab him now, sir?" Philip asked. "He might get away."

"We follow this rat wherever he goes. He will lead us to the nest and then we shall stamp on the entire infestation. Wake the men."

Black Hood hired a good horse from the stables on the north side of town and set out at once. We had followed him ever since as he approached London.

There are ways to follow a man without him noticing. We four took it in turns to ride ahead to keep watch while the others rode out of sight behind. We swapped horses with each other and regularly changed items of outer clothing. When Black Hood slept at an inn, one of my soldiers slept there also the first night and another the second while the rest of us slept in the woods like vagrants.

Late on the third day, he went into an inn at Epsom, just fifteen miles south of London. I told the men it was my turn to sleep in a bed and watch Black Hood.

But our quarry did not go there for a room. He instead met another man. One also attired in a black cloak and hood who kept to the shadows while they whispered across their table. All I could see of the second man was his oily black hair and the flash of a long nose. My heart raced as I watched them from the other side of the ale room. I suspected that both men were immortals, made by my brother William, and both were here in England for some dark purpose.

I considered striding across the room and striking off their heads before riding away but that would be a bloody and public crime to commit when I had no proof that they were immortals. Besides, I believed they would lead me to even more agents.

Black Hood and the new man soon left the inn.

In two directions.

The new immortal went east and Black Hood north and I rode hard back along the road for my men, finding them building a small fire in the trees in the lee of a low hill.

"Quickly, or they shall both be lost. Digby, Finch, you go east after the new man but do not stop him, do not challenge him, simply track him and do not lose him, understand? Philip, with me. Swiftly, now!"

Racing back to the inn before slowing to a restrained pace and continuing along the road, we found him just before the sun went down.

"He's not going to London," Philip said. "We're too far west. Up this road lies Richmond, does it not? Dear me, sir, you don't reckon he's going for the Queen, do you?"

"God's teeth, he better not be. Come, let us hurry."

Not long after, my horse went lame.

His knee was swollen and hot to the touch. He was old, that leg had been troubling him for a while, and I had ridden him hard but still I cursed my luck for the sudden onset. I tried to continue while he tossed his head, complained bitterly, and stopped altogether but I forced him on and on, his leg growing worse with every step, until he would have it no longer.

"Shall I go on ahead, sir?" Philip asked, hopefully.

"Do not be absurd. Give me your horse. Walk mine back to the inn, see if you can hire another and come after me, quick as you can."

Philip hesitated. "You can trust me, sir, I'll not lose him."

I was in a state of rising panic that the man I followed might be about to murder our queen and so I spoke far more harshly than I would otherwise have done. "Well, I don't trust you, you Protestant fool, so give me your horse and go!"

And then as night began to fall, the heavens opened.

Rain fell in a downpour that turned dusk into night in an instant. Such a deluge that I could hardly see to the end of my horse's nose and I lost the man before we reached Richmond. The road was deserted and I could find no trace of him in the downpour. We were yet far from the Royal Palace and not in the village either. When the wind gusted and the sheets of rain parted for a moment, I caught sight of lights close by through the trees beside the road.

Lightning flashed silently in distant clouds and I recognised beside me the gates of the house of Dr John Dee the renowned astrologer and wizard, who lived at the edge of a village called Mortlake, between Richmond and London. The gates were open.

I knew Dee. He was favoured by the Queen for his astrological abilities and my friend Stephen had consulted with him on several matters, for Dee's knowledge was both deep and wide.

Dee did not know what I was but he was friends with a man who did. That man was Robert Dudley, one of the most powerful noblemen in England. I had saved Dudley's life a few years before at the Battle of St. Quentin on the northeast borders of France. We thrashed the French but Robert's younger brother had been blown to pieces right in front of us. Robert Dudley was no great lord, back then. In fact, he was merely the son of a traitor and he had been stripped of all titles.

Still, I had admired his energy and strength of character and considered offering him a place in the Order, going so far as telling him some of our history and demonstrating my abilities. But then his old friend Elizabeth was crowned Queen of England and Dudley was suddenly restored to his lands and immediately became the royal favourite.

Robert Dudley and Dr Dee were friends. Indeed, Dee had been Dudley's tutor.

It occurred to me as I sat there in the rain looking at Dee's front gates and the house beyond through the trees that there was no coincidence in me losing my quarry outside Dee's Richmond residence.

Was Dee a traitor? It was possible. I had been betrayed so many times, and had seen so many treacherous men, that I could well believe it.

And if Dee was a traitor then what of Dudley? No man in England had better or more intimate access to Elizabeth than he.

My mind whirled with possibilities but it was mere speculation until I caught them. I would take great pleasure in torturing Dudley and Dee before slaying them. Both were cynical men, I thought, warming to the idea as I dismounted at the open gate, and clever, too. Cleverer than me and both quite capable of deceiving me and abusing my goodwill. Too much I had trusted Protestants, that was true and I would do it no more.

Tying up my horse at the stables, I found no groom or servant ready to help, despite there being over a dozen horses crammed under the roof, some steaming from recent exertion. It was too dark for me to tell if Black Hood's horse was amongst them but there were fifteen saddled horses crammed into Dee's small stables and no sign of the riders.

It was a meeting of traitors, I surmised. A full meeting of immortals come to plot at the house of the treacherous Dr Dee. For a moment I was struck by the fear of facing at least fifteen immortals at once and I considered riding to London to rouse Stephen and his agents or going back for Philip and chasing down Digby and Finch to assist me.

But I could not risk my enemies escaping in the meantime and so I went on, towards the front of the house. It was an old building with sagging timbers and crumbling plaster but a large one with two storeys and two wings. Rainwater poured from the corner of the building where a gutter had broken and it spattered violently across the path as I rushed through it to the entrance.

The front door was open.

Only a crack but no servant in his right mind would leave the front door ajar during a storm. Lamplight glowed between the shutters upstairs. Lightning flashed overhead and the rumble came as it faded.

Drawing my sword, I pushed the door open and stepped into the dim entrance hall.

The smell hit me first. Then I saw it. A servant lay dead on the tiles, blood spreading beneath him.

From upstairs, a man roared a challenge and a woman screamed.

I took the steps three at a time and had reached the landing when I heard a pistol discharge from a nearby room and moments later another one. I launched myself along the upstairs landing and through the open door into a chamber.

The assassin was bent double as I entered, with his back to me.

In the chamber was Dee in his grey robes and ash-blond beard quivering. Near him stood Robert Dudley, with a pair of smoking wheellock pistols in his hands.

There were servants in the room, cringing away from the violence.

What did very much take my attention was the other occupant in the room. Behind Dudley, with a look of indignation upon her face, there she stood.

Queen Elizabeth.

She was in her early thirties and had been queen for a few years. I had seen her at a distance many times and knew her at a glance.

I was stunned to see her there in Dee's parlour.

Black Hood was hooded no longer. His cloak and hood lay discarded upon the floor. Instead, he wore a close-fitting doublet with belts across his chest holding four pistols and he held two more, one in each hand.

I saw all this clearly as the assassin stood and turned to me, his swarthy face twisted in anger. One of Dudley's pistol shots had hit him in the side of the neck and a shredded flap of skin there suddenly gushed forth with blood. The second shot had taken him in the chest and the wound there was soaking his doublet.

And then he shot me.

I had caused a ruckus flying up the stairs but still his reactions and accuracy were most impressive.

He discharged both pistols at me in the same instant. I flinched as he fired them so that one shot buried itself in my shoulder while the other hit me in the flank. I hit the doorframe and cried out in surprise and in agony, the injury causing me to drop my sword. How I despised firearms.

But the Queen's life was in danger and I forced myself into action.

The assassin tossed his used pistols down and drew out two more from his belts. Dudley likewise dropped his pistols, whipped out his sword and thrust his blade into the assassin's chest.

A fine thrust.

Unfortunately, it did nothing to stop the man.

Instead, the assassin smacked Dudley on the side of the head with one pistol, sending him sprawling as he aimed the other at the queen's bosom.

She did not flinch, as I had.

Elizabeth stared at her assassin with fire in her eyes, as if daring him to try it.

For all her bravado, however, she would certainly have been killed had I not been there.

Charging from the doorway, I knocked him aside with such force that he flew across the room, knocking over a table covered with glass vials and books. Before he had even finished falling, he managed to shoot me again. One shot hit the ceiling while the other ripped into my chest.

I was on him before he could recover, kicking him in the face and punching him down. It would have killed a mortal man but he was tough, even for an immortal and he kicked upward from his back, knocking me down.

Dudley rushed in to help as the assassin got up but was tossed across the room as though he weighed no more than a child. He struck the sideboard, sending glass vials, alchemical ingredients and mechanical devices crashing to the floor.

I came up at the assassin again in two strides but he ignored me. Even in the moment when he was close to failure, he almost succeeded. Drawing a small blade from his sleeve, he tossed it with an expert flick of the wrist at the Queen. I made a grab for the knife, convinced I could snatch it out of the air. It slipped into the flesh of my palm and buried itself up to what slender hilt it had so that all three inches of the blade stuck out the back of my hand.

Wrapping my arms around him, I threw him to the floor and rained punches onto his face until it was a bloody mess. I ripped the blade from my palm and used it to stab him in the chest twice, puncturing a lung. He collapsed, his strength finally leaving him. But he was not dead and was therefore still dangerous.

"Bring me rope, Doctor Dee," I said, glancing over my shoulder at the stunned faces. "John!" I snapped at him. "I must have rope to bind him."

Dee muttered to his servant who hunched quivering in the corner of the room. Behind me, I heard the Queen's ladies attempting to draw her from the room. Dudley, dazed and clutching his head, got to his feet and promptly fell over. As he got up again he too mumbled that she must return to the palace.

Dee's servant, a hunchback, came back surprisingly quickly with a coil of damp rope and I bound the assassin's hands behind his back and roped them to his ankles while the Queen argued.

"Where are my soldiers, Robert?" the Queen asked. Her powerful voice was remarkably steady. "Are not my soldiers supposed to stop assassins from reaching me?"

"They may be dead," he said, holding on to the sideboard with one hand and the side of his head with the other.

"Are there other assassins, Robert?" she asked.

"There may well be, my lady," he replied. "And so we must flee at once."

"And what if these assassins are outside, waiting for that very thing?" the Queen said. "Bring the soldiers in here and they shall escort me."

"I believe it is just this one," I said, holding the dazed and dying assassin in place. "But that is a wise course of action."

"Be silent, Richard," Dudley snapped.

"You know this man?" the Queen said, surprised. "He is one of yours?"

"Yes," Dudley said.

I scoffed and coughed up a mouthful of blood.

"But he is gravely injured, Robert. He saved our life. You must aid him, immediately."

"I am well, Your Majesty," I said as I stood and bowed but as I did so I felt my legs give out. I had been shot three times and two of those were in the chest. Rather terrible wounds, even for me. When I came to my senses a few moments later, Dee and his hunchback were propping me up, opening my doublet and cutting away at my undershirt to see my blood-soaked skin.

I was sitting upon the floor with my back resting against a chest. There was an ornate carpet covering it that smelled of dust.

"You are gravely wounded, Richard," Dee said, his face inches from mine as he prodded the bleeding wounds. "I fear you do not have long for this world. You must spend your last moments praying with me."

I slapped his hands away.

"All I need is a cup of blood, John," I muttered and looked up. Dudley and the Queen of England were peering down at me. It hurt to breathe but I forced myself to speak carefully while taking shallow breaths. "Robert? Can you fetch me a cup of blood?"

"What is this?" the Queen asked. "He calls you John and he calls you Robert. Does everyone in England but its queen know this man?"

"I do, somewhat," Dee said. "He serves Stephen Poole, the London merchant who is my friend."

I grunted and looked for Dudley. His face was a mask of anguish.

11

"Robert," I muttered. "You know what I need." I coughed blood again into my hand and looked down at myself. I was drenched in blood from chest to hosen.

"You may have what you require after Her Majesty and I have gone." Dudley nodded to his valet. "Go and bring the captain and his soldiers here. Or any soldiers you can find. Hurry, man! We must be away."

I shook my head and struggled to my feet. "If you will not give me blood, I will make my way home. My true friends I can trust, Robert."

"How dare you," Dudley said. "My only concern is the Queen's safety and she needs to know none of your devilry, your sorcery. Come, Elizabeth, we shall meet your soldiers down the stairs."

She turned on him, then, shaking off his hand. "Robert, will you cease your prattling. I am not some frail and witless country maiden who must be coddled. I command here, do I not? Well then, it is my command that I stay here until I am satisfied. What is it that this injured man needs? Did I hear him ask for *blood*? And how is it that you stand when you are so gravely wounded? What does this mean?" She glared at the men and women around her.

Dee frowned. "I know nothing of this, Your Majesty."

All looked at Dudley, who glared back. "It is nothing that any of us need know or see."

The Queen looked at me, then, at my face and at my bared chest and stomach and at my sodden loins. "And are you so injured, dear saviour, that you cannot yourself explain to me your want?"

Her brown eyes were wrinkled with concern and compassion. She had a long, rather narrow face and a pointed chin. Her hair was red and framed her face like the halo of an autumn sunset. It was said that she was no beauty and I suppose that was true but her features were attractive enough for any man. More than that, though, when she was animated she was filled with something indefinable that made her come alive with the beauty of her person. The knowing arch of her brow, the twinkling of her dark eyes, the twitch at the corner of her lips could stir a man's loins who was fixed by such a glance. Believe me, I know. And her voice was sweet and clear but with an earthy depth that most women achieve only in the deepest throes of passion. Her voice bathed me in its golden depths.

Dee shook my arm. "Answer your Queen."

"Blood," I said, looking right at her. "I shall be healed in moments if I drink a cup of blood. Human blood."

Dudley had a hand over his eyes. The Queen frowned and her lip curled. Dee tilted his face the picture of curious enquiry.

"I have heard talk of such men," Dee muttered, nodding. "I had dismissed that talk as mere rumour."

"Please," I said to Dee, holding on to him so that I could stand. "Bleed a servant." I nodded to the young man with the crooked back who turned his face away from me in the corner. "That one will do, your valet. Or anybody."

Dee turned to Dudley. "You knew about this, Robert? Can it be true?"

Dudley glanced at his queen, whose look back at him held by far the greater authority. He sighed. "I have witnessed just such a healing, that much is true."

"Will any blood do?" Dee asked.

"Any," I admitted. "But younger is better. Stronger is better."

"But you will take mine?" he asked.

I would rather have a warrior's, I thought. Or a queen's.

"Yes," I said.

"Bring me the physician's bag, Boote," Dee commanded his servant. "Be sure it is the one with the lancets."

"And a cup," I said to him.

"Oh yes, and a cup also, Boote."

At the sound of voices and footsteps, Dudley crossed the door with his sword in hand and went out to the stairway. "Where were you?" he cried. "I shall see all you men punished for your incompetence and if it be treachery you all shall hang!" Dudley came back. "Elizabeth, we must go. *Please.*"

The Queen looked at him. "My soldiers will guard me from there." She turned to me. "And I will witness this sorcery."

Across the room, the assassin writhed in his bonds.

"Watch him, Robert," I said, my vision clouding. "Keep your eye on the criminal."

Though I could not see it, I could hear the shrug in Dudley's voice. "He is well trussed, Richard, and bleeding to death."

"Watch him, you fool!" I snapped. "Surely you know he is another like me?"

Dudley drew his sword. "I shall strike his head from his body."

"No!" I growled. "He must be made to answer questions. One most of all. *Who sent him?*"

The Queen nodded at me. "Quite right. Robert, you shall not behead that man. Not until he has been thoroughly investigated."

Dudley glared at me as he paced back and forth across the

room. He was almost six feet tall, in the prime of his life in his middle thirties, and he was a remarkably handsome fellow. The hair under his hat was a reddish shade of brown, as were his beard and moustache. He was blessed with every fine feature a man could wish for, from his aristocratic nose and shrewd eyes to his slender fingers and long, shapely legs. He had worn nothing but the most extravagant and fashionable clothes even when he was in disgrace in his youth.

He was a proper gentleman. He danced and sang but also he jousted well and excelled at the absurd court game called tennis. Dee had taught him the secrets of mathematics, geometry, astronomy, cartography and navigation, he had studied the masters of Greece and Rome and spoke French and Italian almost as well as I did.

A talented former noble would have been a fine addition to the Order of the White Dagger, or so I had believed. But I was almost glad when his circumstances changed. There was a darkness to Dudley. A pettiness and jealousy that seethed always beneath the surface. He had almost everything a man could wish for, from his looks to his abilities and his wealth. But it was never enough. He wanted more money, always more. He wanted all women to love him, which many did, and he wanted all men to fear and respect him, which many did not.

And most of all, these days, he wanted to be king. Everyone in England knew he wanted to marry Elizabeth and she claimed to want it also while always delaying. He pretended that he could wait for eternity for her to come to her decision and that he wanted only what was best for her and for the kingdom, it was clear that he seethed with anger about it.

"Keep away from him, Elizabeth," Dudley said, referring to me. "He is dangerous."

She did not stand upright, nor did she take her eyes from mine. "Is he, indeed? How so?"

"I am dangerous," I said. "To the Queen's enemies." I smiled at her, with blood in my mouth, and she smiled back, glancing down at me again.

Dudley sighed and stopped pacing before me. "He is cursed. He is unholy. A demon in human form."

"He is?" the Queen said, raising an eyebrow. "And yet he is a friend of yours?"

"To my eternal shame," Dudley muttered.

"I kept my lord Robert alive in battle," I said. "When he was a young man."

"When he was young?" The Queen frowned, looking closely at my face. "Then you must have been a child."

Dudley scoffed loudly just as Dee's servant scuttled in with a leather bag and a cup. Dee whipped back the loose sleeve of his robe and sliced carefully but without hesitation into himself, whereupon his blood spurted out into the cup.

"You do not need to witness this vile thing," Dudley muttered.

"Have you witnessed it before now?" the Queen asked.

"It was unpleasant then and it shall be so again here," he replied. "I would not want you to see."

"It is rather clear that is what you want. However, what I want and what I will have is to stay and see with my own eyes this vile thing."

Dee passed me the cup. "Is this enough, Richard?"

I took it and drank it down. Warm and delightful, it slid down my throat and into my stomach where the strength of it flowed into my body and into my limbs. I felt the warmth of it on my skin and on my wounds.

From being narrowed and apprehensive a moment before, Dee's eyes widened as he saw my wounds begin to stitch themselves together.

"A pen, Boote!" he cried to his servant. "Ink, paper, parchment, anything. Hurry, man!"

I laid a hand on Dee's bare forearm. "No, John. I am sorry, you cannot."

"This is a marvel, Richard. A wonder. It must be recorded."

"None can know about this."

"None shall know. None but me and the walls of my study. This is a phenomenon never before recorded, as far as I am aware."

I sighed. "There are references to us in many texts, sir. I am told hints can be found in Pliny and Aristotle."

"No!" Dee breathed. "What hints?"

"Not my area of expertise. You must speak to Stephen."

"Stephen... Stephen Poole knows about this? Do not tell me he is one of you also! How many of you are there?"

"Never mind all that!" Dudley snapped. "We must leave, Elizabeth. I shall have my men bring this creature to the Tower."

I got to my feet. "No, Robert."

He turned on me. "No? No? You do not get to tell me no, Richard. Who are you? You are nobody! A bloody soldier, nothing more. You do as I command, not the other way around."

I grabbed Dee's wild-eyed crooked servant. "Listen, man. Boote, is it? Do you know the house of the merchant Stephen

Poole?"

He would not meet my eye. "Yes, sir. It's that new road, off the Strand."

"Good man. You go there now, quick as you like, and you rouse him up no matter what and you tell him a message from me, Richard Ashbury, do you hear? Richard says come at once to Dee's house at Mortlake. Richard has captured the object of our pursuit and he must be borne forthwith to Stephen's house. Then you wait there and return with him and the cart. Do you understand? Repeat the message." He did so and I sent him on his way.

"This is not a matter for you and your little band, Richard," Dudley said. "This man tried to kill the Queen. It is a civil matter."

"He would have killed the Queen." I bowed to her. "Begging your pardon, my lady, and it breaks my heart to speak the words, nay even to think them, but it is true. You would have saved her life, Robert, had he been mortal. You shot him well and skewered him to boot but it was not enough. And where he has come from, there may be more. Indeed, there *shall* be more. Only my little band is capable of dealing with this and so that is what we shall do."

I had gone too far. Not with Dudley, for at heart he did not think enough of himself to stand up to me. Elizabeth, on the other hand, knew for certain that there was not a soul on earth who stood above her, in any measure.

"How dare you," she snapped. "Your impudence knows no bounds. How dare you speak to my lord Robert in such a manner. I am disturbed, greatly disturbed. I was nearly murdered this night, not an hour before now, but what disturbs me most of all is not the assassin's bullet. What disturbs me, sirs, is to find a great conspiracy at the heart of my kingdom. I find my beloved friends are keeping secret from me that there exists this sorcery in my kingdom. Did you know that there were creatures such as these with designs on my life, Robert?"

"No, my lady." He bowed his head.

"Did you?" she demanded again.

"I did not. I swear it. I knew of Richard and that there are a handful of others but I did not know they meant to harm you."

"Does Cecil know?"

"Not from me." Dudley was growing ever surlier.

"You there," she said to me. "Is William Cecil one of your friends also?"

"I do not know him," I replied.

"Walsingham?" she asked.

I bowed. "A little. My companions on occasion send information to him that aids in his work in defending England and its queen from all enemies."

She threw up her hands. "Who can I trust, if not my closest friends? What else are you keeping from me, Robert?"

"Perhaps we should discuss it when you are safely returned to—"

I cut him off, drawing another scowl. "This is a battle that has been waged since long before you were born," I said to the Queen. "Any of you. With my friends, I have been keeping this kingdom safe for centuries."

Dudley scoffed while Dee began scratching at the parchment he now held in his hand.

"Centuries?" the Queen said. "What on earth do you mean?"

I smiled at her. "When your father was a young man, I saved his life from an assassin like this one here."

"When he was a... how could that be possible?"

"How, I do not know. But it is the truth."

Elizabeth took half a step forward. "You knew King Henry?"

"Ah, I am afraid I did not have the pleasure of his acquaintance. I only met him briefly and alas we did not engage in very much conversation. But save him I did."

"So you say," Dudley scoffed. "You could say anything. Come, my lady, please. The hour grows too late. You shall be missed."

"Very well." She lifted her chin. "I find the air grows foul in here anyway. Let us return."

I bowed at them as they began to waft by me but Elizabeth stopped before me. She was tall. Very tall for a woman.

"You will come to me tomorrow, first thing in the morning."

I bowed again. "Certainly, Your Majesty."

With that, she was gone down the stairs to her soldiers who escorted her out into the night and away to her barge on the Thames.

Dee looked at the unconscious assassin. "He is another creature like you?"

"More or less. But where I fight for this kingdom, he has another purpose. Chaos, evil, and destruction."

"May I examine him?" he asked, his eyes full of hope.

"No. But I shall," I said, clapping the astrologer on the back but looking into the assassin's wild eyes as he breathed heavily in a pool of blood on the floor. "I shall pull out his entrails and cut him to pieces until he tells me where to find his friends, his contacts, and his master."

2

Elizabeth

1568

I ARRIVED AT THE PALACE of Whitehall in the morning as instructed but I was kept waiting for hours. While I waited, I was ignored.

After midday, Robert Dudley came marching toward me with his retinue clattering down the hall behind him.

"Come with me," he commanded, snapping his fingers and marching on without breaking stride.

Following his men through the palace at a distance, we came at last to the stables. The grooms rushed about preparing horses while Dudley stood impatiently, scowling at everyone who approached.

Dudley had been the Master of Horse since the Queen's coronation and it was a position of great honour and no small influence. While the Queen's ladies would dress her and attend her all day, every day, the man who held the position of Master of Horse would have as much access to the royal person as any man could have. It was a mark of his importance to her and therefore of his importance to the kingdom.

I was in my very best clothing which was enormously expensive without being overly ostentatious. There was a little embroidery on my doublet but no gold or silver anywhere. And yet it had been fashioned some years before and as I cast my eye over the men in Dudley's retinue, I noted that they were all wearing clothing of a rather different style. In fact, I saw a group of four men whispering and giggling like maids while they looked me up and down. Whispering and giggling, that is, until I looked hard at them.

I approached Dudley. "Are we going for a ride, my lord?"

He turned his gaze on me. "Are you loyal, Richard? Truly loyal?"

"You know that I am, my lord."

"Do I?" he asked, glancing over my shoulder to look at the sky.

I wondered if he was seeing that cannonball again, the one that had come screaming out of the blue to dismember, behead and eviscerate his sweet brother on a battlefield in Picardy ten years before. I did not need to remind Dudley that I had saved his life that day and saved it more than once. If he did not remember, then he would never have given me so much leeway already.

"All I do is for this kingdom, my lord," I said.

His voice was low and gruff. "But how can we know it, Richard? How can we trust a man who is not a man?"

"I am a man."

"A corrupted man, perhaps. A twisted one."

I would not waste my breath in arguing the point. "Then trust me by my actions, my lord. I thought we were friends?"

"Your actions in revealing yourself to the Queen, you mean? If we were friends, you would have taken my side and helped me remove her from Dee's parlour before she witnessed your bloody sorcery. And now look where we are."

"Robert, if it means we can be friends again, and it means you trust me once more, then I apologise for offending you."

He pressed his lips together while glaring at me. "Trust must be earned, Richard. A man must have the utmost faith in his friends or they are not friends at all. Now, tell me the truth. Do you, a devilish follower of the old religion, have faith in me, your lord and follower of the true religion?"

I opened my mouth but could think of no answer.

Dudley scoffed. "Precisely."

I sighed. "You ask me to have blind faith in a man who is revolted by what I am."

"Not blind!" he snapped. "Not blind faith but trust. We are both Englishmen, are we not? And we both want what is best for the Queen and for England? I am not some snivelling youth, Richard, yet that is how you still see me, I know it."

I saw him as a man whose self-regard was greater than his ability. A man filled with righteous Protestantism, a religion than I found abhorrent and I did not think he could keep either the Queen or England safe.

"Robert, I see you as the Earl of Leicester and as the Master of Horse and I have no wish to fall out with you."

He scoffed, shaking his head.

When the Queen suddenly emerged from across the

courtyard, Dudley turned on his charm and drifted toward her. It was like a light being lit in a dark room. Suddenly, all his sullen followers were likewise grinning and standing straighter and Dudley's voice was loud and melodious. The Queen did not glance in my direction as she mounted and rode away. She rode side-saddle, of course, but she rode as swiftly and gracefully as a man.

We were a great party of almost sixty people. I had only ever been at the periphery of her court and did not recognise any but a handful of her courtiers. None of them knew what to make of me so they ignored me entirely. We rode out into the grounds of the palace, past the fine bowling green, then by the cock pit, and on by the tiltyard where the men of the court practised and competed in jousting. All the sporting areas were quiet and unoccupied and on we went into the park that stretched away in all directions. Whitehall was the largest palace in England, possibly in Europe for all I knew, and the grounds were enormous.

"The Queen wishes to speak with you," Dudley said, riding back to tell me himself. "Whatever passes between you, I shall know of it, do you understand?"

Whether he meant he expected me to tell him or if he was hinting that the Queen tells him everything, I did not know. Perhaps he meant that he had spies in the Queen's entourage and so every word spoken in her presence was relayed to him whether he was there or not.

"I understand perfectly, my lord."

He glowered, suspecting sarcasm. They were surrounded with it at that court, so it is no wonder.

I stared back, smiling and cantered up to where the Queen

rode. She sat well in her women's saddle with its lopsided pommel hidden beneath her skirts. She wore a dark red coif tied over a close-fitting green cap and I could not see much of her face.

"Your grace," I said as I fell in beside her and matched her pace.

"You ride remarkably well," she said without looking at me. That meant she had been watching me before I had approached.

"I was just thinking the very same thing about you, my lady," I said.

She looked at me then, turning with a smile in her eyes. "I spoke no flatter, sir. You ride as though you were born in the saddle. I take it you have had long to practice?"

"It is my profession."

"Your profession? What is your profession, sir? You are a huntsman, perhaps?"

I smiled. "In a manner of speaking. All my life, I have been a knight, my lady."

Her eyes grew wider. "A knight? But who knighted you?"

"His name was Earl Robert de Ferrers." I did not add that he was my father.

"An earl... but when was this?"

I thought for a moment. "It has been so long. I believe it was the year of our Lord eleven hundred and ninety. I won a melee against many a veteran knight and soon after we went to put down a little band of Welsh rebels raiding across the border. It was not much to be knighted over but knighted I was."

In fact, it was not for many years, even after I discovered that Earl Robert was my true father, that I realised he had only knighted me because of that fact. It might have caused me to question if I deserved the honour of knighthood but I had already saved the life of Richard the Lionheart by that point and if I had not been a knight by then he would surely have made me one.

The queen eyed me. "Do you truly expect me to believe such a thing?"

"It is rather incredible and yet it is also the truth."

"Do you take me for a fool?"

"Quite the opposite."

"My lord Robert tells me that I should not trust you."

"He tells me trust must be earned," I observed, flatly. "When a few hours ago I saved my queen's life."

She glanced sharply in my direction. "You do not think much of my Robert?"

I left the briefest of pauses. "I am certain that you know him better than I do, my lady."

I saw a flicker of amusement in the corner of her eye. "So you say he is wrong when he warns me not to trust you?"

"Trust me with what?" I asked, innocently.

She did not smile. "Trust you with questioning the assassin from yesterday, for one thing. He says I should claim him so that he can question the beast. After all, how can we know what the assassin will say?"

"I believe my friend Stephen Poole has asked Francis Walsingham to attend the questioning of the assassin today and, indeed, to lead it, if he so wishes. And Francis is utterly devoted to you, of course."

"I see," she said, clearly approving of that decision. "But how can we trust anything that you say when there is so much we do not know about you and your friends?"

"What would you care to know?"

She turned her big brown eyes on me. "I would care to know about you, sir."

"I will tell you everything," I said to her, meaning it as I spoke, utterly and willingly seduced by her gaze. "I will tell you everything about me and the things I have done in my life."

Elizabeth smiled and spoke before riding ahead and leaving me behind. "Then that is what you shall do. We shall begin when you return tomorrow, Sir Knight."

Thirty years earlier, we had used our funds to construct a new house for the Order of the White Dagger just off the Strand, the road between London and Westminster. The Strand was lined with the houses and palaces of the richest lords in England and when a new road had been built off from it at the London end we had quickly purchased the largest lot. It was pleasing to be beyond the filth and stench of London and still close enough to obtain all the benefits of it.

Stephen had wanted to build the most ostentatious house in England but Eva had burned the plans before any money was exchanged, much to Stephen's chagrin. So the house was grand but not more than the home of other wealthy merchants and the interior was conservatively decorated, though Stephen had continued to quietly purchase paintings to hang on the walls, as they did in Antwerp and Amsterdam.

When I arrived at the house that evening, I found yet another new piece in the entrance hall by the stairs. It was a small portrait of Stephen in fine black clothes with a small ship over his shoulder and his hand on a map, his finger touching the coast of Flanders, which is where much of his business went. I shook my head as I took it all in. Even in the painting, Stephen looked embarrassed.

"It is expected these days," he said when he came in. Even before I could chide him. Before I could even give him a look. He knew me well.

"Stephen..." I said. "You have adopted yet another Protestant affectation. How long before you convert to the new faith?"

"You can save your condescension," he said, sniffing. "And anyway, you have a man to torture."

"Have Digby and Finch returned yet?" I asked.

He hung his head. "Either they have abandoned us and gone rogue or the immortal they were following killed them both."

I ran a hand over my face. "I told them to stay back. To keep out of sight. Not to engage."

"Perhaps they had no choice."

I shook my head. "These Englishmen these days, Stephen, I swear they have no discipline. It is as though they cannot control themselves."

"Since when have soldiers been able to control themselves?"

"I tell you they are not the same as they used to be. Damn Digby and Finch. If they ever turn up, I will kill them myself, I swear it."

"Perhaps they follow him still?"

I shook my head, sighing. "We should assume they are dead." I felt guilty and I felt foolish for letting them go. Thank God Philip was well. "Anyhow, come on, let us get to business. Is your friend here?" I asked as we made our way through the house.

"Walsingham?" he asked. "He is, why do you ask?"

"I wanted to ask you about Dudley."

Stephen frowned. "There is a problem?"

"He appears to be rather troubled by all this coming into the open and I agree with him. It is a strange situation that we find ourselves in. For so long we have toiled to keep the truth about us hidden but now I find that the Queen knows, Walsingham and Dee know. And so William Cecil will know also."

"If it goes badly, we may find ourselves exposed by this. An armed mob at our doors. Soldiers, even."

"The worst that could happen is we have to flee for a decade or two until everyone dies of old age."

Stephen placed a hand over his eyes for a moment. "It is your fault for being so open with Dudley back in France."

"He would have made a fine member of the Order!" I protested. "He was a gifted man and was also in despair and lacked purpose. The son of a traitor, his lands lost, and looking for a grand quest. Perfect for us."

"This is why you should always speak to me about such things first. Or Eva. We could have told you he was close to Elizabeth and that she might—"

"Yes, yes, save your damned lectures. Anyway, Dudley has held his tongue all these years and all would have been well had the Queen and Dee not witnessed my wounds and my recovery."

Stephen narrowed his eyes. "And I have no doubt you wished to flaunt your gifts before the Queen."

"Nonsense. Anyway, she is intrigued by us. We must be sure to embrace this opportunity, use our influence to steer these powerful people. I will manage the Queen and Dudley, you must manage Walsingham and Dee. With the power of the Crown and the Privy Council behind us, we could find William and his agents in no time. If only Dudley was not so set against us."

"What has he done?"

I shook my head. "We might have been friends. He was so intrigued by us, Stephen, you should have seen him when he was young. But now he is warning the Queen about us. And I know that the Queen trusts him."

Stephen shrugged. "She loves him. They have been friends, companions, since childhood."

"And lovers, so they say."

He shrugged again. "Oh, I don't know about that. It is possible but would she really give up her virginity so cheaply? It is her most precious asset. On the other hand, Dudley is handsome and charming. There cannot be many young women in the kingdom who would resist his advances and the Queen has blood in her veins as much as any of us."

I raised my eyebrows. "You fancy this man for yourself, do you?"

He frowned. "What happened with the Queen today?"

"I think she likes me."

"Oh, dear God."

"I must tread carefully, Stephen."

"You can say that again."

"I will need to outwit her."

He stared at me. "You will not be able to do that."

"You think me witless, Stephen?"

"Her virginity may be her most precious asset," Stephen said, shaking his head, "but it is far from her only one. From the age of six she was educated like a prince. She was tutored especially well under the supervision of old Queen Katherine who engaged William Grindal and Roger Ascham."

"Am I supposed to know those men?"

Stephen sniffed. "They are scholars rather than soldiers so I very much doubt it, though Ascham was also a tutor to your friend Dudley. He is a Cambridge man and a humanist, dedicated to the classics in Greek and Latin and also to the education of women."

I scoffed but Stephen continued.

"He and his fellows are also converts to the reformed faith."

"Oh, for God's sake. The Queen is surrounded entirely by Protestants and has been her whole life. Imagine the horrors they inflicted on her impressionable young mind."

He pursed his lips. "The point is, Richard, that her mind by all accounts is remarkably acute and she has a faultless memory. A few years ago, I intercepted a letter by Ascham who said in it that he had never known a woman with a quicker apprehension or a more retentive memory."

"That's because the only women Cambridge scholars know are tuppeny prostitutes."

Ignoring me, Stephen ploughed on. "Elizabeth's mind appears to be free from all female weakness, Ascham wrote, and she is endued with a masculine power of application. She can discourse intelligently on any intellectual subject and that is a fact I have had confirmed. She can read and speak Latin, Greek, French, of course, but also Spanish, Italian and even Welsh. She has studied the New Testament in Greek, and also the orations of Isocrates, and the tragedies of the great Athenian playwright Sophocles, as well as—"

"My God," I said, stopping to point at Stephen. "You are in love with her."

"Do not be absurd," Stephen said, waving a hand between us. His dismissive tone was rather undermined by his flushed cheeks. "But certainly she would enjoy the level of discourse I can engage in."

"Sounds like she enjoys Dudley's shapely thighs more than she ever will your brilliant mind."

"My point is that you must not attempt to be clever with her. You will not succeed."

"She may be a queen," I said. "But she is still a woman. And I am not one to be outwitted by a woman."

He scoffed, openly, right in my face. "What about Eva?"

I frowned. "Come on, take me to Walsingham and our guest."

We descended into the cellar and opened the door into our secure gaol. When building the house we had been sure to construct extensive underground rooms where we might have absolute safety and security. We had built a row of goal cells, each cell walled with stone and oak doors with iron reinforcement strong enough to resist even the strongest immortal.

Outside the cells was an area for a gaoler to make himself comfortable. Since we now had a prisoner, we also had a gaoler sitting at the small table outside the row of cells. His name was John Leeche, a decrepit immortal servant of Eva's, and he pulled himself to his feet and bowed as we came down the stairs. Dragging himself to the cell that held the assassin, he opened the door and stepped back.

Francis Walsingham was inside with two of his men, one

looked like a clerk sitting at the table at the side of the room with his master and the other was a burly sort standing at the rear.

The prisoner sat tied to a sturdy chair in the centre of the cell, glaring at me, with a gag tied hard around his mouth. I gave him a wink and his face twisted in hatred.

"How do you fare?" Stephen asked as we came in.

Walsingham stood and bowed. "I can get nothing from the man."

Francis Walsingham was in his mid-thirties, of the same generation as the Queen and Dudley. Educated at Cambridge, Gray's Inn and Padua, he was also the Member of Parliament for Lyme Regis down in Dorset. He was utterly loyal to Elizabeth's chief minister, William Cecil. And because Walsingham was loyal and diligent as well as clever, Cecil had recently been tasking Walsingham with uncovering plots against the Queen.

Almost from the start, we had helped him.

Rather, Stephen had. His and Eva's networks of spies and agents had helped gather information but also Stephen had advised Walsingham of the methods he might use to manage this great network. Methods we had first learned from the Mongols in the East and since cultivated and developed.

Walsingham always wore sombre black clothing, like the Puritan he was. That was the insulting term we used for those English Protestants who complained that the new religion did not go far enough. The new Church of England may have been Protestant in doctrine but it retained many of the structures of the old, proper Catholic Church and some men, like Walsingham and Cecil, wanted it to be reformed again. Some even wanted us to have no priests. All of them were miserable pedants and the fact that they had taken control of the Privy Council and directed English policy was tremendously concerning.

But Walsingham was tolerable, despite his extremism. He was a doleful but disciplined man who spoke many languages and was a skilful diplomat with a wide knowledge of international politics that he enjoyed discussing at length with Stephen, given half the chance.

I stepped up to the assassin and peered at his face while he glared at me. It had a little dried blood on it but they had washed the worst off him last night.

"Spanish, is he?" I asked.

"He smells like one," Walsingham said. "And looks like one, also. But most tellingly of all, the fool left a note in his belongings, containing directions from the port to an inn in Epsom. A note written in Spanish."

Like many Puritans, Walsingham also had a loathing for Catholic Spain which I did not share in the least. I had always loved Spaniards. Still, it motivated him to do his work and do it well.

But torture was not his work and nothing else would serve with our prisoner.

"We could always take off his skin," I said in Spanish. The prisoner jolted and squirmed. "Why are you struggling? Certainly you understand you will be spending the rest of your life in agony before we eventually cut off your head?"

He stopped fighting and glared at me.

Stephen spoke up from the doorway, also speaking Spanish. "We have informed him that we will drive him mad with the blood sickness to get him to speak and that he would save himself pain and indignity if he does so first. He appeared to find it amusing."

"Oh," I said. "I am sure he does. But you do not like the thought of being flayed, do you? Of course, no one does. But in your case you will survive for days. Usually we remove the skin from the hands and feet and also the face, if necessary. What was our previous greatest achievement in this regard, Stephen, was it six days the poor man lived?"

"Eight," he replied.

We were lying and would not have flayed a prisoner in this manner. But the man chewed hard on his gag and shook as I spoke.

"Eight days, that is right. I have never seen someone suffer so long and so deeply. Not in all my centuries." He snapped his eyes to mine. "Yes, centuries. I am as old as your master and just as powerful. You will tell us what you know. You are already feeling the hunger, are you not? I can see it in the red of your eyes and the sweat upon your brow. For how many days have you ever gone without drinking?"

I nodded to Leeche. "Remove his gag."

Leeche shuffled forward and cut it off with his knife.

The assassin tried to spit but his mouth was too dry. "My life means nothing," he said.

"It speaks," I said to Stephen and Walsingham. "I wonder what else it will say."

"Nothing." He spat at me but it dribbled uselessly down his chin. "I do not fear death. I go to God. You heretics will go to Hell."

"Ah," I said. "He is a theologian, Stephen. No doubt you and

Francis would prefer to discuss the topic of eternal damnation with him. I am going back upstairs to drink a pint of fresh virgin's blood and, I pray, a delicious hot pie."

Stephen followed me into the chamber outside the cell. "How do you do that? Get them to talk just like that? I do the same things you do but it had no effect."

"Oh, I do not know. It is always different. Likely that the blood sickness is working its way through him, making him weak at the knees. Question him now, at length, but then give him plenty of time alone with his thoughts and his hunger before resuming."

Stephen nodded. "I know you don't trust Protestants but Francis is a diligent and relentless questioner. Leave it to us."

I nodded and made my way up to the entrance hall where I found Eva coming in from the yard. She was wearing men's clothing and her netherstocks and shoes were covered in mud, right up to the top of her hose.

"Richard," Eva said. "I heard screams from the cellar and so I knew you had returned."

I smiled because there had been no screams at all. "Only to bask in the brilliance of your wit, my dear. Where have you been riding, dressed like that?"

"I had to see a man at the inn in Chiswick. He and his son watch the road for us for sign of our black cloaked immortal but he has not come their way, so they believe. Not that we have much in the way of a description to go on."

"Hope you did not ride by Westminster Abbey with your shapely thighs and buttocks on display. You will only confuse the poor canons. Will you join me for a cup of wine?"

"I should change my clothing and take off my shoes. I shall

tread mud into the house."

"That is what servants are for. Come on, old girl, pull up a stool."

A good fire burned in the hearth and it was pleasant indeed to sit in my home, our home, and listen to the crackling of it and the familiar creaks of certain floorboards. I called for one of the servants and he brought wine, tutting about the mud. Eva sat staring at her drink, clearly troubled.

"You will find this man," I said. "And then I will kill him. We always do."

"I will not rest easy until we find him, Richard. Who knows what mischief he might be up to, what subversion he might be about, what other assassins he may meet with, or recruit to his cause."

"Our prisoner downstairs will give him up soon enough. A tough fellow but we shall break his spirit, do not doubt it."

Eva nodded. "He's a tough one?"

"Strong indeed," I said. "He must have been feeding well for months. Years, perhaps. William must have a host of blood slaves."

"He hurt you when you fought," she said, concern on her face.

"Come, dear, you know I am never hurt for long."

"Not in the body, perhaps." She drank. "I was dismayed to hear of your encounter with the Queen. We must proceed with extreme caution."

"She likes me."

"I'm sure she does. She has always had a passion for handsome young rogues."

"What woman does not?"

She was not amused. "This could be extremely dangerous for us, you do realise that? Now that she knows about us she might order us watched, limiting the effectiveness of our work. She may wish to interfere and so put us and even her in danger. Worse, she might take against us on a whim, or even with good cause, and order us arrested. Beheaded even."

"You are right. She is foolish enough but then she is surrounded by those damned councillors. Being a Catholic may not be illegal but many of them would like it to be, I am sure. It is bad enough to have a Protestant on the throne, and a female one at that, but at least she is a moderate, unlike the lord of the Privy Council."

"You will be careful with her, then," Eva said. "Moderate she may be with Catholics but she is a fickle and emotional woman, prone to rages and to violent passions."

I snorted. "Stephen claims she is Aristotle reborn."

"He is quite taken by her and I don't doubt her intellectual abilities. Some say her outbursts are not true emotion but are in fact entirely affected, applied strategically to get her own way in things."

"She is a woman." I shrugged. "Both are likely true."

"Yes, precisely," Eva said. "And so you must tread carefully indeed. You have a habit of allowing your pridefulness to be seen by your superiors and you must not do so with Elizabeth or you shall find yourself banished from court."

"Nonsense."

Eva banged her cup on the table. "Anger her and you may find the Gentlemen Pensioners breaking down our doors here and dragging you off to the Tower."

"Eva, I know how to control myself."

She did not bother to argue. "You must do more than that. You must charm her as if your life depends on it. Because it does."

"I know how to play a prince."

Eva shook her head. "Elizabeth likes her courtiers to be modern gentlemen."

"Well, I am not dancing for her."

"Use your wit then, you have one. But temper it with excessive courtesy."

"Excessive? I say again, I have known kings before. Kings who called me friend. I need no further instruction on how to speak to them."

She sighed, exasperated. "The only monarchs who ever liked you were the knightly ones, the ones who knew your value *in spite of* your manner. Soldierly kings overlook it. They enjoy it, even. With Elizabeth you must be charming. She grants favours most of all to the handsome young courtiers who tell her she is beautiful and profess their love for her. And so, Richard, you must seduce her."

I smiled and reached for her hand. "Well, that I can certainly do. As you well know."

"Good God Almighty." Eva rolled her eyes. "You're going to end up on the block."

* * *

Elizabeth had a nickname for everyone she favoured at court. Her greatest advisor, William Cecil, she called Sir Spirit. Because

Walsingham was of dark complexion and wore always dark clothes, she named him her Moor.

She called Dudley her Eyes and her new young advisor Christopher Hatton she named her Lids and later he became her Mutton and then her Bellweather. Later, she would name the dashing but idiotic Earl of Oxford her Boar.

Even foreigners who came into her circle would find themselves nicknamed, if they were lucky. The Baron de St Marc became her Monkey and her suitor the Duke of Anjou would forever be her Frog.

And I was her Knight.

Dudley hated me for that. Hated me more for that than for anything else. Even more than the fact that I had saved his life in Picardy and comforted him while he was unmanned, sobbing, and soiled while pieces of his brother's flesh still spattered his breastplate.

Despite being Master of Horse, and never far from the Queen's side, he was not there the next day when she came down for her daily ride. She trailed a dozen ladies and as many courtiers, however.

"Not so many on this day, my lady," I observed when we set off the next morning.

"As we shall ride hard today, we have left behind the slow and the aged," she replied from the saddle.

"All the aged," I said, looking around and nodding. "All except me."

She frowned, still not believing me. "Well then, Sir Knight, do try to keep up."

With that, she rode away, gaining speed as she went.

I was old enough to know that when a woman rides off in that fashion, she wishes to be chased, and I was young enough at heart to want to do so. And I was off like a shot after her.

Her courtiers and servants struggled to keep up, or understood she wished for them to stay back for they kept their distance even when she slowed. Flushed from the ride, she turned in the saddle and watched me come up beside her. Strands of her springy red hair had bounced from beneath her headdress and a few hairs were plastered to her brow by the sweat she had worked up.

"Did you let me beat you?" she said, breathlessly and with a smile on her face. "Or am I to not trust your claims of knightly excellence, sir?"

"I stayed behind, my lady, so I could better appraise your seat."

She gasped at my forwardness and flushed even more than she had before. For a moment, I thought she was about to admonish me but her flirtatious side won out. "And what is the conclusion of your appraisal, sir?"

"Alas, my lady," I began and I saw her frown. "It is impossible to say without seeing more of you."

She was scandalised again, I think, but I knew enough already to know that she liked that. From me, at least, she liked it. "Well, sir, appraise this, if you can."

With that, she rode off again and I gave chase. She rode as well as a squire and her horse was as fine a beast as ever created by God and honed by man. Still, I could have caught her but decided to stay back and to the side so that I could watch her. She looked back at me twice and both times laughed to see me watching her. It was not long, however, before she slowed again. She treated that horse better than she treated most of her courtiers.

"Do you have any further observations?" she asked, flushed once more as we slowed to a walk.

I looked back to gauge the distance from those following. "Your life may yet be in danger," I said. "And the kingdom itself most certainly is."

Her smiled fell and her face hardened. "I spoke to Francis this morning," she said, meaning Walsingham. "He tells me you have your very own private gaol where you conduct illegal torture."

"Only immortals, my lady."

"Is that what you call them?"

"Some of them."

"I command you to elaborate."

I inclined my head. "There are three kinds in the world. One which we call immortals. These immortals do not age and they are stronger than ordinary men and yet they must consume human blood every three days or so, otherwise they shall fall ill, grow mad with hunger and eventually they will die. Also, the immortals must not allow the full light of the sun to fall upon their skin, else they burn as if scalded by boiling water. The second kind we call revenants. These are much the same, though they suffer more from the hunger for blood and from the light of the sun. They must drink every night and if the sun touches them, their skin bubbles and blisters and soon cracks and blackens as if touched by flame. Also, they are more like madmen, driven by the blood thirst to raving and to untameable violence."

"And the third kind?" she prompted.

"They are the strongest and the least afflicted. They can walk in the sun without trouble and may live ageless without resorting to blood. But the consumption of it does heal them and make them even stronger."

"And which kind are you, sir?"

I took off my hat, turned my face to the sun for a long moment and inclined my head.

She looked me up and down again. "And which kind is the man in your prison? He is one of these... revenants?"

"He is an immortal. A very dangerous one."

"Well then you must be careful of him, sir."

"It is they who must be careful of me, my lady."

Her neck flushed red and she turned away. "You say you keep my kingdom safe by stopping these creatures, of which you are one. What of my other enemies? Do you wage your secret war on the enemies of England?"

"Your councillors and lords, your soldiers and your sailors, your loving people are engaged in keeping all England safe from her enemies. I do what no mortal can."

"That seems rather selfish, do you not think? You have extraordinary strength and power. Should your strength not be employed in every way it can be?"

"Even a man as strong as I cannot create more hours in a single day, nor can I be in many places at once. However, we remain loyal servants of the Crown and will do as commanded."

"But who are you loyal to?"

"My queen and to God."

"Robert tells me you are a Catholic."

"All my long life. The new religion is—"

"It is the truth, surely you see that now. Many of my subjects were born and raised as Catholics before they were brought to the true religion. I see not why you cannot do the same, no matter how old you claim to be." I began to answer her but she returned to a previous point before I could get a word out. "If you were truly loyal, you would have made yourself known to me when first I was crowned. You have hidden yourself, your strength, and never would I have known of you, were it not for that monster almost killing us. Tell me, how can I trust such a secretive man as you?"

"It was terribly uncourteous of me to do so and I wished more than anything to make myself known to you. And yet to do so would have been entirely selfish, serving only my own desires, my own heart."

She eyed me like a hawk. "How so?"

"There are evil men in the world who would do you harm. I have toiled to keep them away from you. To do that I have had to come and go as I pleased, in secret, and to be unknown not only by you but by most of your court."

"But now you are here. Does your presence not now do me harm?"

I pulled the reins and my horse inched toward hers. "They have shown their hand in their recent attempt. We know that there is yet another out there and so I believe now it is best that I remain close to you."

"Is that so?" she asked. "How close?"

My horse's belly was now touching hers and our legs were inches apart. "As close as can be."

She tore her eyes from mine and looked across to the west. "Tomorrow we are to travel to Windsor. My lord Robert does not wish me to go. It is not safe to travel, he says, not even twenty miles."

"If I am with you, you shall be safe."

She turned slowly and looked into my eyes for a long moment before she spoke, causing my heart to race. "Then you shall accompany me."

We set off in the morning and it was a fine day for the court to transfer from Whitehall to Windsor. The journey would take a full day but the path was a well-travelled one and the courtiers and servants knew what to do without fuss. Soldiers rode at the head and at the rear while in the centre Elizabeth's great carriage was surrounded by servants. At first, the courtiers were clustered nearby but almost immediately they grew bored by the slow progress and rode ahead.

Robert Dudley was nowhere to be seen and I summoned one of the servants. "You, man. Where is the Earl of Leicester?"

"Her Majesty sent my lord Robert on ahead late yesterday to make safe the way, sir."

That was strange, for the way could be safe one day and not the next, and Dudley was the Master of Horse and supposed to travel with her. But I did not think much of it at the time. If I had, perhaps I would not have been so surprised by what happened later.

There were far fewer people than I had expected and I was surprised to see the Queen use her carriage. It was large and entirely enclosed and where I had been looking forward to riding beside her all day, in fact I had not so much as laid eyes on her all morning. Our group spread out further and I rode in silence behind the carriage, ignored by the few servants and small company of soldiers and I tried to simply enjoy the air. When the

Queen's carriage drew to a stop, some of the servants continued to plod on and I made to do the same when one of the Queen's ladies approached and waved at me. I turned in the saddle to see if there was some lord or other behind me and then dismounted and went to her.

"Her Majesty commands you to converse with her," the young woman said.

"Then I shall obey," I replied, smiling. The woman did not smile in response but walked away.

Confused, I knocked on the side and pulled open the door.

Her voice came from the darkness within. "Hurry yourself, Sir Knight, elsewise I shall believe you have no desire to sit with me."

I climbed up and ducked inside. It was surprisingly spacious within, with room for four people to sit in comfort or six to sit closely.

Elizabeth sat alone.

She smiled as I came inside her carriage and offered me the cushioned bench before her.

"Your Majesty," I said. "I am, as ever, at your service."

"Shut the door, sir, so we may depart."

I hesitated. "Surely your ladies—"

"What we must discuss is for no ears but ours, sir. Now, do as your queen commands and order the driver to continue."

I leaned out, called out and shut the door. The windows were covered with thick canvas screens that allowed in little light and a single lamp hung from the roof. After a few moments, the carriage wheels turned and crunched and we began to bounce and sway as the procession got underway again.

She was smiling at me, expectantly.

"This is a very fine and remarkably private carriage, Your Majesty," I said and perceived as I did so that she frowned slightly, so I rushed on. "And may I say how radiant you are this morning, my lady, truly my heart races as I lay eyes upon you."

She smiled once more and lifted her chin and turned her head to the side. It was a surprise to see her in her travelling clothes, which were of course made for comfort more than grandeur and her skirts were soft and so thin I could see the outline of her thighs. Despite all this, her dress was cut remarkably low and her breasts were exposed almost to the nipple, and I fancied I could see the edges of those, though I dragged my eyes away soon enough when she looked back at me.

Elizabeth was not displeased by my ogling. Far from it.

"I am greatly pleased to see you also, Sir Knight. My heart races as does yours. Perhaps you can perceive the beating of it through my skin?" She gestured at her chest and I could do nothing else but stare at it once more as she breathed deeply in and out, her breasts swelling again and again.

"How right you are, my lady." I tried to think of something charming to say but nothing came to mind.

"I have been imagining you, Richard," she said, breathlessly. "Imagining the life that you have led. Imagining the events that you have seen and the people you have known. I imagine it would take hours to speak of it all."

I smiled. "Days, perhaps, or even weeks. And I would be glad to tell it all, if you would hear it."

"Oh, I would. You have been a soldier all this time? You must have fought and killed a hundred men with your own hand!"

I shifted in my seat. "It must be, my lady, at least so many."

"But surely you have kept a count of them, sir? When first did you fight?"

"Oh, at first I was a perfectly ordinary young man-at-arms in Derbyshire, in the household of the earl. Back then, the men of Powys would still raid the Marches and we went to help put down an especially resilient band, chasing them from one valley into another. Just a few hundred men on each side but it was quite thrilling for a young fellow. I am sure I thought us Arthur and his knights." She smiled. "And then later I went to the Holy Land, with Richard the Lionheart. There was much killing there, as my lady will know."

"Oh," she sighed. "Oh, Richard, what grand events you have seen. I still do not believe it, not truly. It is too fantastical to be believed."

"I understand."

She leaned forward, her bosom straining at its constraints most alarmingly. "But I do believe you, of course. I have seen your..." She looked down at me. "Your remarkable strengths for myself. And Robert tells me you are quite unchanged in all the years he has known you, retaining your youthful aspect and vigour. You do look so very young, do you know that?"

"Why, yes, when first I became—"

"Your skin is so smooth and unblemished," she said, reaching for my face before snatching her hand back and sitting upright. "And so you knew King Richard... you knew him well?"

"I knew him briefly but I believe we were friends, of a sort. I know it seems absurd to hear it but his men adored him and he them and he admired his knights for their deeds as much as their station. Within reason."

"It does not seem absurd, sir, not in the least. We are quite the same way inclined, you know."

"Of course, my lady."

"He took his wife with him to the Holy Land, did he not? What was she like?"

"I never had the pleasure of conversing with her but from a distance she appeared quite lovely."

"Did many of the lesser men take their own wives with them or was it the king alone who did something so extraordinary as to take a woman into such terrible danger?"

I thought better of trying to explain Richard's wife was never close to danger. "There were ladies with us, certainly, and their safety and comfort was always our first and greatest duty."

"And you?"

"My lady?"

"Your wife, sir. Was your wife with you there or did you leave her sensibly back in England?"

"Indeed, I met my wife during the campaign. Or rather, on the journey to it. We were married in the Holy Land itself."

"I see. You must tell me about her."

A thousand images and feelings flashed through my mind, of Alice's face and her smooth skin and her softness, the sound of her laughter and the shine of her fair hair.

"It has been so long since I thought of her at all, I must take a moment to recall it. Her name was Alice de Frenenterre of Poitou. A widowed lady with two young children. She was... good to me."

"You married a French lady? Of course, they were there also. How the world changes. Was she beautiful?"

I considered playing her looks down but I could not do it.

"She was."

"Well, you must tell me more. Was she dark or fair? Tall or meagre?"

I tried to keep the smile from my lips as I recalled her voluptuousness and the golden cascade of her tresses. "Rather small and fair-haired."

"And beautiful."

"Yes."

"She had children, you said. How many did you father with her?"

"None. I thought that perhaps she was with child but now I doubt it was true." I thought it was possible that I had been capable of fathering a child before the first time I was killed and reborn. And William also was said to have fathered children before he was killed at Hattin. But I would never know for certain.

"It is apparent that you are deeply saddened, sir. Please forgive me. You were never blessed with children with her."

"Never with any woman, my lady."

"What is this? Never? What on earth do you mean? How often have you been married, sir?"

"Married? Not more than twice."

"I see. How odd. But there have been other women, of course. Other great loves."

"Yes."

"You are a cagey one, sir. I thought I heard you say that you would tell me all, over weeks if necessary, but here you are biting on your tongue."

"How right you are, my lady. I should explain, then, that we immortals are cursed not only with long life but with seed that can never take, no matter how fertile the womb."

"God's body, you mean you have no sons? No daughters?"

"None, my lady. And never will have."

She pursed her lips. "You have tested this fact thoroughly, I take it?"

"It is true not for me alone but all others like me." I was not about to divulge the existence of Priskos and the other immortals of my father's generation who were capable of fatherhood.

"Oh, you poor man," Elizabeth said and she crossed from her side of the carriage to sit beside me, her eyes glinting in the gloom. "Gifted with eternal youth and yet cursed never to be a father. I fear I may be similarly cursed with barrenness. And yet I am cursed also with the fact of relentless decay." She reached up and stroked my face with the back of her hand. Her fingers were hot. "My own beauty has long since faded, gone away along with my youth." She dropped her hand and turned away.

"Indeed, not at all, my lady," I said. I began to reach for her and then I recalled who she was and I snatched my hand back. "You are both youthful and beautiful and utterly enchanting."

She turned back and grasped my hand in hers, pulling it onto her lap. "My heart races for you, Richard, more than ever. Here, feel it beating like a drum."

Taking my hand, she pressed my palm against the bare skin of her breast where it was exposed. Her flesh was soft and yielding and so hot to the touch it was as though she had a fever. For a long moment, I stared at my hand and her bosom as she breathed heavily and then I looked in her eyes.

She leaned in and kissed me on the lips, forcing my hand onto her breasts and pushing it into them. Then our hands were all over each other and she opened her mouth to kiss me more deeply and her tongue was in my mouth.

A small part of my mind suggested that I should stop her at once but it was a small part only and easily ignored. Other parts would not be restrained and I found her hands pulling at my doublet, which I helped her to open, and then she pulled out the tails of my shirt where they were tucked into my hose and then she was pulling my hose down to reach inside. She pushed me back, hitched her skirts and straddled me. Holding herself over me, she stopped to look at my face.

I could be beheaded for this, I thought. Well, came an answering thought, some things are worth dying for and I grasped her and pulled her to me.

She was filled with such passion that it was not more than a few moments before she cried out, shuddering and fell forward onto me with tears in her eyes. I held her in that way for a time before her passions were aroused once more. I do not know for how long we were thusly engaged but it was certainly a good while and it was with extreme reluctance that we withdrew from each other and helped one another to dress. Though her makeup was disturbed, Elizabeth glowed with life and she laughed lightly at this or that small thing, such as my inability to correctly re-lace her bodice.

When the carriage suddenly slowed and stopped due to some obstruction in the road, she grew sad and quiet. It started up again but the spell had been broken and once more there were tears rimming her eyes.

"I hardly need say it and yet I must..." she trailed off.

"You will have my absolute and everlasting discretion," I said.

"Of course I shall," she replied. "I intended to say that... this must never happen again."

I bowed my head. "I wish that it could be otherwise. But your situation is... it is unique."

She smiled. "It is that."

"If you were not Elizabeth... I apologise, I should know better than to fantasise."

"Please, Richard," she said. "Let us fantasise. If I were not Elizabeth the queen..."

"Then there would be no impediment to our love. We could take off to some distant and delightful place."

She smiled. "To Derbyshire, perhaps."

I nodded. "That would be perfect. Though, I know how you feel about the north."

"Oh," she waved her hand. "It is hardly north at all. And I am certain I could stand it if you were at my side." She lowered her voice. "And in my bed."

"Do not... do not think of it overly much, my lady," I said. "Even if such a thing could be, we would still live with my curse."

"Childlessness is hardly a new curse for me."

"But one which will be lifted when you find someone suitable."

She sighed, a touch of anger in it. "I fear I have found someone suitable to my heart. But to nothing else."

"Your heart," I said, reaching for her and laying my hand gently over it. "And your lips." I leaned in and kissed her for the last time. She grasped me and kissed me back so hard our teeth clashed.

Sighing, she pushed me away. "You must go," she said. "Go

and stay away and do not come back. Already they will talk and there must be no more of it."

"I understand," I said.

Straightening my clothes, I opened the door a crack to see one of Elizabeth's ladies riding beside us at the edge of the road. "Are we at Windsor yet?"

"It was reached and passed some time ago."

"God's bones. Well, have my horse brought up. I shall take it and be off while you turn back."

With a last glance at Elizabeth, I stepped out into the evening.

3

Blood Fever

1568

"OUR PRISONER IS NEARLY out of his wits with the blood sickness," Stephen said when I returned to our house. It was full dark by then but we were outside the city walls so there was no one to stop our coming or going. Convenient indeed for a secret society.

"So soon?"

Stephen shrugged. "He says he has not fed since the day he left his ship and abandoned his servant. We have also given him just a few sips of water and no food and have not allowed him to sleep more than a few minutes at a time. His suffering is profound."

"Good man. What secrets has he coughed up?"

Smiling, Stephen led off through our entrance hall towards

the door down to our cellars. "He said he was sent from New Spain."

I stopped. "He was in the New World?"

"That's what he said. At least, I think that's what he was saying, it was rather difficult to follow due to his extreme discomfort. He was ranting."

"And your Spanish is appalling."

"My Spanish is exquisite."

"Well then, lead on, *señor*."

We started down the stairs and Stephen spoke over his shoulder. "It is good fortune you have returned but I thought you were supposed to be staying at Windsor?"

"I saw her there safe and then she sent me back."

"Ah," Stephen said, smirking. "I knew you would anger her."

"Your wisdom knows no bounds."

Outside the cell, Walt sat at a small table with the remnants of a meal on a plate, picking his nails with his eating knife. Leeche sat beside him at the table. It was ironic that we employed him as a gaoler, seeing that in his mortal life he had been a professional criminal in London but he was dutiful enough. He was already old and scarred when he was turned and he was unpleasant to look upon and had rough manners indeed but he was not a bad fellow for all that.

"Master Ashbury," Walt said, smiling. "I had not thought to see you."

"Nor I you," I replied. "How long have you been back, Walt?"

"Most of the day." He gestured at the closed cell door. "Lucky we come back or else you wouldn't have got Alonso chatting away."

"Alonso, is it?" I said. "He told you his name?"

"He told us so much that Stephen couldn't write it down fast enough."

I gestured at the door of his cell. "Quiet now, eh?"

"We tired him out. Letting him get his head down for a bit, then we'll start on him again, winkle it all out proper, you know?"

I nodded. "What happened to Walsingham?"

Walt shook his head. "Stephen's boy ain't got the acorns for this sort of work."

Stephen cleared his throat. "Sir Francis had other pressing duties to attend to."

Walt smiled. "That's what I said."

"Where are your men?" I asked him.

"Callthorp's in Plymouth, Adams is at Dover. Few more of the boys here and there, watching this place or that, keeping an eye on a few men."

"You trust them to keep their heads down? Bleed their slaves quietly?"

"Callthorp and Adams are solid and they control their lads. The others..." He pursed his lips. "They'll be alright. Anyways, they know what will happen if they ain't."

Stephen pinched his nose. "They had better not cause trouble or else they shall be sorry."

Walt scowled. "I just said, didn't I?" He turned to Leeche. "Ain't that what I just said?"

Leeche squinted at Walt. "Your men can't be trusted," he said in his scratchy old voice. "Master Stephen's right to be worried."

"Oh, who asked you, Leeche?"

"Keep it down now," I said to them. Opening the cell door I

saw our immortal Spanish prisoner had been shackled to the wall. He was stripped to his stained shirt and dirty hose, shivering and soaked with sweat.

"He's got the blood fever pretty bad," Walt said at my shoulder. "Eyes running, nose pissing snot, fouling himself inside out all day long." He patted me on the back. "He's all yours."

When I approached and crouched beside him, I heard his breath rattling in his chest. I dragged him by the chains until his back was propped against the wall of the cell. "Alonso," I said softly. "Alonso, time to wake up, my friend."

He groaned and I held a cup of water to his lips. Alonso coughed and spluttered it out.

"Not too much," Stephen muttered behind me.

"Thank you, Stephen."

The prisoner lurched forward, lunging for me and the cup went clattering across the cell. I shoved the man back and stood up while he coughed, glaring up at me.

"Ah, Alonso, you are awake. Now, let me see you. Oh dear, you are not looking well, my friend."

"Blood," Alonso said, eyes flicking left and right as he tried to focus on Stephen behind me. "He promised me blood."

"Only if you told us all that you know," Stephen said. "Then I will give you fresh blood. Good blood."

Alonso's head rolled. "You lie. Already, I told you. Told you. I told you."

"What did you tell us, Alonso?" I asked. "Tell it again. I am the master here and so you must speak to me."

"No, no. Give me blood, I must have—"

I slapped him hard across the face. The sound was like an

arquebus firing. His head flopped over and he fell sideways to the floor.

"Now you've done it," Walt said. "You've killed him."

I dragged Alonso upright again and shook him a little. "You came here from New Spain, Alonso, yes?"

He frowned, confused. "Did I speak of this?"

"You did, at length. What were you doing there?"

"I did nothing," he said. "Only my duty."

"Tell me about your master, Alonso. Who gave you the gift of immortality?"

He shook his head. "I failed. He will kill me."

"No. You are mine now. You live or die at my say so. Do you want to live, Alonso?"

"Kill me."

"Not until you tell me the truth about your master."

Stephen sighed and muttered under his breath. "Too much to ask him such a thing now. Too precious."

I agreed and tried another path. "Where in New Spain did you come from?" I shook him and lifted his head. "Was it the city of Vera Cruz? The island of Hispaniola?" I looked at Stephen for help. I knew little about the New World.

"Panama?" Stephen said, bending down to Alonso's level. "Was it Panama?" He sighed and thought some more. "Alonso, were you in Chile? Or... Peru?"

Walt leaned in the doorway. "You're making these words up, Stephen."

"Borburata."

We all turned to Alonso, who raised his shackled hands to wipe his nose while glancing up at us.

"What did you say?"

"Borburata," he repeated. "They took me to feed at Borburata."

"Feed?" Walt said, stepping forward.

"You ever heard of it?" I asked Stephen, who stepped across the room and sat at his writing table.

Stephen shook his head as he dipped his pen in the inkwell. "Keep going."

I smiled at our prisoner. "That is good, Alonso, very good. You know, I think we shall become good friends. Tell me about New Spain."

* * *

The next morning, after some rest, I called a meeting of the senior members of the Order and we sat down to a late breakfast of bread with sage butter, and sweet omelettes of eggs, butter, sugar, and currants, washed down by some good small beer.

"Have we got any pickled herrings?" Walt asked the servants and they went off to fetch him some.

Eva pulled apart her small loaf and spread butter on a piece. "You broke him, then?"

"Alonso was very accommodating," Stephen said. "Though close to insensible by the end. We gave him a little blood and water and a piece of bread but still he was raving by the end. He's sleeping now and perhaps he will come back to himself."

"What did he tell you?" Eva asked.

Stephen took up a sheath of notations and spread the sheets

on the table while he sipped his beer. "He came from the West Indies to England, with a slave who provided him blood along the way. An African, if you can believe it. The mariners took the slave away with them so he is lost to us, sadly. Then he went to his rendezvous with the other fellow who is still at large. It was this fellow who informed Alonso of the Queen's whereabouts and sent him on his way. It seems he expected to die during or immediately after he had assassinated the Queen. If he lived, he was to go to some other place but we have not managed to get that from him as yet."

"That surely is our most pressing concern," Eva said. "As is the identity of the man he met."

Walt put his cup down and belched. "We'll winkle it out of him, if he ain't too far gone. But it might be too late. What was he ranting about, houses of blood and going on about crows all the time? Half mad, he is."

Eva dismissed that. "Did he say nothing else about the man?"

Stephen nodded. "This is, perhaps, the most important piece of information at all. It was confusing but I believe what he was saying was that the man he met was a Jesuit priest. A Jesuit here to provide services and guidance to England's Catholics. And it is possible that Alonso himself is a Jesuit."

"That was exactly what he was saying," I said. "Whether it is the truth, I do not know."

Walt rubbed his hands as the pickled herrings were placed before him and he began loading them onto his bread while he spoke. "We need all the proper priests we can get in England these days but why do we allow foreign ones in? And Jesuits above all of them ain't to be trusted."

Stephen shook his head. "The Jesuits are a religious order founded almost fifty years ago in Paris by a group of mostly Castilian Spaniards who were students at the university there. As a Catholic, you should appreciate their work."

"Ha!" Walt scoffed. "They was Jews, not Spaniards."

"Dear me," Stephen said. "Some were from families of *conversos*. That is, those who had once been Jews before embracing Christ. But there is nothing to suggest the founders were anything but good Christians."

Walt scoffed again. "Good Christians would never have named their order the Society of Jesus. It's blasphemous, ain't it."

"Well, perhaps. But never fear, for the Inquisition purged all *conversos* from the order years ago. Whatever you may think they once were, they are now no more than Catholic priests working to subvert the new religion. And that is enough, is it not?"

"And we know they are working in England to subvert *us*," I said, before looking at Stephen. "And we know there are immortals amongst them. What more is there to know?"

"All I'm saying is, we need English priests, not Spanish ones," Walt said again. "That's all I'm saying."

"Not all Jesuit priests are Spanish," Eva said. "Many are French and you will be pleased to know, Walt, that the Jesuits have begun recruiting Englishmen in France and Spain to return to spread the old faith in secret."

"The true faith, you mean," Walt said, pointing at her with his knife.

She shrugged. "We may think it so but an increasing number of our countrymen do not. Our Queen and all her ministers included, and every other powerful man and woman in the kingdom, barring a few exceptions."

"The truth is the truth, no matter who believes otherwise, nor how many of them," Walt said, irritated.

I cut in before it descended into the same arguments we had been having for decades. "Save it, Walter, if you please. We know that the Jesuits are working in England in secret, sent by Spain, by France, and by the Pope. They want England to become Catholic again and we around this table want that."

"On our own terms, not because of foreigners!" Walt said.

I raised a hand. "Yes, yes, I quite agree. They are certainly foreign agents working against the Crown, even if they are doing God's work as well. And now it seems they are William's agents, also."

"Not all of them, surely," Stephen said. "Alonso may be a Jesuit, or he may have been raving, and he may even be mistaken about his contact who is at large. I imagine a handful of William's spawn infiltrated the Society of Jesus for their own ends. I shall speak to Walsingham on what is being done by the Crown about these Jesuits making mischief in England."

Eva agreed. "I'll tell Goodie and Leeche to gather word on any Jesuits working around London."

"What do I tell the boys?" Walt asked. "Stop looking for immortals and start hunting secret priests?"

Stephen rolled his eyes. "Have you not been listening? It is the same search."

Walt slowly placed his cup on the table and was about to argue so I spoke quickly. "Tell them nothing for now, they are watching the main ports and that is enough."

"What did Alonso tell you about William?" Eva asked.

I nodded. "It took him a while to speak of it at all but he claims not to know the master of his master, who was a priest. He said that his lord bled him in the crypts of a church and he drank many cups of blood but he does not know where it was. That was before they sent him to New Spain to collect and carry off some sort of treasure."

"Treasure?"

Stephen nodded. "That is what he said but there is only one way to discover what William's men are up to."

Eva narrowed her eyes while she chewed on her eggs. "And what are you planning?"

Stephen shook his notes. "Alonso gave us just one place he remembered being, a place where he was given blood and then a blood slave. That place is in the New World."

There was a moment of silence before Eva swallowed loudly and responded. "You want to send a man to the New World?"

"Amongst his babbling about treasure, Alonso told us he would receive blood from port towns on the islands and the mainland of the New World. We know the name of one of those places. Borburata, he said, and later he clarified that a man can buy a cup of fresh blood in the *taverna*. So we must investigate it."

The New World, I thought, my heart racing. "We must find an agent of some kind and have them go and report back."

Stephen shook his head. "We already have as much information as an agent would be able to gather. Alonso has given it up. Now, we have to send one of us."

All eyes turned to me. "I am not going to the New World."

"I cannot do it," Stephen said. "As I have too much business here, finding the agents William sends against England. Eva likewise has far too much to attend to. For example, Goodie and Leeche will be lost without her to direct them every few days. And Walt has Callthorp and Adams and the rest of the men to manage. They would fall into chaos without his guiding hand."

Walt bowed. "Why, thank you, Stephen."

"Take a ship?" I said. "Across the sea?"

"How else would you get there?" Eva asked, clearly warming to the idea.

"Hold on a moment, friends, only the Spanish go there," Walt ventured. "And the Portuguese, I suppose. But that's near enough the same thing, ain't it."

"Some Englishman have been to the New World in English ships," Stephen said. "But not more than a handful of men, just a few ships, just in two or three voyages."

"Englishmen have been to the New World?"

"If you were as involved in the business of the London sea merchants, as I am, you would know about such things." Stephen wafted a hand in the air. "It is primarily the sea captains of Devon who have on occasion ventured into Portuguese and Spanish waters in Africa and the New World in order to force their way into the local trade. And I must say they are hardly better than pirates. Indeed, I'll go further and say that they *are* pirates."

"And you expect me to put my life into the hands of these Devonshire scoundrels?"

"We must investigate this place and there is no other way to get there. These men may be rough countryfolk but they are a hard lot and have few ways of making a fortune other than through the sea."

I thought for a moment. "Devonshire men, is it? I suppose

they are Protestants?"

"Certainly, the merchants, sea captains and mariners of England are Protestants to a man. But don't hold that against them."

"I bloody will hold it against them. Sailing the high seas with a boatful of Protestants, Stephen, you cannot expect me to agree to this."

"Come, come, Richard. You have faced entire armies unflinching and yet you are afraid of getting a little wet?"

"I am not afraid," I said. "Not at all. I simply have no wish to be enclosed for weeks on end with men constantly falling to their knees to converse with God."

"I will at the least find out the names of some of these men who sailed to the West Indies. Any of my London contacts will know of it."

Eva knew it already. "The chief among them is a mariner named John Hawkins. He returned from a venture with a squadron of ships just last year and made a good profit. Half a mark back on the pound."

Stephen peered at her over his papers. "You are very well informed."

"I should be. I was one of the investors."

He gaped at her. "You were... why did I not know of this voyage?"

"It is all in our accounts, Stephen, as you will find if you examine them. We went through Thomas Ballard so you shall find the entry under his name. Anyway, you will find this John Hawkins knows his business."

I sighed. "I suppose he must if he sailed all the way across that

67

great sea and back."

Stephen wafted a hand. "Oh, Richard, your mind is stuck in the world of fifty years ago. Now, the Spanish do it all the time, back and forth, dozens of ships a year."

"Oh, it is so simple, is it, Stephen? Perhaps you would care to make the journey after all and tell us the state of things in New Spain when you return. If you ever do."

His face fell. "As I have said plainly, I cannot leave London because I have too much business to attend to here." He cleared his throat and ploughed on. "So, this Captain John Hawkins might be the man to speak to about how to get Richard to the New World. Perhaps we could encourage him to undertake another voyage. If he can be so persuaded, he would need financial backing to purchase and outfit the ships and to pay the crew."

"We could pay him whatever he needs, could we not?" I asked Stephen.

He pursed his lips and sucked air in, like a thatcher who is about to tell you that your entire roof needs replacing. "We could, I suppose. But that would be very unusual. No ordinary investor would commit so much when the risk is so high."

"Risk?" I said.

"Walt laughed. "What you even worried about? You can swim, can't you?"

"Not from the Americas."

"You should not go alone," Eva said. "A gentleman needs his valet."

"Agreed. I will take Philip."

Walt rolled his eyes. "He's too young."

"He is nearly eighty."

Walt tutted. "You know what I mean. Young when he was made immortal and he has stayed young in the mind. And he's a bit slow."

"The same affliction has not held you back."

"He's a Protestant!" Walt snapped.

"Unfortunately," I admitted. "Despite that affliction, Philip is dutiful enough."

"What of the sun?" Walt asked. "It is hot in the New World, hotter and brighter even than Spain, than Italy, more even than Anatolia. How will your boy protect himself?"

"He can wear a hat. If William's men are there, it can certainly be done, just as you all survived the places you just mentioned. Eva, Stephen, please make the arrangements with these mariners. Now, please let us stop talking about a sea voyage and let us enjoy our breakfast."

Before I could get a mouthful in, our porter came into the parlour and approached Stephen. "Apologies, master, but that young fellow Martin Hawthorn is here to see you. He claims to have an appointment."

"Ah, yes, have him wait in the hall, would you? And bring him some beer while he waits."

"Who is this?" I asked Stephen. "A friend of yours?"

"You might say that. Martin is a lawyer. A very capable young man and one I have long taken an interest in. Indeed, we have funded a goodly portion of his education and I now engage him in small legal matters whenever I can. I have high hopes for him and I intend to rely on him for business of the Order more generally, as he grows older. In time, by that I mean a good few years from now, I thought I might put him forward as a candidate for permanent, long term membership."

"You want to make him one of us?" I asked. "What on earth for?"

Stephen scowled. "I have an awful lot of business to attend to, Richard. When we needed more soldiers, you and Walt found them and vetted them and turned them and now you have a veritable company running around England doing your bidding. Well, it is high time that I had an assistant of ability who can help us in the coming centuries. He is one possible candidate, that is all. We shall have to see how it all turns out."

"No need to be so testy, Stephen, that sounds perfectly reasonable. Speak to me again in twenty years and we shall see about it." I sat back, finding myself suddenly uninterested in eating more. Breakfasting was still rather new to me and it did not take much to fill my belly in the morning, as good as the eggs were. "But tell me, why have we funded the education of this young gentleman? He is the son of a friend of yours, perhaps?"

"Oh, indeed. Of all of ours, in a manner of speaking. You see, he is the direct descendant of Robert Hawthorn. As you know, Rob always took an interest in his descendants, from afar, and I continued to do so after his death. This Martin is the eldest son of John Hawthorn, who was a yeoman of means but suffered a long illness where he was most taken advantage of and his wife quite mismanaged things. The eldest son, Martin, held it all together. I first saw him arguing most forcefully with a magistrate using a clever point of law regarding land rights. Too clever, it seems, and the magistrate ruled against him but I have looked after him ever since and he has done very well indeed."

I nodded. "Well done, Stephen, very well done. You are a good man and I know Rob will be most grateful."

Walt rapped his knuckles on the table, nodding also but then he smiled. "Clever tricks and law, though? Don't sound much like Rob."

"Nonsense," I said. "And I think it is quite right that you seek to employ more good men to help you in your business. Of course, Eva has Goodie Sprunt for her protégé, taking care of whatever business is required when Eva is otherwise engaged."

Eva put down her knife. "It is clear that you want me to do something," she ventured. "So let me say that I am not travelling to the New World with you. A woman on a long voyage is considered bad luck, you know that. And believe me, they would find me very bad luck indeed."

"I would not allow you to do that, no. But I have been thinking about the Queen."

"I am sure you have," she said.

I had told no one even that I had been alone with Elizabeth, let alone the rest, but Eva seemed always to see everything and know everything. Which is precisely why I needed her.

"I mean I have been thinking about the Queen's safety. Since I shall no longer be at the court, we need someone to watch over her closely. A bodyguard. But a secret one."

She narrowed her eyes. "Have Walt made a guard at Whitehall. Or Callthorp or Adams."

"The Queen travels often. And she is often with her ladies, away from the presence of men. She needs someone strong and clever to be near to her all the time."

Eva's mouth was tight when she replied. "Goodie can enter

the household as a servant."

"Goodie is very bright but she was a tavernkeeper and has the manners of one. Besides, she may be an immortal but you are a warrior, even if you are terribly out of practice. No, I am afraid the only reasonable choice is that you, Eva, become one of Elizabeth's ladies in waiting. I will speak to Robert Dudley and, if he has any sense, he will persuade the Queen to allow it. This way, if any immortal assassins strike at the Queen, you shall be at her side to save her life."

She sighed and pinched the bridge of her nose. "I will do it. But I doubt my services will be required."

"Let us pray that it will be so."

4

Hawkins

1568

THERE FOLLOWED MANY MONTHS of organising, directly and indirectly through agents and proxies. I met with several captains who promised the earth but none were so experienced as John Hawkins. After agreeing to certain terms, I left Plymouth to travel here and there in England, meeting with our men and pursuing this or that line of enquiry.

One of the most pressing concerns was the lack of suitable vessels. A truly impressive ship capable of sailing the wide ocean, storing hundreds of tons of cargo, and carrying large cannons, was astonishingly expensive and rare indeed in England. I could perhaps afford to have one built but that sort of thing takes years and I could not spare the time.

"The Queen has some fine ships," Hawkins said during one

early meeting in a room at a tavern. He was a confident and wealthy man of Plymouth and one of the most important gentlemen in Devon. He was tall and dark haired with piercing green eyes and a long straight nose. "Might be Her Majesty would lend us the use of one or two in exchange for a share of the profits. Such things have been done before. Indeed, my father used the ships of old King Henry and then of Queen Mary to sail all over, including to the New World."

"Indeed? Your father sailed to the New World? I am astonished."

Hawkins beamed with pride. "First Englishman who ever did it, my father. And I learned my business from him and learned it well."

"I am sure you did, sir. So, we shall use the Queen's warships, wonderful idea."

He spread his hands wide and his men winced and pursed their lips. "Well, you see, Richard, a king is a king but our queen is a woman and she can be mighty fickle about such ventures. We can petition Elizabeth but without significant support from the leading gentlemen of the kingdom whispering in her ear on our behalf I can't say it will be successful."

I smiled. "Leave that to me."

Eventually, word came that all was ready. We had six ships for our expedition, two of them warships that belonged to the Crown, granted under terms that would earn the Queen a sizeable portion of any profit made. The largest, the *Jesus of Lubeck* was to be our flagship under Hawkins, and the other royal ship was the smaller 300-ton *Minion*. The other ships, privately owned, were the *William and John* of 150 tons, the 100-ton *Swallow*, the *Judith* a bark of 50 tons, and the tiny *Angel* of just 32 tons.

Officially I was representing a company of merchants that provided much of the funding and so I was to be a passenger on the flagship. The *Jesus* was a vast and mighty ship. At least, it seemed so at the time and it was certainly the largest I had ever boarded at something like 700-tons. It towered over the *Minion* and that ship was twice the size of the next biggest.

I left my immortal servant Philip down on the dockside to find men to help carry our belongings and victuals aboard. Gentlemen brought their own supplies on a voyage, so I had been told, and I meant to eat and drink as well as I could on what I knew would be a long and uncomfortable voyage.

Walking along the gangplank up to the main deck, I stood marvelling at the size of the fore and aft castles rising high and all the big iron and brass guns lashed down at intervals between them. Mariners hustled hither and thither, their arms always laden and their mouths spewing oaths.

"You lost?" a commoner's rough voice called out.

Realising with a start that I had been addressed, I turned to see an officer staring at me, his hands on his hips, from the edge of a raised deck twenty feet aft.

"I beg your pardon?"

He shook his head and stomped down a short stair toward me and drew to a stop an arm's length away. The fellow was both younger and shorter than I had initially thought. When he spoke, it was with a Devonshire accent so thick that I had to concentrate to be certain of his words. "What I said, friend, was that you look as though you are lost. You sure you be in the right place?"

"I am looking for John Hawkins."

"Oh?" he said, growing even more suspicious. "What you be wanting him for?"

I smiled. "I am sure that is my business. Is he on board, yet?"

"What's your name?" he demanded.

"What's your name?" I shot back.

The short fellow scowled. "By God, you better have a reason for being here or I swear me and the boys is going to toss you over the side into the dock." He turned his head to the side without breaking eye contact with me. "Won't we, boys?"

"Too right," a mariner said, placing his load at his feet and swaggering closer.

I looked around at the gathering group of men and turned back to the stocky little man. "How many men does this great ship carry as crew, sir?" I asked mildly.

Confused, he sneered. "Why?"

I leaned forward and lowered my voice. "Because if you mean to lay hands on me, you are going to need every one of them."

The young fellow scoffed and a few of the mariners laughed. He looked me up and down, seeing no doubt the quality of the cloth I wore, and the physical confidence of my stance, the excellent quality of my sword and dagger, and wondering who I was to be so fearless in the face of his threat. I could have been some official from the port, or the town, or more likely he thought me a middling sort of merchant come to offer him some cargo or victuals.

Whatever he thought, though, he decided he would throw me overboard anyway.

"We don't need nobody else, friend," he said, a grin spreading across his face. "No one comes aboard without permission, no one." He nodded at the men next to him.

I readied myself. It was a long way down the curving side of the ship into the narrow strip of utterly foul, black dock water below.

But the mariners hesitated.

"What about his sword?" one man said.

The officer rolled his eyes. "Where is your club, Perkins?"

He shrugged. "Stowed."

A few of the men laughed and more came to gather behind them, so that I was fully penned in from three sides, with just the side rail between me and the water below.

"I merely wish to speak to Hawkins," I said.

The short officer stuck a finger in the air. "You insulted the ship. You don't get nothing, my friend, not nothing."

"How in the world did I insult the ship?"

He puffed his chest out. "You did so by coming aboard without permission."

"I gave myself permission."

That got another laugh from our audience and the officer snorted, angered by my casual defiance of his authority. "You're a Catholic, ain't you," he said. "Only a Catholic would be so arrogant. Go on, admit it."

"Who are you to speak of arrogance, you purple faced little turnip?"

He stared at me, his mouth open, before boiling into anger. "Right, that's it. You're going in. Come on, boys."

A few of them rushed me. Not all, not even close, but enough that they came at me from all three sides in a rush and fists punched my face and my chest and guts and, worst of all, my kidneys. Someone tried to kick me in the balls but of course I was ready for that and caught most of it on my thigh. I lashed out and smacked a couple of them across the face, kicked out another man's knee and butted another.

As they went down, I grabbed the short officer and shoved his back against the rail, pushing him halfway over and holding him there with one hand grasping the neck of his doublet and the other holding the point of my dagger at his throat.

"Easy, there," I said over my shoulder as the mariners rushed forward. "Don't want to jostle me now, do you?"

They backed away and I looked at the officer who was at my mercy. His eyes were fire and they were burning with rage.

I smiled and touched the point to his skin. The urge to push it into his neck was quite powerful. I imagined the point pushing in the skin until it could resist no more and split aside, and the blade sliding in as they do, and the pause before the hot blood came gushing and spurting out.

A voice split the air.

"Hold!"

There was an approaching commotion coming from aft, and in the corner of my eye I saw the mass of mariners parting as the owner of the voice pushed through them.

"Hold, I say, hold!"

It was Hawkins himself, not dressed in his London finery but in black wool and rough linen beneath.

"Oh, there you are, John," I said, without releasing my prisoner.

"What in the world are you doing, Richard?" he cried. "Unhand my officer this instant."

"Only after he swears not to have me thrown overboard."

Hawkins blinked, confused, and shook his head to dismiss his unspoken questions. "Of course he will not."

"I want to hear him say it."

Hawkins exploded in anger. "He serves me and I say no one will throw anyone off my ship. Now, release him at once!"

"Certainly," I said, smiling. I pulled him off the rail and let him go.

"What in the world is happening here?" Hawkins shouted, looking between me and the outraged young officer. Then he turned to his crew. "Get back to work, you laggards!" They reluctantly slunk away, the injured men amongst them muttering and being supported by their friends.

"I asked to see you," I said to Hawkins. "And this fellow attacked me."

Hawkins glared at his officer. "Is this true?"

"That ain't what happened, John, this bastard strolls on and starts—"

Hawkins reddened and glared before speaking over him. "Richard's insistence that we keep his involvement secret forced me to keep you ignorant of his name and position until now but this man is both a gentleman serving on this ship and one of the foremost investors of the voyage."

The officer gaped. "I didn't know, John, he never said nothing about—"

"You will apologise to Richard Ashbury this instant. As you may have guessed, Richard is an experienced soldier and we are fortunate to have him."

The young man straightened his doublet, took a deep breath

and bowed. "I apologise, sir, for any offence given by my uncouth behaviour. It was unacceptable."

I pursed my lips and nodded, impressed by his ability to accept responsibility so readily. "It is already forgotten, sir. And I apologise for crippling your men and putting a blade to your neck."

He bristled and his fingers brushed his throat before he answered. "Think nothing of it, sir."

Hawkins smiled. "Splendid, splendid." He held out a hand to indicate his officer. "And this, Richard, is the master's mate and my assistant navigator, Francis Drake."

I shook his hand. "A pleasure to meet you, Francis."

***

What can I say about my first impressions of Francis Drake? Not much, other than I was not impressed by the man. He had been a mariner since he was a boy and knew all there was about boats, ships, rivers and the sea. He was also a raving Protestant, the son of a preacher, and not to be trusted for that reason alone. I certainly had no notion at all that he would become one of England's greatest heroes.

A couple of days at sea caused me to regret ever coming aboard the enormous *Jesus of Lubeck* for the motion of the vessel made me sicker than I had been for a long time. Indeed, I was vomiting by the time we passed the Lizard and I did not stop until we were well southwest of the Isles of Scilly.

Clutching the rail with one hand, I wiped the spittle from my lips and muttered curses as I raised my face to the spray falling upon it. I found the most relief by staying amidships as much as I could and so had to contend with the amusement and muted mockery of the mariners as they went to and fro and climbed the ratlines above my head.

"You have never been to sea before, I take it?" a voice said at my elbow. I turned and groaned to see the master's mate, Francis Drake, beaming at me.

There was a moment's irritation but I felt no lasting anger at him. After all, he was a young man and young men can generally be trusted to be pleased with themselves and contemptuous of others.

I shrugged. "Mostly, I have crossed to France and Flanders. But I have also crossed the Aegean, the Ionian, Adriatic. Let me see, through the Balearic sea and the Tyrrhenian. The Pontic, and the sea of Marmara by Constantinople. And I have been down the coast of France and around the Iberian coast, in ships far smaller than this one. But I don't recall ever being so sick as this."

Drake laughed and shook his head. "If what you say is true, you'd be the most experienced sailor in this whole squadron." His Devonshire accent made him difficult to understand. "It ain't nothing to be ashamed of to be a land-leaper."

"What is wrong with this ship?" I said, ignoring his disbelief. "It rolls like an old drunkard."

He laughed. "Well, she is. Old that is, almost fifty years old, so they say."

"Why does its age cause this terrible motion?"

Drake parted his lips and slapped a hand on the rail next to me. "She's in a right poor state, all in all. Timbers well on their way to rotten."

"Rotten?" I said, my voice cracking. "What do you mean, rotten?"

"Just as I say it. Some of the lower timbers are so soft, you can poke your finger right into them. Just like that." He mimed a jabbing motion in the air. "Texture like cheese, some of them. You can scrape pieces out with your fingernail."

"You are lying, certainly. How can we be safe, if that is the case?"

"Safe?" Drake chuckled. "Certainly, we are not safe. We are leaking already, with every big wave the seams between the planks bend open and water pours in."

"Pours?"

"Oh, we have bilge pumps and the men to pump them, every watch. As long as we keep the men at the pumps, we should be well enough to get us there and back, God willing."

"And that is why the ship rolls like this?"

"Partly. Mainly we roll because the ship had a great forecastle and sterncastle when she was built and for all her life until we got hold of her recently." He pointed fore and aft. "We had them cut right down so she would sail better and she does. Far better. But still, her balance is high on account of the masts and spars being too big, too heavy. Reckon we'll need more ballast when we come to a safe port and restow the holds. We'll get her right as she can. But she'll never sail nice like the *Minion*." He shook his head. "Forecastles and sterncastles. Madness."

"The castles are for fighting boarding actions," I said, because I had been fighting from ships for hundreds of years. "The taller the castle, the better for fighting other ships. If our castle is higher than that of the enemy ships, we can shoot down at their decks, and we can jump down onto their ship but they will struggle to climb up to ours."

Drake smirked. "Who told you about war at sea? I'll wager it was your grandfather! At least it was some old sod who ain't never been to sea since the days of old King Henry, right?" He snorted. "We don't build ships like this no more, let me tell you how it is, we build ships that sail proper. See, weight way up high causes the ship to roll back and forth."

"I am sure. And yet high towers served us well for more than a hundred years."

Drake shrugged. "In calm waters close to shore, in the Channel, that served well enough. Not these days, though, sailing out into big seas. This ship ain't fit for it."

I stared at him. "We begged the Queen for weeks for the use of it. If it is not fit, why in the name of Christ's balls are we sailing in it, then?"

He scowled and squared off at me. "I do not accept blasphemy in my presence, sir."

Scoffing, I waved a hand at him. "Then leave my presence, you damned lunatic."

Drake jabbed a finger in my face. "Land-leapers have no place crossing the sea. You should have stayed in London, where you belong."

For all I was insulted, I could not help but laugh as he stomped away aft. In all my days, I believe that was the very first time anyone had suggested I belonged in London.

Philip approached with a flask and held it out to me. "Some wine, Richard."

I pushed it away. "It will only overturn my stomach again."

"No, sir, it will settle it just fine, you'll see. Go on, get it in you. Sort you out, make you right as rain, it will."

I took a sip and it burned my sore throat but in a soothing way and the warmth spread through my guts. "You were right, Philip, as always. I feel much restored already." I shoved the flask back into his hands. "Are you not affected by this appalling motion?"

Philip beamed. "Oh no, it's most invigorating. I never been out of sight of land before, not proper, like." He breathed deeply, sucking the sea air in through his nose and letting it out dramatically. He wore a hat with a wide brim and had it tied tight under his chin. "To be at sea is thrilling indeed, truly it is."

I shook my head and was entertaining the notion of tossing him overboard when the hearty voice of our captain called out from a few paces away. "Splendid words, young man. Philip, is it? Well, Philip, sounds like you have the makings of a fine mariner." Hawkins smiled. "Unlike your poor master, here. Richard, I am saddened by your sorry state of being but I beg you not to fret for all men's stomachs settle in time."

"Why in the name of God would you choose to captain such a vessel across deadly seas? By the sounds of it, the *Jesus* should be beached, broken up and burned for firewood."

Hawkins scowled and stepped closer. When he spoke, in a low voice, his Devonshire accent was more apparent than ever before. "I just spoke to Mister Francis, who informed me of your blasphemy whereupon I defended you on account of your afflicted state. And now, mere moments later, I find you once again using the Lord's name in vain. Worse, you speak ill of our good ship and threaten to bring evil luck on us. I will warn you never to say words of beaching, nor breaking up or burning the very timbers that must keep us afloat and provide us shelter from home to destination to home again and everyplace between. Now, I will make allowance for the fact that you are a friend of the royal council and from what I hear a friend of the Queen herself. I will allow also that you are a land-leaper that knows not one end of the ship from the other, currently weak in your body which has disrupted your wits. But all that being allowed, I will not have either blasphemy or words spoke aloud about my ship. Will you agree to my terms, friend?"

As much as I wanted to scoff at his self-righteous Protestantism, he was the captain of the ship and captain-general of the entire expedition and I had no desire to create an unnecessary conflict. "I will better harness my tongue. It would not do to bring ill fortune on us."

He clapped me on the shoulder. "And I also ask you not to make an enemy of Francis. He is a vigorous fellow, full of his own importance, but he has the makings of a fine mariner and it is my duty to see he makes good his potential."

"You are a dutiful captain, John. I also make it my business to get the best of each of my men."

"Each of my men, yes indeed, that is true. But particularly true when a man is my cousin."

"Francis is your cousin? That surprises me, I confess. There is little resemblance between your stature and his, for example. And you have the manners of a gentleman."

"He is a... distant cousin." Hawkins lowered his voice. "If you two come to blows, I have no doubt you would knock him down in an instant. But no matter the causes, I would have to punish you, publicly. I would not want to, you understand, but I would have to. The maintenance of discipline is the most vital aspect of commanding a ship."

"Of commanding a company of soldiers also." I bowed my head. "In my youth, I would already have lashed out. But after an age, I have grown able to resist such impulses. Fear not, I shall not come to blows with your charming cousin."

We shook hands and when he strode off to continue reviewing his ship and his men, I reached for Philip's wine flask once more. "Give me that."

He obliged and pulled a face. "Are you sure you can avoid coming to blows with that young man, sir? He already seems set on making you an enemy."

I sighed, watching Hawkins as he berated a group of mariners for something or other. "All my life, I have known sailors to be the singularly most superstitious, sour and unpleasant men there are anywhere. But now I find that there are men even worse than that. Do you know who they are?"

Philip shrugged.

"Protestant sailors."

He frowned and looked down. Of course, he was a Protestant himself and so he had taken offence. They were such a prickly bunch, as a rule, always ready to be offended on behalf of their tedious new religion.

"Come on," I said to him, pointing at his hat and smiling. "We should get you out of the sun before you start to burn. Thanks to that wine, I feel restored enough to be bled."

That cheered him up and we went aft to the tiny cabin at the rear of the ship. Even back then, I had had wardrobes larger than the cabin we shared. I found myself unable to stretch out to my full length and the mattresses were absolutely appalling but at least there was a modicum of privacy with which I could keep Philip supplied with blood.

My seasickness subsided and soon I was well enough to join the other officers and gentlemen in the main cabin for the daily meal. We took turns supplying certain items from our own personal victuals in order to add variety to the otherwise rather plain fare. The ship's rations may have been uninspiring but they were at least plentiful and I found myself eating well.

Across all the ships we were four hundred men and our holds were laden primarily with cloth of many kinds for trading. Each ship bore the red cross of England flapping at the mastheads and hopes were high for a profitable and swift voyage. I began to enjoy the stirring sight of those flags and the white sails billowing against the blue sky and the smell of the salt spray in the air.

Then a few days in a great storm blew up and scattered us in a gale that lasted four miserable days and threw us about most terribly. The leaks on the *Jesus* grew worse and the men worked the pumps furiously to keep us afloat. I made one of the few contributions I could make to the practical business of keeping the ship afloat and took my turns down in the cold, wet, dark hold beside the common mariners. Even so, the water continued to rise and the sailors began to mutter and look sideways at each other in their growing anxiety and it was clear our old ship was in genuine danger.

On the third day of the storm, Hawkins summoned both watches—other than the men actively engaged in wrestling the storm—to the main deck and held a service in which he cried out a prayer over the wind, beseeching God to save us by sparing the ship. Men dropped to their knees and clapped hold of anything that was tied down while the sodden deck tilted and bucked beneath them. As frightened as I was, I did not pray along with the Protestants.

Nevertheless, their prayers must have been heard because the storm faded and we limped on toward the Spanish colony of Santa Cruz de Tenerife in the Canary Islands, off the coast of Africa. When we made the harbour, I was thankful indeed. It was a Spanish place but unlike the New World, they had never closed the Canary Islands to the English or to anyone else and they allowed us to refit and to take on fresh goods. However, we were tolerated rather than welcomed and the sailors told me the Spanish suspected, accurately, that we were bound for illegal trading in the New World.

Wary of a sudden attack from land, Hawkins repositioned the ships in our squadron by moving us further out so there were Spanish ships between us and the guns of the shore forts. I was pleased to see that for all his adventurous spirit, he was also tactically aware of possible dangers and decisive enough to act swiftly.

As it turned out, he was right to do so.

When we were preparing to depart one of the men noticed the Spanish in the castle moving their guns so they had a line of attack on us. The sun was going down, and it was felt any treacherous Spanish attack would likely come at first light so word was sent between our ships and in the dark of the night we warped and towed the ships further away still, so that by morning we were out of gun range in the mouth of the harbour.

"They were actually going to attack us," Philip said to me, rather surprised. "Even after our fair relations with them here these past days."

We stood at the side of the command deck of the Jesus, in hearing of the gentlemen and the officers and many of them scoffed at Philip's naivety. Yet I was almost as shocked as Philip.

Hawkins did not join in the discussion but stared back at the shore, waiting for them to take some action that would require from him some sort of response.

"The Spanish guard their trade as if it were their wives," Drake quipped. "Or their own children."

"No," Hawkins said without turning. "They protect it far more than that. The gold, the silver, the slaves, all of it together is more precious even than their own lives. It has made Spain the greatest kingdom upon the earth. Without it, what would they be?"

I considered pointing out that it was Spanish explorers and conquerors that had discovered the lands, conquered and subjugated its people and mined the silver and gold. The Spanish *people* made the Spanish Empire and the wealth was a consequence of it, not the cause. But I knew such observations would not be welcomed and so held my tongue.

The soldiers of Santa Cruz de Tenerife did not fire on us in the night, nor did they put out any ships against us, and soon after sunrise we sailed away south with the full squadron toward the coasts of West Africa.

What a strange country that was.

Africa was wild and terrible. Hard coasts, rocky or dripping with vegetation or dry as powdered bone, and hot weather, first parched and then sweltering and the air sopping like steam.

During the day, Philip spent as much time as he could in the cabin as the sun was almost more than he could bear. At night, he would enjoy the relative coolness of the air while I slept. In my travels across the world, I had never yet been anywhere as alien as was Africa. Stepping upon those shores to guard men collecting water and trading with locals, I felt in my bones that it was not a land for us. The air, the earth, the water, all felt intrinsically hostile.

But other men did not feel the same way. Plenty saw in Africa a land of great potential. There was abundance of superb timber, of exotic and fabulously expensive animal hides, and ivory. For decades by then, the Portuguese had been establishing outposts along those pestilential coasts to facilitate trade and it was through those small towns that Hawkins wished to do much of the necessary work.

Coming first to a place named Cape Blanco, we discovered half a dozen Portuguese fishing caravels that were entirely deserted, just bobbing away at anchor with no men and nothing else of value.

"Why would they abandon them?" I asked the mariners as we took one of the caravels as a prize to add carrying capacity to our squadron. No one knew then but later we traded with the locals onshore and they told us that another ship had come, a French ship of war, and the Portuguese mariners had fled together in a single boat, terrified no doubt that they would have been taken for slaves or killed.

"Where is the French ship now?" we asked the locals. They had no idea but were keen to sell us patterned hides and piles of ivory and we were happy to oblige them.

I had seen Africans before, of course, many times. Even

centuries before I had encountered Ethiopes in Egypt and Outremer, trading or living as slaves or servants, or performing tricks or playing musical instruments in troops. In Baghdad there had been some, mostly I heard they had been worked in the marshy fields in the south. The Arabs liked to use them as slaves, for outdoor work in the sun, mainly, but for all kinds of things. They took men in the main and when they bought them they had them castrated, the balls and cock both. As with oxen, it made them easier to control. Their black slaves died at astonishing rates from the castrations and were also kept in poor conditions but then there were always more to be had. Arabs sucked slaves out of Africa like some mighty and unceasing pump, just as the Turks and Moors had sucked in Christian slaves from all over Europe for a thousand years.

The Arabs and Moors had slave traders even in the far west of Africa and that was where we meant to do business. But there were native slave masters there, also. African lords with enormous wealth with whom we could go to directly to barter, legally and fairly. And yet the Portuguese did not want Englishmen taking away any of their business and some of the slavers, yielding to Portuguese pressure, declined to do business with us.

"Another one!" Hawkins roared when the shore party returned empty handed from a third port town. "If we cannot buy them, we shall have to take them!"

Our squadron headed south along the coast, looking for prizes. The Portuguese purchased slaves in Africa and took them to their own colonies in South America and to Spanish colonies further north. Portugal was at peace with England and we certainly had no royal commission with which to authorise actions against them at sea. However, they were Catholics and the English mariners were Protestants and that was enough justification for what amounted to base piracy.

When our fleet came across three Portuguese vessels a few miles away to the south, I thought I would witness a grand sea chase, with guns firing and men leaping from our decks to board the enemy vessels with weapons in hand and I was excited to see it. The reality was deeply disappointing. We approached and fired a gun or two, they pulled in their sails and waved flags of surrender.

"What on earth are they doing?" I asked a passing seaman. "Why do they not run?"

He laughed at my ignorance. "They couldn't get away from us, sir. Why bother trying to run? Waste of time. They reckon it better not to risk angering us."

I nodded as he carried on with his work and I turned to Philip at my side. "Much like taking a castle. Surrender immediately and be spared but resist and face death. Makes sense."

Philip reached under his broad-brimmed hat and scratched his sweaty scalp. "But their ships are smaller and lighter. Surely they can sail faster than us and escape."

A different sailor turned and scoffed at us and turned to his friends and relayed our words to them, whereupon they scoffed also while he spoke to us. "Small ships don't go faster than bigger ones. Not necessarily, anyways. Ain't how heavy you are, it's how much sail you can put up, and your lines and your draught, how you're rigged, and how fouled you are and how close to the wind your ship might sail, you know what I'm saying, sir?"

"Quite," I said, nodding sagely. "How right you are."

We came up to those Portuguese ships and I was surprised to see how orderly it all was. Boats were lowered over the sides and our men were rowed over. They were armed but there was no resistance offered as they climbed aboard and discussed the contents of the cargo with the poor captains. Logbooks were inspected by Englishmen who read and spoke Portuguese and the items Hawkins and his captains were interested in were unloaded. These items were essentially anything that could be readily sold in the New World but most desired of all were their Negro slaves. Every one of these were taken from the Portuguese ships and brought over to ours, where they were inspected, logged, and taken down into the darkness of the hold.

The slaves were miserable and sullen, as might be expected, and it was unpleasant to see them slumping off like whipped dogs. Most did not even look up as they shuffled in rows along the deck to be logged and escorted below.

"What vile wretches they are," Philip muttered that first evening as the last of them were brought across. "Utterly pathetic."

I agreed with him. "God forbid we ever find ourselves in such condition."

"Us?" he cried, horrified. "How could the likes of us ever be thus?"

I almost laughed at his naivety but of course it was no laughing matter and I spoke in a hushed voice lest anyone hear us through the thin wooden walls of the cabin. "If we find our ship taken by the Turks or the Moors, you will find yourself in just such a condition. Worse, in fact, for they may very well take your balls and your cock for good measure and then you would be chained up and worked until the blood sickness drives you mad and kills you. Then again, you're a smooth-skinned lad and you might end up face down in a Turkish lord's bathhouse, being rogered senseless from your first day to your last."

He scowled. "I'd kill them to get away. And I'd die before letting them violate me. A man is only a slave if he allows himself to be." He brightened. "Besides, we are not likely to meet any Moors out here, are we."

I shrugged. "They are sailing farther afield all the time but it is not just they who will take you. The Spanish will make you a slave and have you chained to an oar in one of their great war galleys and again you would starve without blood. They would torture you as a heretic first and make you Catholic, of course, before you died."

Philip gritted his teeth. "Never," he growled under his breath. "I will die before converting to the false religion, I swear it to God." He glanced at me. "I mean no offence to you."

I clapped him on the shoulder. "Let us hope it does not come to that."

Taking Portuguese ships was one way of gaining cargo. The other way was by raiding the coast directly. Wealth was concentrated in large settlements, mostly those Portuguese colonies and outposts and these were beyond our means to assault. The rest of Africa was poor indeed. There were strange and valuable animals but we had no means or skill with which to hunt them.

The only other thing of value that could be taken by force for future profit was people.

"There is a village," Hawkins said to the assembled officers.

The main cabin of the *Jesus* was packed with captains and masters and other gentlemen come from every vessel in the squadron for the meeting. "Half a mile inland or less. My men saw it when collecting water from the river there. I have decided we shall go tonight and we shall take off as many prisoners as we can. By my calculations, by using all boats from every ship we may land two hundred men quite rapidly, assemble on the beach and advance on them. Once the village is subdued, we can load the prisoners in daylight. With God's will, we shall have taken so many that we can strike out for the New World immediately."

There were many nodding heads and half the officers grinned. I noted that it tended to be the younger half, with many of the older men apparently harbouring concerns. After waiting in vain for them to be voiced, I spoke up.

"You wish to attack at night, sir?" They fell silent and turned to where I stood, at the back of the cabin, pressed against the wall. "Would we not do better to wait until dawn?"

Hawkins scowled. "They will be asleep at night. We shall catch them by surprise. I was assured that you were an experienced soldier, Mister Ashbury, but if I have to teach you such an elementary lesson then perhaps I was misinformed."

Laughter flowed through the cabin. I waited for it to die down. "It is precisely that experience that has taught me to be wary of night attacks. Too much can go wrong."

"What can go wrong?" Captain Hampton from the *Minion* said. "They are unarmed, undefended, ungodly savages."

"I agree completely. So why go at night? Such easy prey can offer no resistance no matter the hour."

Men started to shout me down and others argued with them

until Hawkins raised his voice and they fell silent. "We go in full dark. It was already decided before this assembly was called and no matter what the more nervous amongst us fears, we shall take the entire village tonight and carry off the men in the morning."

An officer raised a hand. "But the Spanish will pay for women and children also."

Hawkins shook his head. "More trouble than they're worth, James. Just the men. Now, if there are no more questions, we should give—"

I raised my voice again. "How big is the village?"

Hawkins and most of the others sighed. "How big? I don't know, however big Negro villages are. It hardly matters, Richard."

"So there might be a hundred men there or even more. Each man armed with a spear and perhaps men with bows and arrows. There may well be more than a hundred. What should you do if your men find themselves outnumbered and—"

"I never met a more timid man than you, sir," Hawkins said, staring at me. Silence followed. All held their breath, including me. "A true Englishman is worth ten of these savages, in stature, in physical strength, cunning, and mental prowess. They may have spears and bows?" He smiled and his men chuckled. "We shall be armed with pikes, swords, and firearms. What is more, if we face any danger, we will have the benefits of your renowned soldierly ability." The officers tittered and Hawkins glared at me. "Now, we shall pray on the main deck, then you shall return to your ships and ready your men."

His jibe about true Englishmen was aimed at my Catholicism, I was sure, and I knew they would suspect my advice for that reason alone. If they did not trust me, there was nothing more I could do. And as for the praying, every morning as the day watch came up, and every evening as the night watch took over from them, Hawkins would assemble all the men of the *Jesus* for religious services. The quartermaster, Paul Hawkins, who was our captain's nephew, would preach to the crew in a bellowing roar. Kneeling, the men recited the Psalms, the Lord's Prayer and the Creed, all in English of course, while the young Hawkins would denounce and rail against the Pope or he would inform us that we should only ever pray to God. Not the Pope, not Our Lady, nor any of the saints, could intercede for us. Our relationship was to God alone, directly, with none between us.

No matter how many times I heard it, it always sounded like utter nonsense. It was a miserable religion, I thought, filled with condemnation and criticism rather than with glory and highness, as with Catholicism. But I stomached it, twice a day, and kept my doubts to myself.

But that evening, listening to their righteous piety, I could not help but think of the Godless wretches under our feet in the hold and the others on the shore who would soon be joining them, and I wondered what they made of it all.

While the boats were lowered, and weapons brought up and sharpened, the men who were going on the raid laughed and jostled each other, talking about how many slaves they would capture. I stood back and watched.

"You do not wish to go ashore," a voice said at my back. "But as our captain said, this is your usual line of work, is it not?"

I turned and was surprised to see it was Francis Drake, standing in a drab suit of clothing and clutching a short club.

"It is a low business," I said, shrugging. "I like to fight men,

97

not savages."

He pursed his lips. "But a necessary business. How else will we make a profit? You are an investor, no? This is how the voyage pays for itself and makes us rich. Why did you come if not to trade in slaves?"

Sighing, I looked at the dark shore. It was almost full night and the stars were coming out. It was to be a half-moon, so there would be enough light to see by.

"All I want is to reach the New World," I replied.

He lowered his voice and stepped closer. "The men say you have personal business in New Spain. Is that true?"

I wondered who had been talking and reflected that Philip was too witless to be subtle and too trusting to be wary. "My business is my own. But there are Spaniards I would like to speak to, once we reach the Spanish Main."

"But why?" he lowered his voice to a whisper. "Is it secret work? For the Crown? For the Council?"

"If it were, why in the world would you expect me to speak of it?"

"Ah," he said, straightening and grinning. "Then say no more, sir, say no more. I can hold my tongue, you see if I can't. But if you should need any assistance then I am your man."

"Assistance?"

He nodded. "We can help each other. Perhaps, for an example, once we cross the seas you might need someone to speak with you in the council of officers and I can back your arguments with my own. Or, it might be when the squadron is trading about the islands you will need to take a ship to some secret place and then I can command that ship for you. Even if it's a pinnace or our prize caravel. You might ask our captain for me by name and he might grant it to me. What do you say?"

"You?" I said. "I thought you were barely an officer and here only because you were some poor and distant relation to Hawkins. Why would I have you command anything?"

He took great offence and swallowed three times before being able to respond. Then he stepped right up to me and his voice became low and steady. "I am the most skilled mariner on this entire voyage. I commanded my own vessel in English waters for years, and soon I shall have a command of another. You would do well to make a friend of me, Richard."

I had an urge to laugh at him, and to mock him, but he seemed a fragile sort and I did not have the heart to make another argument. Not when the slaving raid was ahead of us. "I appreciate a man who knows his own value, Francis. I shall remember your words, when the time comes."

Drake smiled, nodded, and looked at the second boat going over the side. "You say this is a low business." He lowered his voice. "And you are not wrong."

I turned and realised that he was speaking to me in the first instance because he was nervous about the coming venture. Of all the officers and gentlemen, I was the only one who had expressed concerns at the meeting. Concerns he appeared to secretly harbour himself.

"Do you expect trouble?" I asked him, gesturing at the shore.

"With the Negroes?" he asked, scoffing. "Not likely." He fell silent, fiddling with his club.

"Worry not, Francis. My objections were presented for discussion, and to make the officers aware of some of the dangers involved. There should be light enough to see by and it is hardly a long way to this village."

He scowled. "I am not afraid."

"I did not say you were and I do not think it. All men are worried before a scrap, even me."

"I am not worried, either. Certainly, we shall take the slaves and add them to the men we have already. It is simply..." he sighed. "When we brought the Negroes from the other ships, I could not help but notice your reaction."

"My reaction?"

He cleared his throat. "You seemed... repulsed."

"Certainly," I said.

"You were?" he asked, surprised and relieved. "You find the slavery business repulsive?"

I shook my head. "These *people* are repulsive. Who knows how long the Portuguese had them in their holds for, they were fetid. God knows how you expect to keep them fresh all the way to the New World. The ship will reek to high heaven. It does already. What a squalid business you do. I wish I did not have to come on this raid at all, and I do not mind admitting it but I will come in order to keep your men safe, if I can. Though I will not take any slaves myself, mark me."

"I see," he said, though his tone and expression suggested he was confused.

"You can stick by my side, Francis, if you like. I'll keep you safe."

He frowned. "I am an officer. I must lead and must do so from the front."

I clapped him on the shoulder. "That's the spirit, son. You'll do well."

Nodding absently, he moved away to the side ready to climb down into the boats.

"Do we have to go, Richard?" Philip asked from the shadows nearby.

"Are you afraid also, Phil?"

"Hardly that. It is just so... ignoble."

I smiled. "That it is. Come on, let us be slavers, shall we?"

The raid was disastrous.

The mariners who had seen the village led our parties through the brush beside the river but there were so many of us we made the most God-awful racket. Worse still, one of the men fired his arquebus into the air before we were halfway there and so by the time we reached it, the men of the village were out front, whooping and shouting at us and shaking their weapons in the air and pinging arrows from the darkness.

I stayed back, at the edge of some spiky bushes, and watched by moonlight as our men spread around the houses of the village. They were round buildings with cone-shaped brush roofs and there were a surprising number of them, perhaps as many as fifty stretching away into the shadows. More and more Negroes came forward while our men rushed them in groups, coming to blows before dragging off a man or two back toward our boats. Shots were fired and men shouted not to kill the Africans, for each dead Negro was a loss where there might have been gain. The night air filled with the curses and shouts of angry Englishmen and outraged Negroes and Philip urged me to help.

"Help how?" I said, almost laughing. "This is a thorough chaos."

"Rally them," he said. "Lead them."

"Use your head, son, they will not follow me."

"Find Hawkins," Philip said, "and advise him to pull the men back."

I scoffed. "You think he will listen to me? Philip, please."

"We can't let our own men die. And they're killing the Negroes!"

I crossed my arms and waited, satisfied at least that I had been proved right. More guns were fired and Englishmen shouted again to stop their shooting, for they were there to take captives, not to slay anyone. The noise faded for a while but then a great commotion rose up in the centre and men began rushing back toward the shore, shouting in fear. I grabbed at a sailor and held on to his arm to stop him.

"What is occurring, man?"

He turned his wild eyes to me. "Captain Hawkins is shot."

"Shot?" I asked. "By an arquebus?"

"By a bloody savage!" he shouted, shaking off my hand. "He's dying, sir, he's dying! And he ain't the only one."

"You go," I said to him and drew my sword. "Philip, come with me."

"We go the wrong way," he said but drew his own blade and joined me. Ahead, men struggled in the darkness and we came to half a dozen tribesmen beating on a couple of floored mariners.

"Oi!" I shouted and rushed into them. I kicked one in the belly and smacked another in the face with the flat of my blade, breaking his nose. A third man got my fist in his eye and then they were running from me. Philip helped up both of our lads and we started back. Just then I felt a jab high in my back and I whipped around with my sword out but there was no one there.

Another sailor came rushing up out of the dark and grabbed me. "Back to the boats!"

"Yes, yes," I said, feeling suddenly lightheaded.

The cry went up everywhere and we retreated all the way back to the shore. I found a group fighting off a handful of blacks who pursued us and helped drive them away. Two of them were cracked on the head and dragged behind us like sacks of apples.

I stumbled and Philip caught me. "You are hurt!" he cried.

"No, no. I am well," I said but my words were slurred and my mouth was incredibly dry. My legs felt very strange and my head ached.

"You bloody ain't," Philip said, running his hands all over me.

"Get off," I snapped and pushed him off as we came to the beach.

We piled back into the boats and the men pushed off and rowed hard. With a start, I realised we had a wounded man in the bottom of our boat. He was groaning and clutching his chest and Francis Drake, who held aloft a lantern in one hand, had the wounded man's head on his thigh while he muttered soothing words.

"What happened to him?" I asked Drake.

"Arrow got him," Drake said.

"That's why we run," a mariner said, pulling hard on his oar.

The rower opposite added a crucial piece of information. "Poison arrow."

"Poison!" Philip cried. "Mister Francis, is it truly poison?"

"Certainly," Drake said, holding the lantern close to the man who was breathing rapidly but who otherwise looked dead.

"How do you know?" I asked, bending over to have a look at the man in the lantern light.

"By Christ!" a mariner shouted. "You got one, too!"

"Don't move!" Philip said and placed a hand on my back. I felt the arrow come out. It was not a broadhead by any means but it hurt.

"You feeling all right, sir?" a mariner asked, gaping.

"Fine, fine," I said and leaned over the side to vomit. "Perfectly fine."

Twenty men had been poisoned, plus Captain Hawkins.

The spindly little arrows of the Africans had floored twenty-one Englishmen and all of them fell ill. Of those, eight worsened and over the next day developed a strange ailment like lockjaw. They could not open nor fully close their mouths and they were wracked with paroxysms of shaking and then of full immobility. Struggling for breath, they groaned in the most appalling fashion and one by one, before midday, all eight of them died.

The others who had been struck recovered almost as swiftly and thankfully Hawkins was one of those who got better.

For our troubles, we took just nine slaves in the raid.

"How is it that you were also shot with poison?" Drake asked me right after the dead men were buried at sea. "And yet you alone had but a moment's sickness before you were well again."

Philip glanced sharply at me but said nothing.

"I have always had a robust constitution."

Drake frowned. "Perhaps your arrow barely penetrated your flesh."

"Perhaps."

I think he was offended that I had shrugged it off while friends of his had suffered so terribly. He went back to his work with a final resentful glance at me.

Our voyage continued, taking more Portuguese caravels along the coast and we came across the French ship that had caused the fishing vessels to be abandoned at Cape Blanco. Our squadron was so mighty that we took it with ease. One look at the monstrous *Jesus of Lubeck* was enough to frighten any other captain in those seas. Surprisingly, young Francis Drake was given command of the newest addition to the squadron, and he grinned at me and winked as he disembarked the *Jesus*.

"He mocks you!" Philip muttered, shocked.

I smiled. "By that look he says merely that he told me so. And he did."

"That he would be given command of a ship? But this is only because he is Captain Hawkins' cousin."

"Distant cousin."

"Still, though," Philip said. "He does not deserve it."

"Perhaps," I said. "And what is wrong with that? It is the way of the world. If he succeeds, it was a good decision. If he fails, all men in the squadron shall see it and he will be restored to his proper, lowly position. All men find their level."

Philip, who was a born valet, lowered his head. "Yes, sir."

Between Cape Verde and Sierra Leone, the shore consisted of nothing but rivers and inlets and it was there that Hawkins declared we would find enough slaves to fill our holds. Using many smaller boats and the shallow-draught ships, we set off up rivers to find settlements to raid or Portuguese traders to take.

At first, it was easy pickings. In a single river we found six Portuguese ships and their handful of slaves were offloaded. Up the next big river we found a laden caravel and took all the victuals it carried.

But our luck turned, or the Portuguese got wise to our presence and then we found no slaves on the water at all. After finding a series of ten ships with no slaves on them, Hawkins was growing desperate. So we loaded our boats and assaulted a small and undermanned Portuguese settlement named Cacheo. Incredibly, the local Negroes decided to fight beside the Portuguese and we retreated from the place without taking a single slave while losing four men to the enemy. We set fire to their buildings as we fled and took some plunder but in all it was a miserable affair and I did little more than observe from the rear.

Two weeks after this debacle, the captain summoned the senior men from the fleet to his cabin and told us that he had a plan which would bring us all the slaves we could possibly want.

"Another raid on a village?" I asked.

"Not a raid but the reduction or destruction of a great place of the natives." Hawkins lifted his chin. "And rather than a village it is, I believe, more of a fortress."

The fortress was on an island called Conga in the Tagarin River. During our usual low-level local trading onshore, the chiefs of the Sapi people along the coast had come to our men with a proposal.

"Our new friends the Sapi are being invaded by the Mande people. It is the invading Mande who have taken control of Conga and who are using it as a fortified base to attack the poor Sapi. I have agreed with the chiefs that we will destroy Conga. The Sapi will be rid of a vile new enemy, while we will keep all the prisoners that are taken."

I raised a hand. "How big is Conga?"

Master Barrett had been upriver already and he stood to answer. "It is a sizable island, half a mile wide and three long. The fortress is far smaller but it is protected all the way around by a wall of rough logs at least six feet high. Because the Negroes there are conquerors, almost every inhabitant is a warrior. The few women are captives taken as wives by the marauding Mande."

"Sounds bloody dangerous," I said.

I was mocked by some but others nodded their head in agreement.

"I thought you understood the necessity of this venture, Richard," Hawkins snapped. "And I hoped that you would finally contribute your supposed military experience to this action."

"Surely, sir," I said to Hawkins, "you have enough slaves now. Let us sail from Africa for the New World now and make the best of it."

He was irritated. "I have heard how you hang back from every assault, and how you refuse to lay a hand on a Negro. Perhaps you think yourself above such things but if you wish us to travel across the sea rather than return home, you should help to fill our holds. All trade with the New World is closed to us, all, I know you understand we can trade nothing else but slaves. So desperate are they for men to work the land, any men, even Negroes, that we can perhaps induce them to bend the rules for this single thing. We have, as of this morning, just one hundred and forty slaves in the holds of all my ships. We must have many more if we are not to return as paupers. If this voyage is not a success, I will never find investors enough for another. And nor will any other Englishman. However important is your nefarious business for the Council, how will you ever travel to the New World without true Englishmen to take you? Help me, and you help yourself, you help the Privy Council, the Queen, all England. Will you help me, Richard?"

The gentlemen and the officers crammed into the main cabin stared at me, even those who had to turn right around to look. I knew they were all thinking the same thing.

Your nefarious business for the Council.

Any hopes I had that my true purposes on the voyage were secret had been dashed. Either everyone already knew, or they now did anyway. I did not doubt that Hawkins had spoken the words not thoughtlessly and in anger but deliberately, intending to force my hand by shaming me, and to demonstrate his power over me by flaunting his knowledge. Did he expect me to explode in anger or shrink under the gaze of the officers?

Instead, I shrugged and smiled. "If it is so necessary, perhaps we should take as much care as we can this time, captain. This fort is filled with warriors, it has timber walls. Might I make some strategic suggestions?"

We took ninety men on the two smallest of our ships, the *Angel* and the *Judith*. We crept up the wide river taking soundings ceaselessly to avoid running aground.

The Sapi tribesmen massed on the banks and swarmed along on foot beside us. They were a horror to behold. Angry brutes, shaking their spears in the air over their heads and making faces, shouting in strange grunts as they ran. Many had painted themselves in white and reds and some wore feathers or furs dangling from their bodies or from their weapons. Standing at the rail of the *Angel*, I eyed them almost constantly, fearing them turning on us. There were hundreds of them.

"Reckon they're trustworthy?" Philip asked me, wincing in the bright light from under his big hat.

"No."

The fort was larger than I had expected and the timber wall, a picket made from logs driven into the ground side by side, was taller in places than six feet. More like ten or even twelve in some places, and there were a few taller towers on the inside and fighting platforms so they could shoot their arrows and throw their javelins at us. Despite the size, it was all roughly done and there was an air of general incompetence and decay, not to mention a foul stench.

We disembarked on the shore of the island and took positions a hundred yards from the walls while the Sapi began to swarm across the shallow and narrow ford, as well as crossing on rafts, branches, and by swimming with their spears in hand.

I commanded my men to start their fires and they unwrapped the pitch-soaked linen and lengths of frayed hemp. The timber walls and especially the roofs of the houses with them looked bone dry. We would fire them as we attacked, terrifying the savages and snatching them up in their panic. At least, that was my intention.

When most of the Sapi were across, three hundred of them at least, I ordered my men to signal our ships.

Almost at once, the *Angel* fired her cannons. They were small guns when compared to the ship smashers on the *Jesus* and the *Minion* but they made short work of the fort.

The guns roared and the balls ripped through the hot African air over our heads to smash into the palisade. Shards exploded up and whole timbers cartwheeled inside. One of the rickety towers collapsed, throwing the Mande from it like a child tossing his toys.

Further along the shores of the island, the masses of Sapi flinched and screeched and ducked and ran around like madmen, terrified and thrilled by our display of power. While the cannons of the *Angel* and the *Judith* were reloaded, the furious Mande warriors charged out through the gaps they had wrought, streaming toward us shaking their clubs and knives.

"Oh Christ save us!" one of the mariners shouted but the others were steady.

We were waiting for just such an attack.

"Arquebuses, ready!" I shouted.

The men so armed raised and clutched their weapons while our pikemen lowered their points.

"Fire!"

Our arquebusiers fired into the charging Mande, bringing down a dozen and sending most fleeing for the safety of their fortress.

But others kept coming and I ordered our arquebusiers back to reload while the pikes took two steps forward. Our men were not soldiers and it was a rough and ragged line but it was all I had. I drew my sword and told Philip to stay behind me. Shaking and sweating, he nodded and held his blade ready.

The Mande never reached us. Instead, the Sapi charged into them from the flank and they began murdering each other.

From the river, our cannons blasted again, ripping more great holes through the walls and the remaining warriors retreated with the Sapi going after them, hacking and bashing their enemies as they ran.

"Come on," I said to my men and the other officers. "Now is

the time. Stay together. Forward!"

The Sapi had driven most of the townsmen away but we still had to fight our way inside, shooting or spearing any who came at us. They were a frightening sight up close, all wild-eyed and mad with murderous fury but they had no cohesion at all and were easily cut down while we attempted to capture those we could.

One group of sailors marched too far inside without defending their flanks and just as I was sending a runner to bring them back, they were fallen upon by a massive crowd of warriors. Still, even they were fended off by sword and buckler, and even by fists and kicks. The mariners were not soldiers but they were used to fighting at sea, which is half chaos at the best of times.

"Come on," I shouted at my small company. "We're going to drive off those bastards and save our boys. With me!"

We charged and I reached them first, cutting a swathe through the attackers almost single handed and in just a few moments they fled. I had defended a few wild blows but no more.

"You saved us," a voice said.

Drake was the captain who had led his group into danger.

"I said to stay together," I replied. "Why are you rushing off like a madman, Francis?"

He gestured with his sword, pointing it at my face before I slapped it away. "Your face," he said, frowning. "You are hurt."

I touched my cheek and felt the gouge which was almost all the way through my flesh and down to the bone. "It is nothing," I said, turning away. "Now let us take the men back and protect ourselves correctly."

In truth, it was not hard work for us because the Sapi fell upon the defenders with a frenzy the like of which I had never seen before. Blood spilled into the soil everywhere I looked. Some were armed with clubs of shiny black wood, some had bows and arrows, and others were armed with steel axes and knives, stolen or traded from the Portuguese. The Sapi prised out eyes, hacked off limbs from the living while they wailed, they held prisoners upside down and sawed men in half from the balls while they screamed. Heads were taken, and hands were taken, and prisoners were castrated and the organs shoved into the mouths of other prisoners while the Sapi themselves shrieked with glee. Guts were ripped open and hearts cut out, eyes gouged from their sockets and eaten.

"Look!" Philip said, grabbing my sleeve and pointing. "Look at that!"

In a large clearing in the centre of the village, two score of Sapi restrained a handful of writhing, screaming prisoners and cut chunks of flesh from their thighs, chests, and bellies and ate it. The flesh, still living, still warm, was eaten while the men it had been cut from died in the dust, watching their own blood running down the cheeks of their captors.

"You ever tasted Negro blood?" Philip asked.

"Keep your voice down," I said. "And forget it, you are not having any."

"I was merely asking," he protested.

"It turns my stomach," I said. "Let us rescue our prisoners before the savages kill them all."

We took just over two hundred and fifty slaves from that attack and lost just eight men of our own and two of those were killed as we rowed downstream when a monstrous hippopotamus overturned one of our boats. We shot it and threw spears into it and though it did not die, it bounded away tossing its enormous head with its immense, murderous teeth shining in the evening sunlight.

It was a victory and yet when we got back to sea with our prisoners, all who had been on the raid seemed stunned by the violence and the blood.

Francis Drake found me after evening prayers standing beside the ship's lantern and handed me a cup of wine without speaking. I drank it off in one gulp and we silently stared over the stern at the dark shore. The air was alive with insects of all sizes but at least it was getting cooler.

"I must return to my own ship," he said after a moment. "But I wanted to thank you. For... you know."

"It was nothing."

"I also wanted to thank you for impressing upon us all the need for caution, and for insisting on starting by properly using the guns, and for letting the Sapi do the hard work."

I shook my head. "I wish I had never seen those savages at all."

"We could not have done it without them," Drake countered.

"No."

"Might I ask, Richard. Do you still wish we had not attacked?"

I turned to him. "It is a rotten business. Sometimes, on quiet moments, or when we see some strange beast upon the shores, or some mighty trees, I like it here. But most of the time, I am filled with the sense that I do not belong here. And yes, I wish we had not attacked. I wish now I had found some other way instead of dallying here these long weeks. It is... it is ignoble."

I could tell he was pleased with my words but he hesitated before answering. "I mean never to do the like of it again."

Surprised by the bitterness in his voice, I looked at him closer.

Half his face was yellow, illuminated by the lantern, the other was silvered shadow. "You do not want to make a fortune?"

"Not like this."

"Hawkins says this is the only way it is done."

Drake shrugged. "There must be other ways. There must be." He shook his head and sighed. "Either way, I'll not do this again. I swear it to God, I'll not."

"Fair enough."

He frowned and looked closely at me. "Turn your head this way," he commanded. "What happened to your terrible wound?"

I touched my cheek. "Thankfully, it was a mere scratch."

Drake's mouth hung open. "But the blood..."

"It was not mine."

"I saw the bones of your face beneath that gouge."

Smiling, I clapped him on the back. "Clearly, Francis, you were mistaken."

He was utterly confused and I felt guilty for deceiving him. For all his bluster, he was not a bad fellow by any means. We shook hands as friends and he went back to his ship.

With holds filled with slaves, the first part of our voyage had been completed.

We sailed west, away from Africa and towards the New World.

5

The New World

1568

SAILING ACROSS THE ATLANTIC was deeply unpleasant. The sun was hot, the wind changeable, but the ships trudged on through the high seas day and night. The mariners appeared enormously satisfied by our progress and as much as I was happy to be travelling finally to the New World, being so far from land was extremely disconcerting. There was also the ever-increasing stench of the crew and the human cargo in the hold. It reeked of ancient sweat and shit and the throat-scorching taste of dried piss. As often as I could, I made my way forward to breathe the hot, damp, but clean air coming straight off the blue sea in front of us.

And then there was the constant praying and singing of psalms and reading from prayer books and more praying. It was as though some madness held my countrymen in its grip and I could do nothing to shake them out of it. Worst of all was the realisation that they saw me as the strange one. I was the outsider, the heretic, I was the one not to be trusted. I had never felt so out of place with my own people before.

Looking at the horizon, I willed us across to the land unseen beyond with every inch of my body and my soul.

We made landfall after four weeks sailing. Hawkins knew we were close, of course, through his employment of the navigational arts and told us at dinner we would see it on the morrow. But we smelled it first. An almost intangible whiff of something in the air. Something not of the sea, and not of the ship, a taste of black soil and a tang of green foliage. Then there were the birds in the distance, black specks dancing against the blue, and then the cry came from the man atop the mainmast.

"Land! Land, dead ahead!"

The men cheered and Hawkins had the officers served a cup of wine, which we drank off before our captain called us together for yet another tedious service where we knelt and offered thanks to God for delivering us safely across the sea. By the time it finished, I could see the strip of dark ahead of us by leaning against the rail on the command deck and looking forward beneath the underside of the mainsail.

"The New World," I said under my breath.

"An island," Hawkins said, grinning as he came up beside me. "There are other islands north and south of it, many of them, in an arc. You have seen the charts. But I believe we are looking at the higher land in the centre of Dominica."

"I never thought I would see it," I said. "When we first had word of it decades ago, men were excited beyond measure, thrilled with the revelation. To tell you the truth, I never really understood all the fuss, it seemed like just another distant place. Because, I suppose, I felt I had travelled the world already. I had been everywhere there was to go. Months of travel to the Holy Land and then even farther, half a year or so, to the distant East. It seemed there could be nothing beyond. How could there be? I had travelled to the edge of the world. But every day that I am on this mighty ship, I understand just a little more how wrong I was. The world is vaster than I understood and it seems only to get larger with every passing year, and with every mile that I travel upon it." I sighed. "And there it is, finally, a new land that no one ever suspected. How strange it is to live to see the world change so very much."

Hawkins was silent for some time and when he spoke I saw at once how thoroughly I had baffled him. "It is just one small island, Richard, not thirty miles long."

I smiled and shook my head. "Do not listen to my ramblings, John. They come from a man... a man too long at sea."

He nodded, able to sympathise with that at least. "We must have fresh water immediately. While we are at anchor, we will have the men properly scrub this salt from the timbers and we must air out the slaves and clean the holds. Another one died this morning."

"I saw him tossed over the side."

"Hardly tossed, Richard, we performed a proper Christian ceremony."

"I am sure the heathen savage appreciated it."

Hawkins frowned. "I pray we are able to sell them soon." He picked at a lump of salt on the rail and lowered his voice. "Soon you shall be free to undertake your... personal business. If you were to explain to me precisely what you wanted, I might be able to better assist you."

I was wary of men who asked such pointed questions. "You are very kind. If I am allowed to explore every town we come to, I shall make a few quiet enquiries here and there."

Hawkins nodded. "Might be difficult. Depends on the governor with these places. We can force some, if you want, but it will cost you in bribes and even then..."

"I understand. All that truly matters is that you simply put me ashore at Borburata and I shall do the rest. That is all for now."

He bowed. "Alright, I'll press you no further. Excuse me."

The Spanish in the colony on Dominica were wary indeed and would not allow us to come ashore and would not purchase a thing from us, though during the days we spent at anchor they did let us buy water and a quantity of wood that the carpenter needed to make running repairs to our ageing monster of a ship. From Dominica we ran south to an island called Margarita, just off the Spanish Main. Again, they were wary but Hawkins went ashore personally and met with the governor for much of the afternoon and when he came back he was drunk and had to lie down in his cabin. I do not know how much Hawkins bribed the governor but soon our squadron was bobbing in the harbour and offloading quantities of linen and iron and bringing back victuals. The fresh food was most welcome but I was not allowed to go ashore to speak with the officials or locals and I did not press the matter. The governor of Margarita refused to buy even a single slave and so a few days later we sailed west along the coast for three hundred miles.

Often, we were out of sight of land but at other times we could see the coast clearly and it was vast and almost entirely devoid of settlement. When Hawkins showed me the entire Main on his chart and I saw what a tiny fraction of its length we had travelled, I was awed once more by the scale of the New World. It truly was as though our world had quite suddenly doubled in size and the new half was empty and full of promise. I sat on Hawkins' finely carved chair and shook my head in wonder while he regaled me once again with tales of the riches that were to be had in that land. Riches that were currently being had by the Spanish alone.

We came at last to the port of the town named Borburata on the Spanish Main and the officers and crew were in a high state, knowing that we would shortly be making an enormous profit.

"We must be subtle," Hawkins said, after calling me to his cabin. He was seated at his desk and writing away with confident strokes. "We must be subtle indeed when dealing with these Spaniards and I know for a fact that you are a most subtle man, Richard. An agent of Her Majesty must be subtle, is that not so?"

"I suppose it is," I said, warily. "Until such time as a punch in the face is required."

He smirked as he wrote. "Yes indeed, how correct you are. Subtle and precise, sir." He finished with a flourish at the bottom of his sheet, returned his pen to its place and read over what he had written. "And we must employ subtlety with these Spaniards if we are to trade with them. I have written to the governor to explain that we have been blown off our intended course and have sought refuge in his waters. We have been blessed in finding victuals at other ports but now we find ourselves in need of paying our soldiers and without the coin to do it. It is for that reason that we humbly request permission to sell a few wares and sixty Negro slaves in order to overcome our difficulties. Now, I say as much in this letter. But I would like you to deliver it and to persuade him to agree."

"And by having me carry the letter, you are fulfilling your duty to put me ashore. Perhaps you would like to send another officer with me, who better understands the nature of these exchanges."

Hawkins frowned as he sat upright, stretching his spine. "I will send Thomas Hampton of the *Minion* to be the senior man in appearances only. And I know you have your own business here and that is all very well and you will have the time to do it. However, you will bear the letter, you will lead the negotiation, and you will make this trade happen. I believe now that you have a gift for such things and of course you are a Catholic. They will like you for that, at least."

The captain was starting to understand that I had some cunning but he did not know that I was learning to play him like a lute. "How much will this governor expect for a bribe?"

"Whatever it is, it will be steep. Bargain him down to the ground but be sure to give in, at the end, and pay up promptly. We must get rid of some of this cargo before they all perish. Every day their condition deteriorates further."

"You say you have made reference in that letter to your soldiers that need paying. I assume that by this you are making him aware of our strength? That we have angry, armed, drilled men aboard the fleet who might make trouble if we do not get coin? Trouble for Borburata?"

Hawkins smirked. "You see. A subtle man indeed."

"Could we take the town by force?" I asked. "Sack it, take the riches within?"

He jerked as if he had been slapped. "*Take* the town? We will not make war on the Spanish, sir. We risk bringing the might of their empire down on us, and then on every Englishman in all the seas, and then on England itself. Take riches within, he says, by God, what madness."

"I do not say we should do it. Merely ask if we have strength enough to do it. You see, if I am to allude to our strength as a point of negotiation, surely it will only have an effect if we do in fact have strength enough to storm his town. So, do we know how many guns they have? How high are their walls?"

Chopping a hand through the air to shut me up, he got to his feet. "He's protected by the walls of Spanish might. He knows we will not destroy him, that is not the point I wish to make. But he will not want angry English soldiers sitting on his doorstep, either, because we can certainly make trouble. Now, take this letter and just sell my damned slaves, man."

Captain Thomas Hampton came across from the *Minion*, along with John Garrett, the *Minion*'s master, and picked me up and I brought Philip with me. Both of us had slipped knives into every sleeve, pocket, and hidden place we had. And we wore thick linen arming doublet to protect our torsos, which made me sweat terribly in the sweltering tropical air. Before disembarking the ship, I had bled myself and given Philip a good drink of my blood so that he would be at full strength.

Of course, I prayed that none of these precautions would prove necessary.

Captain Hampton leaned forward from his seat at the rear of the boat as we approached the harbour. "Now, listen here,

Richard Ashbury. I know you believe yourself to be a man of considerable importance and claim some connection with certain men at the court but I have contacts there myself and they had never heard of you. Most of all, you must understand one thing. I am in command here. Do you see? Me. And after me comes Master Garrett. We are faithful men and you are simply a country gentleman that has come along for the voyage."

"You think me untrustworthy, Captain Hampton?"

He wagged a finger. "You shall do as I say in all things, or I shall have my men here take you back to the dock. Do you understand?"

The rowing sailors grinned to hear a gentleman get a dressing down in front of them and they relished the idea of laying their hands upon me. Philip, however, tensed as if ready to spring the length of the boat to lay into Captain Hampton with his clenched fists.

Restraining Philip with the fingers of one hand, with the other I reached inside my coat and withdrew Hawkins' letter to the governor. "This is for you, Captain Thomas."

Hampton snatched it from my hand and settled back, exchanging a look of profound smugness with Garrett.

The harbour of Borburata was within a large sandbar that hooked around almost closing the entrance. On the mainland stood a few timber buildings, little more than square huts. They did not seem to be houses so I assumed they were warehouses for produce. Standing on the shore watching us come in were a group of small, underfed men with golden-brown skin. Their faces were strange indeed and they were almost naked, clothed with dirty fabric wrapped around their waists, though one wore a filthy and torn undershirt, the tails flapping at his knees. Further along slouched a gang of Negroes, halted in their carrying of sacks to gape at us as we glided in toward the dock. Another Negro, sitting on the back of a donkey, barked at them in Spanish and waved a switch in the air until the group carried on lugging their sacks away.

We were met at the dock by three soldiers, all armed and wearing steel helms but scruffily dressed in dirty doublets.

"The English may not trade here," the oldest soldier said as we stepped up to the dock.

Hampton puffed up his chest and bellowed loudly, in English. "How dare you address us in that fashion! You, a damned commoner militiaman speaking to a gentleman like that. What manner of greeting do you call this, eh, Spaniard? You should be ashamed of yourselves. Now, you will take us to your governor, immediately!"

They scowled and shook their heads, perhaps not understanding the words but certainly not liking the tone and Hampton's gesticulations.

"You must go back to your ship," the senior man said, jabbing his finger out at sea.

I pushed past Hampton and smiled, waving my hand in the air so that the gold coin I had palmed flashed in the sunlight. "Good day to you, my friends," I said in my best Spanish. "Of course, the captain here and I are not here to partake in trade of any sort. We simply have a letter to convey to the governor, from our wealthy admiral who waits yonder on our mighty fleet." I grinned as I flicked the gold coin from one hand to the other, snatching it from the air with a flourish. "Which of you gentlemen

123

would like to escort us?"

It was a small place, barely warranting the label of a town, with more slaves than free men, and hardly any women at all. But the governor's house was rather pleasant, built in stone with a good roof and whitewashed plaster gleaming in the sun. When we got up to it, though, I saw the green growth of some terrestrial tropical algae spreading along that whitewash and the plaster at the base of the walls was crumbling into damp mush here and there.

The governor kept us waiting for five hours. Hampton spent the time fuming and demanding wine and other refreshments from the disinterested slaves that sloped by every now and then. Rather than waste my time, I decided to stroll about, casually, while one or more soldiers followed close behind, watching me like cats watching a mouse hole. Philip started to come with me but I sent him back to the shade of the governor's house.

"But be ready to come to me if I need you," I muttered.

"How will I find you?" he asked, eyes wide.

"If I am in such straits that I need you, I have no doubt you will hear where I am."

After a few minutes wandering here and there through the town, I strolled by a small, dark tavern. I had seen it on the way in, particularly the four women sitting in the shade beneath the veranda and nodded to them as I walked to the door.

I had long been at sea but even so they were not especially appealing to look upon. They were all black haired with light brown skin and all had bare arms and half had bare shoulders as well, with their hair fluttering loose in the breeze. But their clothes were ragged and unclean and they sat slumped, half-drunk already and miserable. Rather than arousing my ardour the sight of them aroused only revulsion and pity.

They all looked closely at me and I smiled at them and touched my hat. "Good day, lovely ladies," I said and they smiled and one laughed.

Stepping into the tavern, my eyes slowly adjusted to the gloom. At the rear was a staircase leading up to a mezzanine with five doors, all rather close together. A woman upstairs squealed and in response came the muffled sound of a man laughing. Beneath the stair was another doorway leading to storerooms or perhaps more bedrooms. There was a counter along one side with no one behind it so I sat at an empty table and waved a hand at the dozen or so men sitting at the other tables in the room.

"Good day, friends," I said, brightly.

An old man stood up and spat on the floor. "Lutheran filth." He turned to another fellow that sat slouched in the shadows. "Throw this English dog into the street, Antonio!"

Antonio muttered something in reply that I did not catch.

The old man spat again but it dripped down his chin and he cuffed it away. "You either throw the Lutheran out or you're no true Catholic and no true Spaniard, neither."

The fellow in the shadows named Antonio took a sip of his drink before replying. "Stop spitting on my floor, Luis."

"Ha!" he cried. "Go to Hell, if you want. I shall not." At that, he staggered away and immediately all the others stood, with much banging of chairs, and stomped out behind him, glaring at me as they went. Sixteen men in all and I nodded and smiled at each one, occasionally wishing them a good day.

"What do you want, Englishman?" the one remaining man said from the shadow.

I shrugged. "Wine?"

He sighed and heaved himself to his feet and limped from his corner toward me, into the light from the door and the half-shuttered window. One of his eyes was gone and the socket was a mass of scar tissue. That scar, or another, reappeared on his jaw, twisting his face into a terrific sneer. He wore a thin, light jerkin and loose hose. His muscular arms were bare, which was understandable in the heat, and the thick black hair on his arms was plastered flat with sweat.

"You will get nothing from Governor Coloma," he said, his voice like a growl. "You may as well leave now."

I nodded, pursing my lips. "I do not doubt you. But I must deliver the letter from our commander and then we shall go." I pointed at him. "So, Antonio, is it? How about a little wine while I wait, Antonio?"

He shrugged and limped away to his counter where he grabbed a cup and clanked around amongst bottles of wine.

"Give me the best stuff you have," I said.

Antonio grunted as he wriggled the stopper from a bottle. "There is no best stuff."

"That is well," I said, "as I prefer to sup on something more nourishing." As I spoke, I set a gold coin spinning on the dirty tabletop and watched it slow and fall, wobbling back and forth until it rattled to a stop.

Antonio limped closer, his eyes fixed on the gold. "I'm nothing but a tavern keeper and I will serve Lutherans wine but I'll not sell them secrets."

I shook my head. "It's not secrets I want." I leaned forward. "Because I already know everything."

He frowned. "What do you know?"

I shrugged and looked around. "I know you are not just a tavern keeper. The women outside, and the ones upstairs, tell me you are the keeper of this brothel house. Surely, I would wager, a more profitable enterprise than selling cups of wine alone. If I am not mistaken I saw a large storehouse behind this building. I would be surprised if you did not also engage in the trading of wine, buying shipments as they come in for sale here and for trading on. You are clearly an enterprising man who embraces all opportunities to make money."

He nodded, relieved by my words, and his eye darted again to the gold coin sitting between us on the table. "You want a whore." He ventured a grin, which was hideous on his scarred face. "A good one."

"Oh? You do not have good wine but you have good whores?"

"The best," he said, still grinning. "Best for a thousand miles."

"And is that how this works?" I asked.

Antonio was confused again. "How whores work?" he looked around his tavern, back to the coin, and then at me. "You pick one and you take her to a room. Not just Negresses. You saw my *mulatos* out front? I have lots of *mulatos*. Very pretty, very nice."

"*Mulatos*?" I asked. "That what you call the native girls?"

"Native girls?" he almost howled with amusement. "You can't make the Indians into whores, they don't do well with it. Breaks their spirit, don't last six months at it before they die. No, no, a *mulato*, you know, like a mule? A mule, half horse, half donkey. A *mulato*, a half Negro, half Spaniard. Lots of them around, more all the time. Very pretty, sweet girls. The beauty and grace of a Spanish lady and the lust and strength of a Negress, you'll see."

He eyed the coin again. "This will get you my best two, one after the other or at the same time."

I did my best not to show my disgust. "I see, how intriguing. And do they speak Spanish?" I asked.

He spread his hands. "What else would they speak?"

I thought for a moment. Would it be best to try to get the information out of these ignorant young women? What if they knew nothing at all of the matter?

Or should I try to bluff my way through the tavern keeper himself? If he was not forthcoming, I could hardly try to force the information from him without creating a terrible commotion, risking violence, ruining our squadron's chance of trade and possibly getting innocent Englishmen captured or killed.

"And is that how it works, then?" I asked Antonio. "I just drink straight from their flesh? Will they be expecting that or will I have to restrain them?"

He froze, his hand drifting towards the small of his back where he no doubt kept his knife. "What did you say?"

I shrugged. "It is simply that I do not know how it is done here, at this tavern. Personally, I would prefer a girl be bled into a cup. I am a civilised man, after all. A Catholic man, that is." And I looked at him knowingly.

"Get out," he said.

"Please," I said. "I am in desperate need of sustenance. It has been a long voyage and there is much more to go before we get home. I beg you, I just need one cupful. That is all, one cup of what I need, for one gold real."

He hesitated. "One cup?"

I smiled. "One cup, and the names of the other places on the

Main where I might get more."

"Coin first."

Antonio summoned a golden-skinned girl, took her into a back room, and emerged a few minutes later with a cup of fresh blood. It was smoothly done, without fuss, and I wondered how often he did it. Were there many people like me here? To ask it would certainly arouse suspicion and I doubted I would get an honest answer, so I held my tongue for the moment.

Sipping the cup, I nodded. "It is the proper thing." I lowered my voice. "Not that I heard this about *you*, Antonio, but some places try to serve up old pigs' blood, or some such thing."

He crossed his arms and watched as I gulped the blood down and wiped my lips. It was perfectly fine. As I was drinking, the *mulato* girl strode back out holding a cloth over the inside of her elbow and she glared at me with open revulsion.

"Now, tell about these other towns, will you, my friend?"

"Other towns?" he asked.

"As agreed, you will tell me of the other towns and ports and fortresses on the Spanish Main and the islands where I might find more men such as yourself who offer such a unique service."

He hesitated and he was no doubt thinking of cheating me. "I only know of Rio de la Hacha," he said, eventually. "Up the coast from here."

"That's it? Come on, you must know more. I paid you for the knowledge. Cough it up."

He shook his head. "I swear it by all the saints. There are more, but I know only of Rio de la Hacha for certain. Governor Castellanos knows about it, got a couple real nice girls for it, too, real nice. He'll do anything for money, Castellanos, because he was born a pauper, so they say. And they pay him to look the other way. Go to the big tavern and ask for Juan."

"Who pays him to look the other way?" I said, keeping myself still.

He froze. "Don't know."

"All right, who paid you to offer this service?"

He scowled. "No one."

"Alright, give me my coin back," I said, mildly.

He jumped away as if stung by a wasp. "It is mine, given in fair exchange."

I got to my feet, feeling the fresh blood of the slave girl warming my stomach, and considered beating it out of him. If I could get him into a private room, I could torture him quietly and perhaps the whores would not hear it. I would have to work quickly and so I closed on him as he limped away with his hands up.

But footsteps in the doorway caused me to turn. A group of soldiers barged in and, believing I was about to be set upon I reached for my sword.

But the foremost of them spoke in a mild tone. "Governor Coloma commands you to come. He has an answer for you."

*　*　*

"Damn him!" Hawkins said, crushing the governor's letter in his hand. Our commander looked around the cabin. "Damn him to Hell."

All the captains, senior officers, and gentlemen were crammed around two dining tables in the main cabin of the *Jesus*. We had arrived back at the squadron in the middle of the daily dinner and Captain Hampton, furious, had thrust the letter at Hawkins and stood fuming at his side while the diners looked on in silence. I stood to one side and eyed the meal, my stomach rumbling.

"Damn that man," Hawkins repeated and looked around the faces of his officers. "Coloma refuses to buy our slaves," he said, though those words were entirely unnecessary. Then Hawkins turned on me and on Hampton. "I sent you there to persuade him, did I not? Why have you failed?"

Captain Hampton, already angry, exploded in rage. "If you think you can do better, you go and converse with the man! He is as immobile as a mountain, as stubborn as a mule. He is a shit, a foul shit, a foul Catholic shit, the damned bloody Spanish bastard shit."

Hawkins got to his feet and glared at Hampton for a moment before pointing a finger at me. "Richard. Why did you not convince him?"

I shrugged. "He was not minded to be convinced."

"Not minded?" Hawkins spat. "Where is the gold?"

I handed the purse over. "He would not take it."

Hawkins hefted the purse in his hands, judging the weight. "It feels light. Where is the rest of it?"

I was surprised. "You have a good hand for judging weights, John. Some had to be spent to get us an audience at all."

Hampton scoffed dramatically. "Do you know what the swine did, while I was conducting our business? Do you know, have you heard this? I shall tell you, then. He strode off to a brothel house!"

All the faces turned to me.

"Is this true?" Hawkins said.

I sighed. "I would hardly be the first mariner to rush into the arms of a whore." That brought forth a few chuckles and just as many mutters of condemnation.

"You spent my gold on a whore?" Hawkins said, his face glowing red in the lamplight.

I leaned in between two seated men and plucked a cup of wine from the table and took a sip, walking to the head of the table beside Hawkins with my cup in hand. "We do not have a bribe large enough to convince Governor Coloma to trade with us, and I doubt all the gold in England would be enough. Do you know what happened to the last governor, John? The one you traded with last time you were here?"

Hawkins frowned. "He returned to Spain."

I pointed at him with my wine cup hand. "He was arrested and returned to Spain as a prisoner to stand trial. A trial where he was found guilty of trading with the English. He had his lands and titles stripped. Our new governor will not risk his position in the nobility for the chance to buy slaves. Even hundreds of them, even at a good price. Nothing we can pay him is worth his lands and titles back in Spain."

A voice from down the table spoke up. "Can we force him?"

I looked for the speaker and found it was Francis Drake.

"Force him?" I said, nodding. "The bay has a battery covering the entire approach, which we could take if we landed men to assault on foot along the spit. But there is another battery on a hill covering the dock. It could be done. But we would lose men. Perhaps as many as fifty of them." That brought groans from every man present.

What I was serving up to them was the truth but I was laying it on thick.

Hawkins held up a hand. "You are talking about taking the town by force and then compelling him to purchase our slaves?"

Drake cleared his throat. "If we did take the town, we wouldn't need to sell our slaves at all. We could just take the wealth for ourselves and sell the slaves further up the coast." He shrugged. "Or we could just free them."

Everyone began speaking at once until Hawkins shouted at them to be silent. "We are *not* taking the town by force. Even if I wished to risk our men's lives in such a venture, we would be condemned as pirates everywhere on the Main, and in the islands, too. We would ruin our chances of trading evermore and we would bring down the wrath of Spain on us and on to England, also. No, we must simply move on. There are other towns in need of slaves."

Captain Bolton tutted loudly and shook his head. "With the example of the convicted former governor fresh in their minds, who amongst them will dare trade with us?"

Again, many voices issued forth at all angles across the tables, with some suggesting the trades might happen in secret and others pointing out we needed just a single buyer, assuming he had enough money. On and on the arguments went, fuelled by the wine all drank with their dinner. I let them argue it out for a while, waiting for them to talk themselves in circles.

"Rio de la Hacha," I said, projecting it over their narrating with my battlefield voice.

They fell silent.

"Did you say Rio de la Hacha?" Hawkins asked. "What of it?"

133

I looked around, to be sure I had their attention, and answered him. "My visit to the brothel house was, tragically, not conducted for the sake of carnal pleasure. The coin I spent was not for a woman but was for certain local knowledge, of a kind otherwise unavailable to outsiders."

"What knowledge?" Hawkins barked.

I had thought about what I would say on the way back to the ship, and I added plausible details as I spoke. "The brothel keeper was also a trader in wines. He informed me that Rio de la Hacha is desperate for slaves. They even tried to buy some from here a few weeks ago."

"So?" Captain Bolton said. "Everywhere needs slaves. If they are still afraid to trade, what good is this knowledge?"

"My point, sir, is that they are in special need for our cargo. But that is not the best of it. It seems the commander of this town, a man named Castellanos, is willing to bend and to break laws when necessary. Indeed, he is not a minor noble, like so many others, but a man risen to his position by his own cunning. By taking risks, so they say."

Hawkins nodded. "I have heard of this Castellanos. A difficult man to deal with."

"Yes indeed, a man who may be dealt with," I said quickly, raising my finger as if Hawkins had proved my point rather than countered it. "But the advice I paid for suggested the size of our squadron would destroy any hope of conducting business in a subtle fashion."

"You mean send only one or two ships," Hawkins said, nodding. "It will have to be the *Jesus* and the *Minion*. We have most of the slaves between us."

Drake laughed. "Hardly subtle, John. The largest two ships of England."

I cleared my throat. "The business need not be conducted with us all bobbing in port. Indeed, the business could be conducted by a single man alone. When the business is conducted, then our ships could come up to offload the cargo... anywhere the buyer wishes. In the town or along the coast, perhaps, in secret and the authorities would never know..."

"A man alone?" Hawkins said, narrowing his eyes. "You refer to yourself?"

I spread my hands. "Merely an exaggeration to make my point. You could send your smallest ship by itself. If the *Judith* came into Rio de la Hacha without flying any English flags or pennants, then this Governor Castellanos could plausibly deny we were ever there, or that we did no real business."

Hawkins nodded and looked at his master and his senior captains. They exchanged looks, passing information between each other with shrugs, raised eyebrows and nods.

"Very well," Hawkins said presently. "We shall send the *Judith* and the *Angel* both together. That way they should be strong enough to see off most trouble, should any trouble occur. Francis?" he said, addressing Drake. "You will be in command of the detached squadron. Richard? You will go with them to Rio de la Hacha. I would like you to bear my letter to this Governor Castellanos, and to lead our negotiations for the slaves."

"As you wish, Captain Hawkins," I said, bowing.

* * *

The *Judith* and the *Angel* were tiny when compared to the *Jesus* and the *Minion*. I was on Drake's ship, the *Judith*, and though it was supposedly able to carry 50 tons of cargo, it looked to me more like a ship's tender than anything else. And the *Angel* was even smaller, considered able to bear 32 tons. And yet both had sailed with the bigger ships across thousands of miles in all kinds of seas, so I supposed them to be capable enough. Though the surface of the ocean appeared disconcertingly close to the deck and the quarters were crowded.

Worst of all, there was no privacy to be had for me to feed Philip so I had to find a quiet area forward or aft or in the hold and bleed myself swiftly and subtly into the mouth of a flask, which I could later pass to Philip for consumption. Twice, I was spotted. Once, the mariner asked if I was drinking wine and said he would not tell Captain Francis if I shared my wine with him.

The second time, I was as far forward as I could get, past the heads with my back turned and leaning against the base of the bowsprit with the spray coming up over me.

"That be right sinful, sir, right damned sinful indeed," the sailor said behind me as he settled his buttocks down against one of the two holes through which the crew defecated. "And before doing it one usually waits until nightfall."

"I was doing nothing of the sort," I said as I made my way aft, tucking the flask away.

It was about four hundred miles west along the coast of the Spanish Main to Rio de la Hacha and though I knew the *Jesus* and the *Minion* and the rest of our squadron were coming up behind, it was disconcerting to be so far from home in such small ships. Many a time I found myself cursing my own cleverness in bringing this very situation about. It would serve me right for being a deceiver if we were smashed upon the shore or sunk by some angry Spanish warship.

Still, the weather was fine and the coast was clear. The shoreline for hundreds of miles was verdant and overgrown but gradually turned drier, with stretches of desert interspersed by what looked like brittle scrub.

"You're sure about this town?" Drake asked me as we approached it.

"Not at all," I admitted. "We could find anything in there. Anything at all."

"This is something to do with your duties for the Crown," he said, narrowing his eyes.

I shrugged. "It may be. All I wish to do is speak to the tavern keeper. Of course, I will do my duty with regards to the sale of the slaves."

He hesitated. "I must say, the way you manipulated Hawkins to get us to bring you here ahead of the squadron was something to behold."

"I do not know what you mean."

He scoffed and ordered the cannons be readied, and the weapons brought up and set up on deck.

Rio de la Hacha was built beside the mouth of a river, and we anchored just off the coast and launched the ship's boats to take us in. Though he was greatly tempted to go himself, Drake allowed himself to be convinced otherwise.

"I will be ready with the guns, should anything untoward happen," he said, his eyes darting left and right as he glared at the coast.

"I am sure it will not come to that, Francis," I said, reassuringly. "I will be polite and restrained and as courteous as a lord."

He nodded and lowered his voice. "Just as long as your other business does not hinder that of the squadron."

"I would not even consider it."

But as the mariners rowed me into the mouth of the river, I could consider little else. Beside me, Philip sat hunched beneath his ubiquitous hat, miserable and nervous and yet armed to the teeth with a sword, a short sword, a long narrow dagger in the small of his back, and knives at his wrists and ankles. Anticipating that I could find myself searched and disarmed before being admitted to the presence of this wily governor, I intended to use Philip as a walking armoury and to leave him outside but close at hand, should the need for more weaponry arise.

A low fortification at the edge of the town hosted the battery that guarded the approach to the harbour, the mouths of the guns thrust through the walls. There were men there, moving slowly about and watching us come in.

"Please God," Philip muttered. "Please Jesus, let them not fire their guns."

I elbowed him in the ribs. "Shut up, Philip, you bloody old maid." I turned to the rowers, who were peering over their shoulders in alarm. "Do not listen to the quaking fool beside me, men. The gunners are leaning most casually on the walls of their meagre battery, not preparing to fire. I doubt the guns are even loaded. Why would they be? We are but traders, posing no threat, and offering possible reward. Row on, lads. We are almost into the river."

I raised a hand to the watching soldiers, then removed my hat and waved that over my head. They ignored me.

As our two boats came in to moor at the harbour, two black men came down to catch our hawsers and tie us up. I was sure to be the first to jump out and I pushed through them to stroll up the bank toward the town. The residents scattered about the small town had halted in their daily activities to stand and watch us. I noted the low defensive wall beside the road that separated the harbour from the homes and other buildings. There was another wall around the church and another, also low, surrounding the grandest house in the town.

"Good day, friends. Is that the governor's residence?" I called out to the nearest group of men, sat on benches working on their fishing nets.

They stared at me, silently. I looked back at them. They were all rather young but there were no boys with them. Perhaps this town also suffered from a lack of suitable women.

"Richard," Philip called from behind me, pointing up at the town.

"Ah," I said. "Here we go."

A company of soldiers marched down the main street, their arquebuses on their shoulders, in three rows of eight. And then another group of twenty-four came marching behind them carrying pikes. At the rear, three horsemen rode. Two with lances held high and the man between them wearing a shining breastplate.

"Richard?" Philip asked again. "Should we run?"

"Run?" I asked, surprised. "They could shoot us to ribbons and their battery could blast our boats to kindling before we get free of the river." I clapped him on the shoulder. "Stand up straight, man. With your strength, you could knock down an entire company."

"Mister Richard, sir?" the master's mate said, his eyes wild. The mariners were standing in a group behind him, their hands on their knives, clubs, and axes. "We having a scrap, sir?"

I smiled. "You lads go back to the dockside until I sort this out."

He touched his hat. "If you say so, sir." With that, he chivvied the men back to where the boats stood and though they made an effort to appear nonchalant, they were in a state of high agitation.

As was I, but still I strode up to meet the advancing soldiers with a big smile on my face and stopped in the road at the point where the walls either side denoted the entrance to the town. At a barked command, the soldiers came crashing to a stop in formation and the riders came on around them and stopped a few yards away.

"What a splendid display!" I cried in Spanish, like a jolly buffoon. "How marvellously your militia are drilled, sir."

"Who are you and where are you from?" The rider said, looking down his long nose at me.

"Ah, a formal introduction, is it? Yes, well, you see we have been tragically blown entirely off our course and are now rather in need of fresh water. I wonder if you would allow us to purchase good water from here before we get on our way once more. Is the river suitable or do you have wells to draw from?"

He frowned and pushed his horse a few steps closer. He handled the beast very well indeed. "Are you Englishmen?"

I bowed low. "How very perceptive of you, sir. My name is

Richard. Are you the governor of this fine town?"

He glanced over his shoulder at the magnificent house before looking back at me. "You want water? Only water? No trade?"

"Water would be most welcome, my lord. If it pleases you, we have drafted a letter of introduction for the governor. It goes without saying that we come here in the spirit of goodwill and swear to obey all reasonable laws and commands without question." I fished out the letter and held it out to him. "For the eyes of the governor, my lord."

He hesitated before reaching down to take it. "You will remain here," he said.

"We will not stray from here." I bowed and waited until he began to turn away before raising my voice to make a request. "With your permission, I shall purchase some wine for my weary men while we wait?"

The officer considered it for a moment before nodding and riding slowly away.

The soldiers turned and marched away up the hill in formation, before being dismissed near to the governor's grand house. There, they sat against the wall, or slouched against other buildings nearby. Their weapons they propped up and left alone while they relaxed.

"What was that for?" Philip muttered, nodding at the militia.

"A display of force. Showing us how quickly the men of the town can turn out, how smartly they can march. They knew we were English when we came over the horizon, or they suspected, at least. Must have summoned them from their trades, from their farms, and got them armed and formed up ready for our landing. And they're leaving the soldiers there where we can see them in case we try anything. The governor here must be a cautious man indeed."

"Is that bad?"

"It's not good."

"What will they do when the rest of the squadron arrive?"

"We will have our business concluded well before then. Or so I hope. Come on, let us buy that wine for our boys. There is the tavern up there, I believe."

"Another brothel house," Philip said, licking his lips.

"Calm yourself. You shall not be partaking in the poxed local harlots."

"Don't want to partake in them," he said, sullenly. "Just want to have a look at them."

I sighed and led him into the town, where I waved and nodded, and called greetings to every face I saw. Most simply turned away.

The tavern was sturdily built and the front was open to the elements along most of its length, with an awning providing shade from the roasting sun. I was wet through with sweat and right glad to come into its shelter.

"Good day, gentlemen. May you point me to the proprietor of this delightful establishment."

A chair scraped and a tall man loped over. He was old, thin, but with big hands and big bones in his shoulders. I did not doubt he would have been trouble in his youth and his eyes still burned with aggression.

"We don't sell to Englishmen. Get lost."

I smiled. "Well, how lucky for us that I am a Welshman. And my servant here is Irish, aren't you, Felipe?" Philip pressed his lips together and nodded. "So, as there are no Englishmen here, you can sell us your wares."

He scowled. "Welsh, English, what's the difference?"

"Oh, my goodness me. You clearly have never met a Welshman before. We are good Catholics, just like our friends in Ireland, and we hate the English more than any other race on this earth. Isn't that right, Felipe, my Irish friend?"

With his mouth pressed closed, he nodded again.

"Your men are English," the tavern keeper said. "Your ships are English. You can go back to England, back to Welsh land, wherever you came from."

The men around the tavern rapped their knuckles and cups on the tables and growled their approval.

I shrugged. "You're right, sir, you're absolutely right. Let those rowers die of thirst out there! I couldn't agree more. I'm sick to death of the damned Lutherans praying away like the heretics they are. Tell you what, me and Irish Felipe here will have a quick drink and go find your town's priest. We'll sit at that table just there and take two cups of your best wine, my friend, with our most sincere and humble thanks." Though he frowned, he moved to get us our drinks.

Philip eased himself onto the bench, so weighed down was he with awkward weapons that he could not relax but instead sat like a bird ready to take flight.

"What's wrong with your friend?" the tavern keeper said as he brought our cups and jug of wine.

"He's a lusty young fellow and after so long at sea I fear his balls are about to burst," I explained. "You wouldn't happen to know of any suitable women in the town who would be kind enough to take care of his affliction... in exchange for a fair price."

He looked around before looking back at me. "What do you call a fair price?"

I shrugged. "Whatever the girl calls fair, and of course the standard fee for the man who keeps her."

"Thought you were going to the church," he muttered.

"How can a man address his spiritual needs without first addressing the needs of the body?" I indicated the wine before us.

He shrugged. "I have a few girls who you might like. Just the one, is it? For your uncomfortable friend?"

I sighed. "Well, it is true that I have needs also, sir, but you see mine are quite special. I'm willing to pay, of course, whatever it costs."

He frowned. "I'll not have my girls hurt. Not for any price."

Spreading my hands, I lowered my voice. "I'll not hurt them beyond drawing a little blood. If they would be so kind. Just a cup's worth will ease my thirst."

He drew back, scowling and looking left and right. "Who are you?"

I shrugged and took a sip of wine. "A man of particular thirsts, just the same as other men who come here from time to time to partake in the specials on offer here."

He hesitated before nodding slowly. "You know the price?"

"Remind me," I said.

Narrowing his eyes, he looked long at me before replying. "The price is the price. You have not partaken before. Who told you about this?"

"Indeed I have partaken before. Just a few days ago to the east, at a charming little establishment with a fine young *mulato*. But I am not the sort of man to talk his coins out of his own purse. Your price?"

This time he nodded. "You take it in the cup or straight from the source."

I sat up straighter. "Oh, from the source, my friend. From the source."

He wagged a finger at me. "It is still just a cupful. No more."

"I understand," I said, winking.

"No, you don't," he snapped and bent low, speaking softly but with a growl in the back of his throat. "Just a cup's worth, mark me. Twice now, I lost girls because your master couldn't control himself. Two of the best girls, here for this purpose alone and only one remains. I will not have it again, not from the likes of you, at least. You kill my girl, you pay double her price and you never come here again, understand?"

"My master?" I said. "He killed two girls here, yes. When was this?"

"Yes! I told him, this is not the Blood House, there are rules."

"The Blood House?" I said. "What do you know about the Blood House?"

"I'll not speak of it, don't worry. Now, tell me you understand."

"Just a cup, I swear it. Now, let me tell you something. I must have a girl who has done this before. One who is used to the act itself. I cannot stand it when they struggle and whimper and go on."

A smile spread across his aged features. "You want *her*, I know."

Confused, I nodded. "Yes, I do indeed. How did you guess?"

"She's the one you all want. How far have you come for her?"

"Thousands of miles. Now, how much is it?"

After he took my money, went upstairs and returned alone, the woman took some time to appear. But when she did, my heart palpated for a few moments at the sight of her. The young woman descended the stairway from the upper floor and all conversation in the tavern stopped. From the corner of my eye, I saw Philip choke on his wine and his coughing spoiled the moment somewhat but I could not tear my gaze from her as she glided to my table, her skirts swishing on the floor.

The woman was young but in the full blooming of womanhood, and rather tall and slender but with a softness and roundness to her, with wide hips and deep breasts threatening to spill from her low-cut bodice with every breath. Her face was beautiful, with a delicate nose and huge brown eyes and a wide mouth. Her curling black hair was piled high on her head, with strands falling loose about her face. By the golden-brown skin of her face, bosom, and her smooth bare arms did I see she was, perhaps, another *mulato* yet she truly did possess the grace and poise of a Spanish lady.

When she came to a stop and curtsied I snapped shut my gaping mouth and scrambled to my feet, bowing low. Philip continued to gape up at her and I winced to think I had moments before displayed the same low manners as he.

"My dear, you are a vision. My name is Richard and I am delighted beyond words to make your acquaintance."

"I am Catalina," she said, her voice as clear and sweet as a fine bell.

Behind her, I caught a glimpse of the tavern keeper standing with his arms crossed and a satisfied expression on his face.

"Forgive my surprise, Catalina," I said, "because surely there has been some mistake." She frowned, a lovely crease appearing between her eyes as she furrowed her brow. "After my long voyage from the other side of the world, I was expecting to make the acquaintance of a young woman so that we might spend some time together in private company. But I see you are in fact a fine lady of considerable importance. Are you the wife of the governor, perhaps? Or more likely his daughter?"

She looked confused for a moment and then she laughed at my terrible jest, flapping a hand at me as if to bat away my nonsense. Turning with a flourish she spoke to the tavern-keeper before retreating up the stairs. "He will do!"

Snatching my cup and drinking off my wine, I winked at Philip and lowered my voice. "Stay here and watch the door. Call me if there's trouble."

His eyes were wide. "What about taking care of my affliction?"

"Watch the bloody door, Philip," I said and rushed to the stairs before Catalina got away. She turned at the top and laughed at my eagerness.

Again, she waited in an open doorway and then stood aside to let me in before shutting the door behind her. In the quiet of her chamber, I looked around to be sure no man was hidden and ready to jump out at me. It was a rather pleasant accommodation, large and bright and with well-made furniture, including a huge bed with what appeared to be very clean linen sheets. Being a corner room, the two great windows showed the town out of one and the sea out of the other. Both windows had the shutters inside and out thrown open and I went to the seaward one and leaned on the sill. There, a mile or so off the coast, sat the *Judith* and the *Angel*. Both looked so small against the infinite blue.

"So, you have come all the way from England, Richard?" Catalina said, gliding up behind me.

I turned and looked at her in the bright light. She was fresh and soft and clean and I sighed, breathing her in.

"I'm sorry," I said, smiling, "but I have been at sea rather longer than I realised."

She laughed lightly and she did it so well that I could almost believe it genuine. "It is quite alright and perfectly understandable."

I nodded, glancing now out of the other window where stood the governors house and the company of lounging soldiers. "I wish I could sit in your company and get to know you a little."

"That sounds very nice," she said. "Let us do just that."

"Sadly, I do not think I have the time. Now, Catalina, do you know what I paid for?"

Before she turned away, I saw the sadness and disgust in her eyes. "Certainly, sir," she said, feigning lightness. "Would you please join me here and take a seat?"

She eased her skirts into a chair beside the table by the window and as she sat, she leaned forward and it was a miracle that her breasts did not tumble forth. When seated, she opened a leather-bound box on the table. Inside was a polished lancet, a red silk cord and a glass cup. These she removed, tying the silk cord around her upper arm using her teeth to hold one end.

"How often have you done this?" I asked her.

"Oh," she said, smiling. "I do not mind. Indeed, it is my pleasure to do so. Of course, it is good for one's health to be bled regularly."

"It certainly is. How regularly do you do this?"

She smiled but could not hide the sadness in her eyes. "Whenever I have the pleasure of certain gentlemen's company."

"When was the last time?" I asked.

Picking up the lancet, she stopped and chewed her lip. "I know that you paid Juan to take it from my vein but that makes ever such a mess, my darling. It is so much more delightful when supped from a glass, do you not think?" She held her breath, watching me.

I rubbed my mouth and sat back. "Do you have any wine to drink here? Why do we not share a drink together first, what do you say?"

She all but jumped to her feet. "Wine? Yes, of course, I shall serve us." With that, she found cups and wiped them clean, unstopped an earthenware bottle and poured.

"How long have you lived here?" I asked, remaining seated while she wandered around the room, sometimes in sunlight and sometimes in shadow.

"Here? Oh, I don't know. Four years?"

"So you came here as a child?"

She laughed, her smile as bright as the sun. "Not a child. I was fifteen, I think."

"Where were you before?"

She shrugged. "My home."

"Back in Spain?"

Catalina smiled again. "New Spain."

"Ah, I see. And how did you come to be all the way down here?"

Her smiled faded, though she fought to keep it on her face. "My father was sent here, to be the secretary. But soon after we..." She strolled to the window and looked at the governor's house and fell silent.

"I am very sorry, Catalina."

"Oh," she said, attempting levity. "It was so long ago, I hardly remember it. I am happy here."

"There must be something I don't understand," I said and she turned to frown at me. "Why on earth has no man taken you for his wife?"

She scoffed and turned away. "Who would marry me?"

I put down my wine and rubbed my eyes. "What man would not marry you?"

Scoffing once more, she crossed the room and filled her cup with a little more wine. "I cannot marry and that is the end of it."

"That tavern keeper, Juan, does he own you?"

She glared at me before looking away again. "I am no slave."

I raised my hands. "Certainly not, my dear. Forgive my ungallant question and it is entirely your business, of course it is. In my defence, I must say I am baffled beyond words that no man to your liking has yet asked for your hand. You must have an endless line of suitors. I am minded to ask you myself after having known you for just a few moments. If you asked it, I would take you away from here in an instant."

She snapped her eyes to me again. "You mustn't joke about such things."

I dropped the last remnants of my jolly demeanour. "It is no joke. And you need not marry me either way. I would want nothing in return but to protect you."

She scoffed. "What man wants nothing? And I know what you want." She slapped her arm.

"Unlike all the other men you have done this for, I would never take your blood against your will. Not even if I paid for it."

Her false jollity was slipping away. "But you did pay for it."

"I paid Juan so I could be alone with you." Her eyes darted to the bed and I shook my head. "Not for that, either. All that interests me is..." I sighed and lowered my voice, well aware that we could be overheard. "My dear, would you mind sitting down with me once more?"

Warily, she stepped back to the chair before me and lowered herself into it until she was perched on the edge. I leaned forward and she did also so that our heads were almost together and I stared into her cleavage while speaking in little more than a whisper.

"I have sworn an oath to rid the world of every evil blood drinker. I kill them, you see, because they kill others. Just now I heard that two girls who worked here were killed by these men, who drank from them too long." Catalina stiffened when I said this. "They are killers and no one can harm them but me and my men. Killing them is easy for me but finding them is not. You see, I have already slain many in Europe and in the East but I find that they are now here in the New World and I do not know how to find them. I do not know their names or what they look like." I turned my head a fraction so that I looked at her, and our faces were almost touching. "But you do."

She pulled her head away, big brown eyes so wide they were white all the way around. "I cannot."

I leaned back in the chair, picked up my wine and said

nothing. Oftentimes, especially with women, it is best to keep quiet while their minds work away at a thought.

Catalina stood and walked away, her skirt swishing on the floor. When she turned, she was about to speak but there came the sound of hoofs outside and we both crossed to the window. The officer had emerged and was riding with his two men down the main street.

"Captain Marcos comes," she said beside me.

"He is coming to send me away," I said, noting the swaggering manner with which he sat on his horse. "And listen, Catalina, I still want to take you from here but I cannot take you now. They would try to stop me and you might be hurt. But if you want me to take you, and to keep you safe, I will do so."

"To marry me?" she said, with anxiety in her voice.

"Oh," I said, almost chuckling. "I should be so lucky. No, my dear girl, but I would see you safe, somewhere suited to you here in the New World or in Spain or even in England, if you wished it. I have a..." I struggled to find a word that would quickly convey what Eva was to me. "I have a sister, of sorts, in England who would be delighted to take care of you until you found your way."

She stared through my body at something distant. Perhaps she looked through me at two possible paths, one which kept her in Rio de la Hacha, shut up in her fine chamber and one that led to parts unknown, with a strange man spouting wild promises. The hooves echoed against the buildings as they came closer.

Her dark eyes narrowed. "And in return you want from me..."

"Just your words. Your memories. Of every man who came here to take your blood or the blood of the other girls. That is all. With what you know, I might be able to find them and kill them."

"What if you take me and what I know is of no use? You will be angry. I cannot trust you."

"I understand that you feel that way. Whatever you tell me, I will help you anyway. I am not poor and it will cost me nothing of note to help you. If you say yes, I will come for you."

The horses stopped outside and a voice commanded us to come out.

"I cannot," Catalina muttered. "I am safe here."

"Safe?" I said. "Like the other girls who died here after the blood drinkers could not control themselves?"

She shook her head. "He would not do that to me."

"Who?" I snapped. "Who do you speak of?"

She jumped as a hand rapped twice on the door, paused, rapped once and then twice again.

"That is my fretful servant, begging me to come out," I said, as the soldiers shouted from the street for me to come out again. "But tell me, who do you speak of?"

She shook her head as Philip opened the door. "Richard, they're coming in." Behind him came the clanking sound of soldiers climbing the stairs.

"Keep them out there," I snapped and turned to her again. "Do not tell me, then, my dear. But please do bleed yourself immediately so that no suspicion falls on you, should Juan scrutinise your arm or your implements." Taking her fingers, I bent forward and lifted her hand my lips while the commotion grew in the hall outside. "Catalina, you are a great beauty and I pray that you do not waste your days here. But whatever life you choose, I wish you good fortune."

I turned as the soldiers barrelled Philip into the chamber and

I lifted my arms. "Boys, boys, what are you doing? How can you interrupt a man in the midst of his pleasure? You uncouth barbarians, this is a lady's chamber, you must get out at once. How dare you! Come on, we shall all go together, let us leave the young lady in peace, you oafs, you ruffians, out, out with you all!"

Waving my hands, I herded and shoved them back out, roaring with bluff good cheer while treating them rather roughly and when I reached the doorway, Catalina rushed to me. She grabbed my arm and squeezed my flesh hard with the fingers of one hand and threw the other around my neck and pulled my head down. She placed her soft lips against my ear and whispered before I was dragged away.

"Come for me."

***

"You want to do what?" Drake said.

We were in the tiny cabin on the *Judith* and I stood stooped over with my head lowered but Drake stood upright with room to spare.

"All I ask is for a single boat and the men to row it. Land us west of the town at the beaches and Philip and I will go in, take the girl and bring her back to the boat, and then we are back here by daybreak."

Drake rubbed an eye and sighed. "You want her because she has important knowledge that will help England's struggle against the Catholics?"

"Yes, that is it."

"You swear it is not because you took a fancy to her? You just want your own harlot for the voyage? Or perhaps you mean to hire her out for my men? If that's the case I tell you it will not happen, not on my ship and not on Hawkins'. We should not have a woman on board at all, it will cause a terrible problem, terrible. Is she pretty? No, it doesn't matter if she is or not, just her presence will drive the men to distraction, there will be fights and discipline will be a constant battle, I seen it before. Woman on my ship, I'll be mocked by the older captains, that much is for certain. Why can she not wait until the squadron arrives?"

"I fear she is already at risk. Her master may have winkled out of her what we spoke of in her chamber and she knows secrets about powerful men. Powerful Catholics. She may be silenced by her keepers."

"Silenced?" Drake rubbed his mouth. "I would not have a woman harmed due to my inaction but I do not know this is the best way. If discovered it would ruin any chance of a reconciliation with the town."

"The governor has already commanded us to leave. Our only choices now are to take the town by force or to leave. Whichever Hawkins and the captains choose, the girl is at risk."

"What could she know that could be so important, Richard? She is just a cursed whore."

"I believe that she is kept in fine style so that she may be used by particular men who frequent this town on voyages around these seas and when travelling to and from Spain. They call here to... to use her, in a particular fashion. I am sorry that I can say no more, the details are secret." I gritted my teeth and ploughed on. "But yes, I will say that by saving her we will help the Protestant nations against the Catholics."

Drake shook his head. "I suppose that be reason enough. Yet I wish it did not risk our primary business. We came here to smooth the path for trade. We must offload those slaves, Richard, if this voyage is not to be a disaster."

I lowered my voice. "One boat, one night, one girl. What can go wrong?"

After full dark descended, we rowed along the coast and slipped quietly into shore. It was dark indeed but we could see well enough to pick our way through the farms and spindly orchards. The town had a few lanterns lit, here and there which served as beacons, drawing us in. As a rule, the Spaniards everywhere liked to sit up late, drinking and gaming and so Philip and I followed the sounds and lights to the outskirts of the town. There was another low, drystone wall on the western side but it was chest high so we hopped over and carried on, bent almost double to stay in the shadows.

Philip hissed and grabbed my arm. We stopped.

Like all the immortals I had made, while bright daylight made him wince, he could see in the dark better than I could and so I trusted he had seen something. I strained to hear over the breeze some indication of what it was he had seen. After a moment, he tapped me on the arm and we moved off again, moving obliquely to behind the buildings on the main street. We passed the great mass of the church and then that of the governor's house and then we were into the rear of the houses. Even in the night air it reeked of latrines and the rot of refuse.

Raised voices and laughter drew us through the sandy scrub to the rear of the tavern and the large latrine frequented by patrons. We crouched by a fence and watched for a few minutes to be sure no one was lurking nearby.

"Wait here," I whispered into Philip's ear and went forward toward the tavern. I knew well where Catalina's room was and I was relieved to see both windows were wide open and there was a lantern lit inside. Praying that she would be in there too, I began to climb the timbers to the window, listening for voices or for the rustle of sheets. If she was entertaining a man, I would knock him out and truss him up, if possible, or I would slit his throat if necessary. Although I had no designs on the girl myself, and knew a man using her services did not deserve death, I still half hoped I would have to do it. It did not make sense but then beautiful women have a profound effect on a man.

Reaching the window, I pulled myself up and peered in.

The room was empty.

Cursing inwardly, I pulled myself up and in swiftly, thinking to wait for her to return or to search in other rooms, if possible.

Stepping down into the window beside a table, I sensed something behind me.

A man had been standing against the wall, waiting for me. When I saw him, he was already wheeling a cudgel through the air, aiming for the top of my head.

Slipping aside, it struck me on the shoulder but then I was on him, grasping him and slamming his head into the wall. He was a hefty fellow but still his skull made a terrible sound and he dropped into a heap at my feet.

Behind me the door burst open and three soldiers came in, their faces twisted in anger and ready for a fight. The leading man had a sword in his hand but the two behind had arquebusiers and these they raised as they braced themselves just inside the door.

They were only mortals and I rushed forward and knocked them down, one after the other, with three punches.

However, one of the men fired his weapon.

The ball hit the ceiling but the sound was like a thunderclap and I winced at the pain shooting through my ears into my head. Before the echoes died away, I heard through the ringing of my head, the sound of footsteps clattering on the stairs and shouts from down in the tavern and even from outside in the town.

Rushing the window, I jumped straight out just as more guns fired behind me. Landing hard, I ran through the gardens, past the latrines to where Philip stood with a sword in hand.

"Are we fighting?" he cried.

I snarled an answer without breaking stride. "Run, you bloody idiot!"

Running hard, we cleared the town and leapt the wall while further gunshots sounded behind me. Shooting at shadows, I thought, and thanked God for the incompetence of the soldiers. Still, there were hooves drumming on the street and coming closer and the shouts grew louder as riders and soldiers rushed after us.

When we came to the boat, the mariners already had the thing in the surf and were holding it ready.

"Thank the Lord," one shouted as Philip jumped right in like a deer. "Where's the whore?"

"Wasn't there," I said, putting my shoulder against the boat and pushing it into the water. "Back to the ships!"

They rowed hard, those lads, pulling with strong strokes in perfect unison and we made it back to the *Judith* moments before the town battery began firing.

Whether they had prepared in the daylight or if it was just a lucky shot, the first shots they fired smashed into the *Judith*'s main deck and instantly killed two English sailors.

They had been standing together lowering the ropes to hoist the boat back onto the deck when their bodies were blown apart. I was right there, just a few feet from them when we were showered in a spray of splinters from the rail and blood from their bodies. Most of their remains were scattered onto the deck, including both men's legs and their heads but the rest was flung out to sea.

There was no time to mourn the poor fellows, and young Captain Drake was everywhere roaring orders and in no time our cannons were returning fire, the guns shooting as quickly as their crews could fire them, run them in, reload them, run them out, and fire them again. At the same time, the mariners were pulling up the anchors and lowering sails to take us out of range of the shore battery.

"Two of my men are dead," Drake said in the light of the false dawn. "They are dead because of your excursion. Your failed excursion. Where is the girl?"

"They have her. Taken her, no doubt they questioned her. She was not there but they were waiting for me so she must have told them I would come for her." I shook my head. "I am very sorry indeed about your men."

"So, she's dead, then?" he said. "Your damned whore."

"I do not know. I will pray that she is alive." We stood and looked at the dark town on the black shore. "What will you do now?"

Drake grimaced. "Blockade the harbour until Hawkins comes

159

up with the squadron. I suppose we'll have to bloody well move on somewhere else, now. Maybe Santa Marta, about a hundred miles west." He shook his head. "I made a right pig's ear out of this, ain't I. Doubt John will give me another command after this."

"I am sorry, Francis."

"This is the last time I listen to you," he said and left me alone at the rail.

I looked back at the town. Catalina, if she was still alive, was still in there. She had met the New World immortals, seen them face to face. The girl was worth her weight in gold.

And no matter what Francis Drake said, I was not leaving Rio de la Hacha without her.

***

It was five days before the squadron arrived. In that time, we effectively blockaded the harbour because no ship seemed willing to risk running by us and on the second day we chased a caravel that came along from the west. The ship, in a panic, drove itself onto the shore and surrendered. At first, our crew were delighted to have taken a prize but all it carried was crates of glass and stacks of rough native pots which were essentially worthless.

On the third night, a small two-masted ship slipped out of port and escaped in the darkness.

A lookout heard her, and saw her, and we lit lanterns and gave chase in the *Judith*, shooting a couple of cannonballs into the darkness in the hope of frightening them into surrender.

But we lost her.

"Running for help," Drake said glumly when we gave up the chase. "Running to bring ships down on us, or to raise the alarm further up the coast. Now nobody will trade with us. Imagine the tales they will tell. English pirates are coming, do not trade with them."

"Probably just a local crew making a run for it," I suggested. "Let us not worry."

Privately, I was sure he was correct. In fact, letting that ship get away turned out far worse than either of us expected.

On the morning of the fifth day, our squadron arrived. The mighty, ageing *Jesus of Lubeck* and the massive *Minion* came up over the horizon in the glory of full sail with the sun rising behind them, reducing sail as they came up to anchor beside us.

They were a sight for sore eyes but when we went over to the *Jesus* for the officer's conference, Hawkins became furious.

"You are to blame," he said to me in front of all the assembled officers. "You have caused me nothing but trouble. So much for your foolish ideas."

I bowed. "You are quite right and I apologise for my errors of judgement. I believed that the governor would be a reasonable man but clearly I was mistaken. Some other forces are at play here."

That gave him pause and in the silence, Drake stood and bowed. "The fault is mine alone, John. We were told no and we intended to wait but I allowed Richard to go ashore in the dark to attempt his rescue of the lady."

"Ha!" Hawkins said. "*Lady*, is it? Quite a promotion from moments ago. Yes, you are at fault also. Why did you have to destroy the governors house?"

In the exchange of fire that night, we had inadvertently sent a cannonball right through the middle of the governor's house and the facade had crumbled. From a distance in the morning we had watched his men clear the rubble away and erect boards to cover the gaping hole, much to our amusement.

"It was a lucky shot," Drake said, unable to hide his smile. "And he had already rejected us, most forcefully, so I say sod the bugger. Anyway, we have taken a prize in full view of the town so there'll be no treating with him now. We must away for another town and I believe the next one of any size at all is Santa Marta."

Many of the heads in the room nodded and I steeled myself to speak up. I was on thin ice so I had to use my words carefully. Too much force and I would fall.

"Francis," I said softly. "I am afraid we must inform our friends of the other ship on the third night."

His head fell and he sighed. "You are quite right." He relayed the events and spoke up the chase of the ship in the darkness as if it was some thrilling hunt, instead of us fumbling about like blind men in a wheat field.

"So they sent word out," Hawkins said, dumping himself back into his chair and holding his palm across his forehead. "Why did you not chase them down, Francis?"

Drake shook his head. "We had to maintain the blockade and I thought it best to keep both my ships together. Alone, my ships are vulnerable and that Spanish ship could have gone anywhere."

The officers were disappointed but they must have known he was right because none challenged him.

"Where do we go, then?" Captain Bolton said. "Keep going

along the Main to Santa Marta? Or might we do better back up into the islands?"

I forced myself to stay silent for as long as I could while they muttered amongst themselves. There was no obvious solution but I did not wish them to talk themselves into one.

"Why do we not sell the slaves here?" I said quietly.

The men around me stop speaking and stared at me, confused and one by one the rest fell silent.

"What did you say?" Hawkins asked. "Sell them here? Have you lost your mind?"

I shrugged. "It has been suggested before." A couple of men chuckled. "But I simply mean to say that we have the men and the town is poorly defended. Let us force them."

Hawkins and Drake exchanged a look and the men's heads swivelled.

"Poorly defended?" Bolton said. "It has a battery capable of killing two of our men. Good men, I will add!"

I nodded. "The battery defends the harbour in the mouth of the river. But the rest of the coast is all beach. The town has walls just four feet high on the west and east with great gaps between them and we can always go around them, if necessary."

"There is the militia, of course," Drake said. "A company of arquebusiers and another of pikemen. There are mounted soldiers also."

I shrugged again. "I suppose if they put all their soldiers out plus every able-bodied free man they might have a hundred or a hundred and fifty." I was underselling the strength but not by too much. "How many can we field?"

"Two hundred and fifty," Drake said, before anyone else.

I nodded slowly, as if I was only just thinking of it then. "If we were to bring them ashore to the west, we could attack together and overwhelm them."

"You want us to kill a hundred and fifty men?" Hawkins snapped.

I affected a look of shock. "Why, no, John, not at all. They will not stand against us, the militia might march down the main street well enough but those men spend their days tilling their dried-up fields outside of town, whereas our men are tough and eager. The militia will fall back from us and we will simply push them out of town. We will leave clear the wooden bridge upstream of the harbour so the townsfolk and its defenders can flee across it to the far bank where there is a scatter of homes, no more. Then all we need do is guard the bridge and the town will be ours."

Hawkins was nodding as I spoke. "Then we will ransom his town back to the governor, with the stipulation that he buy all our slaves at a fair price."

Bolton coughed and grumbled. "We'll lose men."

Eyes turned to me. "We will," I agreed. "Perhaps as many as a dozen when we close on them. I suppose we could try Santa Marta instead. We'll probably have to attack it first anyway but, what did you say, Francis, there are perhaps forty houses and farms there? We might be able to offload as many as forty or fifty slaves and then we can look for another town to take in order to sell the next batch."

"No, no," Hawkins said. "That will take too long and may end up being even more of a risk. We'll be whittled down at every town, losing a man here and there, until we lose more than a dozen. No, we shall sell our slaves here. Go to your ships, arm your men and begin bringing them ashore."

"Now?" Bolton asked. "Today?"

Hawkins stood, a wolfish expression coming over his face. "Let us show these Spaniards what Englishmen are made of."

* * *

"What is your plan?" Drake said as we assembled the men on the shore. The boats brought them in and the officers herded them to the farmland and began spreading them out into a single line.

"To attack the town?" I asked, shrugging. "Take our boys in at a run, making a lot of noise so the enemy run. No chance for anything more complicated."

"What if they don't run?"

"We'll have to kill them until they do."

"How can you be so certain about it?" he asked, tugging at the wisps of beard at his chin.

"I have been doing this sort of thing a long time."

He frowned. "Yes, I have heard you assert that often and yet you are such a young man. How can it be so?"

"I am older than I look," I said.

He looked around as our men busied themselves with their armour and weapons. "I know you manipulated John once again so we would launch this assault and I assume you did so in the hopes of seizing the whore. So, assuming they all flee from us, what is your plan for getting her?"

I looked at him. He was cleverer even than I had thought and I saw no need to continue to lie to him.

"She may be beyond my reach. It is possible that they already killed her, the poor girl. But if I can, I will cross the river at night and take her back."

"You failed at that once already."

"I will try harder next time."

He smiled at that and we turned as Hawkins roared his orders to get in line and to make ready. We were more than two hundred mariners spread across the fields and dry pastures looking back at the town where the enemy were gathering along their defensive wall. It looked a little more of an impediment than it had before due to the hundreds of armed men standing against it. Dozens of them were already aiming their arquebuses at us. Here and there were blacks and Indians standing with weapons, ready to fight us beside their masters.

"When we go, we go together at a walk until the final fifty yards!" I shouted down the line, ravaging my throat with the volume.

The captains had wanted to advance to firing range and trade shots but I argued we would lose more men that way. If we rushed them, we would see a few men hit but then at worst, we would be amongst them, fighting hand to hand. At best, they would turn and run.

"Get ready, men!" I shouted.

"Hold!" Captain Bolton shouted further down the line. "There are still boats coming in!"

"How many men does he think we need?" I said to Philip.

"He's a mariner, Richard, not a soldier. Ain't used to scrapping with dry feet. Same as all the lads, really. Reckon they'll be alright?"

"It is hardly a complicated manoeuvre, is it," I replied, just as a few men around began calling out warnings and jabbing fingers at the town.

I turned just as their words registered.

"A gun! They've brought up a gun!"

It was a small cannon but they had unloaded it from a cart into a carriage in position in the road, with the men manning the walls either side. The gun crew were busy preparing it to fire and already a man stood ready with the linstock, blowing on the length of slowmatch at the end. The ball it would fire was about the size of a clenched fist and I doubted they would be able to reload and fire again before we were on them. But men do not like charging a cannon, it seems worse than charging a line of firearms even though they are hardly more deadly to a single man.

I raised my voice and lifted my sword. "We go now! Before it can fire! Forward, men, forward! Come on, come on!"

Philip took up my cries and walked with me, gesturing with his blade and shouting at the men to come on, come on, we were going to kill them, let's kill them.

God, it was a ragged advance. About as ragged as I have ever seen, with half our men left behind when the other half were almost to the wall. Some men cringed away from the enemy and took cover behind their comrades who found themselves out in front of a small trailing group.

But others were up for murdering the Spaniards. Some cried out the names of the dead sailors who had been killed by the town guns. Others appeared motivated to shove their steel into the enemy because they were Catholics. And, as always, a few men simply loved partaking in violence. I do not condemn any of them, for few men delight in killing more than do I.

Our feet pounded the dry, sandy earth and the air was filled with dust and heavy breathing and the rustle of clothes and the clanking of steel. Spanish arquebuses banged in a ragged volley, if it could even be called that, and puffs of smoke billowed out into the sun. I heard men shout as though they had been hit and shot flew over my head but no one near me fell, as far as I could see. I waited for their cannon to fire, waited to hear that huge sound rip through my men. But it did not come.

And then we were rushing at the wall. Pike heads thrust out over the top and one spiralled down at my face. I swung my sword to parry it aside and ducked beneath it, coming up to the stones and thrusting my blade into the throat of the man behind it. All along the wall steel clanged on stone and grunts and cries filled the air. I saw an Englishman to my left come pounding up at a full sprint and launch himself over the wall with a guttural roar.

The Spanish fled.

As if on some signal, though I did not hear one, they turned on their heels and ran for their lives. Many dropped their weapons right away, others flung them aside during their flight. They crowded the main street, though it was wide, and the echoes of their feet on the hard-packed earth filled the town.

"After them!" Philip shouted with his sword in the air and I had to grab hold of him and pull him back.

"Hold up, boys! Wait! Let them get away a bit first!"

A sailor beside me, his eyes wild beneath a wide gash on his forehead, scoffed openly. "We can kill them all! Let's kill them all!"

I slapped him across the back of the skull, hard enough to

knock off his hat and stagger him. "We don't want to kill them!" I shouted, loud enough for dozens of men to hear me over the din. "We want to sell them our slaves! Let's see them out of the town! We push them out, do you hear me? Just push them out! Come on!"

Some of the mariners hard charged ahead to thrust at the stragglers but mostly we walked as a great mass.

Philip marched beside me as we stomped down the street after the fleeing enemies. "Why not harry them closely?" he asked, catching his breath. "Might they not regroup and start the fight again."

"Perhaps." I shrugged. "But sometimes you find men who are convinced they are about to die will turn and make a last stand. Or they will simply take the opportunity to whip about and run you through if you get too close. Better to give them room to get away, even at the risk of losing them." I looked over my shoulder at the handful of fallen Spaniards lying at the wall, being picked over by sailors. "And I think we have taken enough revenge for our lads."

Philip nodded and I thought he had learned the lesson.

The townsmen fled across the bridge to the other side of the river where the women, children, and slaves were already sheltering in the farms. Hawkins set fifty good men, most with loaded firearms, to watch the bridge and the rest of the men were set to searching everywhere for valuables.

We had lost just two of our own in the assault, and these poor fellows were looked after, while the fallen Spaniards, blacks and Indians were also treated with respect. Whatever else they were, the sailors were good Christians.

I rushed to the tavern but found it empty. Then I went to the governor's house where the men were already stealing everything they could get their hands on. It was picked clean in the few minutes it took for me to get there and men were ripping up the floorboards looking for more.

Catalina was not there, either.

There were people left behind the town. A few older people, mainly, who stubbornly refused to flee or to comply with any commands, and some slaves and Indians who generally stood and watched us make ourselves at home.

Hawkins used one to take a letter to Governor Castellanos, in which he threatened to burn the town to the ground if the governor did not buy our consignment of slaves. The governor sent one back saying that we could "set all of the Indies afire" and still he would not grant us licence to trade.

"Set it all afire," Hawkins growled when reading the letter. "I bloody well will set it all afire."

"You don't mean that," Captain Bolton said, warily.

Hawkins scoffed. "A figure of speech. Of course we will do no such thing. Even if it could be done."

"But it could be done," Drake pointed out, almost to himself. When the officers glared at him, he looked surprised. "Of course, we will not. But I was thinking how easily we took this town. We could have taken every single town we have yet called at. And I was thinking how we could probably take every town in these seas, barring the greatest of them. I suspect Cartagena would be beyond us, and Vera Cruz and the like. But the rest are pitifully undefended. It is quite incredible, is it not, that the greatest empire on earth should be so terribly vulnerable?"

We all stared at him, astonished.

"Francis," Hawkins growled. "You could not take this town yourself and neither did you so much as blockade it effectively. Cease your childish fantasising. We have other concerns, like our cargo rotting in our holds."

He bowed his head, chastised.

"What courses might we take?" Hawkins asked his officers.

"We won't burn the Indies but we could burn the town?" John Garrett the master of the *Minion* said. "See if that don't bring them about."

"That is an action I would rather avoid," Hawkins said. "A reputation as a town-destroying pirate will not be conducive to future trade, do you not think?"

"We can leave and find somewhere less obstinate?" Bolton said. "We are merely pulling against the tide here."

"Attack them," Rounse said. "Across the bridge, take their persons and force them to trade. They may not value their houses but they will value their own bodies."

"And their own wealth must be with them, for it is not here," Garrett said. "Think of all the gold and silver across that river."

"Richard," Hawkins said. "Tell me, considering your experience as a soldier, whether there is a way to take the enemy as prisoners without killing too many? I will not have a woman or a child killed by my command."

Garrett scoffed. "There are so few women and even fewer children, other than those of the slaves, that we are hardly likely to—"

"Let him speak," Bolton snapped.

I inclined my head. "Nothing would please me more than to

bring an end to this impasse. To do it, we would have to surround them on all sides. Landing men behind them, and also cutting off their escape inland. We would have to advance together so that they see there is no way to escape. Perhaps then they would surrender but I do not think that they would. You see, I expect they would shelter in the largest of the farmhouses, firing from the walls and windows and protecting the gates." I shook my head, imagining it. "It would be terribly bloody, for us as well as for them."

Hawkins looked to the heavens and sighed.

"Should we ask the slaves?" A voice said. It was Drake, nodding at a group of black men slouching in the shade of the tavern.

"Ask them what?" Garret said, speaking what we all were wondering.

Drake shrugged. "I don't know, ask them if they know anything that might help us."

The officers laughed at that.

"Know anything?" Bolton chuckled. "What do slaves know?"

Drake pursed his lips. "Probably nothing. But they live here. And surely they have no love for their masters."

Hawkins sighed and flicked a hand. "Do what you will, Francis. We will retire to the governor's house for dinner." They moved off and Hawkins turned back for me. "Richard? I hoped to discuss your suggestions for the assault."

I jerked my thumb. "I will keep an eye on Captain Francis and will join you soon."

Hawkins shrugged, one of the officers said something I did not catch and they all laughed as they walked away.

Drake looked at me. "Is it such a bad idea?"

I smiled. "That remains to be seen. Come on."

We walked up the street and crossed to the tavern. "Good day to you," Drake said stopping before them. "I assume you speak Spanish and I would like to speak to you."

They looked us over with blank expressions and looked away. I strode over to them, kicked the legs of one, slapped the next across the face and dragged them all to their feet, cursing them for lazy dogs and for not knowing their damned place. They stood with rounded shoulders and heads down, radiating surliness. I could have slapped them all senseless for such impudence but I restrained myself.

"I need you boys to help me," Drake said while I stood to the side with my arms crossed, glaring at them. "I want to force your masters to give in. To give up. Do you... do you know if there is anything in town that they value? Anything we might burn, perhaps, in order to anger them?"

They stared, their faces blank and unreadable.

"This was a bad idea after all," I said, speaking Spanish. "These witless slaves are too stupid to know anything, to have seen anything. Their heads are empty, look at them. Too mindless to see an opportunity when it presents itself. Too foolish to get rewarded. They have no use for a gold coin, what would they do with it? Let us leave these ones and find others. Surely one Negro or Indian in this town will know something valuable."

I turned and strode off, pushing Drake ahead of me.

"Wait!" a voice called. One of the slaves, the shortest of them, ran forward. He was a slightly built young man with the hint of a crooked back. "I will show you. But you must free me."

I laughed. "Free you? For what?"

He glared at me. "The treasure."

***

It was buried six miles out of town. A cache of the town's most valuable possessions, including chests packed with silver bullion. It took the men all night to load it on oxcarts and bring it back to town. The cheering filled the streets as the treasure was counted out and recorded.

"It must be all above board," Hawkins said. "Every ounce accounted for."

In the morning, Governor Castellanos sent word that he would like to negotiate for the return of his goods.

"Take me to negotiate," I said to Hawkins as he was dressing in his finest clothes.

He looked me up and down. "This has something to do with your whore?"

"Very perceptive of you, John, it does indeed. I would like to negotiate for her."

"You want to buy her?"

I was going to explain that she was not a slave but I did not wish to complicate matters. "Yes."

Hawkins sighed. "Very well. But nothing must interfere with the trade for the Negroes. With all my heart I pray we can be rid of them."

"I understand," I said, bowing.

We met on the bridge under an awning erected by the

mariners to provide shade. Stools had been provided and two tables and writing equipment, held down by rounded pebbles from the river. The Spaniards massed on the far bank with their weapons ready and the civilians loitered beyond in the shade of the trees there. Our own men stood ready on our side. I did not expect trouble because we also had the town's cannons aimed at them.

Governor Castellanos was both younger and trimmer than I had expected, with an erect posture and neat black beard. He barely gave me a look as he sat down and he and Hawkins thrashed out a deal rather quickly. Castellanos would take every one of our slaves, he would pay us 4,000 pesos' worth of gold himself and his people would pay the rest.

"Everyone needs slaves," he said, spreading his arms and smiling a little, though his eyes were as inscrutable as a shark's. "And you will return what is mine."

"We will," Hawkins said.

Castellanos leaned forward and pointed a finger. "All of it. Every piece."

Hawkins scowled. "I have said it. I will not say it again."

The governor thought about it and then nodded. "So we are done."

"No," I said. They turned to me, surprised. "We are not done. You also have something that belongs to me."

"Richard," Hawkins said and I held up my hand to him.

"You know who I am speaking of," I said to the governor.

"No," he said, feigning a laugh. "I have no notion of it."

"Return her to me, now."

"Catalina is not yours," Castellanos said. "How can I give you what you do not own?"

"I own her. She is mine. You will bring her to me or I will take your treasure and burn your town and then I will lead my men over this river and I will kill every one of you."

Castellanos stared at me and dragged his eyes to Hawkins. "You let this one speak for you? Who is in command here, you or this—"

Hawkins, who was more surprised than angry, turned to me and was about to speak. But I looked at him, and I let him see me. I let him see into my eyes for the first time, let him see the rage and the violence that was in me. Disturbed by my expression, Hawkins said nothing and I turned back to the governor.

"Bring her. Now."

He licked his lips and looked over his shoulder and back at me. "You do not know what you are dealing with. She is not mine to give. She belongs to—" he broke off. "She belongs to another. A powerful man. He will kill me when he returns here."

"I will kill you," I said. "Right now."

He hung his head, sighed and called his man over and commanded Catalina be brought out. It took a long time and we sat in silence, with the wind blowing and the men on both sides speaking softly to one another.

"Do not do this," Castellanos said. "Take my gold. Take my silver. I have twenty-five thousand pesos of it in my treasure, you take that and leave the whore with me."

Hawkins head snapped to me. That much wealth would pay for the voyage twice over with more to spare.

I shook my head. "I will take it all, and take your lives, if you do not hand her to me."

By the time Catalina appeared, Castellanos had tears brimming in his eyes. "He will come for you, also. When he finds out, he will come for you and there will be nothing you can do."

"Who is he?" I asked. "Tell me and I will pay you."

He scowled, deeply unhappy. "Not all the money of the Indies will bring it from my lips."

I considered taking him, killing his men and torturing the information from him but then I saw Catalina and all I could think of was getting her away.

Her dress was ripped at the shoulder and her black hair was blowing wild in the breeze. Dirt stained half her face, as if she had been laying pressed against the ground and perhaps she had for she was also rubbing her wrists where they had been bound together. Her face was twisted in worry, eyes darting about trying to take it all in; all the men and the weapons and the hundreds of eyes on her. And even in such a state as that, she was beautiful.

I got to my feet, pushed past the governor and took her from the men escorting her.

"Richard?" she said, taking my arm. "What is happening?"

I smiled and patted her hand. "Time to go, dear girl."

As I passed Hawkins, I slapped his shoulder and took Catalina up into the tavern so she could clean herself, get dressed and collect any belongings she had.

"You did it," Philip said while we waited. He had a huge grin on his face. "You bloody got her."

We laughed and our laughter echoed in the empty building.

Perhaps God was laughing, too.

6

San Juan de Ulúa

1568

WE SAILED FOR HOME, happy at last with our successful voyage and the £15,000-worth of gold, silver, and pearls that had been made. It was enough to make a decent profit for the officers and investors.

And I had Catalina.

She would tell me her secrets but I decided to give her a few days to come to terms with her new situation and left her in my cabin on the *Jesus*. Philip and I took turns to sleep in a bunk in the officers' cabin beside that of the captain's. It was unpleasant but I needed Catalina to trust me, so I took care of her most carefully, escorting her for exercise and air every day. The men gawped but mostly they were very respectful, bowing and wishing her a good day as we passed them in our turns about the deck. We spoke of small things, like the weather and the ship and long voyages and about animals we had seen in our lives and the trees they had in the New World. She did not speak of her situation and her personal history, though she knew it was of profound interest to me, and as we had such a long journey ahead I did not press her on it. There were hints, here and there, of her story. I found quite early on that she had received an education of sorts at the hands of a tutor before coming to Rio de la Hacha and she could read and write and outperformed me in feats of mental arithmetic. But that was not so difficult. Her father had been a relatively wealthy man, descended from mere merchants but successful ones. Of her mother, she was less forthcoming but I understood her to have been a *mulato* who had died some time before her father. Perhaps that was all there was to tell.

I found myself warming to the young woman all the more as she began to relax into life on the *Jesus* and when she would burst into a smile or even laughter it lightened my day and I could forget I had only rescued her for her information, not her company.

The squadron was in fair shape. Hawkins scuttled one of the Portuguese prizes we had taken, on account of not needing so much room without the slaves, and so we sailed with eight remaining ships. The *Jesus, Minion, William and John, Swallow, Judith, Angel, Grace of God* and a small caravel prize that everyone just called "the caravel". We sailed together but each captain knew the route home. North along the Main to sail between the Yucatan and the western tip of Cuba, and then north of Cuba through the Florida channel, out into the Atlantic and on, eventually, to England.

A storm caught us north of Cuba. A truly vast storm, the like of which I had never seen at sea. The relentless wind brought waves that pounded us and rain that drenched us and nothing could be done to resist it. Day after day, it blew us away from home and deep into unknown seas west of Florida. We knew there was a coast to the north somewhere but we had no good charts and all we could do while the mariners battled the storm was to pray.

And pray we did. The crew prayed outside, shouting their services over the wind, and they prayed in the main cabin and below deck. Catalina and I prayed quietly together in Latin in what was now her cabin, kneeling and occasionally holding hands when not bracing against the walls or bunk.

Eight days, we prayed and fought and I did what I could to help by manning the bilge pumps and heaving on ropes when directed to do so. On the eighth day, we sighted the coast and turned and ran west along it, looking for safe harbour. There was none but the storm slowly blew itself out. Still, we found no good anchorage to make repairs for many days and despair began to set in until we came across a Spanish trading ship.

They were terrified of us but Hawkins simply asked where we could find a port. The Spaniards replied that they were headed for San Juan de Ulúa in New Spain and that we could follow them there.

San Juan de Ulúa.

I had never heard of it. And why would I? It was nothing more than an outpost for the town of Vera Cruz about 15 miles distant from it. There was an anchorage of deep water about 250 yards long between the mainland and a low-lying sandbank offshore, made of shingle. On that bank was a battery and a chapel used by the seamen and labourers who lived in the scattered huts that dotted the sandbank and the mainland.

That was all there was to San Juan de Ulúa. A safe harbour, and a defensive batter to guard it.

In that harbour sat eight Spanish ships. Just small traders and nothing for us to worry about. The local authorities, such as they were, were not happy about our presence. But Hawkins assured them we meant no harm to anyone. We would not disrupt local trade. We would pay for every piece of timber, every cask of water and wine, and all we wanted was to repair our storm damage and be on our way.

For two days, those repairs were made and we bought as much fresh food as we could. Local traders sailed for Vera Cruz to bring back more of what we needed. We had the money and we were happy to pay.

Early in the morning, I took Catalina her breakfast in her cabin and we prayed together before she ate.

"We'll be home in England soon enough," I said to her while she sipped her cup of watered wine. "Nothing worse than that storm can trouble us now."

"I cannot even imagine England," she said, running a finger around the rim of her cup. "Are there people like me there?"

"Catholics? Certainly, it is not illegal."

She smiled. "*Mulatos.*"

"Oh. Well, no. There are not even a dozen Negroes in England and all of them servants of wealthy men. Actually, I saw a Negro fiddler once at Arundel House, he was very good. Though they have no families, I'm afraid, as their servitude is very close and is hardly different from slavery. But listen, the people of

London will love you for your beauty and your charm, of that I have no doubt and you need never fear otherwise. And you do not have to come with me at all, you are free to do as you will. Tell me what I need to know and I will take you anywhere you like in New Spain. Do you know anyone in Vera Cruz?"

She shook her head. "I am happy to go with you to England." As she spoke, she reached out and took my hand. "As long as you promise to protect me."

"I consider it my duty to do so," I said and reached up to brush a strand of hair from her bronze cheek. She looked up at me through her lashes and smiled.

A cry went up from the deck and scores of feet pounded as the sailors dropped what they were doing and ran to see.

"Sails!"

Thirteen ships, big ones, coming up from the south. As they came closer, they were sized up and compared to our own squadron. The Spanish fleet had two massive, modern warships and eleven armed merchantmen. They were more powerful than us, there was no doubt about it.

The *Jesus* was old but massive and we had twenty-six big guns. The *Minion* also could have fought them but the rest were small. The *Grace of God* had eight, the *Swallow* six and the *Judith* just four, as did the other tiny ships. Whatever the intentions of the mysterious Spanish fleet, we could not fight and expect to win.

I had a cold feeling in my guts. If we had been facing a larger force on land, I might have formulated plans to move to a better position, to attack or to retreat or I might have fortified a nearby hill, something, anything. But standing on the deck of that ship, I had no idea what might be done.

But Hawkins did. He was roaring out orders when I could barely count the ships. He deployed a force on the island and ordered new batteries to be erected that could fire across the approaches into the safe anchorage where our ships were.

And our own ships were prepared for action.

The gun crews cleared the decks and readied the cannons for firing, bringing up powder and shot and loading every weapon. Pikes and arquebuses and shields and breastplates were brought out. The handful of archers on every ship went up into the fighting tops ready to shoot down at enemy crewmen.

All was ready before midday.

"Can we beat them?" I asked Hawkins quietly from the stern.

"Well..." he began.

His face was set hard but I noted his hands were shaking. With a start, I realised mine were, too. I kept recalling those two crewmen on the *Judith*, being blown to pieces in an instant by a single cannonball.

"John?" I prompted. "How many guns do they have?"

"Say twelve each on the merchantmen and twenty-five on the warships and that makes a hundred and eighty-two. Perhaps over two hundred."

I hung my head. Two hundred cannons. It was like a Turkish siege train, powerful enough to bring down the walls of Constantinople or Belgrade. Yet our walls were made of oak.

"We will have to talk," I said.

He nodded, already planning it. "If they will talk."

"Who do you think they are?" I asked.

"That many ships? There's no man in the New World who can put out such a fleet. No man except the Viceroy of New Spain."

"Who would he have to command it? Is it some famed Spanish mariner?"

Hawkins pointed at the largest ship. "That is the new viceroy's flag, I believe. His name is Enríquez. Two golden castles on a red field with a lion below, you see it? I assume he is a man of aggressive tendencies as it seems he has come in person."

I shook my head. "What could bring him here? Have we so angered them?"

He looked at me. "Did your woman tell you who she used to service down in Rio de la Hacha?"

I swallowed. "I haven't asked her yet. I thought we had time."

"You know what I keep thinking, Richard? I keep thinking about that ship you and Francis let escape from the harbour. It escaped after you tried to nab the girl."

"Dear God," I said and went down to her cabin. I banged a fist on the door and went in when she called.

"What is it?" she said, her face anxious. "What has happened?"

"Won't you sit?"

She stayed standing and set her face. "Speak, tell me, please."

"We have a Spanish fleet coming up on us. We are trapped and outmatched. I will think of a way out of this and I will protect you but I have to ask you a question. You were kept in that place, to be available to provide your blood for certain men who travelled through. I do not doubt that they kept their own blood servants onboard their ships but I also do not doubt yours tasted all the sweeter. And of course they had the pleasure of your company in that delightful room. A luxury, for them. I believe there are others like you in the New World, in towns on the Main and the islands, for the pleasure of the blood drinkers as they travel to and fro. The man who set it up must be powerful, and wealthy. Perhaps you have seen him. If so, I must ask. Did he, perhaps, did he look like me? Slightly taller, a little older. But similar?"

She frowned, confused. "Not at all."

I sighed. "Then it must be one of his men. We believe that the commander of the fleet bearing down on us is the Viceroy of New Spain."

Catalina gasped as if she had taken a blow and sat down heavily on the bunk. She closed her eyes and muttered a prayer to the Blessed Virgin before addressing me. "His name is Martín Enríquez de Almanza. He was not the viceroy three years ago but they say he was made so this year."

I hung my head. The most powerful man in the New World was an immortal. "He drinks from you?"

She shook her head. "I bleed for him into my glass. He drinks it but it makes him angry, I think, and he takes the cups from me to his men. And then he comes back for me. Just for me. He likes to talk."

"It makes him angry?" I said. "He does not savour it?"

She sighed, her eyes red. "He breathes it in, as if it is warm wine, and he drinks. Sips, then gulps it down quickly as if he does not enjoy it. But yes, it makes him... angry. Or sad, I do not know."

I pondered this. "Not all men take to it. Especially if he is new to it. Perhaps he was forced. Turned against his will." Catalina frowned, not understanding. "And you say he takes your blood to his men? What men?"

She shook her head. "I do not know. One is a giant, I have

seen him."

"A giant?" I said, suspecting an exaggeration. "Is he taller than me?"

She laughed, suddenly. "Yes." Her laughter died away. "Now they are here. Have they come for me? To punish me? To take me back?"

If they have come for you, I thought, they mean only to stop you talking. Forever.

"I suspect, if they have come for anyone, then they have come for me. I have been asking questions in these waters and I fear I have alerted these men and their leader means to stop me. This Viceroy Enríquez de Almanza." I shrugged. "Or they could be here to drive off an unwelcome English fleet. Or it may be a coincidence and we will sail from this place unharmed." I did my best but she looked entirely unconvinced. "Have no fear, Catalina, I will keep you safe."

She did not reply and I had no doubt she was regretting ever having met me. Not the first woman to think so and not the last, either.

When I came up to the deck, the mariners were lowering a boat and Hawkins waved me over to his crowd of officers.

"Catalina says the new viceroy there did use her services a number of times and it may be she knows certain terrible secrets about him."

"Oh? What secrets are they?"

"She has not told me yet but I suppose it is possible he has come to silence her. Or to silence me before I can pass her knowledge to the Council."

"These must be considerable secrets."

"Or they may not be here for us at all."

Hawkins nodded at the boat that was now in the water. "We must find out."

Robert Barrett went over along with the senior official from the settlement, a nervous fellow named Delgadillo, and they were gone all day. When they returned in the late evening, we breathed a sigh of relief as Barrett relayed the terms.

"All they want is to shelter here at anchor. The supply ships have come from Spain and the warships came out to escort them. They did not know we were here and though they expressed extreme displeasure at our trading, I assured them we had harmed no Spanish citizen anywhere and had been blown off course by that storm to refit here for our way home."

"You admitted to trading?" Hawkins asked, pointedly.

Barrett shrugged. "They were implacable and they had heard of our ports of call. I admitted trading slaves and merchandise but would not accept we had used force or harmed a soul."

Hawkins rubbed his temples. "Very well, go on."

"As I say, I explained we had already begun to disassemble elements of our vessels for repair and as soon as we remounted spars and fixed rigging and so on, we would leave. And they said they needed to refit also and so asked for space beside us at the anchorage. There is room for all of them to come in, a hundred and fifty yards beyond the *Minion*. As a gesture that they meant no trouble, they say we can continue to occupy the island and its batteries. As surety, we are to trade hostages. Ten apiece."

"Ten gentlemen, I take it? Very well, perhaps they mean us no harm. Richard? It seems they were not here for you after all."

I nodded. "It seems so."

The thirteen Spanish vessels crowded into the narrow anchorage beside us, so that both fleets sat side by side across two hundred and fifty yards. Our bowsprits overhanging the island and our sterns facing the mainland. We were side by side, at point-blank range. The *Minion* was nearest the Spanish ships, with the *Jesus* beside the *Minion*. And then our small ships in a line.

And work continued on the ships. At first, it was very tense indeed but as the days passed, the men began to relax and the English and Spanish, the Protestant and Catholic, conversed and laughed and drank together on the shore and on the island.

I was sure to keep out of sight as best I could and Catalina was forbidden to leave her cabin.

"But I thought they had not come because of me?" she asked, hating to be so contained.

"All the same, if they see you…"

She nodded and spent her days praying. She did not know it but I made sure that Philip or I was stationed outside her door at all times. On the night of the fourth day, we were ready to depart and were preparing to do so. The men had been commanded to cease their drinking and to get as much rest as they could as we would be heading back for the Florida channel north of Cuba and then into the Atlantic again. It was late September and it was supposedly the worst time of all for the big ship smashing storms so the men talked of their fears as they went for their rest.

But I did not rest and nor did many of the officers.

"They're up to something," Hawkins said as we looked out across the *Minion* at the forest of Spanish masts. "No doubt about it."

"Barrett has not returned?" I asked.

Our captain-general had sent him across that morning and he had returned with assurances that the Spanish were doing nothing untoward. But still, the Spanish were doing several subtly strange things and so Barrett had been sent yet again to check on our hostages and to urge the Viceroy to maintain the truce.

Hawkins shook his head. "Perhaps they are treating him to a fine dinner."

"Perhaps they have killed him," I said.

The officers with us growled their displeasure. It was unlucky to speak it aloud but we were all thinking it.

"Surely not even the Catholics would stoop so low as that," Hawkins replied without conviction.

"They might if they meant to take us," I said. "We have had enough reports now, John. The Spanish merchantmen cutting additional gun ports into their hull would be enough alone. And last night, there was so much coming and going from the mainland, they could have brought over a whole army."

"You are imagining things," Hawkins said but it was clear he was nervous, as were the others.

"Arm the men," I said. "Rouse them but quietly and send word to the other ships."

"Barrett may yet return."

"How would you do it?" I asked Hawkins. "If you were the Spanish and you wanted to take us all as prizes. What would you do?"

He shook his head. "I suppose, if I was the Spaniards, I would assault the *Minion* first. And then... send other ships out to close the way out of the anchorage. Difficult to do in this wind and with such a slight tide, they might have to warp their way by us and our smallest ships could slip out."

"Might we not order the smallest ships out now?" I asked. "And send more men across to the Minion, in case they board her?"

Hawkins rubbed his face. "How could they try such a thing? It could be nothing. Nothing at all."

I forced myself into silence while the officers argued back and forth. If you push men too much, they will take an opposing position despite themselves. Eventually, Hawkins hushed them all and ordered the men awakened and armed.

"But do it quietly," he said. "I will not needlessly antagonise the Spaniards. If they see armed men on our decks, they may believe we are about to attack them."

The officers said that they understood and moved off to do as they were ordered. I grabbed the master before he left.

"Do you know who are your best four men in a fight?"

Without hesitation, he nodded.

"Then arm them and bring them here and command them to stay by Captain Hawkins' side until they are relieved. We must keep him alive at all costs."

The master's eyes were wild but he did it immediately and I went down to see Philip.

"Looks like trouble. Anyone comes down here who's named Pedro, you run the bastard through, all right?"

Philip put his hand to his sword hilt, gulped and nodded his head once. "I will."

"Good man. Now, knock and tell her to be dressed and ready to run, if need be. Otherwise, you keep her safe inside."

"Run? Run where?"

I shrugged. "The island, the mainland, another ship. Hopefully nowhere but if we start getting shot up with cannons or there is a fire, we must get her out."

Clenching his jaw, he nodded again. He might have had the strength of an immortal but he was no soldier and yet his sense of duty was enough to steady him, and to give him courage to do whatever had to be done. Without dutiful men, civilisation does not function.

I reached the main deck and just moments later, English voices on the *Minion* were raised in cries of warning. An arquebus was fired somewhere nearby and then, almost immediately after, a trumpet was sounded from the Spanish fleet.

The trumpet sounded over and over, blasting out a signal that could mean only one thing.

I rushed to the rail along with dozens of mariners and we watched as grapples flew from the nearest Spanish ship onto the *Minion* and instantly they were heaved taut and the Spaniards moved their vessel against ours. On her decks stood at least fifty men and from below came fifty more at a run and then more kept coming up.

Most of the soldiers were armed with arquebuses and they were preparing to assault the *Minion*. Our men there were preparing to stop the attackers but already they were outnumbered and more Spaniards kept coming up. At a glance, I estimated one hundred and fifty soldiers all with firearms, and mariners on top of that pulling the ships together.

I raised my voice to shout orders but Hawkins beat me to it.

All his nervousness and hesitation was gone in an instant and along with every other sailor on the *Jesus*, I looked up to where

Hawkins jumped up onto the rail of the sterncastle with one hand to steady himself on a rope and in the other he held his sword aloft where it flashed in the lamplight.

"God and Saint George! Kill these traitorous villains and rescue the *Minion*! I trust in God the day shall be ours!"

The sailors roared as our trumpeter began blowing the signal to stand to arms and everywhere was filled with shouting. I was astonished to see the sailors throwing out ropes and heaving on our anchors to pull us out into the channel while at the same time others lowered all four of the ship's boats into the water. All the while, firing from the Spanish arquebuses filled the air.

"What are we doing?" I asked a sailor, grabbing him as he rushed by me.

"Putting the *Jesus* in the channel, sir, and sending men to the *Minion* by the boats. Please release me, sir!"

I rushed to the side and climbed down to a boat that was already crowded with armed men just as they pushed off from the *Jesus* to cross the mere twenty yards to the *Minion*. Behind us, our flagship inched out away from the island and into the channel. The arquebuses were firing constantly at the *Minion* and the unmistakable sound of men fighting could be heard even over that. The three other boats were coming up behind ours and when we reached the side we all threw ourselves up but I made sure to be first.

Launching myself bodily over the rail, I came up on a deck filled with slaughter. Englishmen lay dead and dying all over the main deck and the timbers were slick with black blood. Flashes and bangs came continually from the enemy ship, which was pressed against ours at the stern but was a few yards distant at the bow. At the rail, our men fought with clubs, axes, and pikes to keep the Spanish away but more poured across at the stern all the way to amidships.

Drawing my sword, I rushed toward the stern where the fighting was thickest and pushed my way through the pikemen to the heavy press of men. A sailor beside me fell suddenly, his head thrown back in a shower of blood from the shot that took his life. With my sword up high, I thrust it over the heads of the men in front into the eye of a Spanish soldier who cried out and fell back.

"Give me room!" I shouted and eased my way forward, stabbing my sword out through the gaps between the sailors.

A flat-bladed axe hacked into the shoulder of the man beside me and he let out an inhuman howl and fell away from the blow, as if his body knew before his mind that the wound would be fatal. And suddenly I had the room I needed to fight. My sword stabbed and cut and parried and I punched with my off hand and kicked at men's knees and stamped down whenever a Spaniard slipped. Soon, they were edging away from me and I pushed on until I was standing at our rail, fighting over it and over the lower rail of the Spanish ship. Our extra height meant they had to climb up to us and so I swept it clean with ease and threw down any man who came near. One man I saw using a rope to pull himself up with one hand and I shouted at my men.

"Cut the ropes! Cut us free! Cut the~"

A shot hit me in the chest and I fell back, tasting blood. I had bit my tongue on the way down and I found myself being dragged back along the sodden deck by two English sailors I recognised from the *Jesus*.

One looked at the bloody hole in my doublet and his face said he knew I was dead. "Well done, sir," he said, placing a hand on my shoulder. "You done it, sir. You cleared them away. Know that and pray now. Pray and think of home, sir."

With that, he and the other lad jumped up and ran into the mass of men where the mariners were hacking at the ropes fixing them to the Spanish ship. I dragged myself to my feet, gingerly touching my wound. It hurt rather a lot.

Worse, though, was that I had lost my sword and I went to get it. The sailor from a moment before saw me as I straightened up, sword in hand and smiling at my good fortune in finding it again.

"You alright, sir?" he asked, astonished, looking from my face to my chest.

"Oh, yes. Perfectly well. Only skin deep. I suppose it must have hit a rib."

He frowned. "Suppose so, sir."

"Lucky it wasn't a cannonball!" I said, grinning.

He stared as if I was mad.

Men began shouting from the bow and I made my way forward, ducking as I ran and trying to not slip in the blood. Arquebuses fired from the Spanish ship and I did not wish to be shot again. Near the bow, I heard what the frantic cries were about.

"Spanish boats came up from all directions, sir!" a sailor shouted while pointing at the island. "They overran our batteries there. They're repositioning them."

"Where is Captain Hampton?" I said.

But I need not have worried. Having taken back control of his ship, he was also manoeuvring away from the island and out into the channel, where the men of the *Jesus* had already pulled their ship. Beyond the Spanish vessel beside us, the enemy flagship was next and beyond that was the other warship.

They also were warping out from their mooring.

"Are we fleeing?" I asked a sailor.

He looked at me sideways, as if I was a fool. And in sailing terms, I absolutely was.

"Can't turn our backs, they'll blow us to bits."

"What then?" I asked. "Is it to be cannons?"

Scoffing, he pulled away and ran to a hatchway. I noted the men bringing up powder and shot and saw the gun crews loading their cannons.

Philip and Catalina were on the *Jesus* and there was about to be a battle. I ran to the rail, looking for a boat with which to cross to our flagship when the batteries on the island opened up.

A dozen guns began firing as fast as they were able so there was continuous firing from that moment on. But they were not firing on the *Minion*, nor were they shooting the *Jesus* while she took a position closer to the mainland.

Instead, the island batteries began shooting at the rest of our ships, the smaller ones. The shot smashed through their timbers at close range, ripping them to shreds in explosions of smoke and splinters. Ropes whipped loose and spars shook.

"Where are the boats?" I shouted at a man.

He did not know but another fellow did. "On the larboard side! Keeping them there, sir, so's to stop the Spaniards pulling against us again."

I understood at once that the width of the boats between the hulls would stop us being boarded from deck to deck but I had to get across to the *Jesus*. Had Philip got her out, I wondered? No, he would not have sense enough to remove her without my say so. Surely, he would at least have her on the starboard side of the ship, farthest from the Spanish.

And then, at an order from Captain Hampton, our guns began firing. The sound was appalling and I winced even in the open air. I assumed we were firing on the ship that had boarded us but I was wrong.

The two Spanish warships were out in the channel, like us pulling themselves out by their stern fasts and aft anchor ropes so that the *Jesus* was firing at the Spanish flagship and the *Minion* at the other great warship.

And they fired at us.

Their cannons smashed into our hull and our decks, a dozen guns almost at once, blasting us high and low so that the ship shuddered like she was coming apart. What could I do but cringe away on the deck and wait to be blown to pieces?

I ran aft and joined the team still heaving on the stern fasts until our entire length was clear and every one of our cannons could fire at the Spanish warship. When the mariners were given sailing orders that I did not understand, I looked instead at the battle.

We were being hammered, it was true, but the Spanish were suffering more than us. Their ships were bigger, newer, and better than ours. But our gunnery was better. Our men fired faster and more accurately and the enemy ships were suffering badly.

The flagship, in her duel with the *Jesus*, had been hulled at the waterline and she was listing so much that her guns had almost fallen silent. Indeed, though the Viceroy's flag was flying, the men were throwing themselves into boats and I cheered with the others when we noted what was happening.

Through a gap in the drifting smoke, I had a view of the command deck. It must have been the viceroy himself standing as erect as he could on his tilting ship, with a great plume on his hat. And at his side was a giant of a man, towering over every other officer on the command deck. It was Catalina's giant.

Our enemy ship was faring little better. Not sinking but riddled with holes. I wondered if we looked as battered as she did and turned to ask one of the men how the *Minion* was doing when an explosion filled the air.

It was the enemy ship, the one we were shooting. One of our shots must have hit a powder keg, for a roaring blast blew up from her deck into the rigging. The blast itself was not enough to sink her but suddenly there were fires burning from bow to stern and masts and rigging were likewise aflame so that the whole vessel was soon consumed in a mighty conflagration that illuminated everything in flickering red light and deep shadows.

The *Jesus* was already firing on the merchantmen and so too the *Minion* began firing at the other ships.

"By God!" I found myself crying. "We are winning! Thank Christ."

But God was not listening. Before the words were out of my lips, men were shouting that the *Angel* had been sunk.

The small ships had been battered into submission by the shore batteries. The *Swallow*, the Grace of God, the caravel were all smashed to bits and their men were dead or surrendering, waving flags and begging that the Spanish stop, for the love of God. And the tiny *Angel* was below the waves. For a moment, I

197

thought that Drake's ship, the *Judith*, had also been sunk. But the *Judith* had been the furthest out and she was now beyond the anchorage. There was nothing they could do to help us, with their four small cannons they could not even make a dent in the shore batteries.

And so, with most of our squadron destroyed, the shore batteries turned their power against the *Jesus*.

It was a miracle that the *Jesus* had made it across the Atlantic in the first place, and then we had survived a terrible hurricane. For all her great size, she was ancient, her timbers were soft and wormy and those batteries ripped her to pieces. The cunning bastards first fired high and shredded her sails, masts, spars, and rigging so that she could not sail away to freedom. And then they turned their power on the hull. It seemed as though every shot knocked a hole as big as a bull's head through it and soon it looked like it could not possibly hold itself together.

Hawkins stood against the rail in full view of everyone, shouting his commands while cannonballs flew around him from the enemy merchantmen and from the island batteries. He appeared unconcerned, waving with one hand while drinking from a silver cup in the other.

"We must rescue them!" I shouted at Captain Hampton, rushing to him.

"Yes, sir, we must!" he said and of course they were already ahead of me and were pulling closer to take the place of the *Jesus* so we could continue to fire on the enemy while our flagship withdrew. Our battering increased but our timbers were new and sturdy and many of the balls that had hulled the *Jesus* were bouncing from ours.

The boats from the *Jesus* carried her fore and aft anchors out far from the ship to drop them away from the fighting and then the men hauled on the ropes to pull the ship toward the anchor. First the stern and then the bow, as if it was walking away. This was what they called warping and it was impressive enough to me on a calm day in port but they were doing it while the ship was falling to pieces around them and men were everywhere dying while they worked.

Our own ship inched closer to the *Jesus* and as I hauled on our lines, I prayed that Philip and Catalina were still alive. The battle had been raging for hours and the men were exhausted, with bloody hands and blackened faces. We were all deafened by the endless cannon fire and our throats were hoarse so that communication was done more by gesture than anything else. Their eyes were wild and staring and men kept wiping at their dry, wrinkled lips. My wound had long healed but many of the others nursed gashes and some were stricken with splinters as long as a man's forearm sticking from various parts of their bodies.

"Don't, don't!" I saw one lad crying to his mates as they tended to the wooden shard in his belly. "Don't pull it out. You'll kill me!"

Either way, I thought, he was certainly dead.

And then at last, after both ships twisted away down the anchorage, we overtook the *Jesus* and sheltered half behind it so that it would take the brunt of the damage while the men from the *Jesus* evacuated the ship.

I was relieved to see Drake was there in the *Judith*, also nuzzling against the side of the *Jesus* while supplies, treasure and men were taken from our flagship.

As soon as we were tied up, I climbed up from the *Minion* on to the *Jesus* to look for Philip and Catalina.

By God, the ship was a mess.

Debris everywhere, deck timbers jutting up, rigging dangling and swinging like a wild forest. The crew crowded at the bow and stern, passing the items up from the hold to both our docked ships.

"Philip!" I shouted, pushing through the lines of crew. "Where are you, Philip?"

A sailor waved and said he had seen him taking the woman to the bow. Cursing, I elbowed men aside and stomped forward to the other group, calling for him.

He was at the rail with his hand on Catalina.

They were unharmed. Afraid, certainly, but relieved to see me. I looked over the side down at the distant deck of the *Judith*. Already it was heaving with men crowding the tiny ship from bow to stern, and more were climbing down along with supplies and treasure.

"What are you doing?" I said. "We cannot risk getting in that tub. Let us go to the *Minion*, come on, come with me."

They were on my heels as we pushed back to the stern. Cannonballs still crashed into the ship and after a sudden accurate barrage the top of the mainmast came crashing down through the tangle of rigging to slam into the deck ahead of us and spin over the side. Thankfully, it missed both the other ships and splashed into the black channel but the trailing rigging knocked men down and one was dragged over the side.

No one was going to go after him so he was as good as dead,

if he was not already. I ducked and climbed through the quivering ropes and pulled and pushed Catalina until we were clear, while Philip helped from the rear. At the stern we found that great mass of crewmen, some still passing casks and sacks of provisions while others called out to hurry up before the damned ship sank.

"Stand aside for a lady!" I shouted. "Lady coming through, stand aside there!"

At the same time, not waiting for their good manners to assert themselves, I shoved men aside and dragged Catalina after me.

There were dozens of men ahead of us when a terrifying shout rose over everything else.

"Fire ship!"

In the channel, the Spanish had towed one of the merchantmen around the wreck of their flagship, still half sunk on its side and the other warship, now burned to the waterline. That merchantmen now had its sails out and was catching a slight breeze enough to bring it inexorably toward us as the towing boats rowed frantically aside. For on the deck of the ship they had started an enormous conflagration. Fire roared up on the forecastle all the way up the foremast and flames and burning debris spilled over the side, the prow poking through a wall of flame. It looked like some black demon come up from hell, shedding fire from its flesh as it came to destroy us.

The men had been fighting a devastating, overwhelming, confusing battle in the dead of night for hours and they were beyond exhausted. It was the shock, I think, the sudden appearance of that ship igniting out of the black, still exploding with white bursts as powder kegs erupted one after the other as the fire ship bore down on the *Minion*.

And it broke them. The men on the *Minion* were overcome with a marvellous fear and they cast off the lines tying her to the *Jesus* and they pulled the *Minion* away while we were still crowding the decks of the stricken flagship, desperate to be taken away. From the orderly cohesion of a moment before in an instant it was every man for himself. Sailors threw themselves from the *Jesus* down to the *Minion* as it inched off.

"Go!" I shouted to Philip and elbowed my way through with Catalina behind. "Take her and jump!"

I helped her to the rail, guarded them from the crowd and pushed Catalina's backside as they leapt. They fell hard, Philip pulling her on to him as they landed in a heap. Well done, son, I thought.

"Where is Hawkins?" I shouted at an officer who was ineffectively trying to restore order.

His eyes were half-crazed but he answered quickly enough. "He went below to free the hostages."

"Free them?" I shouted. "He should have bloody murdered them!" That honourable fool had got himself killed for nothing.

I pushed back a few paces, looking for the captain while men climbed and jumped behind me.

Hawkins came up at a run and I sighed and turned back to the rail.

The *Minion* was ten feet away. The fire ship seemed to make the darkness even deeper and the blackness between us loomed like an abyss.

"Jump!" I shouted at Hawkins and he looked at me as if I was mad. "Jump, you bastard!" I grabbed his shoulder with one hand and a fistful of his clothing at his lower back and threw him across the gap.

As he fell, I wondered if I might have made a terrible mistake but there was no time to do anything but bend my knees, swing my arms and leap after him.

I held my breath, falling and falling and expecting to smash into cold waters and to sink forever because the fall had taken too long, and I knew I had missed and then my feet hit the deck and my legs buckled and I thumped every bone in my body.

Hands pulled me upright and I limped to the stern rail where Philip stood with his arm around Catalina's shoulders. The fire ship missed the *Jesus* but it illuminated the scores of men still crowding her decks. One young lad stood with his arms laden with a huge golden goblet and a huge silver plate set with precious stones all glinting in the light. Cannons still fired but we pulled further and further away until they could threaten us no longer.

Despite being enormously outnumbered and outgunned, and despite our agreement being so utterly betrayed, we had destroyed the two great warships, two of the huge merchantmen, and had killed dozens of the enemy. Not only that, we had escaped with many of our men and much of the treasure. But there was no doubt we had suffered a devastating defeat.

The *Minion* was crowded with exhausted men but their trials were not over. A wind blew up before dawn that threatened to wreck us on shore and so the mariners worked the ship hard to beat back and forth out to sea. At least there was no shortage of hands.

When the sun came up we found ourselves in a heavily damaged, overloaded ship. And Drake's *Judith*, which men said had certainly sailed free of the harbour, was nowhere to be seen.

The worst of it was that she had most of the victuals on her and we had very little.

Hawkins had no doubt that the young man had abandoned us to our fate. And so, alone and in terrible shape, the *Minion* sailed for England.

There were two hundred and two men on board and one woman. We had so little food that in the coming days, when we had barely made any headway, the men ate every rat on the ship, and they ate the parrots and other creatures taken as pets or as curios to sell. Men even chewed on rawhides we carried as cargo.

It was too much and the crew were immediately close to mutiny. Almost a hundred demanded that they be put ashore and said they would take their chances with the Indians or with the Spanish. Hawkins did not want to abandon them but I was thankful when we did as they asked. I heard much later that those men walked back into Spanish territory. Many of them were murdered by Indians on the way and the rest, weak and starving, were arrested on sight by the Spaniards.

Those that died before being captured were the lucky ones. One can imagine the mistreatment that the English sailors suffered from the start of their confinement in Spanish gaols and it only ever grew worse as our men were passed into the hands of the Inquisition where they were examined and put to the question. Most then died in prison or as slaves. Some, I know for certain, were tortured, whipped and sentenced to the oars of the Spanish galleys. Others were burned at the stake for renouncing Protestantism before taking it up again. Their tales came back to us over the coming years and every one was like a knife in my heart. I can imagine what it did to Hawkins. He felt he was responsible but I knew that I was.

And that was the first battle fought by the English in the New World.

The voyage home was like a realm of Hell, filled with desperate hunger and death. I had to give my blood to Philip and there was never enough water and every drop I gave away made me feel like I was dying. Philip was ever at the edge of the full blood thirst and many a day I saw him staring hungrily at Catalina's soft neck. I cannot deny that I looked at her in such a manner at times myself.

Hawkins was close to despair by the time we limped into Mount's Bay in Cornwall after months at sea. I had suffered with hunger before, and starvation once or twice, but I had never been so thin or so weak as when we reached England.

But reach England we did and never had she looked so beautiful and never had I loved the sight of her more.

All the way home I knew that I had brought the calamity down upon us. I had alerted the viceroy to my presence and I had taken a woman who could identify him as an immortal.

Now I knew two things. Firstly, that William's commander in the New World was the Viceroy of New Spain Enríquez de Almanza. Secondly, I knew that I had to cross the ocean again so that I could tear out his treacherous black heart.

7

Changing Course
1569 - 1572

"SO, IN SUMMARY," Stephen said, looking around at the men around the table, "we might conclude Richard's voyage was not a success."

"We came as close to ruin as I have ever been." I shivered. "But I live. And now we must take revenge on Spain for their treachery. My heart says I must cross the world again, find Viceroy Enríquez and murder him. But I am old enough to know when to seek advice."

I had been in London for a week, still regaining my strength and putting on weight. Every day, I exercised more and soon I hoped to be back to my old self. Bodily, at least, but my wits remained rather shaky especially at night when I lay in a bed that seemed too soft and remembered the sounds of the cannons and the moans of the starving.

We went to see Cecil and Walsingham to deliver my report. I had written to Dudley but he had claimed to be busy and had declined, seemingly quite done with me. I am certain he was jealous of the Queen's affection for me and had decided to pretend I did not exist. John Dee had begged to join us but we told him to stay away and to leave us alone.

Cecil steepled his fingers. "You are certain Viceroy Enríquez is the one you seek?"

"I am."

Stephen pursed his lips. "What evidence did you find to prove this supposition?"

"Our witness."

Walsingham rolled his eyes and exchanged a look with Cecil. "A woman of dubious reputation."

"She is trustworthy."

"Could it be," Walsingham said, "that you trust her because she is a Catholic?"

I looked square at him. "No."

Cecil sighed. "Let us assume that she has spoken the truth and Viceroy Enríquez is what you say he is. But how do you propose to assault his position? He is assuredly the most well-protected man in all New Spain. An entire city, its militia, its forces surround him in Mexico."

"I will raise another fleet and return."

Cecil sat very still but I could see that he was disturbed. "You claim to be an ancient man well versed in war and I have been urged to believe it by friends that I trust." He meant Dudley and Walsingham and perhaps even Elizabeth. "But I fear your actions are bringing us into war against a kingdom that has long been an ally of England."

I leaned in. "As I have attempted to explain, we are drifting toward war with the Spanish in large part due to the devices of the immortal lord William de Ferrers. It is not my actions that brings us into conflict, I am the one seeking to stop it. There is no need for Spain and England to be at war."

"Perhaps you are right," Walsingham said. "More likely it is the fact that Catholic Spain cannot abide a Protestant England. They would crush us, by any means, to install the old faith on us again. At times, I wonder if it is not inevitable."

Cecil frowned. "Nothing is inevitable, sir, other than death and the judgement of the Lord."

Walsingham opened his hands. "As you say. And yet, peace has been maintained these long years while France stood as an enemy between us. As we each bury our differences with the French, we are seeing other points of conflict bloom. Our brothers of the faith in the Low Countries are growing in number and power and ever more are committed to throwing off the yoke of Catholic Spain. Antwerp's decision to close its ports to English traders devastated our volumes of cloth exported and we could do nothing else but close our own ports to them. The anger of the traders has meant we hardly send ships to Spain these past few years and it dwindles ever more, as does theirs stopping here. Our traders go elsewhere now, to Cologne and Frankfurt and so on. And then there is the Spanish army there, just across the Dover Straits, putting down the rebellions of our Protestant brothers. The commander of the Spanish army is the Duke of Parma. Not only is he a devout Catholic but a man of a ruthless nature and there is always the risk that he could cross with his army and invade England."

I was shocked that the situation had degenerated so rapidly in my absence. "Can that truly be a possibility, my lords?"

Cecil took over from Walsingham. "Shortly before your return from the New World, a squadron of Spanish ships put into Plymouth and Southampton. They had all the backpay for Parma's Spanish soldiers. The Queen seized it."

I stared at them. "Surely that is an act of war? Why did she do such a thing?"

"It was against our strongest advices but we learned the money was a loan from Genoese bankers. Her Majesty decided that if it was a loan, it may as well be to her as to him, and she took it. It was Genoese money, she said, and now it is English. She wanted it not so much for England, though God knows we need it, but to deny it to Parma. Without pay, his men might mutiny and then she has protected England, and our Protestant brothers in the Low Countries, without firing a single gun."

"Clever of her."

They rolled their eyes. "The Spanish seized all of our shipping in retaliation. And so of course we had to do the same to theirs. Now our ships are truly embargoed at all Spanish ports."

"You are trying to tell me that the conflict arises due to the failures of men and due to chance and to fate and to other forces. I do not disagree. But there is a hidden hand also, pushing here and there where needed. I have seen it before."

"Perhaps you are right," Cecil said. "But we see no strong evidence for it."

"Above call, we cannot risk accelerating this trade conflict into open war," Walsingham said. "England, I am sad to admit, would fall. They have five times our ships, ten times our soldiers. Above all, we must work to slow, delay, and God willing, abate this crashing together."

Cecil nodded. "War can be averted. It must be averted, sir."

"If you had been at San Juan de Ulúa, you would know the war has already begun."

Cecil waved a wrinkled hand. "A sharp skirmish is not a war, sir."

I bit my tongue until my anger passed. "We should remove the hidden hand pushing our kingdoms together. At the least, I can raise another fleet and take it to the New World. There, I can roust out the immortals in the ports and coastal towns."

They looked long at each other.

Eventually, Walsingham spoke. "And Captain Hawkins has agreed to this voyage?"

I shifted in my seat and looked out of the window. "Hawkins will not voyage again. So he tells me. The losses at San Juan de Ulúa are too much for his soul to bear. He lost a great many men who were sworn to him. Good men, honest Englishmen. God-fearing men, just as he is."

"He will not sail? Not ever again?"

"Today, his soul is broken and I cannot imagine it will heal by tomorrow. One day, God willing." I shrugged.

"So how do you intend to return to New Spain?"

"I shall find a way."

They looked at each other. It was an awfully weak response and I knew it even before I said it but what else could I say? It was the truth. I knew what had to be done. I had to get across to New

Spain and I had to kill the immortal viceroy and anyone there who was his man. I had to destroy the supply of gold and silver flowing to William that was funding his war on us. Funding whatever mischief he was working in Spain.

"You shall find a way?" Cecil repeated, peering at me. "What way shall this be, sir?"

"I will find captains and ships and build a new fleet and when it is done we will sail to New Spain, put it into action, and achieve victory."

"Ah," Cecil said. "It sounds so simple."

More sarcasm. But I smiled, for his doubt was natural. "Yes, my lord, it sounds difficult. But it shall be done as everything difficult is done." I looked between him and Walsingham. "One step at a time."

"And what is your first step?" Walsingham asked.

"I must find an Englishman who is not only capable of leading the voyage but who is also willing to do so."

Cecil raised an eyebrow. "You have someone in mind to replace Hawkins?"

"No, my lord. But I must find one."

"What if you cannot?"

I sighed. They were beginning to irritate me. "Then I shall make one. Or I shall become one."

It was a foolish boast. I knew I could never lead a fleet. Not only could I not sail or navigate, I did not know even the principles of these things. I did not know what ships were capable of, what they could do and what they could not do. I had seen the devastating effects of artillery they carried and yet I knew not how to command such seaborne batteries.

I saw the look pass between Cecil and Walsingham. Saw it and understood what passed between them.

Oh well, that look said. Let the fool thrash around for a while and when he fails, perhaps we can wash our hands with the whole business.

Then they turned to me and smiled.

"In that case, sir," Cecil said, standing. "I wish you good luck."

***

I had to wait an hour for Eva to come from the Queen's private apartments to a small parlour. Eva came in, skirts swishing in a green dress with golden embroidery.

"My dear, you look beautiful," I said, embracing her.

She rolled her eyes. "I can't breathe in these clothes. Nor this place."

"You do not enjoy living in a palace?"

"Don't jest with me, Richard, I'm not in the mood."

"I apologise. I am happy to see you."

She smiled. "It is so good to see you. I can't tell you how relieved I was to read your letter. You were gone so long. And so far."

"And must return. The task is only just begun."

"Tell me what happened."

We sat and I spoke and she listened without interrupting, taking it all in. "This woman, Catalina. She is at the house? Do you need me to return to take care of her, to guard her?"

"Goodie is looking after Catalina. Treating her like she's her long-lost daughter, just returned from a long absence, waiting on her hand and foot. Doesn't seem to care that she's a Catholic. Catalina is rather bemused but appears to enjoy it all the same."

"That is well. And you are home now, so I can leave the Queen's service."

"As I say, I must make arrangements to return to New Spain."

She hung her head. "I pray Stephen unveils this Jesuit plot soon."

"How are you getting on with Elizabeth?"

Eva pursed her lips. "She likes me. That is to say, on some days, she likes me. On other days... she is rather changeable. But I like her also. She has a quick mind. But the other ladies. They resent my presence. They are nobly born, they have heritage, names. They do not know me and when the Queen favours me they conspire together to bring me down in her estimation and they scheme constantly to trip me up over matters of etiquette or my false personal history. It is jealousy, I know, and pettiness on their part but it drives me mad. Literally mad. Most days I could batter them all bloody, I swear. Nothing would give me greater joy. Yet I have had to scheme myself in order to protect my reputation and so I play one against the other and cause them to fall out. I spend my days discovering their secret loves and hoarding knowledge that may prove useful."

While she paused for breath I leaned forward and patted her hand. "It is not your natural state to be so surrounded by women of that nature."

"Indeed not but the worst of it is that, God forgive me, I excel at it. While I play these games, I am the chief amongst them. Every day I break one or the other and find one crying on my shoulder over something they do not know I did to them. It is driving me to distraction." She took a deep breath and let it out slowly. "I'm sorry, I have been keeping such things to myself for ever so long and could contain it no longer. I am returned to myself again."

"Do they not exclude you for being a Catholic?"

Eva pursed her lips. "I pretend to be Protestant."

"Pretend?"

"I have memorised whole passages of prayer books and the Psalms in English and I know all there is to know and they suspect nothing." She looked at me. "Have you found it difficult with the Protestant sailors?"

"Not at all," I lied. "If you are finding all their deceit difficult, perhaps the Queen would allow you to return home for a few days, here and there. In your absence we could send one of Walt's men in as a palace guard. It would not be as safe as you being here but I suspect it will be for the best. I will speak to Cecil about it."

"Thank you. I will have to think of some excuse that does not involve your name."

"Oh?" I asked. "Why so?"

Eva looked at me chidingly. "She asks about you quite often. About what you might think or feel about this thing or that. But most of all she is curious about the precise nature of my relationship with you. How long I have known you, how we feel about each other, and whether I think you handsome and so on."

"What do you tell her?"

"Certainly not the truth, Richard. She would have me thrown out of here immediately, never to return. She is quite taken with you." Eva looked at me closely. "And there are rumours."

"Rumours?" I said, lightly. "Of what rumours do you speak?"

"They tell me you spent the entire day alone in the queen's carriage on the way to Windsor. Of course, no one dares suggest openly that anything untoward occurred, being as you are so lowly a man but it was undoubtedly unseemly."

"It was."

"You should not risk the anger of Dudley and the other court favourites with your flirtatious nonsense. Even though you are back and she may summon you, you must stay away from her."

"It is already done. She does not wish to see me again."

She frowned. "What did you do?"

I scoffed. "I did nothing."

"Then what did you say?"

"Nothing at all, Eva, our conversation was cordial. Pleasant, hence the length of our discourse. It is simply that the queen also realised, as you say, that the private time would set tongues wagging. If we met again, it might do more. No man wants to avoid a scandal more than me."

Eva frowned, looking closely at me. "You did not... Richard, you did not actually do anything... physical with the queen, did you?"

I looked away. "Of course not! I never would, how could I? She would not stoop so low and of course I have too much self-control even if she had attempted it, or even if she would attempt to suggest it again one day in the future."

Eva gasped and cupped her hand over her mouth. "Richard!" she whispered. "You plucked the Queen!"

Holding up my hands to quiet her, I growled. "Speak it not! And I deny it. I did nothing of the sort."

She peered at me sideways. "You must tell me true. So I can

protect you."

I shook my head. "There is nought to tell, woman."

Eva narrowed her eyes like the sly fox she was. "So, how was she? I wager once saddled she rides like a centaur, does she not?"

Anyone else would surely have missed the nature of the smile that leapt onto my lips before I clamped it down and saw it off. But Eva jumped to her feet, gasping once more and clapping both hands over her mouth.

Then she pointed at me, whispering. "You bawdy, beef-witted strutting codpiece! Your inability to keep your sword sheathed could ruin her reputation! What then? What of the kingdom, then?"

I waved her to silence. "No one shall know. I shall tell no one and the rumour will be nothing."

She stomped up to me and leaned in and hissed in my ear. "It would be if you could have kept your something out of her nothing!" With that she slapped me across the back of the head.

Rubbing the admonished area, I could not contain my quiet laughter and of course that only angered her all the more, for a moment before she, too, smiled and then laughed while shaking her head.

"You are the one who commanded me to seduce her," I protested.

"Not literally!"

"She practically forced herself upon me. What was I supposed to do, reject her?"

"Mmm," Eva said, taking her seat. "I'm sure that is precisely how it occurred. But if she speaks of this to just one of her ladies..."

"She will not. Of course she will not. Anyway, I am not sure that she had not been plucked previously. She certainly appeared to know what to do and how to do it."

Eva rolled her eyes. "One hardly requires an extensive education on the matter."

"My point is, she managed to keep her previous dalliances quiet and she will do the same again."

Eva jabbed a finger at me and whispered so quietly I could barely hear her words. "You plucked the Queen's sheathe and now she will have a taste for it. Stay away from her. If she summons you, we will write that you are sick." Her eyes sparkled. "We will hint that you are syphilitic! No, no, that will only alarm her. But it must be something unpleasant, something foul, to do with the guts."

"This is all unnecessary, it will not happen again."

"You are lucky that I am here to protect you from yourself."

"I tell myself that very thing daily."

"I must go now." She stood and turned to the door.

"Give me a kiss goodbye, my dear."

Stepping to me, she leaned forward and stopped in front of my face. "Go kiss a queen, you ruttish lout." With that, she pinched my nose and swept from the room with a quick glance over her shoulder before slamming the door on me.

Giving her a few minutes to get clear, I left the parlour and made my way out to where Walt waited with the palace servant. I paid the man and walked out with Walt at my elbow.

"How's Eva doing?" he asked.

"The same as always."

Walt shrugged. "Have to say, I miss her terribly at the house."

"You do? How unusually sentimental of you, Walter."

He nodded. "No better bosoms in all London, our Eva." Pausing, he pondered it. "Except Saucy Edith down Pie-corner, perhaps, though there's nought but a gnat's cock between them."

I sighed. "And she calls *me* a ruttish lout."

He laughed. "Why she call you that? Oh?" A sly looked crept over his face. "Did you and she just..." He made an obscene gesture with his fist and two servants and a priest saw him, all of them scowling in disapproval.

"No and let us change the subject for discussion to something more suitable, shall we? You know where we are to meet these new sea captains?"

Walt nodded. "We got to go there now. Some have come in from Tilbury, most from the port of London. We're already late but if I know mariners, once in there they'll not leave the dockside alehouse until they need carrying out."

"We would not need to convince some inexperienced captains if Cecil and Walsingham would just give us their backing. The bloody bastards. I need a willing captain and they could help provide such a man yet they are content to do nothing. All the power of the kingdom and they're damned useless."

"What did you expect?" Walt asked. "Protestants only care about whining to God and complaining to each other, not about anything important."

"But this concerns them, it concerns all England."

Walt shrugged. "Not real for them, is it. Even that Walsingham, and he's seen immortals with his own eyes. Killing Catholics, that's what they care about." He stopped to spit. "I don't know how you stand it, spending so much time with these heretics. They're all mad, every one of them."

"Yes, they are. But some of them mean well, perhaps."

Walt scoffed. "Ain't proper Englishmen, are they. Lost their wits with this new religion. I pray for the day when all this blows over and England comes to her senses again."

"We have already been waiting for some time. I dread to think what it will take to turn the English back to the old religion."

"Easy," Walt said. "A proper Catholic king sitting his Catholic arse on the throne of England would do it."

I stopped, grabbed him and looked around before pushing him against the wall. "In the palace, Walter? In the palace?" I said, keeping my voice low. "Such words will get you executed, man. Are you mad?"

He pushed me back and dusted his doublet off. "It is not me who is mad but these heretics."

I looked around but no one was within earshot, or so it seemed. "Keep your voice down."

"Do you deny it?" he demanded.

"Of course not," I said.

He pointed at me. "You been spending too much time cooped up with these bastards. It's rubbing off onto you. Don't tell me you're starting to become one yourself."

"Do not be absurd."

"You better not, Richard. It ain't right. These people ain't right."

"Fine, yes, I agree. Now shut your flapping tongue behind your teeth and let us be gone from here."

In the outer courtyard, there were as ever clusters of petitioners and other people waiting on court business, along with servants and messengers going to and fro.

Standing alone to one side, was a young man that I recognised. I was not pleased to see him.

"You!"

Francis Drake stood and drew himself up to his full height, squared his shoulders and puffed out his chest.

"Mister Ashbury." He bowed his head. "Richard."

"What are you doing here, Francis?"

He bristled. "I am waiting to see the Secretary of State."

"You are here to see Cecil? I was with him earlier. Why do you wish to see him?"

Drake hesitated, apparently unwilling to admit his business. But he was too filled with righteous anger to be able to long hold on to it. "I wrote the Secretary a letter when first I landed and rode hard to London to deliver it by hand, which I did. The letter told all that had happened and I begged to be given leave to return."

"Return? To Devon?"

His eyes bulged. "To the West Indies!"

"But why?" I asked, feeling my hopes kindle just a little.

His hands curled into tight fists and his shoulders hunched up halfway to his ears as he spoke with great passion. "The treachery of Don Martin Enriquez must be answered."

I looked closely into his eyes and saw the fire of vengeance burning within. I knew that look well, though such passion was for the youthful and not the ancient. My own had burned down to a smouldering core.

"I understand. And you wish to persuade Hawkins to take up the fight once more?"

The fire died in his eyes. "John prefers to let the matter stand."

"You look for some other captain to lead you back, then?"

He glared at me. "I *am* a captain. That is, I was for a time and will be again. I shall lead the fight against the Spanish. I have sworn an oath to Almighty God to not rest until justice is done."

I could not stifle the condescension in my voice. "But you were the least of all Hawkins' captains, Drake. You were given command only due to your family connections and even then you were given the weakest ship, one with barely any guns. And then, when we needed you most, when all was almost entirely lost, all you did with your ship was to sail it away and abandon your men and your cousin who had placed such trust in you. Hawkins has condemned your actions in a letter written to the Secretary of State. Not by name, perhaps, but the allusion was as clear as day. Why would anyone give you command of a ship ever again, Francis?"

The rage filled him completely. I was certain he would strike me and I had half a mind to let him. Instead, he pushed past me and strode away toward the front of the palace.

Walt shook his head. "Didn't you just say you needed a willing captain? A Protestant he might be but there was one there, with experience, and a more willing man I never saw. And yet you made him into an enemy. How do you do it?"

"I need no lessons in morality from you, Black Walter, and I need no captain such as he. Willing, he may be, but I need a reliable man, someone I can have faith in, a trustworthy man. Not a damned coward."

Walt shrugged. "As rich as you are, in this you're a beggar. And beggars don't get to choose a sixpence over a farthing."

"There are hundreds of sea captains in England. Thousands. I can do better than the coward Francis Drake."

* * *

The sea captains of London were for the most part all bluster. Some men had been to Africa and some to India, or claimed to have done so, on English ships or Portuguese ones. A handful appeared credible but when we attempted to find investors, most merchants and wealthy gentlemen were unwilling to part with hundreds or thousands of pounds on untested men.

I was not the only man attempting to put together squadrons of ships for voyages of profit. Despite our terrible destruction at the hands of the Spanish being well known, it was also known that it was almost the third successful voyage Hawkins had led to the New World. But for that single calamity, men said to me, Hawkins would have returned rich beyond his dreams.

And it was not just the captains of trading ships with the backing of merchants who were keen to get a piece of the wealth. One of England's admirals, a seaman and gunnery expert named William Winter was committed to transforming the Queen's naval strength into a proper fighting force capable of fending off Spanish and Portuguese galleons. More than that, he was one of the men organising the English fleet so that it could be brought together, crewed by veteran mariners and captains and properly supplied when needed. It was a herculean task with many obstacles of tradition and law in his way, and the constant interference of the Queen, her Council, and the wealthy merchants and nobles who wished to balance the security of England with their own personal financial gain.

In the midst of all his reforms, he sent three ships to the Caribbean before the end of 1571. When they returned, I heard that they took a Spanish ship off Jamaica and then utterly failed to take the port of St Augustine in Florida. They returned home in failure but with experience. Eventually, I was granted a meeting with Winter and he apologised for not telling me of the voyage.

"It was to be done in utmost secrecy. We wished to test the strength of the Spanish but we could not have word getting out."

"I would not have betrayed the voyage. All I want is to travel to the West Indies once more. Cecil knows this, he should have told me."

Winter was confused. "It was Lord Burley who commanded me to keep it from you. He said you would only fan the flames of war."

"Cecil said that?"

"He did and requested that we arrange it in secret. Just three ships were hardly a great squadron and they did not go close to the southern part of the Main under control of the Viceroyalty of Peru, which I believe is the only area that you wish to go?"

"No," I said. "There is much more to be done than to simply return to the south. I have business all over."

"And that is why Lord Burley did not wish you to become involved. He said you would have grown our three ships into a fleet of six or ten and we would have started a war."

"They started a war already, sir, at San Juan de Ulúa!" I cried and left him.

I wanted nothing more than to charge into Cecil's house and

thrash him raw but I calmed myself after Philip repeatedly stood in my path. He was a good fellow.

There were more secret and unsanctioned voyages launched, often with just two small ships chancing their luck. One John Harret of Plymouth and James Raunse of the Isle of Wight went to trade, inspired by Hawkins and also Lewis Larder of Plymouth and Captain Trenel of Totnes. They were small in scale and small in success but there was a growing number of English captains and crew with experience of the waters of the West Indies and even of the Spanish Main. Despite all that, building a fleet large enough for my needs was proving an almost impossible task.

"No one in this kingdom trusts me and if they will not lend me ships, or sell me ships, we shall have to build them ourselves," I said to Stephen after months of frustration.

"Do you have any idea how expensive a modern warship is?" he said. "We could perhaps fund one and fit it out but our coffers are not bottomless. That ship would have to make a profit just to keep it sailing and then we would not have enough to fund another."

"Let us at the least do that, then," I said. "What use is the money sitting in a chest?"

"It does not *sit*, Richard, it is constantly moving and, God willing, growing. But if I pull together enough to find a suitable shipwright and commission a ship, if we are talking about a warship of hundreds of tons we will need royal assent. That means Cecil, our newly made Lord Burley, will have to give us permission."

"Which he will not do because he still believes he can avoid open war."

"It is the Queen's belief also."

"She is a woman, of course she believes that. We know the truth."

"Do we? Do we even know that William is working to attack us outright? It seems he is intent on taking over the New World, perhaps that is to where his energies are turned."

"He sent an assassin to kill Elizabeth. There are more of his men here, at least one. He is up to something here and it is your business to find out what and to stop it."

"That is what I am doing."

"Not well enough. You fail, Stephen, you fail every day."

He scoffed. "No more than you."

I began to argue but of course he was quite right.

It was that very day when a letter arrived from Callthorp in Plymouth.

"What does it say?" Walt asked as I read it at the table in the dining parlour. He was slicing an apple in his hand and eating it with infuriating deliberation.

"I do not believe it," I said.

"Go on, then, spew it out," Walt said, chewing noisily.

"Callthorp says a small squadron of ships let out from Plymouth on Monday. Headed for some secret destination all now say is the New World. The lead ship was captained by Francis Drake."

Walt laughed. "I knew it. Little bastard had the acorns enough to get it done. Good on him." He gestured at me with his knife, a slice of apple still on it. "I told you. I bloody well told you."

"Shut up, Walt."

He chuckled and I made my way to my chamber to write a

letter back to Callthorp to instruct him to listen for word of Drake's activities trickling back through the network of ships and ports to Plymouth. But before I could write more than two words, a servant came to tell me that Dr John Dee was here to see me.

"Tell him I am busy. Perhaps Stephen would like to entertain him."

A few minutes later, Stephen strode in. "Have you forgotten your appointment with Dr Dee?"

"I have no such appointment."

Stephen sighed. "I knew you would forget! It was arranged weeks ago and I will not allow you to postpone your meeting again. He is here, come and speak with him. Answer his questions."

"I have no desire to satisfy his absurd curiosity. You speak with him. You answer his questions."

"Which I have done. Many times. He has questions that only you can answer."

"I am not sure I wish to answer questions such as those."

"You can at least tell him that yourself, can't you? It would be polite."

"Yes, yes. I will finish my correspondence and meet with Dee."

Stephen narrowed his eyes. "Do I need to instruct the porter to stop you fleeing?"

I wrote and answered without looking up. "Very amusing, Stephen."

A short while later, I found them in the dining parlour just off the entrance hall and Dee stood and bowed so low his beard reached his knees. "Richard, I am honoured."

"Good to see you, John."

Dee's young hunchbacked servant bowed deeper and muttered a question to his master.

"Yes, Boote, off you go to the kitchens," Dee said.

He ducked and bowed and bobbed away as I stepped aside.

"Hungry, is he?" I asked.

Dee smiled. "I am well aware you wish to keep your secrets. Would you like to speak in your chamber?"

"Here is well enough." I invited him to retake his seat and sat at the table myself. "Are you staying, Stephen?"

"I admit I am rather curious."

"Fine, fine. So, what do you wish to know?" I asked Dee.

"Ah, yes, wonderful. Just a moment." He bent to a cluster of satchels, cases, and bags and took out sheathes of parchment, pens and inkpots, and three hourglasses in various sizes. Stephen and I glanced at each other while he sharpened his implements with his penknife and arranged his things just so until finally he was ready. "Now, Richard. I wonder if you could tell me if that is your true name, or one you have adopted?"

I folded my arms and leaned back. "What does that have to do with anything?"

Dee frowned and Stephen half laughed. "Richard, why not answer him?"

I shook my head. "But why do you want to know? I thought you were interested in our attributes, not my life story."

"I am interested in everything in the universe. But I am specifically interested in the origins of your abilities. Where you came from. Were you born to a woman?"

I laughed in disbelief. "How else would I have been born?"

He raised his eyebrows. "Then tell me."

"Yes, John, I was born to a woman."

"And your father? Who was he?"

I sighed. "What questions did you answer, Stephen?"

He shrugged. "Many. A great many. We have had conversations on multiple occasions. And we performed certain physical investigations."

"You did what?"

Stephen pointed at Dee's implements upon the table. "We made precise cuts of varying lengths and depths in my flesh and recorded the time they took to heal under certain conditions."

"And what did you learn?"

"Oh, very much," Dee said, flicking through sheets of parchment. "Would you like to see our results?"

"No. Do you want to do the same with me?"

"Yes, indeed!" Dee said. "Precisely so. Let us perform the same cuts and compare the healing times with those of Stephen."

"Perhaps later. Tell me what you have learned from your conversations with Stephen."

"Well, let me see. I learned that Stephen believes his abilities come from the consumption of your blood and there is no sorcery or magic at all."

"Sorcery? It certainly is not sorcery."

"Indeed, that is what I believe also. It seems entirely possible that your unique powers are a natural phenomenon. But I do not yet know enough to disregard the chance that there is some form of magic at work here, magic which may even be unknown to you."

"Nonsense."

"Is that so? Well, certainly you know more than I. Perhaps you would tell me about the origins of your powers?"

"Ask me about something else."

He and Stephen looked at each other. "Very well. Let us discuss other important questions. For example, I want to know the worst injuries you have suffered in your life. Also, how fast can you run? What is the heaviest weight that you can lift and carry? What different effects does the blood from different people have on these abilities?"

I looked at Stephen. "How does this help us?"

"It might help in ways we do not yet understand. Knowledge is power. And Doctor Dee may help us learn things about ourselves we never knew."

Sighing, I poured myself a cup of wine and sat back. "What was your first question, John?"

"Tell me, what kinds of wounds have you suffered?"

"I have been cut, stabbed, shot. Run down by horses. I have fallen a long way. Once I was burned very badly indeed."

"Did you ever lose a part of your body to injury? A finger cut off, or an ear torn off?"

"Never. But my men have lost parts of themselves. The wounds heal very nicely but the lost body parts do not grow back."

"So I have heard. But I wonder if you are the same as the men below you in the hierarchy. If you lose a finger, will it grow back?"

"We are not testing that."

"No, indeed. Quite. I am curious also how much damage might be done to an immortal of the various hierarchies before they perish. A leg, an arm, all limbs together?"

"You mention our hierarchies. What do you know about it?"

"Only what Stephen has kindly informed me. You are the

pinnacle, you feed your blood to the drained people and they become what you call immortals. And these men may perform the same process to create what he calls a revenant. These men have the same powers and weaknesses as the immortals, only each is greatly magnified. Light burns all the greater but darkness is more comforting to them. They require blood daily. They lose their minds to some extent and are difficult to control and highly dangerous."

"It sounds like you have it right."

"And may these revenants create spawn of their own?"

I hesitated. "I have never considered it. I doubt that they would be able to do so. When creating an immortal, a certain fraction of them perish in the attempt. When they create revenants, a far greater fraction die before they are turned. If they were to create their own..."

Dee nodded as he scratched away. "It is logical to assume the scale may be severe, perhaps even a geometric progression."

I looked at Stephen. "It gets progressively worse," he said.

"That is what I said. I doubt one in a hundred would survive the process, if any. And if such a creature did exist, he would be a raving beast, a mindless monster that required an all but ceaseless supply of blood. I doubt it has ever been done."

"It would be fascinating to see it done. Perhaps we could perform the experiment on some captive people."

"Pardon me?"

"Criminals, perhaps, or some other people. If they were already sentenced to death, we could experiment on them to turn one into an immortal and he may turn one into a revenant. We might then have the revenant turn one into this raving beast you mention. Of course, we might have to kill a hundred men to find one who lived, assuming your proposed theorem is correct but that is the niceness of using convicted criminals, you see? And then we can perform detailed experiments on each, comparing one with the other. Strength, swiftness, exposure to sunlight and effects of blood satiation and blood starvation. If you would consent to undergoing the same tests, it would provide an ideal base with which to tabulate the effects on each subsequent generation. Indeed, if we could discuss further your own origins we may discover that the scale travels in the opposite direction, where your creator will be stronger still, faster still, with a lesser reliance on blood and other factors which may prove unique. We might even extrapolate further and imagine beings of almost unimaginable power as progenitors of your creator, Richard. Perhaps you are not an angel but you are imbued with an element of angelic power which traces back even to an archangel."

I looked at him for some time after he finished speaking while he continued to scratch away in his coded symbol writing.

Stephen squirmed in his seat and reached a hand across the table as he began to placate me. "Richard, of course this is merely a proposal. Perhaps we could use the immortal prisoner we keep in our gaol for starters?"

Dee's head snapped up. "You have a gaol? You have immortal prisoners? Is it here?"

Stephen smiled, gesturing with his thumb. "Certainly, downstairs we have constructed—"

"Stephen!" I snapped. ""We are done. And you, cease your scratching!"

Dee looked up, a confused smile on his face. "Richard?"

"You are mad, John. I do not doubt your wisdom and your wit but you are also mad. And I am done with you."

Stephen stood. "Richard, please do not—"

"Collect your deformed servant and leave, Doctor Dee. We shall not meet again."

***

There was occasional word about Drake's secret and unsanctioned voyage but it was mostly rumour and not to be trusted. While he was gone, I continued to lobby Cecil and tried to bend Walsingham to my way of thinking. They were serious and dutiful Puritans and still they did not trust me. We also spoke to a number of shipwrights who were willing to build us a ship, once we had the proper permissions. Or they offered to build us smaller ships, two or three of them that would not require any special dispensation. But those kinds of ships we could buy from almost anywhere and indeed we already owned a dozen, through one agent or another. Even all together they would not stand for a moment against even a Spanish treasure galleon, or a single of the warships that sank us at San Juan de Ulúa or even the massive merchantmen there beside them.

I sent a letter to Callthorp commanding him to send Drake to me, should he ever return from his voyage.

This he did, finally, and we arranged for him to visit the house off the Strand. When the day came, I invited him into the parlour and we sat at the table with a little cold meats and warm wine between us.

He looked older than before, especially around the eyes and his skin was darkened from the sun.

"How do you fare, Francis?" I asked and poured him some good wine.

"Well, sir, well indeed. It is good to be home. Though London is no true home to me, nor never will be. My wife spent some time here in her youth but she did not like it either, preferring her own land, which is Cornwall, and accepting mine in its stead, which is Devon."

"You are married," I said. "I thought you a bachelor."

"I married Mary before I went on this last voyage. Thought it was about time I started making sons and she is a good girl and a good wife."

"You have sons now?"

He pursed his lips. "Alas, not as yet. Not for want of trying but I have been away and... well, you know."

"I certainly do. I am sure you will have a dozen of them running around in time."

"Aye, God willing." He eyed me over the rim of his cup. "This is excellent. Now, I can guess why I am here."

I nodded. "Foremost of the reasons is that I must apologise for speaking to you so brusquely when last we met. You did not deserve my ire. I was frustrated most of all with certain councillors and I vented my anger onto you. So, I hope that you will accept my apology."

He smiled, knowing full well that I was only apologising because I needed him so much. "There is nothing to apologise for, Richard. It is all in the past and as well forgotten." He fiddled with a big gold ring on his finger. "Now, I expect you'll be wanting me to tell you about our voyage?"

I was about to agree when footsteps sounded on the stairs, and a woman's laughter, and I called out.

"In here, Catalina!"

She swung herself in through the doorway, her black hair flying loose and her skirts flowing as she came to a stop. "Mister Drake!" she said. "Perhaps you remember me, we met on that terrible bad voyage."

After jumping to his feet, he stared at her for a long moment before bursting into laughter. "Of course I remember you! How could I ever forget so delightful a young woman? And you speak English now?"

She blushed and lowered her head. "Only very badly, I'm afraid. I get everything wrong."

I shook my head. "Complete nonsense, Catalina, your English is faultless. Perhaps you would like to join us?"

"Oh, I would but—"

Philip stepped into the parlour behind her and took off his hat, bowing to Drake. "Sir, it is good indeed to see you again." His smile faded. "Come, Catalina, we must be away." He reached as if to take her elbow and then dropped his hand. "If you please."

She smiled. "Yes indeed, we must."

"You are going out?" I said. "Where to?"

"Lizzie and John's wedding," Philip said. "Then there's to be dancing in the Bell until late."

"Well you best take damned good care of her and Catalina you do not leave Philip's sight, do you hear me?"

She giggled. "Not even when I must visit the privy?"

I rolled my eyes. "And the dancing may continue until late but you two had better be home early."

"Yes, Richard," they both said at the same time.

"All right, go on, then. And have a good time."

As they went out, we heard them laughing together.

Drake raised his eyebrows as we sat once more. "She is yet in your household?"

"Best place for her. To keep her safe."

"I see, yes, of course. And your valet and she are clearly in love. How delightful."

"Oh, Philip is smitten. He waits on her, obeys her every word, is never more than six feet from her. But Catalina... I am sure she knows she can do better. Far better."

"Surely you do your man wrong by such talk. Clearly she has great affection for him and after all she was nothing more than a Spanish whore when you found her."

Placing my cup on the table, I leaned forward and looked him in the eyes. "I shall thank you to never refer to her as such again, Francis. Not in my house and not in my presence, do you understand?"

He stared for a moment before looking embarrassed. "Perfectly, and I apologise. She's a fine young woman, there's no doubting that. She might almost pass for an Englishwoman. Well, perhaps a Welshwoman. Has she come around to the true faith yet?"

I could not divulge the truth that I had a priest on hand to come and perform services to my people on a regular basis and so I shook my head. "She is as Catholic as she ever was and likely to stay that way."

"Ah, well. I will pray for her, as I pray for you. Now, you wish

235

to hear about my voyage?"

"I have heard already that you had some small success in your venture. How did you convince the Spanish to trade with you? Where did you go?"

He sighed and leaned back, drinking more of his wine, savouring it and savouring even more his position. Now he was the man who had what I wanted and he meant to make the most of it, I was sure. I smiled politely and waited for him to speak.

"I put all my profit from the last voyage into it, and everything else I had besides. A mere handful of my cousins put in a little but all I could afford was two small ships, both about twenty-five ton."

I whistled. "Mere pinnaces, Francis. How many men?"

"Forty-six in all. And every one of them sailing without wages, to be paid only in profits from the voyage."

"So you had desperate men."

He smiled. "All Devonshire men and Cornishmen are desperate, Richard. Although a goodly portion were with us at San Juan de Ulúa. They wanted to strike a blow as much as win plunder, if not more. You can trust an Englishman to seek a fortune but you can trust him more to persecute his enemies." Drake raised his cup. "Whatever his religion."

"I don't know about that but I am glad they earned something to ease their troubles. But a pair of twenty-five-ton boats and forty-odd men? You could not carry slaves enough to make a profit."

He rubbed his chin. "I said I will never trade in those poor souls and I meant it. I thought you would know that about me, Richard. No, not slaves. In fact, not trade at all."

"Not trade... you mean you did piracy?"

He scowled. "I mean war, sir. War! War waged upon the

guilty. A war of the only kind I can wage." Drake thumped his chest.

I thought of the Queen and the Privy Council's efforts to stop that very thing.

"What did you do?"

When he spoke, he was picking his words carefully and I had the impression it was a version of a speech he had made before or had at the least practised. "The way I have seen things for some time has been dictated by our former voyages under John's command. We piratically plundered those Portuguese ships and used force to get our way with the Spanish colonies. Indeed, it was only through the application of force that anything came of it at all." He pointed at me. "You were the cause of that success. Without your manipulation of John and the others, we would have flailed around and returned empty handed. We would have had to strand those slaves on a patch of coastline and come home paupers. But you showed how it must be done."

"I had my own reasons, as you well know."

"I hardly know anything at all but it is not your reasons but your actions and their effects that interested me." He leaned forward. "Only by force did we accomplish anything, you certainly agree with that. And how can that be? The Spanish Empire is the greatest the world has ever known, the richest and the most powerful. Their soldiers are the envy of the world, unbeatable, disciplined. Their ships are the greatest and most numerous, their mariners more skilled now than the Portuguese ever were. Their colonies are rich. Silver and gold pour out of their mines and flows across the sea to Spain. Each governor is like a king. But..." he held up his finger. "But it is vulnerable. Even weak. Have you seen the West Indies and the Main on charts and compared them with those of the same scale with England or the coast of Europe?"

"I have not."

"The coast of the mainland is almost four thousand miles. That is not including Florida and the islands of the West Indies. We sailed with impunity here and there from port to port and there was no one to stop us. No one!"

"The Viceroy stopped us at San Juan de Ulúa."

Drake's face fell. "That was our mistake. We should never have negotiated, never trusted them. Why did John trust them? I knew it was madness, I'm sure you did, too. Why would an Englishman trust a Spaniard? Why would a Protestant trust a Catholic? A mistake we shall never make again, never. And it only ever happened because we were blown by that storm so close to Vera Cruz. If we are careful, they can never catch us. They do not have the ships to protect their ports, their towns, their people, they simply do not have them. We can strike wherever we wish, within reason."

My heart was racing because this was precisely what I wished to hear. "What happened on your last voyage?"

"We sailed there and took Spanish traders as prizes."

"You *took* them?"

"We sailed close, blasted them with a little cannon fire if they needed it and they surrendered. Time after time. We took what we wished from each and sailed on, looking for more."

"Ships are all very well but I need to land in ports and then to speak to tavern keepers and the like."

"What you need, Richard, is the Viceroy of New Spain."

"I would need thousands of soldiers to attack Mexico, it

cannot be done."

"What if we could damage him from afar? Not his person, perhaps, but his riches."

"It is well that you mention it as his riches are of profound interest to me. I have no doubt that he is diverting the wealth of New Spain for his own dark interests. And those of his true master, who sits somewhere in Spain, commanding events from the shadows."

"And who is that?"

"We do not yet know the name he is using but we know what he does. He is my enemy. And he is England's enemy. And his secret war against us is surely being funded by the gold and silver of the New World."

"Then it would serve your interests, and England's, if we took all of his treasure."

"All?" I asked, smiling. "What do you mean by all?"

Drake's grin spread across his face. "There is a route. Hidden in the loathsome, pestilential forests of the isthmus of Panama. The narrowest point between the two oceans. The route, over land, through the fetid air of those woodlands, is the Achilles heel of Spain."

My heart pounded. "Go on."

"Gold and silver from the mines in the south are shipped north to a city named Panama on the other side of the isthmus. The gold and silver is collected and collected until it is piled high as Rame Head and then they load these bars and bars of metal onto pack mules that carry it in a great long train through those hills to the eastern side to a tiny town named Nombre de Dios. It is so small a place for what it guards. Produce comes in, bullion goes out in the treasure galleons. These great ships are huge, covered in guns, filled with men. No one thinks of attacking them and with good reason. But we would not need to. Not if we get it *before* it reaches the galleons."

He sat back and crossed his arms, smiling rather smugly.

"Steal the treasure," I said. "That is your plan."

"And become the richest men in England in the process."

I sipped at my wine. There were so many holes in his plan that it would not hold water. But those could be talked away, plugged up, with lots of hard work. I would like to have bigger ships, more men. But with Drake's expertise and willingness to act boldly, I believed I might just be able to do it.

"It is not the worst plan I have ever heard," I said.

Drake grinned, clapped his hands together and held one out for me to shake.

I looked at him. "Francis, we are a long way from shaking hands on this."

"We want the same thing, don't we? I have seen what you can do in battle and you have seen what I can do at sea." He shrugged. "Let us simply shake hands as friends."

At that, I leaned forward and grasped it.

8

Treasure

1573

I LOOKED OUT ACROSS THE SEA from the deck of the *Pasco* at our other little ship, the *Swan*, clipping through the tops of the waves just as we were, in full sail. Our two small ships carried just seventy-five men. Though the mission was dangerous, each one had volunteered in the hopes of winning for himself a fortune while striking back at the hated Spaniards. They were young—all but one or two of them were under thirty—and filled with vigour and anger. Truth be told, some of them were no more than boys. I suspected, as I watched them from the deck of the *Pasco*, that many would die in our little war against the Spanish. And I was right, in a way, but not quite in the manner I expected.

I had my own young man with me.

Philip had been a fine fellow to have at my back but he had

suffered under the relentless sun and keeping him fresh with blood had been a challenge of sorts even on the *Jesus*. What was more, I had no wish to drag him away from Catalina's side, for all the hopelessness of his situation, and in the days before I left for Plymouth, I told him he was not to come. The relief nearly knocked him flat.

"But I must have a valet," I had said to Stephen. "A mortal one. And one who is trustworthy, dutiful. I was thinking to call in one of Callthorp's men, if he has any mortals in training."

Stephen stared at me. "This is divine providence. It is, it surely is. Or fate, perhaps, simple chance, I know not but it is perfection itself!"

"Unwind your smock, Stephen, and shit it out. You have someone in mind, I take it? Not a Protestant, is he?"

"Of course he is, Richard. Everybody is, these days. All our new men are, there is no getting around it no matter who you take. But there is a young man, I spoke of him to you once or twice. Martin Hawthorn is his name, Rob's descendant."

"He's a bloody lawyer! I do not need a writ presented to a magistrate, Stephen, I need a man to darn my hose and keep the rust from my blades. And more importantly one to watch my back in a fight."

Stephen waved a hand at me. "I have seen to it that Martin practices with an instructor of the sword these last five years and as for fighting, well, that is precisely the issue at hand. There was a woman, you see. And some sort of altercation between interested parties, one of which being our friend Martin who unfortunately for the other party defended himself with vigour."

"He killed a man?"

"Wounded a young gentleman across the face, permanently disfiguring him, and cutting two of his friends in less visible but no less painful places."

"Maybe he takes after Rob after all."

"That was my thinking."

"Now, the trouble is, I have tried my damndest to make it all go away but without success. I have bribed two dozen men already and yet I cannot get the warrant for his arrest withdrawn."

"The young gentleman won't let it lie, then? Have you considered, you know? Walt might pay the lad a visit."

"Richard! We may do underhanded things when we need to but surely we draw the line at having the son of a lord murdered in his bed?"

"Merely a jest, Stephen. So, he needs to get out of London for the sake of his own safety and you thought taking him on a piratical raid against the might of Spain would be the best idea."

"Oh, damn you, I was attempting to solve two problems in one but damn you anyway."

I laughed. "I will meet with him. If he seems suitable, we shall ask him. He can always say no."

Martin Hawthorn had said yes.

He was a tall young man, a shade taller than me but as thin as a bowstave and rather serious. I had thought it nervousness at first and hoped he would become more comfortable in my company but after a while I realised it was simply his way. He was not a bad fellow for all that and he was not too proud to be my valet. It takes enormous humility for an educated man to do work below his station without becoming angry at his master.

The voyage across the sea was pleasingly uneventful, though

the small size of our two ships was a cause for concern. We were crowded indeed and there was nowhere to get away from it. My cabin was no more than a bunk with a curtain across it and even that was more than most men had. I was after all a gentleman and the principal investor.

Our initial goal was to once again head to the southern parts of the Main, the northern coast of what would later be called South America, where it curves deeply to join Central America. During the journey through the coastal waters, we chased down a handful of small ships and rifled through their holds and the personal belongings of the senior mariners. It was all remarkably civilised and none of them tried to fight.

We came to the town of Cartagena in late 1572. It was far too strong for us to threaten with our two small ships but we practically blockaded the port and chased and seized traders that came toward the town. Every time we took prisoners, though, we were sure to put them ashore or send them that way on small boats and always we left them unharmed. Drake was very clear about that from the start and to his credit he treated every man with respect.

The Spanish could do nothing to stop us. They tried, of course. How they tried. The local authorities attempted to open negotiations but why would we do so when we could take whatever we liked?

Then we finally headed west for isthmus and the treasure route.

After the crossing and a few weeks of taking prizes, the men needed time ashore to recover, to repair the ships, to restock and prepare for our assault. We found what seemed to be a pleasant harbour along a deserted stretch of the coast and set about doing just that. It was a deep inlet that curled around and provided cover from the sea so that passing ships could not see us and our own were safe from squalls. A brackish river flowed out into the small bay and there was a wide stretch of beach where we set up shacks and canvas tents.

The dense jungle came right down to the beach and the men stomped straight in with axes to start collecting firewood and poles for building and the like.

"We must guard against attacks from the natives," I said when we were making the camps. "Organise landward watches, day and night."

Drake and the other officers looked between me and the jungle.

"But this is virgin land," the master of the *Swan* said.

Drake nodded. "Aye, there's no natives here, Richard."

"I was told there were natives everywhere in the New World." I gestured at the deep shadows. "They might be there right now. Watching us. There might be a thousand eyes on us and we would not know."

They all turned back to the trees. "We will organise landward watches," Drake said. "Day and night."

We began a few revitalising weeks onshore, Drake focusing on maintaining the ship and I took to drilling the men on the beach. One afternoon after a week of work, I was chopping lengths of dense wood while Martin sat close by on the sand polishing my knives, my daggers, and my swords.

"I bet you regret coming with me now, Martin," I said, setting the timber upright before swinging for it. "You could be hiding from your warrant in Scotland or Geneva or somewhere civilised, you know."

"If my friends at Gray's Inn could see me now..." He smiled, shaking his head. "I'd never live it down."

I nodded. "Tell you what, Martin. I'll ask Drake to lend me one or two of his men from time to time and I'll see if he has not some other tasks better suited to your education. Certainly, you can assist him with record keeping and the like."

Martin nodded as he sighted down the blade he was oiling before rubbing the rag along it again. "Very well. Although, I must say I do not find this life as disagreeable as I had expected. The sun and the sea are relentless and yet I find it exhilarating to see so much of the world. It is so very different from home, in every way imaginable. And the men, though uneducated and rough, are remarkably pious and the ships are entirely harmonious. And I must admit that I find myself willing to put up with much discomfort and humiliation knowing that I may return home a wealthy man."

"I do not know that you will be wealthy but, God willing, you will be able to buy yourself a good house in London and with that you should attract a decent wife soon enough. Tell me, how much does a young lawyer—"

There came shouting from the jungle.

Our men crying out warnings and calling for help.

I grabbed my sword from Martin and ran with it in one hand and my axe in the other toward the sound, crashing along a path the men had hacked through the undergrowth.

Upon reaching a rough clearing, I came across a dozen of our men brandishing their weapons at a smaller group of black men, most armed with makeshift spears.

"They just came out of nowhere!" one of the mariners cried. "Jumped out like they was going to murder the lot of us!"

"That ain't what happened," an older man said. "They come up slow, arms out, weapons high. They want to talk."

A few more men arrived behind me.

"What's Negroes doing here anyway?" another asked. "Do you get Negroes here?"

Drake's authoritative voice came from behind me. "They are slaves, Perkins. At least, they were." Drake switched to Spanish as he came to a stop and addressed the wary black men. "We are Englishmen, the great enemies of Spain. You are welcome to join us at our fire. We have food. Please, be our guests."

Those of us that spoke Spanish stared at him in astonishment.

"If they was slaves," a mariner whispered. "Why don't we capture them and sell them? They're a bit scrawny but they got to be worth something."

"Come," Drake said again. And with that he turned and walked back to the beach. As the black men made to follow, we stepped back to allow them to pass. Martin had come up and he inched behind me as the short men trod through our group. We trailed them back to our main campfire where Drake invited them to sit on our log benches and ordered that they be served water and wine.

"Bad idea to give wine to a Negro, Captain-General Francis, sir," one of the men said. "Drives them wild."

"Aye," said the purser. "Wine makes the savage into a wild beast."

"Nonsense," Drake said, smiling, and called for some broth to

247

be served also. I stood near Drake, ready to kill them all should they try to harm him.

"My name is Captain Francis," he said to them. "These are my men. We are here to fight the Spanish and to take everything they have and to grow rich. Why are you here?"

They began smiling at us and at each other and the senior man answered. "We escape the Spanish. We live in a village." He stabbed his stick into the air over his shoulder.

"Of course," Drake smiled. "You were slaves and you fled your masters and took up in the forest. I have heard about men like you. The Spaniards call you the *cimarrones*, do they not? Tell me, my friends, what was the name of the place you fled from?"

"All places. Some, a ship. Some, Panama."

"Panama?" Drake snapped. "Where the treasure comes from? Are any of you from Nombre de Dios, where the treasure is taken to?"

They nodded.

Drake grinned. "Praise God."

Those escaped slaves, the *cimarrones*, had carved a village out of the jungle and they lived off the land and from raiding the towns and villages of the isthmus. Drake treated them well, gave them worthless trinkets like beads that they valued and fed them up with salt pork stews and all the while winkled out their knowledge of the Spanish. After just a few days he had them spying on Panama, watching for the treasure to be assembled for the pack mules. They agreed to come and warn us and also to then lead us through the thick jungle to the line of the route. We waited and prepared and I went over the tactics of ambush with the men until they understood. We were ready and we waited.

Tragedy struck.

Out of nowhere, the men were struck down by an abominable tropical disease.

Dozens fell ill with fevers and headaches and their skin turned an ugly yellow while they shook and wept and fouled themselves while the rest of us could do nothing to help. Nothing but pray and that did not seem to help.

Some said it was caused by the change in weather at the turning of the year causing miasmas to rise from the depths of the trees to settle over us. An almost endless argument broke out about a group of sailors who had refilled our water with the brackish stuff from the estuary rather than rowing upriver to fill the water where it was purer shortly before the disease broke out.

"You have murdered us with your idleness!" one sailor roared before bending over to vomit a stream of foul black blood at his feet.

When they started dying, it seemed as though it would never stop. When the sailors prayed, I watched and then prayed in my own way until Drake, weeping after burying another of his men, asked me to pray with him. I knew he meant for us to offer prayers in the Protestant fashion.

"I do not pray with..." I started to say but looked at the mariners lying all over the camp, writhing in agony. Those who were well tended to the sick, wiping their heads and holding their hands, squeezing water into their lips and washing the shit from their bodies as diligently as if they were all of one family. "I will pray with you. You'll have to teach me the words."

Drake nodded and we knelt together in the sand.

After the pestilence had burned itself out, we had lost four men in ten.

Our little fleet was vastly weakened by that plague and I expected Drake to return us to Plymouth. There could be no doubt anymore. It was an unlucky voyage. We had been cursed and everyone knew it.

"Leave me here," I said to Drake. "You must leave me here when you return. Put me ashore near some town, in the north if you can. Take Martin back with you, he would not do well."

"Why?"

"There must be a way to reach the Viceroy's palace. And there I shall kill him and all his men. All the ones who are... who are like him. And anyone who stands in my way."

"Alone?" Drake asked, appalled. "How will you strike at him alone?"

"I will find a way."

"You are mad, Richard. Are you certain this fever has not struck you after all?"

"I am certain. I do not get ill. I never shall."

He scoffed. "No Englishman will survive long alone here, let alone attacking the Viceroy's palace."

"I will pose as a Spaniard. I have done it before. Gradually, I will work my way to where the Viceroy is. And then I shall make my way back to the coast and find a ship to England. I have plenty of gold, I can buy my way in and out of places."

Drake stared at me. "I think you must have lost your mind, Richard. You may be a soldier and a gentleman and I never saw a man better with a sword than you. But there is no man who ever lived who can do something like that."

"Francis, you do not know what I am capable of. The more I

think on it, the more I realise that I cannot allow the Viceroy to continue to live. You know, he is sending gold to Spain. Every shipment he sends makes my true enemy stronger. As his strength grows, so does Spain's. And as Spain grows, the more England is at risk. His gold funds those who undermine the English. I look at your sailors and our small ships and dread to think of them battling enormous Spanish galleons off the coasts of England. We can stop that from ever happening. My men do their duty at home to stem the tide in our kingdom and it is my duty to do whatever is necessary to cut it off here. And that is what I shall do. So, when you go, you leave me on the Main."

He nodded but he was in a black mood. Drake wanted to stay as much as I did. More, perhaps, as his desire for revenge burned brighter than mine but his men were broken by their losses and by their continued relative poverty. They had found no treasure and instead had found death. Friends, cousins, brothers had died humiliating, stinking, loathsome deaths halfway across the world and the men just wanted to go home. Drake took parties in small boats up and down the coast for a while, giving them a chance to get their desire back but he knew if he attempted to force them to stay, he would face their hostility and perhaps even a mutiny.

But even as we prepared to set off for home, a group of *cimarrones* scouts arrived at the fort. The men crowded around as the leading *cimarrones* bowed to Drake, smiling broadly. He was an older man with grey in his dense black hair and with yellow-brown teeth in his mouth.

"It is come, Captain Francis," the man said in his accented Spanish. "It is come now and it goes across the shore. It is time, Captain, it is time."

Drake stood up straight and waved his men into silence. "What are you telling me? Where is the treasure?"

"In Panama, Captain. The treasure, piled high, in Panama. Soon, they take it across the land." He showed us his yellow teeth. "We take it, yes?"

* * *

The rainforest of the isthmus of Panama was dark and it was quiet in the way that those vile places are. Which is not to say it was silent. Far from it. Brilliantly coloured great birds would cry as they flew through the canopy above, illuminated by the white sunlight touching the tops of the trees. It was cooler beneath the trees than it was on the beaches or out on the water but the air was damp and close and oppressive. Those trees were giants, like ancient monsters from the pagan myths that held their breath, ready to reach down to crush you flat, and up those mighty trunks wound vines as thick around as a man could reach. On the ground sprouted bright green ferns taller than your head.

It was lush indeed and on the march through it the *cimarrones* speared wild pigs with ease and they could pluck lemons, mammee and palmetto fruits almost at will.

"It is no wonder the escaped Negroes can survive here," Martin observed. "Even a fool could avoid starvation with ease. All a savage need do is reach out his hand and feast. It is like the Garden, is it not?"

"You are the fool, Martin. Why do you not return to the camp and tell the dead men we buried there how this evil place is the

Garden of Eden? And keep your voice down about the Negroes, they are helping us."

He was ashamed for having been lost in his own cleverness but still he mumbled something about the savages not speaking English and we walked on in silence.

Food aplenty there was but calling it the Garden of Eden was bordering on blasphemous. The vermin were the worst of it. Lizards and monstrous great things with a hundred legs but the size of rats scurried about through the leaf litter. Beetles as big as your fist and spiders with a span wider than your face.

And through all this we marched, day after day.

We were fifty men.

Twenty of the healthiest surviving Englishmen and thirty *cimarrones*, each of us laden with our weapons and victuals. Some of the *cimarrones* carried bundles of dead monkeys, pigs and other animals I could not name but happily ate.

Wherever possible we kept to the uplands or in the shade where it was cooler but at times we could not avoid crossing the white waters of frothing streams. The rocks in the beds of those streams were so stony that they cut our shoes to pieces and sliced the bare feet of the *cimarrones* to bloody ribbons. Other times we came across open stretches of nothing but thick, lofty grasses that we struggled through while the sun beat down on us.

Each day, we began in the false dawn and marched hard until the sun rose high in the sky and the temperature became unbearable. We would rest in the late morning and set off again when the sun was at its highest. We did not want to but we had miles to cover and if we did not make it in time, we would miss the treasure. After our afternoon march we would make camp late in the day where the *cimarrones* set to work hacking down palmetto to make poles and thatching together plantain leaves to fashion shelters. Rough shelters indeed, and not good enough to last more than a single use but they served only to keep the inevitable night's rain from soaking us. It grew cold in the hills at night, despite the heat of the day, and if it had not been for those industrious *cimarrones* we would have been deeply uncomfortable.

Indeed, we would not have made any headway at all were it not for them. During the march, a group of them would break the trail for the rest of us to follow and a group of twelve formed our vanguard and another twelve made our rear guard.

They were led by a broad-chested fellow named Pedro. He had an unpleasant face, with large bulging eyes and he had a horrible scar across his neck and cheek. When first I saw it, I wondered if he had received the wound during his escape from Spanish slavery or if it had been the suffering of the wound which had caused him to seek escape in the first place. Or perhaps he had received it in his youth, or after he had fled captivity. The *cimarrones* were known for warring constantly amongst themselves.

But it seemed rather impolite to ask the man outright what the cause of his disfigurement was and his Spanish was too poor for us to ever become well acquainted, where it might be broached in a natural way.

Pedro seemed sharp enough, for his part, and his men followed him without question. And he liked Drake and could never do enough for him. Indeed, he seemed committed to never leaving Drake's side for the entire march.

"We call him Drake's Shadow," one sailor named Jack said to me, giggling at the cleverness of it.

"His name is Pedro," Drake said, overhearing and looking across the camp to us. "And that is what we call him."

"Right you are, Captain Francis," Jack replied, chastened.

Later, I found myself walking beside Drake. "I do not know how you have done it. Harnessed these men, I mean."

It was obvious to him and he shrugged. "We want the same thing, do we not? Us and them."

"Treasure?"

He frowned. "Revenge. They despise the Spaniards. They would do anything to serve their vengeance. Anything."

Despite the heat, I felt a chill in my spine at the thought of those savages acting out their fury on Christians and I was not the only one to feel trepidation.

We came to a *cimarrone* village, high on a hillside where a swift river tumbled by. The place was protected by a river and an earth wall almost ten feet high. Although, truth be told it was more mud than earth, for everything was sodden in that land, the earth and the trees and the air itself. The villagers welcomed our party and while we crouched in the central area, their women brought out an abundance of maize, fruit, and meat and sat with us to eat it. While we ate, they told us a tale of woe, how their village had once throve before the Spanish had come and sacked the place, taking or slaughtering the men, women, and children.

Drake was outraged, or at least he affected outrage, and told them how shocked he was at their treatment at the hands of the Spanish. And then he launched into a speech that lasted a full hour, about how the Spaniards and the *cimarrones* were following a false religion.

"Follow the true religion," he proclaimed, "and God will

reward you with peace. Throw down your crosses and take up the true worship and your freedom will be assured."

I was surprised to see it but they seemed very interested indeed in the notion and begged him to tell them more.

"If they can be so easily turned away from the old religion," Martin observed while Drake spoke, "then they can never have been overly attached to it in the first instance. Do you suppose it is because the Spaniards imposed it upon them and the forms and structures of Catholicism does not speak to their race?"

"Salvation is for all men," I replied, saddened to see a woman take down the rough wooden cross from above the entrance to her hut.

"You are right of course," Martin said, stiffly and watched me from the corner of his eye. "But in the proper way..."

Drake finally brought his sermonising to a close. Swearing to return one day if we could, we set off into the jungle once more.

"A trusting and faithful people," Martin observed as we waved goodbye.

"I am as surprised as you are," I said.

"They are even growing crops in the clearings," he said, shaking his head. "Though I suppose everything grows well here. Not a bad life, I suppose."

"They are riddled with diseases and squatting upon the ground while eating unseasoned food. There are not enough women and even fewer children, what does that tell you? Not much of a life at all."

"About the same as Africa, then."

"I suppose so."

A few more days brought us to a very high hill, or rather a

ridge, running east to west and upon the uppermost point of the summit stood an enormous tree. It had vast buttresses and was broader across the base than any I had ever seen in my life. Taller, too, though it was hard to appreciate it from the ground.

"Up, up?" Pedro said, jabbing his sharpened stick at the tree and grinning at me.

"What do you mean, up? You mean it is high? Yes, very."

Pedro frowned. "No, no. You go up." He waved to me and I followed him a quarter turn about the trunk, climbing over one of the mighty buttresses and there, incredibly, was a stairway cut into the tree itself. "Watch from top. See everything."

The steps had been hacked into the bark and they wound their way, very steeply, up the side and into the canopy. They had banged in lengths of rotting rope above the steps, for handholds, and in other places where there was no rope they had hammered in pegs.

At once, I began removing my satchels, my sword and other weapons, and dumped them on the ground or handed them to Martin.

Drake came over and stood beside me. "You are not thinking of going up that?"

"Pedro says you can see everything from the top."

"The top?" Drake said, alarmed and craning his head up. "Surely, you do not trust those tiny steps?"

"I will let you know what it is like," I said and clambered up to start the climb.

After a few steps I looked down and saw Drake stripping off his gear and I laughed.

But I did not laugh for long. The steps were more like

footholds and I had to climb somewhat facing the tree. Much of the rope was even more rotten than I had first thought and hardly a yard could be trusted. Both footholds and the pegs were sodden and I slipped more than once and found myself clutching at ridges in the bark to stop myself tumbling down. I made the mistake of looking to see how high I had come and found myself cringing away, pressing myself into the wet bark. I was a hundred feet up and still I was nowhere close to the top. On I climbed and found myself rising through the surrounding canopy where birds flew and monkeys or some other creatures chattered. Still, I climbed on and I wondered how anyone had ever carved the steps in the first place and then I was above the canopy and bathed in light for a while but I dared not stop to look around as I was breathing hard and wanted above all to make it to the top. And then I finally reached the part where the giant tree spread its branches wide, covering me in shadow once more before I came to an enormous bough over head, the steps and pegs leading to the top of it.

On that wide branch the cunning *cimarrones* had built a platform from rough planks. It even had rails up the sides. The whole thing shook as I got to my feet but still I barely noticed.

Beyond the tumble of green canopy to the west was the glittering waters of the Pacific Ocean. Turning to the east, through the branches I could see the distant shimmer of the Caribbean.

"By God," I muttered.

At a sound below, I looked down to see Drake struggling up the side. "Richard," he growled. "Richard, are you there?"

"Give me your hand! I am here, reach up." I pulled him up to the platform and he knelt there on all fours, quivering.

"Would have thought that was nothing to a mariner like

yourself," I said.

He shook his head. "There is no mast in the world so high. How is it you never tire, Richard?"

"I am blessed with a robust constitution. Come look on this, Francis. It will make you feel better."

Together we stood and looked out at the ocean to the west.

"The South Sea," Drake breathed. "How blue it looks. And we are the first Englishmen to lay eyes upon it."

"I saw it first," I said.

"Do you know Magellan named it the *Pacifico*, because it was so peaceful after his crossing through the continent to the south? Does it not look peaceful, Richard?"

"The Spanish have it all to themselves," I said. "So I am sure it is peaceful."

"Aye," Drake said. "Peaceful and ripe for the plucking."

"As much as I would enjoy looking at these two seas for the rest of the day, we should go down," I said.

"Can you imagine seeing the sunrise and the sunset from this place?"

"Come, Francis," I said and slid myself over the side, praying to God to guide me back to the earth.

By the end of the day we reached the grassy hills above Panama and we crept to the edge of one of the final crests and looked over into the great town. It was still somewhat obscured by trees in between but there it was, the place where the bullion ships came up from Peru sitting at anchor. Smoke rose from the cooking fires and workshops, tiny figures no more than dots moved here and there between the roofs of the houses and on the docksides beyond them. It was the largest settlement I had seen in the New

World.

We grinned at each other and crept back again. Another day's journey away from Panama we found a grove where we made camp. No one from Panama would come out so far and we knew we would be safe there. The *cimarrones* made camp alongside us and we each set guards.

That night, Martin whispered as the sun went down. "Does it not weigh on your conscience to be facilitating the letting loose of such savages upon your fellow Catholics?"

"No," I said, lying so that I might end the discussion. "Go to sleep."

I myself lay awake, wondering if the Negroes would try to murder the Spanish escorts and if we would try to stop them. If we fell out with the *cimarrones*, all our efforts could result in failure. Worse, they might turn on us.

Troubled, I fell into a fitful sleep.

A half dozen of the *cimarrones* had gone down into the city to spy and in the morning they returned with news.

"Captain Francis! The gold comes."

***

There were three vast mule trains with over two hundred mules in all coming along the path. Their escort was forty-five Spanish soldiers.

We just about outnumbered them but over half our number were *cimarrones*. Helpful fellows, and eager, but they were not soldiers. And neither were our sailors.

What we did have, however, was the advantage of surprise, for we were hidden beside the path along a flat stretch with dense jungle to either side.

The mules ambled along with their heads bobbing low, each heavy step an effort, their backs laden with treasure. Barefoot natives and blacks did the work of leading them and whipping them on, while the Spanish soldiers and their officers strolled along with their weapons over their shoulders. Most had probably walked the journey many times before with no incident and they had no inkling that we lay in wait.

The first of the mules was well past us and the men were growing restless. But the rear of the train was still far behind.

"Now?" Drake asked, his lips so close they tickled my ear.

I shoved him back and shook my head while another dozen mules stomped past us on the track.

Drake was straining beside me and I knew it would not be long before one of our men could control himself no longer. Deciding, I nudged Martin and nodded and he rushed off behind us, running hunched low through the trees toward the front of the train. Whistling softly, I sent one of Drake's most trustworthy men hurrying toward the rear.

Then there were shouts ahead and answering cries and I knew either our ambush had begun or we had been spotted. Either way now, we were committed.

"Now!" I roared and pushed forward, crashing through the undergrowth with my sword drawn. The two soldiers I was heading for took one look at me and ran away, one of them tossing his pike as he did so.

The Spanish were stunned but they recovered well when an

officer began shouting at them to form on him about thirty yards to the rear from my position. Soldiers with pikes began to assemble with men armed with arquebuses and I knew we would soon be receiving coordinated fire.

"Someone shoot that bastard!" I shouted, pointing with my sword. Guns banged and there was smoke in the air.

The mule train had stopped and the muleteers were cringing behind their animals. I had feared that they would scatter in panic but the animals were so tired that they simply stood with their heads down while the weapons were fired beside them and men struggled and fought.

At the head of the line, our men had shot down a soldier and grasped the lead animal, bringing everything to a stop. But there were towns nearby and even if we defeated the soldiers on the path, we would soon have scores or even hundreds more Spaniards coming for us.

The cluster of enemy soldiers had grown and they were firing at our men.

"Come on!" Drake shouted. "Men, to me, to me. We must kill them!" He pointed and started toward them in a straight line, right into where they were aiming their spears and their arquebuses.

"Francis!" I shouted. "Not that way. Let us go around."

He glanced at me but the fire was in his eyes and his men flocked to him, as did a dozen of the bravest *cimarrones* and together they advanced directly for the Spanish soldiers.

"By Christ, you fools," I said and was about to join them when I heard a cry behind me.

Martin was on his back, crawling away from an enemy, a black soldier fighting for the Spanish, who advanced and stood over my friend before aiming his arquebus at him from point blank range.

Shouting, I charged down the path and he turned in shock to see me bearing down on him. He still managed to get a shot off and it ripped through my flesh above my collarbone before I sliced through his neck and bore him to the ground.

"My God!" Martin cried. "He was going to shoot me. He... he has shot you!"

"Get on your feet!" I snarled. "Find a weapon. Join the fight!"

I turned and looked for Drake who was rushing the Spanish company. Guns fired and their battle was wreathed in such smoke I could not make out what occurred. Running back by scores of dumbfounded muleteers, I found a pile of bodies, including five dying mules on the path. The Spanish were reloading and our men were sheltering behind fallen animals.

"Francis!" I shouted and the men pointed to where he lay, protected by the body of a dead mule and the boxes of treasure still on its back.

"Richard," he said, clutching a wound in his belly.

"Oh, Christ," I said, kneeling beside him. There was blood in his mouth and it soaked through his doublet. "Let me see. Francis, release your hands, let me see it."

The wound was almost in the centre of his belly. Low, through the guts.

"I am killed," he said, and like all men so mortally wounded, he could not believe it.

"Put your hands back over it, hold the blood in." I stood and looked around me. "Get up! All of you, on your feet. What are you? Are you Englishmen or are you cowards? We stand upon the fortune of the world and it is ours, if we but take it! Stand! Stand, you there, rise and join me. We will kill these—"

A shot hit me in the chest and I coughed, stepping back for a moment before steeling myself.

"We will kill these Spaniards! And we will take this gold and live like kings forever. Rise, I say, rise!"

Martin came up behind me, cringing from the shots but standing with a long dagger in his hand.

Slowly, the others got up and I stepped forward to the head of them until I had a dozen men coming to me and then half a dozen more and I raised my sword as another shot smashed into my upper arm, striking the bone. It hurt, terribly, but I did not react.

"With me!" I cried. "Kill them!"

They fired again before we reached their position but I was not hit. Instead, I swatted away one pike head and grasped another and forced my way into their formation and began killing them. It was not more than a few moments before they broke and we cut them all down. Martin killed a man and stood staring down at the body, shaking all over.

But the Spanish were dead. The treasure was ours.

Our joy did not last long.

"Drake is fallen!" the cry went up and the sailors were shaken to their bones. The *cimarrones* were hardly less so and Pedro knelt beside Drake with tears in his eyes.

"Give him room!" I cried and shoved most of them away. "The Spanish live just a few miles to the south and to the east. Hundreds of them will be here soon and so we must be gone by then, with the treasure or without it. I say we must take it, what do you say?"

"You lead them," Drake said when I knelt at his side. "Lead them to the ships. Then give up command." He smiled, though his face was grey. "You're no sailor."

"Lead them yourself," I replied. "You're not dead yet."

"Pray with me," he said, wincing. "I know it is not your way but I should like it if we—"

"I am carrying you from here."

"Leave me, take the gold."

"Have faith, Francis. Now, I am carrying you to your ship and you must not die before then, I will not allow it." I coughed out a handful of blood and wiped it on myself.

He frowned, seeing the blood soaking. "You are shot."

"A graze, nothing more," I lied and looked around. "Martin! Tend the captain."

We had captured a fortune. Twenty tons of silver and gold, we guessed and there was no way to get it all to the coast before the enemy caught up with us. But that was expected and even a fraction of the total was a vast sum.

The treasure was shared out as best we could, with each man laden with as much as he could carry. A group of the black muleteers directed us to where the gold was stored so that we would carry the greatest value away with us. We thanked them and the *cimarrones* pressed silver into their hands and told them to join them in their hidden villages, free from Spanish control.

We found chests packed with gold coins and these excited our men enormously. Poles were cut and boxes suspended on them so two men could carry a great weight on their shoulders.

Many tons of the silver we took off into the jungle and stashed and buried in the hopes of returning for it later but soon we were out of time and we set off before they could cut off our escape.

We could not retrace our steps so heavily laden. And we had never planned to. The shortest route to the sea was almost due east and so that was the way we went, marching for about two hours.

We carried Drake on a stretcher, two poles looped through two shirts. His blood issued forth without let up and even his belly began to swell where it collected inside his abdomen. It was not long before he grew insensible and every man there knew he was going to die.

"Halt!" a cry in Spanish came from the path ahead. "Who are you?"

I took a deep breath and cried out my reply. "Englishmen!"

From the side of the path a Spanish soldier emerged, scowling, with a sword drawn in his hands. But he bowed and spoke with civility. "In the name of my master Philip of Spain, I command you to surrender."

I laughed loudly and turned to my nervous men. Some smiled with me as they all slowly lowered their heavy loads to the ground and carefully reached for their weapons.

"Give me your pistol," I said to Martin. "Is it loaded?" He nodded and handed it over. "Get ready, boys."

"What are you going to do?" Martin asked.

"Well, we can't go back and we can't go around. Get Drake out of the way when the shooting starts."

"Shooting?" Martin said but he went back to the men and muttered with them.

"Sir!" I cried out to the Spanish officer. "I thank you for presenting your offer of surrender. But for the honour of Queen

Elizabeth, my mistress, I must have passage that way."

And I shot him in the chest. The shot struck his breastplate and did not pass through, though he fell down from the shock of it. In reply, the Spaniards fired a great volley from their positions.

"The only way to England," I shouted. "Is through those men!"

At that, I turned and charged down the track, hearing the mariners and *cimarrones* behind me.

In the brief but sharp fight, a Spaniard skewered one of the *cimarrones* right through with his pike and four of the Spanish soldiers were killed. They had a friar with them and he was killed also, whether accidentally by a stray shot or by one of our zealous men of the new religion. Many more were wounded and the rest ran off into the jungle.

"We cannot let the Spaniards get away," some of the men said. "They will return, they will bring others to us."

"Pick up the treasure," I commanded. "We go on, stopping for nothing."

Drake was unmoving and insensible but no one suggested leaving him behind. Perhaps it occurred to no man but me.

The Spanish militiamen had been protecting their village which was just up ahead and we trooped right through it without stopping. An old woman appeared as we marched though, shouting at us.

"What does she say?" Martin asked. "She speaks Spanish but, in her anger, I cannot make it out."

"She says there are three women in the village recovering from childbirth and she threatens us with eternal damnation should we harm anyone."

Martin reassured her but she spat at him and made obscene gestures at us.

"She must be afraid of our Negroes," Martin said.

"I'm sure that's it," I replied. "Come on, hurry men. No stopping, no slowing. On, on!"

They cursed my name with whatever breath they had but I would not let them rest. All were soaked in sweat and some even wanted to drop their treasure rather than carry it a step further.

"Have pity on them," Martin argued. "What are riches if they cannot enjoy them?"

"It is not for their enjoyment but for the detriment of our enemy that we do this. We must not simply enrich ourselves but deny the riches to the Viceroy. And the Viceroy's master."

"King Philip?"

"Save your breath, Martin. Go on, on!"

We had to push our way through the jungle to reach the bay we had selected. The last light of day lingered in the air when we reached the beach. Out in the anchorage, there were our ships. The men collapsed while we signalled the crew and they came to pick us up, along with the treasure.

Drake was at the edge of death when we got him to his cabin and onto his bunk. We could all smell the foulness of his swollen belly and none believed he would last the night. They brought water, wine, clean cloths, but they knew it was useless.

"I will pray with him," I said to the men. "Stow the treasure, ready the ships to sail at first light and for God's sake set good men to watch the shore and the sea. The Spaniards will be hunting this treasure and I'll be damned if we let them take it from us now."

We had lost so many men due to the sickness that, in addition to the exhausted men, there were not enough crew left to do every task. They grudgingly allowed me to stay with the captain while they moved to do what had to be done.

"Not you, Martin," I said. "I will need you."

He came back, stooping beneath the low ceiling. "How long does he have, do you think?"

I looked at him in the lamplight. "I knew your ancestor, Martin. A man named Rob Hawthorn. A good man. One of the best I ever knew. A fine archer. I knighted him on a hill, after we smashed the French at Poitiers." I smiled. "You know, he actually killed Joan of Arc. It is true. Shot her with an arrow. I wondered how much of him there was in you but I saw you today. You did well. I know Rob would have been proud of you."

Martin stared at me. "Your wounds, sir, have driven your wits from you. Please, you must sit."

I sighed and eased off my doublet. There were holes in it. In addition to the shots that had ripped through, I had been stabbed twice without realising and my shirt was stained through with dried blood. Removing that, I examined my wounds. They had mostly healed.

"I need fresh blood to drink to heal them quickly," I said as I wiped my skin clean. "But I will heal even without it."

"Blood?"

I crouched by Drake. "He is too far gone even to swallow, I fear. But let us see how he does."

I sliced my wrist and held it over his lips.

Martin jumped up so hard he banged his skull on a beam. "What is this?" he said. "Is this sorcery?"

"It is physick," I replied. "Medicine. Healing."

"It is evil," he replied, looking to the door.

"He will live," I said. "If you keep your voice down."

"The captain is beyond help, Richard."

"Perhaps," I said just as Drake coughed and licked his lips. His throat swallowed, up and down it bobbed, and I smiled. "Or perhaps not. I have saved men and women against their will before. Rather, I have not asked them until after they were turned and it is not much of a choice, then. Do you see?"

"No," Martin said. "I pray it is that you have lost your wits rather than you are performing some act of devilry."

I showed him my bare chest. "Where are my wounds, Martin?" I showed him my wrist where I had cut it.

He stared at me and picked up a lantern, bringing it closer. "They heal further?" he muttered. "All but closed. How?"

"A gift," I said, picking what I hoped to be the most reassuring of explanations. "A gift of healing. The esteemed Doctor Dee called it a *natural phenomenon* and it is found within the blood of certain men. I am one of those men. And it is a gift that may be shared."

Drake groaned and his eyes flickered open. "Richard?" he said, his voice a whisper.

I smiled. "Francis, I am here."

"I dreamt," he began and then frowned, licking his lips.

"A cup," I said to Martin and he fetched one and then grabbed the wine but I ignored him and sliced my wrist again, bleeding into the cup. "Here, Francis. Drink this broth."

Lifting his head, I helped him to drink and he frowned. Gagging, he pushed it away.

"What...?" he muttered. "What?"

"Let it do its work," I said and it seemed to bring him back to himself in just a few moments.

"It is blood," he said and tried to sit before wincing and falling back.

"You were shot," I said. "In the belly."

"I know I was shot in the belly," he snapped. "What happened?"

"We got the treasure," I said. "You are in your cabin."

He sighed and lay back, smiling. "Praise God." He patted my arm. "Thank you, Richard."

"But, Francis, you are going to die."

He looked at me. "I feel well."

"There is one reason for that. The blood I gave you to drink."

Drake frowned. "What is this?" he looked at Martin and then at me. "Where are your clothes?"

I smiled. "I was shot in shoulder and in the chest. Also in the arm. And I was stabbed twice."

"I recall that you were..." he looked at me. "But you..." He lay back again, wincing and touched his belly. It was as taut as a drum and tears pricked his eyes. "I was going to do great things."

I nodded. "You already did."

"No, no," he muttered. "The Viceroy..."

"I will kill him one day. You may die knowing that. And the battle against the Spanish will go on. Already, you have taught me much and I will not forget you."

He grasped me. "No. I will live."

"You know you are dying. You would be dead this moment if I had not given you a taste of my blood to drink. It is my blood that makes me strong. My blood that makes wounds from swords, from shot, and arrows heal in hours. You have seen this for yourself."

"Your blood?"

"You tasted it and you could feel its power. You tasted it and you have the strength to speak. But if I give you more, you will be healed by morning."

His fist tightened on my arm. "Yes. Do it."

"My people and I, we call it a gift. The gift of the blood, my blood. But it is not a gift, in fact. It is an exchange. You are granted eternal health. Centuries of life. It grants you strength to heal from great wounds, the strength to fight harder, for longer. Great speed. You can see better in darkness. But you lose also. For these blessings you are cursed with other pains. Sunlight burns your skin and hurts your eyes. You do not see as well in daylight as before because of the pain. And you will never father a child, not if you live a thousand years."

He closed his eyes. "Madness."

"That is not all. In exchange for saving your life, I will expect your obedience."

He looked at me, then. "What?"

"There is evil in the world. Men like me but where I strive to do good, they do ill. One man who grants his followers powers like I do mine but he is committed to evil. He is the one who directs the Spanish against us. He is the one who has made the Viceroy into an immortal, like you will be."

"Immortal?" Drake breathed. "Me?"

"All I do is in pursuit of my enemy. My people are with me. You have met some of them, at my house in London."

Martin sputtered behind me. "You mean Stephen is one? Mistress Eva? And—"

"Quiet, Martin," I snapped. "But yes. Them and others. We protect the Queen, we protect England, but we are not subservient to them. I am my own master and my followers are all obedient to me. If I grant life to you, in return you will take an oath of obedience to me. You will obey me for the rest of your days, even if we live for a hundred years or more. Those are my terms to all and they are my terms to you."

"You are all Catholics?"

I sighed. "The eldest of us are, and always have been. But almost all those I turned in the last fifty years have been English Protestants." I did not add that they were all I could get and I hardly trusted a handful of them.

"I must think on this. Must... consider."

"You will be dead in moments. Already the power of my blood fades. The damage to your body is so great, I am not certain..." I trailed off, not wishing to complicate the matter. "You must decide now. Life and obedience, or death and the hereafter?"

"Then yes," he said, growling the words through gritted teeth. "Give me life!"

9

Ambush

1574 - 1577

"SO YOU SEE, YOUR MAJESTY," I said, "our voyage was a complete and stunning success that has brought great riches for England."

Elizabeth had invited me for a private audience with her in her small receiving chamber and I relayed the high points of the voyage, speaking lightly about the deaths and disease and the failures and emphasising the heroism shown by Drake in particular. He was, after all, my man now.

As I finished, I bowed and waited expectantly for a polite round of applause. When there was nothing, I straightened and looked questioningly at the Queen.

"We are displeased," she said, her face set hard.

I glanced around at the servants who were not paying

attention to us. "Displeased with me? But we stole a fortune from the Spanish, my lady."

"That is precisely the reason for our displeasure, sir."

I forced myself to be courteous. "Perhaps Your Majesty would be kind enough to explain further, on account of the dullness of my wits in comparison to hers."

Elizabeth narrowed her eyes. "You must not start a war with Spain, Richard," she said. "That is all there is to be said on the matter."

It is possible that my mouth fell open. "But I thought you understood that war is coming whether we fight it or not?"

"Careful, sir. Do not suggest I do not understand the world. It is a world I understand far more than you do. A prince sees and understands where lesser men do not and can not."

I said nothing, because a reply was not required.

"Let me help you to understand," she continued. "King Philip has his hands full with the rebellion of our friends in the Low Countries. He begs me to put our differences to rest and I am inclined to agree with him. There is more at risk here than your little secret wars."

"It is the same thing. The same war. Mine and yours. England and Spain, Richard and... my enemies, they are the same conflict."

She scoffed. "Oh, you think yourself mighty indeed, sir. I see it now where once I did not. You think you deserve a throne of your own. A throne of time to sit beside my own, is that how you believe it to be, sir? You wish to marry me and rule at my side while I wither and die so you may go on ruling my kingdom forever?"

"No."

"But you would bring my people into war so that you might settle your own? Well, I shall not allow it. Do you hear? I shall not allow you to return. With Philip, I have agreed to stop my seamen from raiding his commerce either as pirates or as corsairs. In return, he shall command the Duke of Parma to allow the good Protestants of the Netherlands greater liberties and he will prevent the Inquisition from further molesting the English sailors in their prisons. These are good terms. We shall have peace and prosperity and my subjects will not have to kiss their sons and daughters and wives farewell and march off to war in steel hats. They shall not feel a Spanish halberd spilling their entrails on English soil because of these terms. Would you risk that for my subjects, Richard, my subjects of both the old religion and the new? Would you?"

What could I say to her? That she was being absurdly naive? That she was a damned fool woman for trusting anything that cunning bastard in Seville served up for her? Especially with my brother there, perhaps whispering in the King's ear.

I bowed, deeply. "You are wise in ways I could never be. And I am and will remain your loyal and loving servant."

She softened at once, becoming smaller and she came to me and lifted me upright until I looked at her face. Reaching up with her long fingers, she caressed my cheek.

"Dear Richard," she muttered. "My dear Richard."

As I reached to take her arms, she closed her eyes and pushed weakly at my chest and spoke in a soft whisper. "Go, now. You must go before I do something I swore to never do again."

I knew she really wanted me to kiss her. Instead, I raised her hand to my lips and brushed her fingers against them. "Your loving servant," I said again, speaking softly.

She sighed as I left her.

Walter was chatting up one of the queen's ladies outside but he left her alone when he saw me and approached. "How did it go? Off to New Spain again?"

"Not immediately."

"That's good, then." He looked at me. "How's she looking?"

"What do you mean?"

"Elizabeth. How's she looking these days? I ain't seen her up close for a few years but she was a tidy piece back then."

"For God's sake, Walter. She is your queen."

He shrugged. "I'm not appraising her princeliness. All I'm saying is, I like a tall woman in my bed and I like a redhead even more and, given half a chance, well, I would." He shrugged again. "I would in a heartbeat."

"Well, you're not likely to be given half a chance, are you. Not even a fraction of a chance."

Walt grinned. "She looks alright still, then? What is she now, thirty-five? Forty? I like an older woman, me."

"You are over two hundred years old."

"Oh, you know what I mean!"

"We must meet with Stephen and Eva at once. I need a full account of events since I left and, considering the Queen's commitment to this false peace, we must decide on our next course of action."

"I'm just saying I would, is all."

Ignoring him was often the only way to deal with him. "I must now go over to see Cecil. No doubt he will keep me waiting and so there is no need for you to attend me here. I shall meet you at the house."

"He's Lord Burley now, don't forget," Walt said. "And expects to be addressed as such."

"I am ever respectful, Walt, you know that."

As I had known, I was made to wait for hours for Cecil to be ready and his servants, his valet, and his clerks repeatedly asked me to make an appointment and to return another day but I insisted on waiting. Eventually, they escorted me into Cecil's chambers where he sat as usual behind his great writing desk, surrounded by papers. A plate of cold chicken sat uneaten at one side. He did not stand as I entered and he did not offer me refreshments but he did design to look up from his work and speak to me.

"Ah, the pirate returns."

I smiled as I sat on the chair before him and reclined. "What a pleasure to see you again, William, how goes the job of ruling England?"

He frowned and slid his pen into the holder beside the inkwell. "The Queen told you, I take it."

"That I am now doubly forbidden from returning to New Spain, doing great damage to England's enemies and making many Englishmen rich in the process, yes she mentioned it, William."

"Not only that, you are forbidden from making any noise about your recent success."

"There is nothing I want more than to avoid noise of any sort concerning me or my activities."

"I am most pleased to hear it. Perhaps, then, you might consider reining in your rough captain."

"Drake? What has he done?"

"He spreads word of his exploits by way of his absurd letters and public pronouncements and Englishmen everywhere are becoming riled up by his antics. The Spanish will hear of it. You will hush him."

I shrugged. "If the Queen and the Council will not celebrate his exploits, he must do so himself. Anyway, since when do you care overmuch about what Catholic Spain hears or does not hear about England's strength?"

He rolled his eyes and sighed. "Do not play the fool, sir. And in answer to your question, I care ever since my queen commanded it of me."

"War is coming, you know this. Nothing can stop Spain from coming for us now. Certainly the actions of a few men thousands of miles away will not accelerate what is already in motion."

He sighed and sat back, his stern tone softening. "It is possible. And I think the queen knows it, in her heart. She is the most intelligent of women but she is still a woman. For the time, she has convinced herself that war can be avoided and so that is the path that we must take."

"Since my return I have heard that there is trouble brewing in Ireland."

"When is there not? We must put them down, of course. The Earl of Essex is there now, tasking with subjugating the rebellious areas."

"Essex, I think I saw him at court before I left. As I recall he is dashing and elegant and utterly witless."

Cecil frowned. "You think him witless?"

"No man who thinks so much about his own clothing as Essex

can have much room left in his mind for wits."

Cecil was a serious man who wore serious robes and so he understood. Still, he did not think much of the likes of me openly mocking an earl and a favourite of Elizabeth. "We very much hope the earl succeeds."

Later, Stephen told me that Cecil was one of many lords to have invested in Essex's grand expedition to Ireland, hoping to profit from the venture by way of land and booty recovered from the Irish. But the Irish, a people belligerent to the point of self-destruction, would not be pinned down. For two years they avoided engagement with the English, using their skill in the woods and hills and bogs to launch ambushes on Essex's forces.

Soon, Essex would hit upon the need to establish permanent garrisons to protect the new English plantations but he did not have the resources needed for such large-scale colonisation. Gradually, his backing fell away, the fool and he returned to court in bitter disappointment. But all that was to come and I knew nothing about it anyway until after the fact.

"Why go to Ireland at all?" I asked Cecil. "There is nothing there but the Irish."

"Catholic Irish who can be driven off the land which will be used properly, by Protestant Englishmen."

I scoffed. "There is land enough for all Englishmen in England."

"The fact is, if we do not take it then the Spanish will. Do you want that, sir? Spanish colonies on our doorstep? Surrounded by Catholics on all sides? How will the Englishmen fare then?"

I shrugged. I had no answer about Ireland, merely a vague feeling that we had no business over there. What I wanted to say was that if England was to throw off the madness of the new religion, we would not be so afraid of Catholic kingdoms. But the Puritan Cecil would not wish to hear it.

"I do not know."

"No, it appears you do not. Sadly, I am not afforded the luxury of not knowing and not taking action. I must do whatever I can to protect England."

"As must I. And that is why you must change the Queen's mind so that I can return to New Spain."

He smiled. "Ah, change the Queen's mind. Just like that, yes? She has a will far stronger than mine and wits sharper even than that."

I did not return his smile. "You do not fool me. I know you can manipulate her. You have a dozen subtle ways to do so, I am certain of it. And so you can do this, if you wish."

He leaned forward; his smile gone now also as he reappraised me. "I suppose I could spend some hard-won goodwill on your behalf and push her into it. But why should I do so?"

"You disagree that it is in your interest to disrupt the Spanish in every way possible at this time?"

"No. But then I do not agree enough to force the Queen's hand. As it stands, she will do nothing to risk the agreement with Philip and Parma. In the meantime, there is plenty to be done to protect England from within our own lands. That should suit you, considering your opinions on where the English should and should not go."

Rather than listening closely as he spoke, I was thinking to myself that I would have to find and outfit ships in secret and sail anyway. If I proved successful, she would overlook my disobedience. But when Cecil stopped talking and I did not answer, he prompted me for a response.

"I say there is plenty for you to do in England, sir."

I looked up. "What is happening with England? More Spanish agents? Immortal ones?"

"You should speak with Francis." He meant Walsingham. "He will know more about it than I."

"I will do that very thing."

He nodded once as he picked up a paper from his desk and prepared to read it. "Well, I hope your discussions prove fruitful. And I trust that you will not go rushing off across the seas. You do understand that you and all who sail with you will be publicly declared pirates with orders for your arrest sent to every port in England?"

"It had not crossed my mind for a moment," I said as I stood. "You can trust me. I am a loyal subject."

***

"I must go once more to the New World," I said to the assembled men and women of the Order of the White Dagger. "My intention was to terrorise and harry the ports, towns, ships, and above all the treasure of New Spain in order to bring out the immortal lord that rules there. However, our Queen and the Council will not grant us the ships and the men to wage such a war and so I must find another way to destroy the immortals across the sea."

Everyone was there in the main hall of the house, sitting at the arrangement of tables with me at the centre. Beside me at the top table sat Stephen, Eva and Walt. While on the other tables Philip, Goodie, Leeche, Callthorp, Adams, and our soldiers sat watching me.

Martin, now that he knew the secret of the blood, was also there. The warrant for his arrest had been settled by Stephen's cunning and his purse and despite that, Martin wished to know more. He was at times a cautious and quiet man but his sense of adventure ran deep and I expected now that he would one day take our oath and join the Order as an immortal. Stephen hoped that it would be sooner rather than later but Martin was still young and there was plenty he could do even as a mortal.

Drake was not with us. As agreed, he was away in Plymouth and in other ports working to drum up men and investors for future voyages. I had urged him by letter to do so quietly but he had not listened and continued to proclaim his own brilliance in a dozen public ways.

"We shall buy a ship," Stephen said. "or build one, using the profits gained from the recent venture, and it shall take you there."

I nodded. "I think we must. I know the outlay will be immense but a great galleon capable of carrying a large crew and many guns will allow us to overpower many of the ships there. Can you correspond with Drake and find a shipwright and so on?"

"Of course," he replied. "Though even when we find a builder and a yard and agree it all, the construction will take months. Over a year, perhaps."

"That is well, because we cannot yet leave. Remember the Queen has threatened to outlaw us, declare us pirates, if we take such action."

Stephen nodded. "Perhaps Eva can change her mind?"

All eyes turned to her. "I will be unable to convince Elizabeth to change her mind." She glanced at me. "I shall not waste time explaining why, know simply that it cannot be done. Not by me whispering in her ear, at least."

Walt tapped the table. "Lord Burley, then. Cecil is the real ruler of England, ain't he. Convince him, change his mind."

"He is intractable," I said. "How do you suggest we do so?"

Walt shrugged. "Like we always do. Break his fingers, maybe. Threaten to kill his son. Maybe just his daughter, I don't know."

A few of the soldiers chuckled and Walt grinned at them.

"Are there any serious suggestions?"

"Money," Goodie Sprunt said. "The Queen needs money, the Council needs money. Money for ships, for making guns, everything. They never have enough. Make it clear to them that they stand to make a bloody lot of money, for the Crown but also personally, if they back future voyages."

Edith Sprunt was called Goodie by her friends, shortened from Goodwife Sprunt, was a commoner who was made immortal in her middle thirties. She had the kind of figure that makes grown men weep. An unkind fellow might call her plump but she carried her roundness at the hips and in her prodigious bosom. Her wavy red hair often fell in tumbling tresses out from her caps and hoods to frame her handsome face. Her freckled nose was perhaps a touch too large but her eyes were bright and green and full of life while her lips were as full and sensuous as the rest of her. In her former life, she had been an innkeeper, until an immortal had murdered her husband and she, seeking revenge, had come by turns into the Order. It was fair to say that we all liked her very much.

"We granted Elizabeth a significant share of the treasure," I pointed out.

Goodie shrugged. "Seems to me, Richard, when a man gives a woman a present and she don't seem like she's showing the proper level of appreciation then might be that woman was expecting something of greater value, know what I mean?"

I noted in passing that she was glaring at Walt when she spoke and he was staring back with a mixture of confusion and horror on his face.

"You say we should have given her more?" I asked Goodie and looked at Eva.

Eva nodded, smiling. "One thing is for certain. One may never grant Elizabeth too much praise or too much money."

I nodded. "Let us give her more, then."

"And something special," Goodie piped up. "Something unique. Something thoughtful." Again, she was looking at Walt when she spoke but he was now avoiding her eye.

Eva agreed with Goodie. "The Queen adores jewellery. We must have something made, something unique and worth a fortune. Something symbolic to help her think of our need."

I banged my hand on the table because a wonderful idea had occurred to me. "A pendant in the shape of a galleon!"

Eva scoffed. "It is a gift for a woman, not a man. It must also be beautiful. Emeralds, for example, bring increased wealth for the wearer and agates speak of adventure. Leave it to me."

Goodie sighed. "What I wouldn't give for a beautiful pendant made special for me." She shook her head. "Ah, well. Such is life for an ordinary woman."

Stephen nodded. "Eva, you shall commission the piece. And we shall certainly continue to push Lord Burley and our friend Walsingham on this matter. Perhaps in time they shall come to see things our way. Indeed, the Queen herself is liable to change her mind eventually."

"Every day that we show patience and deliberation is a day that William grows richer and stronger. Wherever he is. You must find a way, Stephen, Eva. Do whatever is in your power. Now, Callthorp, tell me about your activities. I understand you had a run in with a Jesuit?"

Callthorp had been turned into an immortal at the age of fifty-one but even then he had been fit and strong, despite his white moustaches and grey hair. He got to his feet and spoke like the grizzled old soldier he was. "We found this servant what said his master used to bleed him and drink his blood. The little fellow took a bit of convincing but we got him to talk in the end."

"Callthorp," Stephen snapped. "You did not torture a mortal, I hope?"

"Oh, no, sir, not at all, sir. We just asked him questions in a particular manner sir?" He kept an admirably straight face but Adams and some of the other soldiers smirked and covered their mouths.

Stephen turned to Walt. "You must control your men."

Walt suppressed his own grin. "They're good boys and they do the job. If they don't, they answer to me. Go on, Nathaniel."

Callthorp nodded. "So he tells us eventually that his master was a secret priest. A Jesuit priest at that. And, see, we knew then we was on the right path, as it were, sir, so we wrote off to Mister

Stephen and asked—"

"Yes, yes," Stephen said. "Tell Richard what you did when you found him."

Callthorp shuffled his feet and cleared his throat, looking down at the table. "Tracked him for days through Devon, sir. Then we nearly got him outside Bristol but then Easton fumbled it, sir."

Easton sat bolt upright at this and turned on his captain. "It weren't my fault!"

Callthorp ignored him and carried on. "The Jesuit run north and we tracked him almost all the way to Coventry but then we cornered him in this barn and we had him." He smiled.

"And?" I said. "What did he say?"

Callthorp shuffled his feet again. "Well, the thing is, sir. He burnt down that barn. With himself inside it."

Walt pinched his eyes and I sighed. "Is that the end of the tale? Did you at least make certain he was inside?"

"Oh yes, sir. Indeed, we waited until late the next day and we found his bones, blackened and part crushed by a timber but it was there all right."

"You compensated the owner of the barn, I hope?" I asked.

His men looked hard at him and he hung his head again. "We told him quite sharply not to speak of it to anyone, sir."

I looked at Stephen and he threw up a hand to forestall me. "I shall take care of it."

"And what will you do next?" I asked Callthorp.

He looked blankly between Stephen and Walt, lost for words. "That is what all your bribery and cunning has brought forth, Stephen? One burnt corpse?"

Eva touched her lips, deep in thought. "If this Jesuit was in Plymouth and the rest of Devon for some time he must have had others sheltering him, supporting him. If they have not fled, which they would have done if they have any sense, they will still be there. I shall send Goodie and Leeche down to Plymouth to find it all out."

Goodie nodded but old Leeche, who had been bent backed and half crippled already when he was made immortal, groaned. "What? Leave London, mistress? Me, leave London?"

John Leeche had been Eva's servant for some decades. She had dragged him up from the filth of London's semi-criminal underworld and used his knowledge and contacts to keep an eye on events that no civilised person would ever have been party to. In his time, Leeche had run a range of schemes from fixed cockfights to pilfering London's docks and had suffered the consequences of crossing the wrong people. His knee had been smashed in his youth, later his face had been carved up, and after his eye had been gouged out he had accepted Eva's offer of steady employment. He knew every disreputable soul in London, and he either knew everything that was going on or he knew who you had to pay to find out. But he was a London man through and through and hated to leave it.

"Yes," she said. "And you will do as Goodie commands in all things, do you understand?"

"What about us, mistress?" Callthorp asked.

"You also shall do as Mistress Sprunt says."

Callthorp grinned across the hall at Goodie, eying up her chest like a vagrant staring at a hot pie. "It'll be a pleasure, mistress, a sweet pleasure, that's the truth."

Walt stood. "I'll go, too," he snapped.

After discussing other Order business and eating a fine meal together, we went our separate ways to carry out the work that had been agreed.

* * *

Many months later, in April, I travelled up to Aldeburgh on the Suffolk coast in the east of England to meet with Drake at the yard where our new ship was being built. It was a fine spring day and the air was filled with the smell of wood being worked and tar being boiled. The sounds, too, of hammering mallets and sawing and lengths clanking to the ground and of good-natured shouting between carpenters at work.

"Francis," I said when we shook hands. "How are you?"

He smiled ruefully beneath his large hat. "Grateful for my life and yet cursing it all the same."

"And I am both sorry for your state and relieved at the same time. I do know what a curse it is, believe me."

"My wife can sense I am changed but I do not dare to speak of it to her. I know, I know, I am sworn to secrecy but I might break that oath if I thought my wife capable of understanding and of keeping the secret herself. She is a good woman but her world is a small one and she would not understand. I have been home a long time now and still she is not with child." He laughed suddenly. "I find myself speaking uncontrollably about private matters, forgive me."

I smiled. "It is because I have abandoned you so long to suffer your fate without my guidance. It is I who must beg your forgiveness. Please, let us tour the yard and look upon our new ship and afterwards perhaps we can get drunk together."

He laughed. "That I can agree with. Come, see what your fortune outlaid has wrought."

It was not yet a ship but it was in the shape of one. Enormous great timbers formed the spine and ribs, though sections were partially screened behind extensive scaffolds and hanging platforms. A score of men worked on the vessel directly while twice as many were occupied elsewhere in the yard.

"What do you think?" Drake said, beaming with pride as we walked through the yard, craning our necks to look up at the timbers.

"It is coming along very well. Though, I must say it seems somewhat smaller than I had expected. We will be crossing the seas in such a small ship?"

"What did you expect, the *Jesus of Lubeck*?"

"Not that, no, but perhaps something the size of the *Minion*."

"She was a warship, this one is built for sailing the high seas."

"But surely the larger the ship the safer that will be?"

He smiled. "It is not the size of the ship but the strength. The *Minion* was sound but still she was top-heavy, with overlarge masts and heavy spars and lacking depth in her hold. And her planks were thick, to protect against shot. But we must first fight the giant waves we will face out there and so our strength must be in the frame, with each part braced and sturdy so she does not bend apart or break when we are pounded by waves and when we come crashing down from the top of a giant wave to the trough between it and another. Here, you see the keel? The very best oak, faultless and thick. The quality of the oak is one reason for her great expense and the slowness of the construction."

"Crashing down a giant wave into the trough?" I said.

He smiled. "She will take it, never fear. The masts will be the strongest there ever were. And she will be sheathed with extra planking, she will resist rot, she will keep us safe and sound, worry not. Yes, sir, the *Pelican* will be the soundest ship ever to sail."

"Excuse me, Francis, what did you call her?"

"Oh," he said. "Forgive me, of course I meant to discuss it with you. Just my idea for the name and it's how I've been thinking of her. But you're paying, I wouldn't want to impose."

"I expected we would name her something more... daring."

"Perhaps I should explain my thinking. You know, of course, that the pelican performs what is called a vulning where she pecks at and wounds her own breast with her bill and with the blood that issues forth, she feeds her young."

I smiled. "I see. All right, I like it well enough, Francis."

He grinned, relieved. "I was thinking of calling it the *Immortal* but it might give us away to our enemies."

"How right you are. No, no, I like *Pelican* just fine."

"Ah!" he said. "Here is the shipwright, Master Chaplain. Sir, here I have with me Richard Ashbury, the principal investor."

The shipwright was a stocky man in his fifties with his sleeves rolled up showing his huge hands and forearms and a scroll of parchment tucked under one arm and a lump of cheese in one filthy hand. He scowled as he approached and his bow was barely a nod.

"I thought that Christopher Hatton of the Privy Council what come up last week was the principal investor?" he said, in a thick

Suffolk accent.

"Yes indeed," I said, "many on the Privy Council have quietly contributed a small amount here and there but we must not let such a thing be known, sir. And I may not be a member of the Council but I do favour privacy, also."

"All right, sir, all right, I know when to keep my mouth shut. So, what do you reckon so far?"

"I do not believe I have ever seen such a sturdy vessel."

"Oh, aye, she'll sail a dream, I reckon. Touch her whipstaff and she'll turn on a farthing, I don't doubt it for a moment. Take you to the moon, she will."

"Not that far, I hope," I said. "Just to Alexandria."

"Eh?" he said, scowling. "She ain't no galley, sir, she's built for the mightiest waves of the high seas. Alexandria? What do you mean?"

"Yes, well, this is another point that we must keep rather private, you see."

He rolled his eyes and strode off back to work, muttering under his breath as he went.

Drake smiled. "He is the best there is, trust me."

"I do, Francis. On this business, I trust no man more. Now, let us drown in wine."

He had taken rooms at a large inn up a little way back from the port at Aldeburgh. The beach was wide and very pleasant that day to look out upon while we drank at the upstairs window.

"I miss the sun," he said. "The feel of it upon my skin is pleasurable but for a moment before the pain begins. I admit, I have taken to subjecting myself to it on the days when I take my regular blood. I find myself reddened and sore but I drink my blood and I am healed in moments."

"You are having no trouble with your servants, then."

"A handful allow themselves to be bled once a week or so and I am never without. I make sure of that."

"Good, good. If you ever need more, send to me and we will have someone sent out to wherever you are."

"You have everything worked out, don't you. The Order."

"We have had many years to perfect it."

"Don't people doubt? Don't you get found out? There are rumours, certainly."

"There are always rumours. I am sorry to say that you will certainly have rumours about you, also, in time. But we must live with it. Nothing too bad comes of it, usually. And if it does, we just outlive the trouble."

"I fear a long voyage with this affliction." He smiled. "This gift, I should say. I shall have to hide in my cabin on sunny days. Bleeding servants regularly, I shall find myself much talked about. Rumour on land is much different to rumour at sea."

"All will be well. I shall be there to help you. Have faith."

He nodded slowly. "And are we any closer to receiving leave to go on this voyage?"

"As you know, I have made great progress with every member of the Privy Council and they are all in favour. All that remains is the Queen. She is digging her heels in. Praying for peace."

Drake shook his head. "The Spaniards have long broken that peace. As our brothers would attest, could they speak to us from heaven."

"I know it, Francis. And we will see to it that the treachery of the Viceroy will be avenged."

"As long as the Queen changes her mind."

"One way or another, we will make the journey. Nothing will stop us."

He nodded. "Let us drink to that."

Drake seemed to have adjusted remarkably well to the immortal life. But then his daily experience had not changed overly much. He was living as he always had done, only with more money and fame. It was the future I was worried about, when he would have to abandon an ageing wife, and put aside the name he was working to make famous.

But that was a long way off and I was satisfied enough to leave him once more to his duties and continue with mine.

I was back in London for five months when a messenger came charging into the courtyard at sunrise before bursting in through the rear and calling my name. I rushed down the stairs in nothing but my shirt, frightening the servants, and snatched the proffered letter from the sweating, exhausted man.

"I have ridden through the night, master, on the understanding that—"

"Yes, you shall have an extra shilling and a hot meal, be silent."

Ripping open the letter, I saw it was in Eva's hand, hastily scrawled in a simple code. I deciphered it on the fly and my heart leapt into my mouth.

"Saddle my horses!" I roared. "Where is Philip? Philip!"

After a few moments he came rushing down the stairs, entirely naked with his member flapping about grotesquely and a long dagger in his hand. "Are we attacked?" he cried.

At the top of the stairs I caught a glimpse of a frightened Catalina, also naked but for a sheet clutched to her chest.

"Not us, no. Get dressed and hurry to the horses, we must ride for Hatfield at once."

"What has happened?" he asked.

"The Queen," I said. "She has been attacked by an immortal."

* * *

The Queen is well, Eva had ended her short note. And I shall recover. *Come at once.*

Despite those reassuring words, I rode hard and my horse was in a bad way when I threw myself from his back outside the Royal Palace at Hatfield. It was just twenty miles north of London and much favoured by Elizabeth. The building was a hundred years old or so and was more of a comfortable residence than a grand palace meant to impress but she had spent much of her childhood there and still visited as much as she could.

There were dozens of soldiers outside the house, standing in the rain as the sun set and a group approached with their halberds lowered.

"State your business!"

I held up my hands. "Richard Ashbury, here to see the Queen."

"No one sees the Queen! By orders of the Earl."

"Which one? Burley? Leicester? It doesn't matter, tell them I am here, as commanded. Also tell Eva, one of the Queen's ladies."

They knew me by sight, at least a couple of them did, but still they guarded me closely for a long while, even making us stand in the rain while we waited. They allowed the horses to be led away, at least. When finally I was admitted and escorted into the hall, a small group was there and they turned.

"Richard!" Elizabeth said and marched through the men around her and embraced me, kissing my cheeks. "Richard, you came. How quickly you came."

"Are you harmed?" I asked, looking her over.

"No, praise God." She snorted. "Praise God, I say, but praise Him for sending me the Lady Eva." Elizabeth grasped me. "She saved my life, Richard. I have never seen such bravery, such skill, such strength."

I steadied myself but still my voice shook. "Where is she?"

The Queen stepped back, holding me at arm's length. "Of course, how inconsiderate of me. You shall be taken to her at once."

Before rushing off with the servant, I stepped closer to the Queen again. "But you are certain you are unharmed, my lady?"

She smiled a little. "Quite unharmed. As is your... friend. At least, I trust she is by now." Elizabeth lowered her voice to a whisper. "I had a number of my servants bled for her."

"So you saved her also, my lady," I said.

Elizabeth brightened. "God's bones, I do believe you are right, sir. Now, you must go, Richard. Go, I say."

Following the servant, I saw Dudley advance toward the Queen while he scowled at me. Also, there was John Dee, smiling and waving a hand at me. I ignored him and strode by through the palace into a chamber where Eva reclined, fully dressed, on a bed.

"Christ Almighty," I said, going to her side. "What has happened?"

She sat up, smiling and taking my hands. "I am well, I swear it. The Queen commanded me to lay down. No matter how much I protested I am fully healed, she does not quite understand."

"Fully healed from what wounds, Eva? What occurred?"

Philip sat on a chair across from us and I sat beside her on the bed.

"There is not much to tell. We were out riding in the park, as the Queen likes to do every day. Perhaps that is where I have failed her, in allowing her to follow the same course each day. Nevertheless, we were riding through the pasture beside the larger woodland in the north and I saw movement in the undergrowth beneath the trees. When I saw it, I was some way back in the party and I called out a warning to the soldiers and to the gentlemen as I rode by them but they simply stared at me. The Queen, I think, when she turned her head at my cry thought I was challenging her to a race. She charged on ahead and a good thing she did, too, as the shots missed her."

"Shots?" Philip cried.

"By God," I said. "Go on."

"One of the shots hit her horse in the neck and the poor thing tossed her head and veered away. But she never threw Elizabeth, not even close. Blood gushed out everywhere and she stood shaking while the men took the Queen off. It died soon after, blood everywhere. The Queen is more upset about her mare than anything else."

"Who cares about the mare, Eva, what happened?"

She sighed. "They shot and they missed and already they were running from the bushes at the Queen. By their speed, I knew them for immortals. I knocked one down with my horse, knocked him flat and then I jumped down upon the other one. He was strong and I could not subdue him so I put my dagger into the back of his skull. The other man needed beating bloody and the gentlemen helped to truss him up tightly."

"You captured one!" I cried, grasping her arm. "You are a wonder, my dear. But are we hearing the entire tale? What of your wounds?"

"Well, yes, I was unfortunately run through the belly twice and received slashes below my neck. And my hands and arms were cut also. My forearm down to the bone."

"And everyone saw all of this?"

"Well, it was over rather quickly but I did look in rather a bad way. Lord Robert carried me in his own arms and offered his own blood."

I raised my eyebrows. "The Earl of Leicester, eh? Are you trying to anger the Queen?"

"She thought him chivalrous indeed and was most impressed by his gallantry."

"Gallantry," I scoffed to Philip. "I wager he is peeved indeed to have failed a second time to protect his love from assassins." Philip sniggered as Eva snapped at us to be quiet. "Where is this man you captured?"

He was in the possession of Robert Dudley, or rather it was his personal retinue who held him in an empty storeroom in the cellar of the palace and so it was to Robert I had to speak to get access.

"Truly, I am not certain this is a matter for you at all, Richard," Dudley said when I went to find him and the Queen. "We have already ascertained that the man is an English Catholic. Not a

Spaniard at all. I would be surprised if he has anything to do with you people."

Nodding, I inclined my head and tapped my lips. "I do suppose, Robert, that it was difficult to perceive their speed and their strength at so far a distance from the fight. But Eva says they were very much our sort of people."

Dudley drew himself upright and puffed out his chest. "He is an Englishman. I have already established it. Motivated by Catholic hatred."

"I see. And is he a Jesuit priest? You do know that there are English Jesuits, Robert."

He scowled and I noted how soft his cheeks were becoming as he aged. "You will address me as Lord Robert, Richard."

Across the room from us, but listening to every word, Elizabeth spoke up. "Oh, what nonsense, Robert. Richard is our friend who has nothing but concern for us, is that not so?"

"Just so, Your Majesty," I said and bowed.

"Let him question the beast," Elizabeth said. "He slaughtered my second favourite mare and he should be slaughtered in turn."

I bowed again. "As you wish, Your Majesty."

Dudley of course came with me and before we entered the dark cellar, I turned to him. "We shall have to torture to him, Robert, I hope you realise that. No word of this can leave the palace and any rumours of an attempt on the Queen must be quashed and denied. No one shall know of his existence. And then, we shall work on him, day and night for days or weeks. However long it takes until he breaks. Can I trust you to hold your tongue and control those of your men?"

"As long as it is you committing these illegal acts, then I will allow them to take place." Dudley pursed his lips. "For the greater good of the kingdom and the safety of Elizabeth."

"Come, then," I said and we went down the steps to where the prisoner was bound, ankle and wrist, and gagged and with three soldiers pointing their halberds at him. "Take off the bastard's gag," I said.

We stood while one of Dudley's men gingerly untied the cloth from around his mouth and pulled out a sopping rag from within.

The prisoner licked his lips, spat and took a deep breath. "I'll tell you everything!"

* * *

"Your Majesty," I said. "Thanks to Eva's actions in not only saving your life but in capturing one of the assailants alive, we now have incontrovertible evidence that a campaign is being waged against you and all England. A campaign dictated by a shadow power located in Spain but funded by gold from the New World."

It was the evening of the day after my arrival and I had spent the night and most of the morning questioning the man. The Queen's small audience chamber was cleared of all but a few servants and there were guards at every door and window. It was raining outside and quiet enough within to hear the rain falling.

"His name is John Brocksby, the son of an English Catholic merchant who attended a college at Cambridge before running to France where he was ordained as a priest. Then he says he was sent to Rome and then to Brussels and then he was sent to Spain and brought into a darker, more insidious conspiracy. It was there, in Spain, that he was made into an immortal by a senior Jesuit. This can only be William de Ferrers, in whatever guise he has adopted. After he survived the changing, he was sent to a place near Panama on the far side of the Americas. Some place he called the Blood House and there he was instructed, along with other immortals, in methods of assassination. Some of the other immortal priests died in the training but the best of them were then sent back to Europe and eventually him and the other assassin were sent to England. They then received instruction to come here."

"To kill me!" Elizabeth exclaimed, outraged.

"Yes indeed. But they had help. Another immortal who told them where to go and when to do it."

"But who?" the Queen asked.

"We know not," Dudley growled beside me. "But it can only be someone who has been watching you, Elizabeth. Watching from afar and passing word of your habits to these assassins."

"My habits?" she asked, suddenly wary.

"Your riding habits," Dudley explained. "Your location here and elsewhere."

"But who?" she cried. "Where are they?"

Dudley stepped close to her and took her hand. "My men are out now, riding the country to look for suspicious characters. Rest assured, Elizabeth, I shall find him. And destroy him."

"Oh, Robert," she said and clasped his hand in both of hers. "I know you will find him. Please, do not let me delay you any longer. You must lead your men, I know they will be lost without you. Go, find him and bring him to me in chains."

He stepped back and bowed. "As you wish, my lady."

With a final glare at me he marched out, calling for his men and for his horse.

"He loves you dearly," I said.

"He does. And I him." She looked at me. "What does all this mean, Richard?"

"It means I was right. But it is worse than I feared. It is clear that my enemy is recruiting these Jesuit priests and turning them into immortal assassins. We know of at least three because these we have killed or captured. But certainly, if this man Brocksby is to be believed, there are more. Many more."

"Is he to be believed?"

"His story will be checked as much as is possible but I believe so. I will take him back to my house, put him into our gaol and have my men question him thoroughly to be sure."

She shuddered. "And all these assassins are sent against me." She held herself very still.

"I doubt that all these immortal Jesuits, if they exist, are set upon your assassination by their own hand."

"Do not lie to me to save my feelings, sir."

"I would not. Not in this. Your life is in danger, of that I am in no doubt. But I know my enemy and he will have many plans in motion and other people he would see dead."

"King Philip is an honourable man, he would not condone this."

I was not so sure about that but I could let it pass. "He may not know of it and if he does he may be powerless to stop it."

She scoffed. "King Philip, powerless? I never heard such a foolish thing."

"But how can he not know what happens in his kingdom, his

empire?"

"Oh, but I did not know about you and your little band, did I, Richard?"

I bowed. "Indeed, my lady, and yet I have always been loyal to the Crown, to England, whereas our enemy in Spain will use whatever means necessary to impose his will."

"You do not mean he would threaten a king with violence?"

"He would manipulate, cajole, bribe, extort, threaten with violence and inflict actual harm on the king or his loved ones in order to get his way. As you can see by his attempts to kill you, a legitimate and rightful ruler of a sovereign nation."

"You truly think Philip is in thrall to this evil rather than ignorant of it?"

"What we do know, my lady is that it must be one or the other. Treasure diverted from the Crown's fleets into private hands, training assassins on the far side of the world, ports across thousands of miles ready to provide fresh blood to immortal men that sail through them. It seems to me that operations of this scale cannot happen in Philip's empire without his knowledge."

The Queen looked sidelong at the door to her bedchamber. "I like this not one bit, sir. Not one bit." She was greatly perturbed by it all and I could see her desire to avoid making any decision at all creeping into her demeanour so I prompted her to think of the danger once again.

"I urge you to do whatever Eva suggests with regards to your personal safety. I know you must have your daily ride. But please change your routes regularly and send armed guards ahead of you and at all times keep some with you. Have Eva at your elbow, for even the most vigilant mortal soldiers will struggle to stop immortals."

She scowled. "You would turn my rides into military campaigns. And for how long? For the rest of my life, is that what you suggest?"

"Not at all. I mean to defeat our enemies at the source while my companions round up those already here in England."

Elizabeth eyed me with suspicion. "What *source*?"

"I mean to stop the training of assassins in Peru, stop the diverted treasure which funds it all, and kill the leaders commanding it."

"Oh do you?"

"I must be allowed to destroy the immortal lord of New Spain, Your Majesty."

She shook her head. "You desire war and death and bloodshed because you are a soldier. A knight."

"There is but one thing I desire in all the world." She peered at me, suddenly interested. I bowed and stepped closer to her and took her hand and held it while I went down on one knee. "With your permission, Elizabeth, I will sail to the far side of the world and destroy England's enemies. I will do so to keep you safe."

She sighed and stroked my cheek with her long fingers as a smile touched her lips.

10

Traitor

1577

WE FITTED OUT A SMALL but strong squadron and set sail from Plymouth. Along with the shining and powerful *Pelican*, we had in decreasing order, the *Elizabeth*, a fine ship of a size with the flagship, the *Marigold*, and the *Swan*. There were about 160 men in total, most on the *Pelican* and the *Elizabeth*.

Drake was the captain of the *Pelican* and Captain-General of the whole expedition but it was my mission. He was also one of the few on any of our ships who knew our true destination was the far side of the world. Indeed, the crew and most of the gentleman had been told we were heading off for a daring trade voyage to the port of Alexandria in Egypt, which would explain why our ships would be so well armed and well stocked with powder and shot. I had no idea what would happen when we told them of our true destination. By then, I had some experience of sailors and the importance of morale on a voyage. It was even more vital in a ship's crew than it was in an army. A ship out at sea beyond the borders of England, beyond civilisation, was like the whole world in itself. When they found out where they were going, they might take it very ill indeed. Would they mutiny?

Drake assured me that they would not but I was preparing myself for such a fight. They were mostly rough men who might well come at us with swords, axes, hooks, spikes, and clubs. But if they chose that course of action, I would not go easily.

Accordingly, I kept my blades sharp and my powder dry. The response and reliability of the crew was my primary fear, along with my terror with regards to travelling into the Southern Ocean to search for the Straits of Magellan. Would we find our way through without charts or pilots? Or would we be wrecked on those savage shores? Might the straits be defended by the Spanish? How could we force our way through those unknown waters against a mightier foe?

And assuming we reached the western coast of the Americas how could I challenge the Viceroy and his immortal followers with so few men of my own? That was assuming the crew did not revolt at some point on the way, which seemed rather the most likely outcome of the whole mad venture.

Even when we started out there was an unpleasant atmosphere on the ship, as if the men were unhappy or angry and everyone was tense. I wondered if it was perhaps my own anxieties that I was feeling and imagining it on the part of everyone else but Martin said he felt it also. There was something dark and unpleasant afoot and the unknown nature of it was the biggest worry of all.

After just a few days at sea, I began to focus my attention on a particular gentleman named Thomas Doughty who strutted about the decks with a face like thunder from dawn to dusk.

"Is all well with you, sir?" I asked him on the fifth day as we stood side by side looking aft over the rim of the wooden wall.

He looked me up and down, apparently detecting some implied criticism in my enquiry. "I have never been clear about your purpose aboard this ship. You will explain it to me."

"I will?" I asked, amused.

"Do you know who I am?" Doughty asked.

"You are one of the gentlemen that our General, the Captain Francis, decided to bring with us on this voyage."

We had dozens of investors who did not join us on the voyage, most of them important men in the kingdom and members of the Privy Council such as Dudley, Cecil, the Earl of Essex, Christopher Hatton, and even the Queen herself. The Queen had not given *official* consent and there was no written warrant giving us leave to attack the Spanish. But the fact she had allowed us to go amounted to the same thing, or so we all thought.

There were also a dozen gentlemen with us on the ship, some were also representatives of the big investors and all of them looking for adventure. Gentlemen in those days still trained in the sword and all could ride and I hoped some of them would prove useful in a fight, if it came to it. They were well-educated and filled with energy and high spirits and a few had been trusted with the secret of our true destination. One who I liked was a naturalist named Lawrence Eliot, a botanist determined to discover and record new flora in the New World. Others were gentlemen merchants like John Saracold and our parson was a well-bred yet dour fellow named Francis Fletcher, who I avoided as best I could on an eighty-foot galleon.

But when I described Thomas Doughty as one of the gentlemen that Drake had brought on board, Doughty stared at me, agog.

"Do you mock me, sir?" His hand drifted toward the hilt of his sword.

I looked at his sword hand and back to his glaring eyes. "Apparently I have misunderstood something. Perhaps you would enlighten me?"

"Drake did not *bring me* on this voyage. Indeed, he did not bring me anywhere and it is rather the other way around. You are ignorant of this but you see it is I that was instrumental in gaining Francis the command of this expedition. In fact, the backers of the voyage fully expect me to be consulted on every decision. Every decision. In fact, there is more to this voyage than most people realise, Mister...?"

We had been introduced and I knew that he knew my name. I stared at him, smiling for a long moment. "Oh, I see you have forgotten. Well, not to worry, there is a lot to remember for those on their first voyage and I expect you have become befuddled. My name is Ashbury, Richard Ashbury."

Doughty turned up his nose. "Oh yes, I recall now. A representative for certain London merchants, is it?"

I frowned. "You say there is more to the voyage than I realise. What do you mean, sir?"

He sighed and looked off across the sea, a small smug smile on his face. "I really cannot speak of it just yet but you shall see in time, you shall see. But just bear in mind what I said and perhaps we shall speak again on these matters."

"On matters of your importance, sir?"

He frowned. "Indeed."

"I look forward to the day, sir."

He nodded primly and ambled away forward. After watching him go for a while, I dragged my way to Drake where he was bent over a chart.

"That man Thomas Doughty," I said to Drake. "He is an investor, I know that but why did you bring him with us?"

Drake stood, frowning. "He is a soldier. He served Essex as his aide in Ireland. One of the most highly educated men I ever had the honour of knowing, for he has studied the classical languages, and philosophy, and is a master of the law. Indeed, he is a member of the Inner Temple. He is a gentleman and this past year he has become my friend. A man of some influence, I would add, who has contributed five hundred pounds to this voyage. His last position was as secretary to Christopher Hatton and so I am surprised you have not run into him before."

"Yes, I would have thought so, too. Perhaps he was avoiding me."

"I doubt that. Why do you ask about him?"

"Oh, nothing, really. I suppose he just has a high opinion of himself."

Drake bristled. "If he has such an opinion then it is one well deserved." He frowned. "Please, do not go making an enemy of one of the noblest gentlemen under my command. Not so soon, at least."

"Whatever you say, Captain-General."

He frowned at my words, suspecting that I was mocking his authority, which I was.

I left it at that but resolved to keep my eye on Thomas Doughty.

Soon enough, we were ploughing the seas along the coast of northwest Africa. The distant shore presented as a line of white sand with rocky, wild country beyond. By then, the men had realised we were not entering the Mediterranean, which was further behind us every hour.

Some were delighted by it, winking and grinning at each other and I heard many a whispered word about filling the hold with slaves and other exotic cargoes.

But not all were pleased. While making my way to the head for my morning shit, I overhead two men hissing angrily. One telling the other to shut his stupid face while the other would not be silenced.

"... hired for Alexandria and if this savage land be Alexandria then I'll be damned thrice over and no mistake."

"Keep your voice down or you'll end up hanged, you fool."

"Hanged? Hanged, is it? If I'd been told I was coming to this God-forsaken land then I'd have rather been hanged in England than come here, mark me, John, mark me."

I said good morning as I came around the corner and the two sailors hurried away, looking guilty and fearful. No doubt there were many more such conversations being had all over the fleet that I was not privy to.

But there was no open objection or challenge to Drake's authority and from there we proceeded toward the Cape Verde Islands, four hundred miles west of Mauritania. These were occupied by the Portuguese and were a place one could find fresh fruit and vegetables and livestock. They used the islands when sailing between West Africa, the East Indies, and Brazil.

"Forgive me for asking, sir," Martin asked Drake at dinner, "but if we are entering their waters, how will you avoid conflict with the Portuguese there?"

Drake looked up from his boiled shark steak with a small smile on his face. "Avoid?" he asked and a few of the men around the table chuckled.

Martin flushed and hung his head. "I apologise, sir."

Drake's smile vanished. "A man seeking truth by honest enquiry need never apologise to me, Mister Hawthorn. But it's as you guessed. We have such strength that we need not avoid conflict with the Portuguese and indeed it's likely our only hope for finding the necessary victuals is through such conflict. That is to say, it's my hope and indeed my expectation that we will need do no more than show our great strength in order to get what we need. And if any think to oppose us or run from us, well, we shall not allow it."

In the morning we sighted the Cape Verdes and in the middle of the day, out from Santiago, a ship was spotted. Drake sent a pinnace off in pursuit on a route that took our boat close enough to draw fire from an onshore battery. None of the wild shots hurt our friends in the pinnace and they soon returned with a rather fine little prize, the *Santa Maria*.

She yielded the victuals we sought but also God smiled on us for we found there a gifted and well-known Portuguese pilot named Nuno de Silva who had sailed the route between his homeland and Brazil dozens of times. He had in his possession written sailing instructions describing the directions for that route and several up to date nautical charts. He also had a very fine astrolabe. The crew we put into a pinnace and sent them off but we took their ship and their cargo.

"This is open piracy," Martin whispered as the crew of the *Santa Maria* sailed away for Santiago.

"Well," I said, drawing the word out. "One man's piracy is another man's practicality. We need the victuals or the men will fall ill."

"It is criminal," Martin said. "The law is the law."

"Laws are made by men."

"So men are free to ignore whatever law they will? Even theft? Piracy? Even murder?"

I had murdered more men than I could count. "Of course not. We must follow God's laws. We must not act immorally."

"And this is moral in your eyes, Richard?"

"Well, no, it is simply a matter of..." I sighed, waving my hand at the retreating boat and growled a frustrated response. "Why have you even gotten your codpiece twisted upside down on this matter when those men are nought but Portuguese?"

"Oh," Martin said, crossing his arms, "so it is only piracy when stealing from Englishmen, is that it?"

I smiled and clapped him on the back. "That's it, son. They told me you were a bright fellow."

The prize was renamed the *Mary* and Drake appointed Thomas Doughty as its captain. I was surprised but then the man had been agitating constantly for some recognition of his supposed value ever since we had left England and Drake liked him, that much was obvious. After a while to think on the matter,

I could see why. At heart, Drake was nothing more than a rough Devon sailor whereas Doughty was well-bred and connected. A friendship with the gentleman could only benefit Drake during the remainder of his mortal life.

It was clear that Doughty was a braggart, filled to bursting with his own importance while being utterly, pathetically incapable of criticism. Drake was usually an excellent judge of character but perhaps he was willing to overlook the man's flaws in the hopes of reaping some future benefit. Or perhaps he was so dazzled by the man's wealth and power that he was taken in by the bluster. I could see it so easily because I had hundreds of years' experience of such fellows whereas Drake was just a young man of thirty-odd.

Still, it was with trepidation that I watched Doughty bobbing across on the boat to take command of the former prize, the *Mary*. It was not long before Doughty's true self began to show to all.

A few days later we were drawn together in open water while almost entirely becalmed and our ships' boats went back and forth with supplies and men. But the sailors on the *Mary* were unhappy with their new captain.

"Mister Thomas purloined some of the Portuguese goods for himself, captain," one of the sailors said to Drake when he arrived on the *Pelican*, clutching his hat in his hand. "John Bone see him do it, pulling this thing and that from the old captain's chests and stuffing them away in his own sea chest without making record of what was what. John come to me and we spoke to Mister Thomas face to face about it."

"*Captain* Thomas," Drake said, his face darkening. "What did your captain say?"

The sailor clutched his hat tighter but looked Drake in the eye when he replied. "Flat out denies it, sir. Says he never done nothing of the sort and threatened to have Bone flogged bloody for spying on him and says I was bordering on mutinous and that I would be flogged too." The sailor shrugged. "He said he would make sure Captain Francis would hear about us lacking all respect for our betters. And we says that be all right with us and beg him speak to the Captain-General forthwith but then he tells us to get out and stop bothering him or he'll have us flogged double. That were three days passed and he ain't not been over to the *Pelican* since. So, begging your pardon, captain, the men ain't happy about things and they need sorting or else there's only one way things will go and it ain't going to be better, if you mark my meaning."

Drake's face gave nothing away but his displeasure. "You did the right thing. As General, I am compelled to investigate. We shall row over at once. Lead the way."

I sighed and turned away, cursing my tendency to be right all the time.

"Richard," Drake said and I turned back. "Will you accompany me?"

His eyes flicked to my sword, which I had no need to wear but wear I often did. The familiarity of its weight at my side was ever a great comfort. Even the absurdly ornate and complex hand guards at the hilt had grown on me.

I bowed. "It would be my pleasure."

Being gracious when providing service is a virtue. One may wish to huff and blow and draw out a grudging acceptance by which to convey the greatness of the service you will perform, yet such behaviour is unbecoming. One must treat all such favours as if they will bring you nothing but great joy. If you cannot do so, then you must decline the favour entirely.

In the case of being conveyed from one large ship to another in the open ocean, I can think of very little that would give me less pleasure. Even with such small waves and when almost devoid of wind, I was ever struck with the terror that a sudden storm or some catastrophe would destroy or scatter the ships, leaving me adrift in a tiny boat to slowly starve to death or to be smashed beneath giant waves and driven down into the black depths.

An irrational fear, perhaps, but then those are the only ones that matter.

"It seems like such a small matter," I said to Drake as we crossed, mostly to keep my mind from thinking of the incomprehensible vastness beneath me. "That he should take some booty for himself. Was the ship that he commands not taken in just such a manner? And a captain receives a greater portion than the men anyway."

Drake pursed his lips before answering. "You shall never be a sailor, Richard. You have sailed further than most men ever will but still you do not understand the sea, the ships, or the men. And if you do not understand it by now then you never will."

It was hard to hear but it was fair. "Tell me, then."

"If it is true, and that is to be determined, then it is not the things themselves. It is not the value of those things. It is not even the act of theft, immoral though it is. You see, we must not steal from each other. When we take a ship, every item is recorded, line by line. We use the manifests from the ships, we make our accounting, and we compare and we make a true list. Every item of value is stored and when the voyage is over we shall tally the total, estimate its value and pay the men their due share. So, by taking something now and hiding it, a thief is cheating the entire crew, though the value will be small."

"Everyone steals," I said. "Every crewman, every gentleman, every captain. I shall never be a sailor but I will always be a soldier. And every soldier knows that."

As I spoke, I saw the two men rowing exchange a brief, blank look of guilt.

"Perhaps," Drake said. "It may be that every man helps himself to a trinket or two when nobody is looking his way. And it might be his mates do not find it, ever, or if they do they choose to ignore it. These thefts are a matter for the thief and for God. This is why I say it is not even the act of theft itself that is of concern."

I nodded, understanding what he was getting at, finally. "It is because he was seen. And we must have no disharmony in the fleet."

"We must be as one. Not only a lack of disharmony but a true community, true solidity. Ships sail not on the wind and the seas but on faith and trust. Trust in one another and in the law. The law must be followed in the strictest possible fashion or we should turn about and make for England once more. But it is well. For the act itself was a small thing and I do not doubt that Captain Thomas will make amends by way of apology and returning and recording whatever it was he took."

Clutching the side of the boat I looked up at the flaccid sails of the Mary looming above. "Let us hope that you are correct."

"Francis," Doughty cried as we pulled ourselves over the side of the prize ship. "Francis, how good of you to come visit."

He spoke as if an old, slightly inferior, friend had just arrived at his manor house for dinner. Coming forward, he held out his hand.

Drake ignored it. "I have heard accusations regarding unrecorded private seizures of goods," he said, without preamble.

Doughty's face clouded over as he glared at the sailors who had returned in the boat with us. "Perhaps we could discuss it in my cabin, Francis."

"Captain Thomas," Drake said, his voice taking a harder edge. "We shall go to your cabin at once and you will show us the content of your sea chest."

Doughty clenched his jaw and his mind churned as he sought a way out. "I will not speak of these matters in front of my men."

"Very well," Drake said and marched aft for the captain's cabin. Following, I made sure to be within two or three paces of Doughty, lest I need to run him through at a moment's notice. The sudden darkness of the cabin blinded me but Drake did not hesitate. "This is your chest, Thomas?" he pointed across the cramped space and marched to it. "You will unlock it, if you please."

Doughty crossed his arms. "I do not please. I am a gentleman and this flagrant disregard for my position will not be forgotten."

"You will unlock it, Thomas, and you will procure the items you took and we will proceed from there."

Doughty shook as he finally did as he was instructed and removed a pair of beautiful gloves, a gold ring with a cluster of rubies, and a handful of assorted coins, placing them upon the table with ill-disguised reluctance. I was certain there was more within but Drake apparently did not wish to argue further, judging that this would be enough to deal with.

"You took these items from the captain's sea chest?" Drake asked.

"No," Doughty said, puffing out his chest. He was taller than Drake and made a point of drawing himself up to his full height.

But most people were taller than Drake and such petty tactics never appeared to bother him. "No? But you admit these were taken from this ship?"

"Not from the ship, Francis, but from Portuguese prisoners. The gloves from a gentleman companion of the captain and the ring from the captain himself. And the coins were pressed upon me by other Portuguese members of the crew before we left them in the pinnace by Santiago."

I scoffed. "Why would they give you such fine things?"

He glared at me, startled that I would address him. Nevertheless, his guilty conscience compelled him to answer. "Understanding the seniority of my position in the fleet and in English society at large, they wished to be in my good graces. And to thank me for our polite treatment of them."

It was all I could do to stop myself laughing out loud. "Then the gifts should go to Francis, for it was he that treated them well, not you. You would have been happy to see their throats cut and their bodies dumped over the side."

Drake turned on me. "That's enough! Thomas has provided his explanation and it is certainly the truth, as a gentleman of his standing would never stoop to petty deceit. Sir, thank you being so forthcoming with your explanation and I can only apologise for this being necessary at all. But I am sure you can understand the reasoning."

Doughty shrugged and smirked. "Oh, think nothing of it,

nothing at all. The lower sorts jump to these petty conclusions on account of their crushing jealousies. It is one of the curses of command."

"Indeed, sir, indeed, how right you are." Drake lowered his voice and slid closer to Doughty. "The men on this ship, in fact, have not the quality of my crew on the *Pelican*. I wonder, sir, if you might do me the honour of taking command of her."

Doughty was stunned but he can hardly have been more shocked than I was.

"Take command of your ship?" Doughty said. "And you would serve under me?"

Drake laughed then, just a little, but it was enough to wound Doughty's delicate pride. "I will continue to be the Captain-General, of course, but I shall take command of the *Mary*. I wouldn't want you to have to bother with the likes of these men. The *Pelican* crew will give you the respect you deserve."

Doughty suspected he was being punished in some way. He was being given command of the flagship but it was a demotion in his eyes. It said to everyone that the crew of the *Mary* would not have him, which was indeed the case. Drake hoped that a fresh start on the *Pelican* would set Doughty straight. That his prime crew on that ship would run the ship well no matter who was in command.

That is not what happened.

Word was passed back to us by Drake's loyal friends on the *Pelican* that Doughty, incredibly, was doing little other than sowing discontent on the flagship. Speaking in private to this man or that, the master, the carpenter, and others, promising to reward them in various ways if they would commit to doing his bidding over Drake's.

"But why?" Drake asked, speaking rhetorically after those men had been dismissed from the cabin on the *Mary*. I had joined him there, along with Martin, for I wished to stick with Drake wherever he went on the seas. There could be nowhere safer. "He seeks to undermine me so thoroughly. All I can imagine is that he means to take the ship and return home. Or perhaps he means to harry Portuguese shipping off Africa, or perhaps he means to journey across to attack the vulnerable parts of New Spain. He has lost his nerve for the grander venture, that must be it."

I leaned forward and held my head in my hands. "I should have seen this coming. Suspected he was a true traitor."

"You had no say in bringing him in, Richard. It was I that allowed him to push his way in."

I looked up. "He approached you, I take it? He offered money, flaunted his contacts, and so on, and wheedled you into letting him come with us. He wooed you, yes?"

Drake squirmed in his chair. "I wouldn't put it that way, exactly. I thought he was my friend, thought he was a good man. I was fooled."

Standing, I reached for my sword and buckled the belt around me. "I shall bring him here."

"No," Drake said. "I will not have his poison back here."

"Ah," I said, smiling and patting my sword. "A more permanent solution."

"No!" he cried, seeming horrified. "You can't just murder him, Richard. That will quite destroy the men's will. It would make chaos for us."

"If you insist. What, then?"

I soon found myself making the crossing back to the *Pelican*. The sea was rather high and the crossing was entirely unpleasant but my anger saw me through it and I climbed the side of the ship as if I was boarding an enemy vessel.

"Where's Doughty?" I asked the master's mate.

"He just now retired to his cabin."

"When he saw the boat was returning?"

The mate's face was grim. "When he saw Thomas and Ned were not in it but it was you instead. He cursed your name, Richard."

"I bet he bloody did. Not a happy ship this, John?"

His face twisted as if he was about to cry. "When is Captain Francis returning?"

I clapped his shoulder. "Take heart, son. It is almost over."

Adjusting my sword belt, I strutted aft for the cabin while the eyes of every man on deck followed me. A man in the rigging shouted something I did not catch and there were a couple of grim chuckles.

I threw the door open to find Doughty standing across the room with a pistol pointed at me.

Rushing obliquely forward, I drew a small knife and threw it at him. He recoiled in terror and flailed at the knife with his pistol. It missed him anyway, banging off the wall by his head and by the time he realised his error and turned to shoot me, I was snatching it from his hand.

I slapped him hard across the head, knocking him down. He cried out as he fell, a self-pitying wail.

"Are you one of his?" I demanded.

He was angry and afraid but also confused. "... Drake? One of Drake's?"

"William's, you damned fool. Are you one of William's?"

His confusion increased, along with his rising panic. "William who? William who?"

"Who put you up to sabotaging this mission?"

He clamped his mouth shut. I was tempted to beat it out of him there and then but Drake had asked, for the sake of the morale of the crew, that we treat Doughty more humanely.

And so it was that I had him rowed across to the flyboat, the *Swan*. It served us as a store ship under the command of John Chester. Doughty complained bitterly that he was being treated as a prisoner when there were no charges and no crime but I simply ignored him. I would leave him there, locked in a cabin for a few days without servants or friends and I would see if he would get the blood sickness. Then I would know.

Whether he was an immortal or not, and if he was an agent of William or of Spain or of some other foreign master, it mattered little now that he was out of the way.

"Once we are in England, you Catholic swine," he shouted from inside his cabin when we nailed the door shut, "I shall refute every charge you lay on me!"

"If you live to see England," I replied through the timber.

That silenced him well enough.

It was not, however, the end of the affair.

***

We were out of sight of land, crossing the Atlantic travelling south-westerly, for over sixty days. Crossing the equator in late February, we got on our knees and thanked God for bringing us so far in safety. And then we had a double ration of wine, which was souring but welcome.

In early April, we breathed the very sweet smell of land.

"It is the coast of Brazil," Drake said, sighing in satisfaction and sweating in his hat and gloves.

I looked across the waves at the dark smudge at the edge of the horizon. "How can you be so certain?"

He laughed at my ignorance but not maliciously. He was happy. "This is my craft, Richard. And I am a master."

"Fair enough," I said, breathing in that fresh green scent.

We were a long way south, having forged our way beyond the busiest Portuguese colonies of Brazil and had arrived precisely where Drake had always intended to make landfall. We spent two weeks at a vast river mouth, bludgeoning seals, filling casks with sweet water, mapping the coastline and exploring. That place was like nothing I had seen in my life. It was even stranger than the jungles of Panama. The Indians were like nothing I had seen before, either. They came out every day to watch us from the shelter of the trees. Our men were concerned about the presence of the natives and their fears were disrupting our work.

"We have nothing to fear from the likes of them," I said confidently to the shore party I was with. We were collecting freshwater and seeing whatever else we could find growing in the trees. Our water was stowed on the boats and we were about to venture further inland to look for fruits but the men did not want to go into the darkness of the trees.

I considered organising an assault to drive them away but I had no wish to murder them simply for making my men jumpy. Instead I sought to alleviate their worries, for I did not believe that the natives would attack us for no reason, on account of our superior size and our steel weapons. As long as we kept our distance and showed no fear, I presumed that we would be in no danger.

"But they're savages," the master's mate said and spat on the sand.

"Of course they are," I replied. "But look at their short stature and the narrowness of their shoulders. What could the likes of them do to us?"

He shook his head. "They're armed to the teeth, sir."

I laughed. "Those little sticks? They are thinner even than the willow switches you whip your sons with. Their bows are like the ones boys make for fun in summertime. Come on, the trees are laden with those dark fruits, I am sure of it."

"Ain't it their fruit, master?" one of the ship's boys said. "Ain't they going to be right put out if we go taking what be theirs?"

"Nonsense," I replied. "How can what grows wild belong to them? Did they cultivate the trees with their own hands? Did they make orchards and tend to them? No, lad, they do not own the wilderness. The fruit belongs to God and therefore belongs to all men equally. Come on, come with me. All will be well."

To be fair to my men, though they were of small stature, the savages did look like horrors. They had long black hair and painted their naked bodies in thick bands and blocks of red, white and black. Worse was the bones and pieces of wood they wore pierced through their noses and their lips.

They followed us at a distance and watched with blank faces as we loaded baskets of the strange fruits and carried them back to the shore and from there along the beach to our boats.

Martin watched them in return and lurked at my shoulder in that way he had.

"What is it, Martin?" I asked.

"Your pardon, Richard?"

I sighed, passing a basket in to one of the sailors in the boat and letting the men stow it properly. "You wish to speak to me about something. Say it or do not. But do not stand dithering like a woman."

"The savages," he blurted, pointing at them up the beach and then speaking hesitantly. "I do not agree with you."

"Oh? What do you not agree with?"

"That the fruits are not theirs. Do you believe, sir, that the land of these parts is theirs?"

I sighed, looking at them standing in a row three hundred yards away at the tree line, staring back at us. "I suppose it is."

"The land we're standing on? And the land those trees are growing from?"

"Unrecorded by deed or title but I suppose they have a moral right to it."

"Well then, how can we just take what is theirs?"

"But they have given us no indication that they consider us trespassers. They have not protested our presence, or our taking of the water or produce. So perhaps they do not see it as their own land at all, perhaps they see it as land belonging to all, just as I said." I grinned. "You did not think of that, did you. See, they are not like us, Martin, one look at them and any man will understand that."

"All the same. We should offer them something in return."

"In payment?"

He shrugged. "It would only be polite."

I nodded slowly. "I suppose so. What should we give them?"

He shrugged.

"Men," I called out to the sailors. "We are going to give the savages some gifts before we leave."

They looked at each other in confusion. "But why?" one called out.

I glanced at Martin. "It would be polite."

The sailors shrugged but they understood at once. "What should we give them?"

John, the master's mate chuckled and called out. "Give them your sword, Richard."

"What about your gold?"

They laughed and I waved them into quiet. A small group of men together for any length of time become giddy boys with the merest hint of excitement.

"It need be no more than a few trinkets, lads. Our meanest objects will be treasures for these fellows. An old cup? A pair of gloves now beyond repair? Any tool you can spare? I do not know, whatever you like."

Once they got going, they were hard to stop. Men were collecting this thing or that and throwing it into a large basket. A broken knife handle, three iron nails, a roughly painted pocket sundial made from baked clay.

"Put your shirt back on, Hopkins!" I shouted.

He stood there in a state of undress. "It is well, sir, I have another on the ship."

"Hopkins, you have boiled your brain dry in this sun, not even those savages want your holey, worm-eaten, filth-stained undershirt. Put it back on or I shall ask one of them to borrow his nose bone and when I return I shall shove it sideways up your backside."

We were having a high old time but of course not one of them wished to accompany me when I walked to hand over our gifts to the Indians.

"You are coming with me," I said, pointing at Martin. "This was your idea."

He hung his head. "Yes."

We strode up the beach with the basket. On top the men had thrown in some ship's biscuit, dried fish, and two fresh fish that were swiftly spoiling and the smell was rather bad. Still, I forced a smile onto my face as we got closer.

"Smile, Martin, smile. You look as if you are a man on trial, ready to hear the judge pass sentence."

He did his best, though he looked as if he was in physical pain and he began to fall half a step behind me.

"Give them a wave, son. You have a kind and gentle aspect. Go on, give them a friendly wave."

He raised his arm and I called out a greeting.

They turned and ran.

Fleeing back into the trees like a herd of deer.

"Oh, for God's sake," I said. "What did you do?"

"Nothing," he protested. "I waved."

"You are carrying the basket back."

Before we left, we cut poles from the woodland and drove

them into the ground, out in the open. Upon these poles, we stuck an array of our gifts. The next day, we found all the gifts had been taken.

"Told you," Martin said, enormously pleased with himself.

"What else can we leave for them this time?" I said to the men.

Each of them immediately pulled out armfuls of stuff they had brought from the ship in preparation.

After a few days, the natives began coming closer and closer and staying longer. We noted that this one or that was wearing the gloves or was brandishing a particular knife a man had left, and so on.

We found them growing friendly in time and they sat and listened while our men sang, sitting around our cooking fires. Soon, they brought animals they had caught in the jungle and we traded them for seal meat and other things. We found they loved our music, especially our drums and trumpets.

One of the most astonishing things I had ever seen was how they could bring forth a fire from no more than a pair of spindly sticks, twirling one upon the other. They lit their own cooking fires near to ours and the bravest men amongst our parties came from one to the other to trade and to attempt to communicate with much pointing and laughing.

We showed them our dances and they performed theirs. There was much joy on the part of our men when Captain Winter spontaneously joined in with the Indians, leaping about just as they did.

It was not all so easy.

A handful of us sat at their fire while they roasted small animals and large insects wrapped in thick leaves in the coals.

"What do you reckon their women look like?" one of the men beside me asked.

"Naked as the men, might be. Just with no clothing covering them at all."

"What, none at all?"

"The men don't favour it much. Why would their women be different?"

On my other side, another nodded at an Indian's pierced lip. "I wonder where the women's bones are shoved through."

We chuckled and the laughter died away as the men began thinking of women generally, and of the fact that there might be some relatively close at hand. Even if they were strange-looking savages, they were still women and naked ones at that.

The man at my side turned to an Indian and began making obscene gestures in the air. "Where are your women, bony? Eh? Women, you know? How much you want for one? I'll trade you a handful of—"

I smacked him on the back of his head. Harder than I intended but he deserved it.

"Mind yourself, Morton," I said. "And all of you, for that matter. How would you like it if these men were in your village and began bartering for your wife, for your daughters? You will bring us to violence with your antics."

I dragged them all away and they grumbled at me.

Perhaps we had made a rod for our own backs by providing gifts in the first place but the Indians turned out to be terrible thieves. When your back was turned, you would find one sneaking his hand into your belongings to pilfer whatever he could get his grubby fingers on. A few of us almost came to blows but we always calmed things down before then.

Yet the Indians would not be put off.

On one of the last days we were there, Drake had joined us and he was in a fine mood, commanding his trumpeter to play this or that while watching the natives' delight. I saw one of them sidle up to the General, casually, looking from the side of his eyes.

"Watch out!" I shouted and rushed to protect Drake, drawing my sword. The men leapt to their feet, reaching for their weapons.

Instead of harming Drake, though, the Indian instead snatched the scarlet cap from his head, a rather fine one with a golden band, and dashed away with it in triumph, brandishing it over his head as he ran.

Our men were outraged and more than one aimed their firearms at the fleeing figure. I came to a stop, irritated beyond belief by the thieving little shit.

For a moment, I thought Drake was quaking with rage. In fact, he was laughing so hard that he was weeping and clutching his stomach. He waved the men down.

"Have patience, my friends, have patience," he said, wiping his eye. "They do not understand our ways. We must think of them like children."

"But... Captain Francis," one sailor said, brandishing his polearm, "he stole your cap. We'll get it back."

"You will not! I will suffer no man to hurt him, or any of them. Do you understand?"

They did not understand, not fully, but they loved him already by then and so they did as he commanded.

"Now," Drake said. "Can someone rather quickly provide me with another hat?"

The weather was not always on our side and wild storms blew up and we had to sail out to sea to avoid being dashed against the shore. Our squadron was separated for some time before making the rendezvous further south.

When the *Swan* returned, we heard that not all was well on the little boat. It had turned out that Doughty was not an immortal after all. After four days in his cabin, he had not suffered from the blood sickness. All that had happened was he had grown even more obnoxious than before. I let him out and brought him back once more to the *Pelican*.

"Perhaps it wasn't long enough," Martin said. "Might be he could control it better. You should have kept him confined another day or two, just to make sure."

"Either way, he is where I can keep an eye on him."

I hoped he would realise he was powerless now and so cease his nonsense. Instead, Doughty had spent weeks spreading his poison, whispering in the men's ears that Drake was a villain, that he was incompetent and that he, Doughty, should be in command of not only the flyboat but also the entire squadron and the mission. Again, he had been spreading the lie that Drake owed his position entirely to Doughty and that William Cecil had sought him as his secretary. He told them he had the power in England to reward any and all followers and to punish his enemies. And his enemies were all who dared oppose him.

When we heard these reports during a meeting with the loyal officers, I looked at Drake. "I should have thrown Doughty into the sea weeks ago."

"We are not at the point of murder, Richard," he said, in a chiding tone.

Fletcher, the preacher, spoke up. "Doughty is. Forgive me, General Francis, but I must say this. Doughty was drunk last night and he told me that he would drive a wedge between all of us, on the ship and off, and he would force everyone who stood against him to cut their own throats!"

"What does that mean?" I asked.

Drake cut in before Fletcher could answer. "It matters not what the meaning was. You were alone when he said this, Fletcher?"

"No, General, there were four of us in all, we all heard him say it. It was—"

"Where is he?" Drake growled.

He did not lose his temper often but when he did it was a sight to behold. Despite most men overtopping him, when enraged he seemed to be ten feet tall.

"Doughty!" Drake roared as he stepped out of his cabin and marched across the command deck. "Your knavery is now over."

"You have no authority over me!" Doughty shouted, jabbing his finger at Drake. "If it were not for me, you would still be skulking on a Plymouth dockside hoping for one of your betters to grant you the—"

Drake struck him.

His fist caught Doughty between his jaw and his neck, snapping his head back and buckling his legs under him.

I pursed my lips and turned and whispered to Martin. "Definitely a mortal."

"Bind him to the mainmast!" Drake ordered.

The crew were growling their support while the other gentlemen protested but not enthusiastically, no doubt fearing they might be next. Doughty was lashed to the mast and Drake stomped away. The prisoner was dazed for a long while and I watched him even as the crewmen were ordered to get back to their duties.

The sun fell squarely on his face and hands. It did not burn.

"Well," I said to Martin. "That settles it. Let us leave the fool be."

His poison had been working its way through the squadron for four months but still it was not over. Something had to be done. Something final.

After a few hours, Drake had him taken down and transferred to the *Elizabeth*.

"He cannot be here," Drake muttered to me. "So there he will stay. We will lock him in and feed him through a hatch."

"Surely we can just throw him overboard?"

"No, no. How many times, no. He will be tried but not here, not now. And he has too many sympathetic ears still now on my ship. We will be rid of him but we must do it properly."

I took Doughty over myself and our General came also, in order to speak to the crew of the *Elizabeth* to let them know what they were in for.

"I am sending to you a very bad man," he said to them as they assembled on the main deck before him, "the like of which I do not know how to carry along with me. Your new prisoner, Thomas Doughty, is a conjurer, a seditious fellow, and a very bad and lewd gentleman. What is more he is a witch, and a poisoner. I cannot tell from whence he came but from the Devil, I think."

Warning them to neither speak to nor communicate in writing with the man, we left him in their charge.

We would be done with him soon.

***

We came in time to Port San Julian at 49 degrees south, a little north of the way into the Magellan Strait. The anchorage there was flanked on the south side by great pillars of black rock and was littered with dangerous small islands. Still, it was the last known harbour on Drake's charts before we entered the unknown waters of the strait.

An ominous sight awaited us. Even more ominous than the black rocks and the mournful cries of the birds wheeling overhead. On a rise on the shore stood a gallows. The same gallows that Ferdinand Magellan had erected fifty-eight years earlier so that he could hang one of his men for mutiny.

We came in to anchor, the *Pelican*, *Elizabeth*, *Marigold*, *Mary*, and the tiny *Swan*. We were further south than any English vessel had been before. About to head into the unknown terrors of the strait and the Spanish South Seas, we could not do so with dissent in the ranks. Doughty would have to be dealt with and it would happen here.

But first, we met with an entirely avoidable tragedy.

Two days after we arrived, we went ashore where stood a large group of Indians. They looked just like the men we had seen miles to the north. Largely naked despite the cold, carrying twiggy little spears and spindly bows and arrows. We smiled when we saw them, recalling the pleasant times we had had with the last Indians we had met. And certainly these fellows would have known

Europeans from the Spanish ships that stopped in the bay the past few years. Indeed, they would be descended from the men who had seen Magellan come almost sixty years ago.

It was foolish beyond words to go so lightly armed but for many reasons we assumed those under-fed men were no danger, trusting to their weakness and our strength. Seven of us went ashore with just one arquebus, one longbow, and six swords at our hips and five of us had small bucklers. They seemed perfectly friendly when we approached and they did not run away. Indeed, they came closer and poked and prodded at us, at our clothing, at our weapons.

"Get your damned hands off me," I said to one and peeled his fingers off my sleeve and pushed him away.

"They mean no harm," Drake said, smiling benevolently. "It is mere childish curiosity, as you can well see. And just as with children, if you treat them properly, they will respond in kind."

"And I would not allow a child to lay his grubby fingers on me either," I replied. "Do we really need victuals so badly that we must allow these impudent wretches to manhandle us?"

Drake shook his head. "Stowing what more we can find will do us no harm but we are in no need. We are here to present our gifts and to make known to them the name of England and of Elizabeth."

I pointed at him. "And the name of Drake, no doubt."

He shrugged, nonchalant. "If we carry out our mission, it will be on all Spanish lips soon enough, why not on the Indian's also?"

"Let us give to them their gifts, then, so we can get some fruit and be on our way. We still have Doughty to deal with."

"I had not forgotten," Drake said as we started back for the boat.

The sailor who carried the longbow was named Robert Winter and he was showing the Indians the power of his bow, demonstrating how much better our weapon was than their feeble things, when the cord snapped.

"Oh!" Winter said, chuckling as the Indians leapt back, startled and agitated. "No matter, good sirs, no matter. It oft does this, you see. But it be no matter, see I have a new cord safe and sound under my cap, here and all I need do is—"

An Indian with a white band around his head standing not six feet away placed an arrow on his own string, pulled and released it in a single fluid motion, faster than you can blink.

The arrow took Rob Winter in the side of the chest, piercing his lung on that side and travelling into his heart or right near it. The poor fellow staggered and dropped dead.

Our sailor with the arquebus, named Oliver, raised the weapon at once and aimed it at the very man who had shot Winter. He had been standing right close to Winter and so there was no chance he could miss. Oliver discharged it but the powder was damp and it fizzled and misfired.

That same Indian, the damned murdering savage with the white band around his brow, slid another arrow onto his string and pinged it straight into Oliver's chest from close range. Spindly little bow it might have been, the arrow went right through the Englishman's chest and the point stuck out of his back. He threw himself down in terror and pain and died just moments after he fell.

Mindless savages that they were, they had become instantly inflamed by Winter's murder and with the death of Oliver they grew ecstatic with joy. Shouting in their barbaric tongue, whooping like monstrous great birds, they shot a stream of arrows at the rest of us.

It all happened so swiftly that we were all yet stunned, even me. But when those arrows fell upon us, I roared at the survivors.

"Get your shields up! Bucklers, get the bucklers over your heads, men!" I pushed them forward. "Francis, get behind them!"

He had no buckler and so had no defence other than the protection of his crewmen.

Drawing my sword, I ran toward the Indians. Arrows fell around me and one bounced off my blade. Before I reached them, they turned and scattered from me like doves from a hawk. Not in blind panic but scattering in a fan-like spread away from me so that if I charged one group, the others could still shoot at me.

I dropped my sword and snatched up Oliver's arquebus.

An arrow hit me in the arm and another stabbed into my foot but I carried on, cleared out the powder, recharged it from Oliver's horn and raised the weapon, clutching it tight between my arm and my flank. Two arrows hit me in the chest and one in the stomach but I walked forward a few paces and found the murdering bastard with the strip of white cloth about his head.

Aiming at his chest, I discharged the arquebus. It banged into my armpit and coughed out a jet of smoke and fire. Tossing it aside, I rushed forward and drew my knife so that I could kill him and the rest of them.

Instead, running through the smoke, I found the entire band of Indians fleeing as fast as their legs could carry them, their cloaks flapping behind.

The Indian I had shot sat on his knees, clutching his guts. My shot had gone low, somehow, but it had blasted his guts abroad and these he cradled in his arms as he looked up at me in anguish. His mouth opened and closed but no more than a tight-throated mewing came out.

"You can die slowly," I said to him and sheathed my knife, leaving him there on the shore. "Come on," I called to Drake and the others. "Let us take our men and be gone before the savages return with the rest of their tribe."

The sailors gaped at me. "But... you are injured!"

"What? Oh." I found over half a dozen arrows jutting out of my body and limbs. Ripping two of them out, the blood gushed down me. "It is well. Come on, grab the bodies!"

They looked at Drake and he nodded at them. "Do as he says," Drake commanded and they rushed forward to collect their comrades. "What a fool I am," he muttered.

I yanked another arrow from my side and tossed the bloody thing aside to grab the next, in my forearm. "Could have been worse," I said, ripping it out. "Anyway, now you know."

"Yes," he replied. "Now I know."

We did not go ashore again but instead pitched our tents on a low stony island out in the bay. The ships were worked on, repaired and re-stowed. The men spent time on the islands, stretching their legs. We were there for a full month making preparations but those Indians never bothered us again.

"Scared of you, I don't doubt. Probably they thought you were a god of some kind," Drake said. "Or a demon."

"What makes you think I am not?" I asked, with a straight face.

He furrowed his brow. "What does that make me, then, Richard?"

I pointed at him. "Lucky to have met me."

When all was ready, and the men were rested and fatter than they had been, and the ship's ropes and sails were in order and the holds were rearranged in some ways that created better sailing qualities in the ships, we began the trial of Thomas Doughty.

Every man in the squadron was called to our stony little island where our general stood grim and implacable at the head of the assembly. Beside him, Captain Thomas of the *Marigold* acted as official clerk. They had prepared well and Thomas started by displaying the pages of testimony he had recorded of Doughty's mutinous talk and behaviour during the voyage. All the while, Doughty stood to the side with the eyes of all upon him, with his head held high as if he was supremely confident. When the evidence was laid out, Drake addressed the accused man.

"Thomas Doughty, you have here sought by diverse means to discredit me to the great hindrance and overthrow of this voyage. If you can clear yourself of these charges, you and I shall be very good friends. Where to the contrary you will deserve death."

At the mention of the ultimately penalty, a murmur went through the men. If they had harboured any doubt with regards the seriousness of the matter, they were now dispelled.

"How should you like to be tried?"

Doughty puffed out his chest and raised his voice. When he spoke, I recalled well that he had trained and practised as a lawyer. It was a very fine voice. "Why, good General, let me live to come into my country and I will there be tried by Her Majesty's laws."

Clever bastard, I thought. He knew if he could delay his trial, any number of things might stop it from ever actually taking place. And what was more, if ever we did try him in London, he would be surrounded by his friends. The London court system was his home territory. He would probably even be friends with the judge, or with the judge's son, at least. It was a good move on his part and one I sensed the men thought perfectly fair.

But we could not allow his poison to continue to work away on the crew, not when we were about to go to war with the immortal viceroy and the entirety of New Spain. And Drake would not consider it.

"No, Thomas. I will here empanel a jury on you to inquire further of these matters."

At that, Doughty looked at me and sneered before turning back to Drake. "By what right do you claim the power to preside over such a trial?"

Drake looked angry but he covered it quickly. "By right of my command, as bestowed by Her Majesty the Queen."

"Ah!" Doughty cried. "Of course. Well then, General, I hope you will now present your written commission before us all!"

Drake had no commission. Our mission was secret and was only condoned in secret and Elizabeth could never had left evidence showing she was complicit in this war we were to wage on Spain.

"I warrant you my commission is good enough," Drake snapped.

Doughty smiled, gesturing expansively at the men. "Well then, sir, I pray you let us see it. It is necessary that it should be here showed, is it not? Else nothing here may proceed in legal fashion."

"Well you shall not see it!" Drake cried, swinging his arm through the air as if dashing away Doughty's request. "My fellows, see how this fellow is full of prating. Bind me his arms, so that I might be safe in my life."

Without hesitation, some of his men moved to obey.

Beside me, Martin hissed. "What is this?"

I shrugged. "You have some objection?"

"It is highly improper."

"Tying a prisoner?"

"All of it. And we have not yet learnt that our leader has the legal right to do any of this."

Tutting, I shook my head. "You have a lot to learn, son."

Doughty cried at Drake while he was expertly bound by the sailors. "I am no threat. You do this only to shame me."

"Nonsense," Drake said, acting as though astonished. "Was it not you that murdered your lord the Earl of Essex by poison?"

Doughty froze, either in genuine shock or in a faultless performance of it. "How dare you accuse me of such a monstrous thing? I served the Earl well. And it was through me that you were ever introduced to that good earl!"

Drake smiled. "I know for certain that Essex held you in small esteem, Thomas, for I that was daily with Essex for a time never saw you there more than once. And it was you that poisoned him to weaken our kingdom, just as it is you poisoned this squadron with your rotten words. Enough of your lies. Now we shall swear the jury!"

Captain Winter was the foreman and Captain Thomas read out the charges, while members of our company stepped forward to recall Doughty's words to them. Many together told how Doughty had tried to enlist them into his party and how he had spoken of breaking away from Drake. One man said Doughty had told him he would bribe the government of England to buy his way out of the trouble he had caused by his conduct.

Doughty did his best. He denied that he knew them or that they had ever spoken of such things. He accused them of lying on behalf of the General, that they loved dearly, in order to bring about this trial and a certain verdict.

"And this entire trial is illegal. I must be tried in England, I must. Or your legitimacy as general of this expedition will be questioned by all. This is your last chance."

"My last chance?" Drake said. "No, sir, as is so often the case, you have things backwards."

"Your last chance, I say, before I disclose the true purpose of this mission! This false mission which you call a voyage of plunder but which true purpose is nought but murder! Assassination, my friends. And there is your assassin, fellows, the murderer Richard Ashbury! Our purpose here is nothing more than to protect that man there, under the pretence that you will all become rich. Instead, he leads you to your doom! He is an agent of the Queen's men, sent to commit illegal murder against the legitimate ruler of New Spain and he wants each one of you to serve as his personal army. You will be cut down by the fire of the Spaniards before ever you see England again, mark my words. Mark them and recall them as you lay dying on some distant shore, seeing your blood pour onto foreign sands, and you will wish then that you had listened to Thomas Doughty over the madness of the false captain Francis Drake!"

All eyes had been on me throughout the stream of accusations. I wanted to stride across to him and punch him into silence. While he spoke, I had wished to slice open his throat and drink him dead. Instead, I allowed him to shout himself hoarse and fall into panting silence.

I left it a few moments until men began to think I had no answer before I raised my hands before me and clapped. After a beat or two, I clapped again, in the slowest applause possible. Just a few claps later and I smiled.

"Truly, sir, if there was any doubt that you were a great liar, you have now dispelled them."

That brought a few chuckles but not from Doughty or his friends. The gentleman and lawyer Leonard Vicary stepped forward and raised his voice. "Do you deny these accusations, sir?"

"Deny them?" I said, affecting profound confusion. "Why ever would I deny them? I likewise do not deny the ravings of any other madman who claims that he speaks to fairies or that he has the power to walk on water."

Again, a few of the men laughed, which enraged Doughty and the gentlemen. They protested that I could not answer serious accusations with flippancy. It was not right morally or legally.

This finally caused Drake to explode. "I have not to do with you crafty lawyers! I know what must be done." At that, he ordered the jury to deliberate on the charges.

While they did so, the men muttered darkly to each other and Martin turned to me.

"How can you dismiss his words so easily? Do you not care that you are found out?"

"I care very much. But I cannot deny what is true, not when the men around us will, God willing, find it to be true before too long."

"And they speak truth about these proceedings. It is not legal, Richard, and when we return to England men will know it also.

What then?"

I shrugged. "We may die before we reach England, so why worry on it now?"

He stared, aghast.

The jury returned a verdict of guilty.

Drake stood before the crews once more. "My friends, you see how this fellow has sought to overthrow this voyage? First discrediting me and Richard Ashbury and he surely then meant to take our lives. My friends, consider what a great voyage we are to make. The like of it has never been seen in England, and when it is done the lowest of us in this fleet shall become a gentleman. And if this voyage fails, which it will if this man lives, what a reproach it will be. Not only to our country but especially to each of us." He looked at them in turn, attempting to meet every eye. "Therefore, my friends, whoever believes this man deserves to die, let them hold up their hands."

Not quite all raised their hands but those that did not instead hung their heads and spoke no dissent.

Before his execution, Doughty was allowed to settle his will in conversation with his friends. After that, he shared the sacrament with Drake and then he and I and Doughty dined together at table out there on the island.

It was a strange meal. For half an hour, we sat and ate and conversed as if we were friends and Doughty seemed to bear us no ill will.

"Who did it, Thomas?" I asked him at last. "Who put you up to this? Who told you about me and this mission? Who paid you? Why are you doing this? You are not an immortal yourself but it seems as though you know too much about it by far."

He shook his head and smiled. "I hear you are fond of torture, Richard. Perhaps if you torture me you will discover more but I suspect you fear turning the men against you by such actions. And so I will take the secret to my grave."

I shrugged as if it was no great significance, though I burned to tie him to a chair and remove pieces of his skin.

"I can think of a way to torture you to my heart's content. Do you know of the power of my blood, Doughty?" I looked closely at him as he smirked. "I see, then you know I can give you my blood to drink to preserve your life."

"I want nothing at all of your devilry."

"Whether you want it or not makes no difference. We can hang you until you suffocate, then I can take your body in a boat to bury you in private on one of the nearby islands, out of sight and sound. And then I shall rouse you and begin taking you apart, piece by piece, until you tell me."

Doughty's eyes were wide and he stared at Drake. "You will not allow that."

Drake leaned back and folded his arms. "You've taken payment from our enemies to murder us, to betray England. I would do it to you myself, if I could."

Doughty shook. "I never took payment, never. Not for myself. Not like that."

"How then?"

He hesitated. "A man came to see me. A man in black. He threatened my sisters, Francis! He had men following Margaret and Susan and he said he would—" His voice broke and he collected himself. "He described all the things he would do to them if I did not comply. They have no one but me to protect them. No one."

"Why did you not speak to Christopher Hatton, your friend and patron? Or some other man of importance?"

Doughty would not meet my eye. "I have debts."

"Must be great debts."

"They are. At least, they were. My estates would have been taken, my family left with nothing, nothing! My sisters would have been destitute, even had they lived. And..."

I nodded. "No doubt there is more here. You have some shameful secret that they preyed upon. Something you did in your past they threatened to expose? A lover, a murder, something. I care not what it was. But you were given a choice. Ruin and disaster for you and your siblings. Or all your problems could go away. Your sisters would not only live, unmolested, but they would still marry well, the family will go on. If only you would do this one thing and corrupt the voyage."

His head was low. "Yes."

"I am pleased that we understand. Who was he?"

"I know not. A tall man, black of hair. He dressed all in black but I believe he is a Catholic."

"Now, tell me his name."

Doughty's head shot up. "His name? He never gave it. Not his true name. But his men called him something and he signed his notes with his symbol."

"What was the name? What was his symbol?"

"They were one and the same. The Crow."

"The Crow. I see. Well then," I said, raising my cup, "I hope you die well."

He lowered his head and raised his cup also.

Doughty did die well.

He and Drake prayed together while I stood apart, they embraced briefly, and then he turned to address the crowd.

"Please my friends, forgive me. I have prayed to God to protect our queen and to grant success to this voyage. And our good captain, General Drake, has sworn that there will be no reprisals against any of my friends on board or my family at home. Indeed, he has sworn to watch over them, for which I am deeply grateful. With my death, the slate is wiped clean." His voice faltered only on the words my death, which was understandable. With that, he stepped up to the block and knelt before it. We had given him the choice of how to be executed and he had chosen to die like a gentleman. And so, our executioner, a burly mariner named Dobbs, swung the axe well. It was sharp and the blow was true and Doughty's head was struck from his neck.

Drake stooped at once, seized it by the hair and raised it up to us. "Lo! This is the end of traitors!"

We buried him on that nameless island beside the graves of Winter and Oliver, murdered by the natives.

We were rid of him but his stench remained. His friends, the other gentlemen and those who liked Doughty still, were concerned for their own safety and the men were not settled as we prepared to board for the final time. Drake was pacing back and forth along the island, watching and reading his men as well as he read the tides and the weather. Suddenly he called them forth for a final assembly there on the shore.

"My friends, I am a very bad orator, for my bringing up has not been in learning but take good notice of what I shall say for I am unashamed of my words and I would say this again in England

and even before Her Majesty."

There was not a sound to be heard other than the wind and the cries of the seabirds. In the silence, Drake looked at each face in the crescent of men, as if he wished to look into the eyes of every one of his men.

"We find ourselves very far from our country and friends. We are compassed in on every side with our enemies, we are therefore not to make small reckoning of any man, for we cannot have another even if we could give him ten thousand pounds. That is why we must have these mutinies and discords that are grown amongst us redressed. We must be as one. There are too few of us for it to be otherwise! Not one man may shirk, not one may not give his all. I must have the gentleman to haul and draw with the mariner and the mariner with the gentleman. Let us show ourselves all to be of a company and let us not give occasion to the enemy to rejoice at our decay and overthrow. I would know him that would refuse to set his hand to a rope but I know there is not any such here."

"Also, if there be any here willing to return home, here is the *Marigold*. Whoever wishes to leave, now is your first and only chance. Step forward and go with my blessing, for I want no man with me who is not with me fully and in his heart."

I looked around, along with every other head in the crowd, swivelling left and right.

No man moved.

Drake nodded, as if he had expected the outcome. "Well then, my fellows, we leave here together as nothing but friends, each and every one of us. And now there is real work to be done. Let us do it together."

They cheered and praised God and we did get to work.

First, the small *Mary* was burned to reduce the size of the squadron and the men and supplies distributed amongst the other ships. It did not make much sense to me but Drake claimed it would reduce the risk of losing too much if and when the squadron was separated by the storms known to plague the area.

And so, friends and equals, we set out from Port San Julian and the three graves on the island in the bay and headed south toward the terrifying Strait of Magellan.

11

The Straits

1578

THE CAPE OF VIRGINS, they called it. A more inappropriate name will never be found. By God, it looked frightening. Columns of jagged grey-black rocks jutting up from the sea in a series of sharp promontories, with shards like sharks' teeth descending into the waves away from them, as if the cliffs were about to rise up from beneath our hulls and rip us to pieces.

I am certain that we all felt a profound sense of dread as we inched closer, taking soundings with every yard.

What Drake felt, though, was not dread at what the seas would throw at us. He felt the dread of the crew and he was ever sensitive to their emotions, reading them like a book and playing them like the virginals. And so he called a stop before we rounded that cape, commanded our guns fire a salute to the queen, held a service on the decks with much kneeling and praying, and then rechristened the *Pelican*. From that moment on, it would be known as the *Golden Hind*.

"Why the *Golden Hind*?" I asked him afterwards.

He shrugged. "That is the family crest of Sir Christopher Hatton. He was one of the first on the Privy Council who gave us our support and it can do no harm to show our continued loyalty by this."

I nodded slowly. "And Hatton is a good friend to Doughty, so you wish to fend off some of the anger he may feel about what we have done."

"You disapprove?"

"Quite the opposite," I replied. "You are far shrewder at this sort of thing than I have ever been. Some of my friends tell me I am too proud while others say I am too foolish."

He smiled. "And which is it?"

"I have had many centuries now to come to terms with being a proud fool. But I like this. A new name, a fresh start. It is a fine idea."

"And a cannonade to blast the old away and welcome the new." Staring up, he started at some sign in the rigging or the sails that I could not see. "See now, sir, the wind favours us finally and we can begin."

He turned and called out to the master, rushing aft, and soon we began to enter the shark mouth of the strait. I clung to the side and stayed out of the way until I was needed to haul on a rope or perform some other task. We crept forward, with every man not actively engaged in sailing instead peering over the side at the shoals, ensuring that we stayed in the centre of the channel. Our other ships came on behind in single file, the only sounds the creaking of the rigging and the calling out and relaying of the depth. After passing the cape, we found the land to either side low and flat but soon the land came closer and closer until we were passing through two sets of narrows with less than a league of water from bank to bank. And then the landscape changed again.

Vast, jagged peaks rose beyond darkly wooded hills, cut by thousands of small streams that poured into the strait. The tallest of the distant mountains were capped with snow. Of course, it was winter in that southern land and that made us feel even more out of sorts. Eventually, the passage opened and led southward but before going on, we anchored by three islands.

Not one man in the squadron, not even our Portuguese pilot Nuño de Silva, had been through those straits before and Drake was as active as I had ever seen him. The qualified men took readings almost continuously and Drake worked tirelessly comparing them to his charts and written accounts, while making his own charts and recordings. Our ships tacked to and fro in the ever-changing winds. The current was with us, most of the time, but those winds were nightmarishly changeable and I did not know how our navigator or our sailors managed. The winds were on occasion behind us but just so often they came from ahead or from one side or the other and they were never steady, only gusting so that the men were always aloft taking in sail or letting it out. On occasion the winds were so changeable and so powerful that, in combination with the current, they churned the water into whirlpools out there in the channel.

That channel was a constant horror. Some parts were crossed with shoals and rocks that poked above the white caps or, even worse, came to just beneath the surface. There were many close calls and changes in direction, under terrible conditions. At other places, the strait was so deep that no anchor could touch the bottom. Those depths terrified me.

"Why?" Martin asked, when I admitted as much to him one night after my double ration of wine loosened my tongue. "A man can drown in a yard of water just as much as he can in a mile of it."

"Oh, you and your damned reason, Martin Hawthorn. Do you know that no one in the world likes a logical man?"

He seemed both wounded and confused so I gave him the rest of my wine and retired to my bunk. There, I tried not to think of the endless black depths beneath my back and dreamed of storms and waves and freezing waters.

That strait was three hundred miles long. Three hundred miles of terror and when we got halfway through, it turned northwesterly and we found ourselves now picking our way through thousands of scattered islands. The seabed became jagged and frayed our cables so that sometimes in the night one broke at our bow or stern and we found ourselves swinging around in the current until a new line could be let down. Those islands were treacherous and we found almost no safe anchorages so that every man became brittle with anxiety.

But we made it.

The strait widened until we came out into the Pacific Ocean.

"Come and see!" Martin said, shaking me awake in the dark of a false dawn. "Come and see, Richard."

Staggering forward to the bow, I pushed through the group gathered there. "What is it?" I asked, rubbing my eyes.

"He has done it," Martin whispered, grinning. "Drake has done it."

Our general was leaning out over the prow and he turned then and saw me. He smiled. "Richard, come and see it again. Come and see the South Seas."

Drake brought us through in fourteen days. It seemed like an age but I heard decades later it was the fastest known passage of the strait. Magellan we knew had taken five weeks, and other ships that came after us in later years had taken months to feel their way through.

We rejoiced, thinking we had passed the greatest test that we would face in the voyage.

We were wrong.

At first, we made a good seventy leagues up the coast of Chile.

And then a great storm hit us from the north and drove us relentlessly southward.

I thought I had experienced fear before. On a battlefield, of course, it was so familiar to me it was like putting on a comfortable old helm and I hardly counted that anymore. At sea, though, the existential fear was greatly magnified by my utter helplessness and I thought I had faced such fears before. Fears of drowning and being dashed to pieces on rocks or set drifting on wrecking and slowly freezing or starving or dying of thirst. I thought I had faced them crossing the Atlantic, and in the Caribbean and when passing through the strait. But I was wrong.

Once, I had suffered in a deadly storm in France that had killed men and horses but that was sudden and then it was over. It was also on land. This great storm was not only beyond my experience but beyond my imagination. Never had I known seas could be so wild, waves so high, winds so strong. Days were so dark they were indistinguishable from night. Lightning flashed to reveal sometimes the black peaks of the jagged coast, at other times we knew we were heading for death only by the sound of mighty waves booming against the rock cliffs. We worked like never before. Sails were destroyed, ropes snapped, spars broken. Our hulls were battered and seams opened and so we bailed and pumped and repaired with timbers and still we slowly filled with storm water. At times we struggled to drag ourselves away from the coast. At others, we fought to come back toward land and search for anchorages in lulls. But our anchors were ripped from the seabed half a dozen times and always we were hammered by waves bigger than churches. Every sailor on board swore it was worse than anything they had experienced before.

The *Marigold* was lost.

It happened one night when we could not see but on the gusting winds we could hear the terrible cries of the men as their ship was smashed and churned up by the waves. In the dim light of daybreak we spied pieces of her but we saw no man, each one already sunk into the depths.

Up and down the coast we ran, in and out toward the open seas. After weeks, we found ourselves at the mouth of the strait once more and a soupy fog descended atop the terrible waves and Captain Winter of the *Elizabeth*, instead of following us out to sea, sought shelter inside the Strait of Magellan. In there, it was calm and they spent some weeks repairing the ship and restoring the men. But instead of coming out to meet us on the coast at 30 degrees as agreed, Winter took the *Elizabeth* back through the strait and home to England.

We did not know it at the time. Indeed, we spent weeks searching for them and waiting for them and even months later hoped they would turn up. But later I discovered that Winter and his crew lost their nerve, and they fled. They had a half dozen excuses and each senior man accused the others of making the decision but I am sure they were simply afraid. They failed in their duty and because they lost their nerve they returned home as cowards, with nothing to show for their months of toil and danger.

I do not blame them. At times in the weeks of that great storm, I would have gone home, also, if given the choice. When you are shaking with cold and terror with swollen and bleeding hands and an empty belly and a throat soured with vomit then duty and oaths and vengeance be damned.

But we had no choice, for our fate was in the hands of that storm. It seemed like something alive, like the pagan god Poseidon himself was tormenting us. And so we ran south, further and further, hoping to escape his clutches. Every now and then we found an anchorage that proved unsafe among the countless islands and then we would be forced south again.

Everyone knew that the Strait of Magellan was the only route between the Atlantic and the South Seas. South of the strait, the lands continued all the way to the pole as the great continent of Terra Australis, the southern landmass.

But we were the first men in the world to discover that was not the case.

South of the strait was in fact simply an archipelago, a chain of broken islands with a vast open sea beyond. Finding this to be the case, we wondered if Terra Australis existed at all. After all, we were further south than any man had ever been and there was nothing there but vast waves taller than the *Golden Hind*.

Indeed, we were driven by that storm of Poseidon to the utmost island, the southward point of the Americas, and there was nothing beyond.

"Do you know what this means?" Drake shouted in my ear over the wind and the crashing waves. "This means there is another route to the South Seas! The Spanish can never stop us, they can never block the passage if *this* is the passage." He waved an arm at the mountainous rolling seas around us. "Is it not the most wonderful news?"

Clapping a hand over my guts, I dragged my frozen body away. "I'm afraid you must excuse me," I shouted.

We worked our way in amongst those last lumps of rock at the point of America and found a sheltered place away from the mighty waves where we could anchor and make repairs. Those islands we claimed for the Queen and for England and so we named them the Elizabeth Islands.

"Come ashore with me, Richard," Drake said one morning as I came on deck for my watch. "Come ashore so we may claim these lands legally and properly."

I looked at the barren wasteland of that island where the storm winds shrieked ceaselessly across the rocks and shook my head. "What use are these lands for anyone? All they are good for is collecting bird shit, Francis."

He was greatly offended. "What lands have *you* claimed for your queen?"

In the end, I went with him just to feel solid land beneath my feet once more. By God, it was bleak, though, and unfit for man.

Even the seals and penguins and birds seemed unhappy about being there. Drake had the men heave upright a mighty stone and carve into it the Queen's name and the date. While they were doing that, I headed south on foot across the land.

"Richard!" Drake called after me. "To where do you go?"

Turning, I raised my arms. "I have stood further south than any man who ever lived!" I cried.

Drake would not be undone and he hurried toward me and then, without slowing, he walked right past me. A few paces ahead, he turned and raised his arms. "And now it is I that have stood farthest south!" He laughed and waved to me. "Come, let us get back before the tide turns."

Instead, I walked by him heading south. I sensed him on my heels and I turned to see him hurrying after me and the rest of our party coming behind.

After a brisk hike, we reached the southern coast. Below, mighty waves smashed into the cliffs sending spray into the air where it was whipped away into the sea again. The rocks beneath our feet resounded with every blast, like tons of gunpowder detonating over and over again. Standing near the cliffs, I turned and raised my arms, smiling. It was too windy to speak.

Drake scowled and marched up to me, edging by me to stand on the wet rocks with the waves shattering far below. He crossed his arms, nodded once with terror in his eyes and marched back inland.

There was no denying that he had won. The only place further south was in the sea itself, or so I thought, until I noticed a few paces away a spit of rock little wider than a man jutting out over the sea. Spray from the waves coated it every few seconds in more freezing water.

I looked at Drake and he shook his head, terrified.

Gritting my teeth, I marched toward it, head bent into the wind and shoes slipping on the slick surface. When I reached the edge I could make no headway against the gale that came gusting up from below and so I dropped to my knees and then to my belly and I crawled out onto the ledge and inched forward until my head was at the very end and my eyes peeped over the precipice into the maelstrom below. Waves soaked me to the bone and my hands were so numb and my limbs shook so hard that I found I could get no purchase on the stone and I feared that I would be stuck there. The shame of suffering such a fate filled me with anger enough that I pushed myself back and back again until I could turn and crawl again onto the land.

Teeth chattering, I made my way back to Drake and the others. He did not speak to me for three days after that. But it was worth it.

The great storm blew itself out after fifty-three days.

During that time, we had fought almost ceaselessly to stay alive. But when it faded into nothing, we found ourselves miles out of position, having lost the other ships, and many of the crew were suffering from scurvy. We all knew the disease could be cured with fresh fruit and vegetables but we had none left. So, in search of green stuffs, we made our way north once more. Exploring an island with a suitable anchorage we found seals and birds on the ground that we slaughtered and took back to the ship in their hundreds but there was nothing green there but grass.

Weary but hopeful, we reached the coast of the mainland again and looked for somewhere to find food. We knew there was no Spanish occupied territory until we reached 30 degrees south on the coast of Chile so we had little fear about where we stopped. Even so, we thought it would be a good idea to stop at a place marked on our charts as Mocha Island. It was flat all around the rim, with shoals and beaches, but in the centre rose a short chain of stubby mountains, so from the distance it looked like some monstrous great hat sitting on the horizon. We anchored there and went ashore.

The natives had spotted us, of course, and came down to the shore in numbers. We were wary, on account of our previous experience, but we were not wary enough, as we would soon discover.

They seemed friendly enough at first and indeed brought gifts with them.

"Do my eyes deceive me," one man cried, "or do they have sheep with them?"

"Where's these savages get themselves sheep from?" another muttered. "Ain't no sheep in these parts."

"Aye," another said, "and I know that breed, and all. That be Spanish sheep, or I'm not a carpenter."

Drake put his hand on his sword. "If they are allies of the Spanish then we may have trouble."

I nodded. "Be ready, men. Spread out. Ensure your powder is dry."

The Indians came closer and we prepared for violence but they immediately handed over the pair of sheep, plus half a dozen hens and baskets of a strange kind of wheat that men recognised as maize.

Relations were cool but friendly enough and we asked in

Spanish for green stuffs, fresh fruit and vegetables and heaped gifts upon them in exchange. At the end of the day, we seemed to have agreed to return on the morrow to collect what we had bargained for and we parted with smiles and firm handshakes.

The next day, I went in a single boat with Drake and eight men to collect water and then meet with the locals to collect the fresh food we had bargained for. We did not take firearms or bows, and we had only the swords at our sides.

How could we have been so naive? We trusted them because we thought them simple. We believed them incapable of deceit. With hindsight, I soon understood that the natives were not all so innocent and childlike as they sometimes seemed. Indeed, some tribes were pleasant folk who wished us only well and were a delight to deal with but others were possessed not only of a warrior spirit but also a deep cunning and malevolence.

We did not know that the Indians of that island, that we approached that morning, were a fierce warrior race. The Spaniards had been at war with them for decades and still the Europeans had not won.

The kindest of the native tribes were the first ones wiped out, usually by disease but also in conflict with the colonists and with other tribes whose territories they were pushed into. It is people who are filled with a deep and enduring preference for their own kind, along with mistrust or hatred of outsiders, who thrive.

The people on that island were from a tribe that had used any means necessary to defeat the Spanish. They learned how to ride the horses left by the Spanish and devised means to fight enemy cavalry by lengthening their spears, reinforcing their warclubs, and attaching nooses to poles with which to snare horses' heads and feet. Some even used captured arquebuses and in at least one case, a cannon. They were courageous and cunning and they were determined to continue as a people.

But we knew none of that as we approached the creek mouth from the sea that morning. We were like children ourselves, or like the penguins standing still while disaster crept closer and not knowing the danger until it was too late.

The two lads in the bow, Tom Brewer and Tom Flood, joked about seeing some native women this time, nudging each other and daring one another to mime a woman's shape to the natives. Beside me in the stern, Drake growled at them to do nothing of the sort and their faces fell as they agreed and assured the captain that they were merely making fun and had no intention of doing anything so uncouth. Drake winked at me and I grinned. It was a clear morning and warm and I was looking forward to filling the casks with water from the creek that we entered from the sea. Our rowers raised their oars as we came into the bank by a massive, dense stand of reeds and we ground upon it. The two Toms jumped over the bow into the bank, carrying the mooring rope forward toward a rotten tree stump a few paces away.

We others stood and made our way forward, still smiling, when the Indians launched their attack.

They were hiding in the reeds, at least a hundred of them and possibly many more. They leapt out and ran at us, screaming terrible war cries and shooting arrows and throwing darts and javelins. They thumped into the boat and into us and the men jumped back into the boat.

"Row us off!" I shouted, pushing the oarsmen into the benches. "Row!"

The natives rushed in at us from all sides, grabbing at the oars and at the boat itself. What is more, we were driven up onto the bank and a dozen of the bastards had hold of our mooring rope and were heaving on it.

Drawing my sword, I stabbed and slashed at all those swarming the sides, cutting off fingers and hands and stabbing one young fellow in the eyes.

When I reached the bow, I lay about me, cutting throats and hacking into heads. I jumped out onto the bank, cut through the taught rope, sending the Indians falling back into a heap and I heaved against the boat with such force that I almost failed to get back in before it floated out into the current.

Even so, the Indians waded in after us, still shooting their arrows and grabbing our oars so that four were lost, half our number.

We smacked them with the oars that were left and stabbed and hacked until we were away from the banks and the creek and I took an oar and Drake took another and we heaved and pulled until we were out and heading back to the Hind.

Every one of us was badly wounded. Two of our men were dying in the bottom of the boat, pierced by the arrows and darts.

Drake had two of the spindly Indian arrows in his head. One in his face was stuck just below his eye.

"How bad is it?" Drake asked as we rowed, spitting out mouthfuls of blood every few seconds.

"By God, sir!" the master cried as climbed came up the side. "By God, sir, you are mortally wounded."

"Nonsense!" I cried. "Our captain shall be well."

The crew rushed us and I shouted at them to move.

"See to these others," Drake growled, pushing through the men and heading to his cabin.

I followed behind and saw Martin, jabbing my finger at him and then at Drake, and he darted aft. The mariners begged me to save their captain and I waved them off, swearing that I would before closing the cabin door on them.

"Give me your blood," Drake growled, his throat thick and bubbling with all the gore pouring down it from his wound. "Pull this damned thing from my face and give me blood so that I may revenge my—"

"Yes, yes," I said, "be silent. You make it worse, man. Hold still. Martin? Find something for him to bite down on."

Martin used a belt and Drake sank his teeth into it, I placed my hand on his forehead and with the other, grasped the arrow shaft. It entered an inch below his eye and I wished to avoid extracting the arrow in such a way that he would lose that eye so I pulled gently at first. Drake screamed through his teeth and screwed his eyes shut. The shaft was slippery with hot blood, mine and Drake's, and my hand kept sliding and I had to grasp it tighter, applying such force that the arrow bent. Drake's legs went weak and he dropped.

I grabbed him and laid him on his desk while he moaned in his semiconscious stupor. "Hold him down," I commanded Martin and then I slid the arrow from his face and then used my dagger to dig out the tiny stone arrowhead that had slid under his scalp and dug into his skull.

Martin kindly bled himself, and I drank his blood and fed my own to the dazed Drake.

"Will that not weaken you, Richard?" Martin asked, as ever

concerned with practical matters. "When you are yourself injured?"

"He needs it more."

After a few gulps, he rose and came back to himself, though he still shook. "I must address the men."

"We will return with three boats," I said. "And thirty men with their arquebuses. You shoot them from the boats and I will cut them down. We can kill every last one of them."

He glared at me and I thought he was going to order just that. I am certain that he was tempted. Instead, he shook his head and let himself out of his cabin.

The men crowded around, astonished by the quick recovery of their leader.

"Cannons loaded, sir!" the master called. "Say the word and we'll blow the bastards to pieces."

Drake went to the side and looked back at the beach. It was packed with dancing natives, waving their weapons and shouting, though we could not hear them.

"Bloody savages!" men shouted. "Let's kill them. Let's kill them back, sir!"

Drake turned to look at his men. "I am at fault."

That shut them up.

"I am at fault. I did not see. But I see it now. The savages believe us to be Spaniards, for that is all they have known. How could they believe us to be any different? And I have no doubt the Spanish have wronged them in some way, or it is more likely they were wronged in many ways. And so they feel they have taken revenge."

"But sir, we can just shoot them!" a mariner called.

Drake shook his head, sadly. "Do you not hear me? They have suffered enough by the hands of the Spanish. Yes, we might take our revenge and it would be sweet enough, for a time. But that would make us no better than the Spanish. And I would give England a better account in these parts. This is why I shall not consent to an attack on them."

"But they killed Brewer! And Flood!"

Drake's head dropped. "They are dead, then. It is my fault. I did not see." He raised his head. "My friends, I hope in time you will come to understand. Now, let us see to the wounds of the injured and once that is done we shall weigh anchor and go north once more. The treasures of New Spain are there for the taking."

With that, he retired to his cabin again. I was left staring after him and I was not the only one.

Martin was breathless with admiration. "A fine thing. A fine thing, is it not?"

"We should go back and kill them," I said.

Martin started as if I had slapped him. "But it is a godly act, is it not, to turn one's cheek if one has been struck? Christ sought peace and so we must do the same, as best we are able. Do you not think his act a chivalrous one, sir?"

"Chivalry is meant for other Christians. Honourable deeds are to be done for our own people, not for those who have no conception of such things. They will forever believe they won a victory, and we shall feel the sting of defeat, because that is the truth and all men know it, be they Christian or savage."

He seemed disappointed in me. "Revenge is for the Lord and we should leave justice up to the wrath of God."

"Our general has a soft heart for the savages and I see you do, too. I may not have read the Bible, as you have, and I may not have your lofty lawyers' education, but I know that our fallen mariners should be revenged."

He thought me a barbarian. Perhaps he was right.

But soon enough, we weighed anchor and headed north towards the Spanish towns and ports of Chile and Peru.

Drake and his men hoped to make themselves rich. And I hoped to find the viceroy and place his head on a spike.

12

South Seas

1578

WE HAD EIGHTY-TWO MEN on the *Hind* but only about fifty of them were fully fit. I had taken every opportunity during the voyage to ensure they were well drilled and every man kept his firearm cleaned and was ready for action at a moment's notice.

Before we began our raiding in earnest, Drake reminded them of the rules. No man was allowed to purloin an ounce of plunder without the express permission of the General. Each man would go home rich enough to last him the rest of his days if only he could control his acquisitive urges until that day. Such things went on, of course, but if there was too much of it, it would lead to arguments, and fights, and seething resentment. We were on the far side of the world, with no Englishmen for thousands of miles, and so we could have no dissent.

I would command the men when boarding enemy ships or when assaulting positions on shore but otherwise I stayed out of giving orders or even relaying them. It was Drake's ship, through and through, and he demanded a certain formality. He would pull at the ropes with the rest of us, and he would carry casks of water from shore with us, but at the same time, he never let any man forget he was our leader.

At the daily dinner when dining with the officers, we would stand until Drake was seated. Our meals were served on fine plates while the musicians in the crew played softly on their trumpets or piped away on a shawm. That was another thing that Drake and I had in common, a love of music. He even had them play during the tedious religious services he insisted on holding during dining, which helped me get through them without striking Fletcher across the face. Often it was our Captain-General who led the singing of the Psalms or who read aloud from the Book of Martyrs. Every Sunday, even when in enemy waters, he insisted that every man wore his finest, cleanest clothing and ordered pennants and flats hoisted aloft.

Those services were the worst part of the voyage, other than the storms. When weather permitted, they would be held on the poop, where Drake or Fletcher would stand at a table to conduct the worship. Him and a small group of the men would kneel at the table and pray for a full fifteen minutes and then they would rise and he would read aloud for a full hour, then the musicians would play to accompany the singing of the Psalms.

He was a good man but all told he usually spent three hours a day at prayer. When he was not required to navigate or sail the ship, he would shut himself in his cabin and paint rather good pictures of birds, trees, seals, leaves, and all manner of other items taken and observed. Or he sat writing of events in meticulous detail.

But unseen by most of the men was his seething anger. When we were alone or in more intimate company, Drake would speak of revenge. He would ask about our plans for putting an end to the Viceroy of New Spain, Don Martin Enriquez, the criminal of San Juan de Ulúa. A bitterness was in his voice whenever we made our plans, and his eyes grew hard. I did not doubt that when he went to sleep at night, he envisioned the destruction of our enemy.

For him, the gentlemen, and for the crew, the treachery and loss at San Juan de Ulúa was cause enough, was justification for all the raids and the attacks and piracy that we were about to inflict on the Spanish.

Our first opportunity to redress the balance was at Valparaiso, the port of Santiago, Chile on 5th December 1578. It was a clear and warm day, with a slight but steady breeze blowing along the coast. A few white clouds formed over the land and out to sea it was a perfect blue. We crept into the harbour and there was a Spanish ship there at the outer part and they had no idea that we were their enemy. No English ships had ever been in the Pacific, no foreigners of any kind as far as they were concerned. And so why would they think anything different.

We crept closer and made anchor beside them and we lowered a boat and set out for that Spanish ship. The poor fools even drummed a welcome and waved and called greetings as we approached.

"Steady men," I muttered, turning from the bow of the boat.

"Keep your weapons sheathed, now. Steady."

When we came alongside, a keen and unpleasant cove named Tom Moone clambered up the side like a monkey, threw himself over the rail. I was up after him with more of the men coming behind. The men were under strict orders to avoid all violence that could be avoided. We would treat every prisoner as well as was possible, as long as he offered no resistance.

But before I could stop him, Tom Moone strode up to the closest Spaniard, formed a fist and swung his arm back.

"*Buenas noches*, Pedro!" Moone roared in his rough Devonshire accent, before cracking the smiling fellow in the jaw. "Go down, dog!"

"Moone!" I shouted and dragged him back from the decked victim.

The Spaniards cried out in alarm and they rushed toward us but our surprise had so thoroughly demoralised them that they quickly gave up as the rest of my boat crew came up and levelled their firearms at them.

We herded them down into the hold and they went obediently enough. But then I heard a cry of warning and then a splash and I ran to the side where our men stared down at the water.

A Spaniard had jumped from the ship and was swimming furiously for the town.

"He'll raise the alarm!" one of the men shouted and Moone raised his arquebus and aimed at the swimmer.

I shoved the weapon up and he cried out in protest.

"Your fire will alert the townsfolk just as much as that man will."

"Might as well shoot the bastard, then!" Moone shouted and tried to aim at him once more.

I shook my head. "Perhaps he will drown before reaching the shore."

"The Spaniard swims like a fish," one of my men said. "Look at him go!"

"Well good luck to him, then," I said. "We will not murder a man for doing his duty. And it makes no matter, for soon we will take the town anyway. It is already too late for them. There is nothing they can do to stop us."

As they walked away, I heard Moone muttering to the others. "Thought he was some big soldier what hated Spanish dogs more than anyone. Strikes me as a mewling runty mutton-headed—"

Grasping him by the back of his neck, I dragged him to the side, turned him about and stretched his back across the rail.

"Can you swim like a fish, Moone?"

"Get him off me!" he cried. "Help me!"

"I asked you a question," I said, not bothering to look at the rest of my men. "You will answer it." I pushed him further out and back.

"No! By God, I cannot swim."

"So, you would not like me to throw you over the side, Moone?"

"Please, no. You will murder me. It's murder! Murder!"

I nodded, bent and grasped him by the ankle and lifted him fully over the side so that he dangled by his ankle. "Perhaps it is time you learnt? You will sink or swim, Moone."

"I'm sorry!" he cried. "God help me, I'm right sorry, sir, right sorry. I beg you, Mister Richard, murder me not!"

I threw him to the deck where he curled up, taking shaky breaths and clutching the planks with his fingers. "Moone, Stobbart, Blake, guard the prisoners and watch the ship. The rest of you, back to the boat!"

Along with another boat from the *Hind*, we rushed the little town so that we might capture it. We were ready for a fight but the inhabitants had fled before we arrived.

My supposedly disciplined men ignored my orders and ransacked the port. Once I saw they were giddy with the thrill of the sack, I left them to it. If I had tried to stop them, I would have failed and I would have greatly reduced my authority. There was not much to be had, in all. Most of the men went straight for the town warehouse, expecting it to be piled high with mountains of gold and silver. Instead, we took sacks of flour and wine. A group of them rushed for the church and came back carrying all the silver that had been contained therein. It pained me to see it and for a moment I considered forcing them to return it but again, it would have diminished me. And so I silently watched them laughing and clapping each other on the back, overjoyed at the value of the silver and thrilled to have dispossessed the Catholics of their idolatrous treasures.

From the ship in the harbour, we took their pilot who knew the local waters, and unloaded their wine and four chests containing a total of 25,000 pesos worth of gold.

It was a perfectly good first engagement but now we had to move quickly. There was a truly vast coast to raid and we had to stay ahead of the news.

"This is what we must do," Drake said that evening to the officers. "We must continue to search for the *Elizabeth*. There is still hope that they survived the storm and if they did they will meet us as agreed." We did not know then, of course, that the *Elizabeth* was on its way back to England. "As you know, we must build a pinnace which we will need for cutting out prizes and generally allowing us to take other actions."

Building a pinnace, a sailing boat large enough to hold a decent amount of men and provisions to operate independently for days at a time would give us the operational flexibility necessary for our plans.

"We must also gather provisions now while we yet have a few days, and of course we must make the repairs to the *Hind* and properly mount our cannon ready for the coming battles." He looked around at his men. "At the same time, we must not linger long. All work must occur at great speed for if news of our presence here passes north ahead of us it will scare away the prizes and the Spanish at Lima or elsewhere will have time enough to mount a great and coordinated opposition to us. We are powerful, my friends. Our ship is strong, our men are trained to perfection but there are thousands of Spanish here, hundreds of ships. If half a dozen ships of war are on this coast and they come for us together, all our efforts so far will have been for nought. So! Speed, my dear fellows, speed!"

It was already too late. Word had already reached the Governor of Chile and he wasted not a moment. He fitted his best vessel with stores, powder, and a hundred men to destroy us. He also sent another ship to Callao, the port of Lima, to tell them of our raid on Valparaiso and then concentrated on fortifying every port in Chile against us.

Two weeks later, we were readying to spring north. Anchored

in a bay south of Coquimbo, two boats went in to shore to collect water.

They were ambushed by the Spanish.

No mere band of local townsfolk, either, but a full company of soldiers and cavalry, armed and armoured, supported by their auxiliary force of naked brown Indians. Our men on shore were not totally surprised, as we knew it was enemy country. But we had no idea they could field such a force so far south. Of course, they were there to protect the settlements against the persistent threat of the hostile tribes. Seeing and hearing the approaching soldiers, our men fled through the surf to shelter behind and amongst a great mound of rocks.

One lad did not escape the charging cavalry. His name was Richard Minivy and one of the horsemen shot him in the back. He fell forward into the waves, throwing his hands out as he collapsed. Indians on foot rushed forward and dragged the dead or dying Minivy out of the surf to where the cavalry were dismounting.

All of us on the ship were watching by this point, shouting from out in the bay as if they could hear us. Quickly, Drake ordered rescue boats to be launched and while the crew rushed to do that, and to arm themselves, I turned and shouted orders of my own.

"Cannons! Load the starboard cannon!"

Martin came rushing forward with his arquebus and mine in hand and I followed him to the boats. Before we got there, the men at the rails roared in anger and I turned in time to see a Spanish horseman hacking into Minivy's chest with a knife, sawing and cutting frantically before reaching in and ripping his heart out. The Spaniard held his bloody prize up to us, shouting defiance. Behind him, other men sawed through Minivy's neck with a sword and soon held his head aloft to us.

"How could they?" Martin cried. "How could they?"

Our men were roaring in rage, the *Hind* growling like some monstrous beast.

"I'll kill them," I said to Martin, then raised my voice. "I'll kill them all. Every bloody one of them. Come on!"

But while we were rowing toward the rocks where our party huddled, firing an occasional shot at any Spaniard or Indian who approached, the *Hind's* cannons boomed.

Our artillery damaged only trees and threw up showers of sand but that and the sight of twenty angry, heavily armed Englishmen coming to reinforce the ones at the rocks caused the Spaniards to turn and flee.

We lined up to fight, pikes and axes, arquebuses and swords, but the enemy ran back to their inland fort and stayed there until we left. Which we did, taking Minivy's mutilated corpse with us.

"They act like savages," Martin said, staring blankly into the distance as our boats crashed through the surf on the way back to the Hind. "How can they do that?"

"Catholics," one of the rowers said and spat over the gunwales.

"It's them savages," another more enlightened mariner offered between oar strokes. "They learnt it off them savages. Don't see that in Spain. Stands to reason."

Martin looked to me. "Have you ever seen anything like that before, Richard?"

I did not return his look but nodded. "And worse."

"But not from Englishmen?"

Not for a few years, I almost said but the flippant words stuck in my throat as Minivy's head rolled beneath the benches to my feet. Before it could roll back again, I placed my foot on it, then picked it up and put it on my lap.

"Sorry, lad," I said quietly to him. "I will pray for you."

That act of savagery by a handful of men only increased Drake's hatred for Spaniards. He thought they were not like us because they were savages, torturers, and Catholics, and above all they were treacherous. I was all of those things except treacherous and I hoped to one day no longer be a savage but Drake had not quite seen those parts of my nature and when we came back he turned his anger on me, going so far as jabbing me in the chest with his finger.

I stood and accepted it, like a good subordinate, and refrained from snapping his neck.

"From now on," he said, still shaking with the frustration and the fury, "you will accompany every shore party. No matter how simple and easy it may seem. No matter how uninhabited the land appears. You will be first onto every shore, with your sword drawn, and you shall be the last back into the boats, do you understand, sir?"

"I would have it no other way."

He caught the look in my eye and flinched, stepping back and nodding before dismissing me.

By the time the pinnace was built, the men were spoiling for a fight. They needed one and I did too. The pinnace had a gun in the bow and was big enough for almost forty men, half our number. With the *Golden Hind* and the pinnace we raided small ports, villages, and took traders and fishermen on our way north.

At the port of Chule, a tiny place with a single ship in its harbour, we pulled alongside in the pinnace and went aboard the small ship while the sailors stood powerless. We took them prisoner and guarded them but as always did them no harm and treated them as well as we could under the circumstances.

I went straight to the captain's cabin and pulled out the books. "Take the charts," I commanded Martin. "And the logs and everything else you can find."

"I know, I know..." he muttered, filling his arms with it.

But I found what I was looking for. The ship's manifest, with its ink barely dried. Taking it back out to the deck, I found Drake questioning the Spanish captain.

"Where is the bullion?" I asked him at once.

Drake looked annoyed for a moment but then turned on the Spaniard. "What bullion is this?"

I handed our General the manifest and placed a hand on the Spanish captain's shoulder. "Captain," I said in his own language, "I am not like these other Englishmen. I like Spaniards. In fact, I can honestly say that in all my life, I hardly met one I did not like. Please, do not make me start now."

He opened his mouth, closed it to swallow, and opened it again. "May I have some wine, sir?"

"Tell me where you hid your bullion and I shall give you a barrel of it."

He shook his head. "It is onshore. It was unloaded."

"You are lying. It is still on your manifest."

"We had word, sir. Word that..."

"Go on," Drake prompted.

"Word that... pirates were coming. English pirates. The mayor of Chule sent all his men. And the bullion was taken ashore to be guarded by his soldiers and all the natives."

It was clear Drake was enraged but he stayed calm and spoke with surprising politeness. "How many days ago did you receive this word?"

The Spanish captain swallowed again. "We finished unloading perhaps two hours ago, sir."

We hung our heads for a moment and the men around us gaped in astonishment.

"Where?" I asked him.

"Just around the headland," he replied, nodding that way. "A small fort."

"Cannons?" I asked.

He hesitated before shaking his head.

"You better not be lying to me," I said. "Because I have to say, as it stands, I like you."

"No cannons, I swear it. Just earthworks, sir." He looked up with a glint of fire in his eye. "But they are well guarded by the militia, with firearms and plenty of powder. And the Indians are armed with bows. You will not get near by land or by sea. The bullion is lost to you."

I smiled and reached slowly for his face. He flinched and I gently slapped his cheek a couple of times. "You are a good man, captain. A credit to your fine people."

We locked the crew away in the hold and left behind just enough men to sail her out after us. Heading up the coast, we had barely begun when we saw the little fort there on the shore, atop a headland. It was heaving with men and bristling with pikes and arquebuses over the tops of the banks, which were topped with low walls. We anchored the *Hind* and the pinnace and discussed how we might assault it and take their treasure.

"What do you think?" Drake asked.

"Can't you blast them to pieces with the cannons?"

He shrugged. "It is not easy to hit something so small and we can go no closer because of the shoals. Perhaps the pinnace can chip away at them but they will duck behind their earthen and stone banks and those we will not damage. Not enough."

"They have men enough to cover the approach and there is no cover. Our boys will be shot to pieces."

"Damn them. Two hours, Richard! Two hours earlier and we would have had it."

"Word is getting out. We should hurry now to get ahead of it."

He did not seem to hear me. "If we wait until nightfall and rush them in the darkness."

"Might work. But even if it does, we'll lose men. Perhaps a lot of men."

Drake rubbed his eyes. "If we could scare them out, somehow. Or wait them out. It looks as though there is no water source within, we could post companies to stop them getting out to collect water. It will be two days, three at the most before they surrender."

I nodded. "Assuming no reinforcements come, that would work. But we are not here just for bullion, are we, Francis."

He looked from them to me. "We are not."

"And every day we spend here is another for word to travel along the tracks and trails north. If they are prepared for us, our greatest advantage will be lost."

He removed his hat for a moment, rubbed his eyes and scratched his scalp, before pulling it back on again. "We will run for Lima."

The local troops jeered us, calling us foul thieves, Lutheran dogs, and mocking us for being too late. We left them sitting on a fortune and headed for Callao, the port of Lima.

* * *

Speed was all that mattered. Drake set all prizes adrift, released all the prisoners other than two pilots, and thanked God for the stiff wind that took us north, the ship and pinnace heeling over as they clipped through the white-capped sea.

Even so, Drake could not resist taking the small prizes we found on the way and though I chafed at every delay it was a good thing for us that he did. From the captain of one small vessel, we had a remarkable tale.

"Anchored at Callao," the portly little captain said, his legs planted wide on his deck, "is a vessel belonging to Miguel Angel named the *San Cristobal*, bound for Panama with a hold stuffed with silver."

We grinned and shook his hand but he was not finished.

"There is another treasure ship, and you may find her nearby. She is the *Nuestra Señora de la Concepción*. They call her the *Cacafuego*."

Drake and I turned to each other.

"*Cacafuego?*" Drake muttered to me and spoke English. "Does that mean…"

I nodded. "Fire-shitter."

We shrugged and turned back to the captain. "You said we may find her nearby. She is not at Callao?"

He shook his head. "She departed on the same tide that I did. She goes north, to Panama, with the treasure shipment."

"How much?"

"All of it."

I nodded. "When you say all, what do you mean?"

He rubbed his soft cheeks. "It carries the entire year's treasure from Lima to Panama."

For a moment, I thought Drake was going to vomit in shock. Our men near enough to hear muttered and the word spread like lightning from the deck of the prize, to our boats, the pinnace and the *Hind* bobbing beside us.

We stepped back to confer, speaking excitedly and Drake seemed weak at the knees. "If it has just departed, we may catch it yet."

I jerked my head at the little man. "Can we trust him?"

Drake glanced around me to look at the captain. "Can we not?"

"Black Walter always says never trust a fat man."

"Black Walter sounds like a fool."

"He is. And yet, somehow, he is rarely wrong."

We returned to the captain. "Why do you tell us this?" Drake asked.

"Because the Viceroy of New Spain Enríquez de Almanza is a dirty cheating, murdering bastard." He turned and spat downwind and his gob of phlegm shot away out to sea. The little fellow spoke with anger but there was real pain behind his eyes.

"And because you will let me go with my crew and my cargo intact."

"A murdering bastard, you say? And do you know if they say he likes to drink blood?" I asked. "Human blood?"

The captain started. "I never heard that. But I would not be surprised to hear it."

"You have strong feelings about him."

Our portly captain shook with anger. "He is a thief, a killer, ripping the heart from this land."

"What precise rumours have you heard about his murderous nature?"

"My wife was..." He shook his head. "They take people. And then they are never seen again. I rarely go north to Panama anymore. Not since Enriquez made his residence there."

"And Viceroy Enriquez is still there, in Panama? Are you certain?"

"He went to oversee the treasure shipments. Some Englishmen stole a great shipment a while ago and so Enriquez squats on Panama like a devil bird on his nest." He spat again and made a sign against evil.

Drake let the man go, with his ship, crew and cargo intact and he even gifted the man an engraved silver platter and a fine velvet cushion.

"Did you hear what he said about the Viceroy?" I said to Drake on the way back to the *Hind*. "We must rush to Panama at once."

"First, we will go to the port of Lima and take the treasure ship, this *Fire-shitter*, and then we will sail on to Panama, where you can do your work."

"All that matters is that we kill Don Martin Enriquez in

Panama."

"We will take the treasure ship at Lima, then fly with all haste for Panama. Agreed?"

I sighed. "Very well."

By chance, we reached Callao, the port of Lima, late in the evening and the officers gathered in Drake's cabin for a discussion on how to proceed. All agreed that it was too much of a risk to raid the ships in the harbour in the darkness, as we would not be able to see the boats we launched and if our boats and pinnace were separated from the *Hind* and we had to flee, we risked either leaving men behind to be captured, or having the *Hind* engaged by enemy ships before we could get away.

"You will be leading one of the boarding parties and yet you have been silent so far, Richard," Drake prompted. "Do you also think we should wait until morning?"

I shrugged. "You all have more experience than I do in this sort of thing. You talk of timing assaults to coincide with wind and tide and I will accept your wisdom in this arena."

The officers nodded in satisfaction but Drake was clearly not getting the answers he wanted.

"What would you do if it were a land battle? If you arrived at an enemy position on horseback or on foot, when tides were not a factor. Would you assault at sundown or sunrise?"

"It depends on the circumstances. I have led men in full darkness before. With good men who know their business, it can be done. But if the men are inexperienced, poorly led, and if things begin to go wrong, you can find yourself in unrecoverable chaos."

"Ah," the master cut in, "so you agree we must wait until

morning? Good, good."

"Not necessarily. Men expect an assault at first light and those on watch are more alert. And, gentlemen, the tides are not the only forces at work here. Our goal is not to raid the port of Callao and return to England. We must hit them, hard and fast, and before they can understand what has happened we must run north once more. And, my friends, think of our men. They are armed, they are ready, their blood is up. We should let them loose now, while the fire is in their bellies. By morning our men's hearts may have grown cold, while the enemy's begins to kindle."

Drake rapped his knuckles on the tables. "We shall begin now. Richard, you will cross to the pinnace and lead us in." He fired off his final instructions and the officers filed out while wishing each other luck. Before I left, he grabbed my arm. "I thank you."

I smiled. "I do not know why you hold these conferences. No matter what any of them say, you just do what you want anyway."

"They must have their say, you know that. And having at least one other voice with me makes me seem less the tyrant."

"Load the cannons, ready the lanterns and be prepared to run out of here at a moment's notice, Francis."

"Always. God be with you."

After I crossed to the pinnace, we slid quietly between the island of San Lorenzo and the mainland and on into the harbour. It was a forest of masts. More ships than I had seen together anywhere since leaving England. The sky was still illuminated and many ships displayed lanterns, and lights in the town were being lit but still it was hard to count how many.

"Sixteen ships?" I asked the master's mate from the bow, peering through the gloom.

He stared at me like I was mad. "More like twenty-six, sir."

Martin was with me, as always and he hissed close to my ear. "So many! Should we call it off?"

"Too late for that, now."

"Indeed, it is not," Martin countered. "It is a brave commander who knows when to abandon his best-laid plans when the situation calls for it."

I turned to look at him. "Did you read that in a book?"

It was too dark to see but I am certain he blushed. "Wisdom is wisdom, wheresoever it might be found."

"Hmm," I said. "Sounds like more book-learnt nonsense to me. All will be well. They can't all come out at once, can they." I turned to the mate. "They can't all come out at once, can they?"

"Bloody hope not," he replied. "And not if we do our job proper."

The *Hind* put out two boats and together we went forward without crying out strokes or directions but instead speaking softly. We peered ahead at the shore and at the merchant ships, waiting for questions or even a cannon firing at us.

But it was quiet. The moon was little more than a slither rising above us and the stars came out in a clear sky. It seemed God was granting enough light to work by.

We pulled the pinnace to the largest ship in the harbour while our boats went forward and began boarding each ship in turn. I came up over the side of the Spanish merchant ship and looked around. My eye may not have been experienced but it appeared to yet be stowed for sea, not for unloading. It also seemed deserted but after a moment I could hear voices below or in the aft cabin. With a handful of my men, I went aft and threw open the door into the cabin.

They were having dinner.

"Good evening, sirs!" I cried in Spanish. "I have come to inspect your ship!"

They took one look at me and knew something was wrong. The captain jumped to his feet, scowling. "The customs officers came aboard this morning. What is this?"

I bowed. "I am terribly sorry, captain, but I have to take you and your men into custody and I think we will also take your ship and everything on it."

The rest of his men jumped to their feet but my men came in behind me with their weapons aimed and the captain told his men to stand down.

"By what authority do you seize our property?"

I grinned. "By the authority of Captain Francis Drake, the English pirate. Now, I am afraid you shall have to take the cheese course in the hold. This way, my friends!"

The captain I stopped with my hand on his chest. "You will regret this," he said.

"Possibly. Now, tell me, are you Miguel Angel?"

He frowned. "I am. How did you know?"

"And so this is the *San Cristobal*?"

"You know me and you know my ship. How?"

"We met a good friend of the Viceroy. He says you have a hold stacked with silver. Please, show me where it is."

Now it was his turn to grin and my own fell away. "It is not yet loaded. It is still in the customs house. We agreed with the officers today that we would load it in the morning."

"You are lying."

"I assure you, I am not. Do you intend to assault the customs house?"

Chewing my lip, I thought it over. "How many men do they have ashore?"

He smiled. "Two hundred soldiers, both foot and horse. Please, I beg you, assault the customs house with your... how many men?"

"What is the value of the silver?"

He hesitated but he could not resist rubbing it in my face. "Two hundred thousand pesos' worth."

"You will get below with your men. I am taking you and your ship anyway and when I have you out at sea, I will decide whether or not to cut your throats before I throw you over the side."

That shut him up, at least, but we searched the ship and he did not appear to be lying.

There was no silver.

I left behind the master's mate and nine men. They reckoned they could together guard the prisoners and also sail the ship out of the harbour and so I took the rest of my men into the pinnace and on to the next ship.

There were twenty-nine ships in the harbour and we searched most of them. Any crew on them we locked away, and my men and the men in our boats set about expertly crippling every ship. They hacked and sawed through rigging and cables and on the two largest ships they decided they would cut down the masts.

"That will rather give the game away, I fear," I said.

"Cripple the ships, the General said!" my men cried. "And this is how it might best be done."

They were angry that we had found no silver and few valuables and so I let them chop away while others cut the ropes that held the masts aloft.

"At least let us do this ship and the other at the same time," I advised and so we went to the next largest ship to do the same thing.

"We don't want to be standing here when it goes, sir," one of the men said, as politely as he could while I stared up at the top of the swaying mast.

"Oh, indeed. How right you are," I said and we ran for the pinnace.

Before we had completed our final tasks, shouts came from across the water and yelling came from the shore.

"Time to go, men!" I called but they were determined to do the job and then almost in the same moment, the mainmasts on those two big ships fell. Both tumbled into the rigging and spars rather than collapsing like felled trees but it was nice work nonetheless.

I counted every one of my mariners back in, other than the ten that sailed the *San Cristobal* out of the harbour. We sailed and pulled hard for the *Hind* while all hell broke loose behind us.

"What happened?" I asked the other men when I came back to the flagship.

The sailors were grinning as they told it. "The Spaniards came out to inspect us. They thought we was a Spanish ship and we called out in Spanish and they came up the side about halfway but then he sees our cannons sticking out. He near enough jumped down into his boat and they bolted for the shore like a shit off a shovel."

"Did you try to stop them fleeing?"

"Wanted to but the General wouldn't let us shoot them." They were disappointed.

The sailors anchored our vessels just offshore until sunrise. We went over every inch of the *San Cristobal* but the silver truly was not there. All the prisoners we had taken up to that point we transferred to the *San Cristobal* and set it adrift. Their friends would tow it back to port, when they came out.

"You failed," Miguel Angel said to me before I went back to my boat. "And now you will slink back to England."

He was goading me in the hope of getting me to reveal our plans. "That's right," I replied. "Back home now. We are already rich men, thanks to the prizes we have taken so far. Tell me, what do you know of the Viceroy of New Spain, Martín Enríquez de Almanza?"

Angel's face twisted in disgust. "I know to stay out his way. Him and his beast."

"What beast?"

"You are a pirate. Why should I tell you anything?"

"Because I am a pirate and I will cut your throat if you do not."

His eyes shone with fire. "You have treated all of us very well. I do not believe you."

I whipped out my knife, grabbed him with my off hand and held him fast, while putting the edge of my blade to his neck. "I will."

He was shaking all over. "Do it then," he said and lifted his chin higher. A brave man.

How I wanted to slit his throat and drink from him as he died. Instead, I let him go and the *San Cristobal* drifted south in the current while the *Hind* and our pinnace raced north once more,

more eager than ever to catch the treasure ship *Nuestra Señora de la Concepción*, known as the *Cacafuego*.

Lima sent two ships after us that very day which were packed with soldiers but they had no cannons, as far as we could tell, and they gave up before sundown. The question on everyone's mind then was the *Cacafuego*. Could we catch it before it reached Panama? Would we even find it in that vast ocean?

It was a busy stretch of coast, between Panama and Lima and we chased down and took every ship we could and asked them for news of the *Cacafuego*. We heard how it had stopped for flour four days previously at a small port, from another we heard it was now three days ahead of us. We came to a small port named Paita and they had no defence against us and so we landed men and demanded they tell us all they could. The *Cacafuego* had stopped just two days earlier.

The men were by now giddy with excitement and I was beginning to feel it, also. Standing at the bow, clinging to the rigging and straining my eyes on the horizon, I felt the sun on my face and the spray of the water slowly drenching me. I knew I would have to comb the salt from my hair later but in that moment, I breathed it in. Below me the ship pitched and shook as it rode the waves, slicing through the water and travelling with it. Every sail was out and full to burst and they caught the sun and shone like some great, strange bird swooping over the water. In my hand, the rope quivered and creaked and all the rigging hummed in the wind. I found myself laughing.

"You alright, Mister Richard?" one of the mariners asked as he and another went forward to adjust some rope tied near the prow.

"It feels alive," I called to him, no doubt seeming like a madman. "It feels like the ship is some mighty beast that we are barely taming."

I could hear the edge of hysteria in my voice but they did not mock me as I thought they would. Instead, they nodded and spoke with deep sincerity.

"She's a beast, alright," one cried, slapping a hand on the timbers. "She's our *Golden Hind*."

The other man looked out across the blue expanse before. "Only she's the hunter now, eh?"

I got so excited by it all that I even made the climb, for the first time in my life, to the top of the mainmast for a four-hour watch. It amused the sailors because they could always tell how frightened I was of going aloft. On a handful of occasions I had climbed the ratlines up into the fighting top which was two-thirds of the way up and provided a platform where the men could shoot down at enemy vessels. And I had found the experience rather unpleasant, much to the delight of the men. But the route above the main topsail to the cross trees was a different matter and I found my hands shaking as I made my way up to it.

"That's it, sir," the sailor said above me. "Up you come."

It was not the height itself, although it was ninety feet to the deck and a fall from that height would at the very least shatter my bones and could dash my brains out. More than anything, though, it was the alarming swaying that occurred at such a height. While on deck, the ship rolled and pitched always but when climbing high above it, those movements were amplified many times, so that one traced a shape in the air with every wave, swinging out and forward and back again in a mighty, never-ending arc.

"Let's just lash you on here, sir," the mariner said, loosening the ropes there so I could slide my legs through them. These he pulled tight over my thighs. "All well now, sir?"

"You will come and get me," I said, "at the end of my watch?"

"Course I will, sir. As long as you don't fall off."

He swung himself down and scrambled down toward the fighting top which seemed a long way below. Below that, the deck seemed impossibly far away and then I found myself swinging far out over the sea. If I fell into it, the fall would stun me, perhaps even break my neck and I would likely drown before the ship could slow and a boat could be launched to pick me up. I clung to the mast, pressing the side of my face against it and wondered why in the world I had volunteered for such a thing.

"The horizon, sir!" the mariner called from below. He was leaning back on the ratlines, holding on with one hand as we began swinging the other way and jabbing his other hand northward. "Watch the horizon!"

I have lived a long time but that uneventful yet terrifying watch was one of the most unpleasant four hours I have ever spent and when I came down I brought with me a far deeper respect for the sailors who clambered about up there in all weathers, in storms, fearlessly. I also swore never to do it again.

The *Nuestra Señora de la Concepción* was sighted at dawn, two days later off Cape San Francisco, right on the equator.

A sail, four leagues to seaward. The chase was on and every man worked the ship with everything he had. Our prey did not even know it was being chased, it had no idea there was any danger in those seas and so we caught up to it steadily while it sailed on.

It was a good-sized ship. Not a ship of war but they believed they had nothing to fear from another vessel coming up at her on the same tack. And Drake, cunning man that he was, contrived to help them believe that for as long as possible. He ordered pots and buckets be tied to ropes and thrown aft which acted as a drag upon our ship and this allowed us to put out full sail without coming up too quickly. From a distance, coming straight at the prize, we must have looked like a heavily laden merchant ship going as quickly as we could.

Our general also ordered the master of the pinnace to hide behind the *Hind* while we approached and this he did with an almost supernatural skill. It took nine hours in all to reach the ship. When we came close, we waved at the crew lining the rails and they waved back, looking forward to trading news with us as we sailed together into Panama.

Instead, Drake ordered the pinnace to surge forward to engage the treasure ship's other flank. Our men pulled in the buckets so that we could spring ahead if she slipped out of our grasp.

While the Spanish crew stood gaping at the pinnace that raced out from behind us to circle them, Drake took the *Hind* across the *Cacafuego*'s stern with our gun ports open and the cannons poking out.

Drake turned to me. "Now, if you please, Richard."

I had the most powerful lungs on the ship and I stood at the rail, cupped my hands and roared across the waves to the Spanish in their own language.

"Englishmen! We are Englishmen. Strike sail! You will strike sail!"

They were stunned and perhaps frantically thinking of a way

out of their predicament. The *Cacafuego* sailed on.

"Call the captain by name," Drake said to me. "Tell him we will fire."

I turned back to them and took a deep breath once more. "Captain San Juan de Anton! Surrender! Surrender or we shall sink you!"

The men on her decks were frantic but they made no moves to lower their sails. Indeed, though they had no artillery, I saw that the crew were beginning to arm themselves. Pikes and arquebuses were being passed up and passed around.

I was not the only one to notice.

"Very well," Drake said, his arms clasped behind his back. He turned to the master's mate. "Give the signal."

The order was relayed and the trumpeter sounded a blast.

From the gun deck, half of our cannons fired one after the other as each came to bear on the enemy ship. The sound even up on the command deck was appalling and the smoke billowed out between the ships.

Our cannons balls smashed into the rigging at the rear of their ship with astonishing force, sending ropes whipping and great splinters flying. With that first steady volley, their mizzen mast at the rear of the ship fell across the decks, sending them into a panic.

Immediately after our artillery fired, our men stepped up to the rail from the stern to the forecastle with their arquebuses and shot across at the crew. From our fighting tops, the men there also fired, shooting down at the vulnerable officers where possible. Those that did not have arquebuses shot their longbows, loosing yard-long arrows over the sea to drive into the timbers of the

395

Spanish ship.

We were not trying to murder them. Drake had ordered the men to shoot the ship, not the men, and only a single Spaniard was injured. But it was enough to send most of them fleeing below.

Captain Anton did not run. He stood glaring at us across the water with his hands clasped behind his back and his legs planted wide, even as he ordered his flag lowered.

Our pinnace threw their grapples and pulled alongside and in no time there were Englishmen swarming over the side to take them all prisoner.

Soon, Captain Anton was brought over to the *Hind* and escorted to Drake's cabin.

The Spaniard was distraught but he hid it quite well, bowing and holding out his sword with his documents under one arm.

Drake stepped forward and embraced him before stepping back. "I bid you have patience, captain. Such is the custom of war."

Still out at sea, over the next two days we transferred everything from the *Nuestra Señora de la Concepción* to the *Hind*. Boat after boat had to be filled.

Martin did the work of tracking it all, toiling tirelessly at Drake's desk. There were fourteen chests of silver reals, eighty pounds of gold, and twenty-six tons of silver bars of registered cargo valued at 360,000 pesos.

When the calculations were made and cross-referenced with the treasure we had brought across, Drake nodded at Martin calmly, though I noticed his hands were shaking.

"And what is that, Mister Hawthorn, in English—"

"It is approximately one hundred and twenty-six English pounds, captain," Martin said.

I could not help but laugh aloud at their expressions. "A tidy sum."

Martin nodded. "I believe the annual revenues of the English Crown are not much greater."

It was Drakes turn to laugh. "The voyage is made." He stared. "My fortune is made. We have done it."

Martin shook his head. "That is not all, however," he said, and took up a sheathe of notes. "There was also unregistered treasure."

Drake nodded. "Of course. How much?"

"I must check it again, you understand, and I will not be held to these figures. The value I have calculated based on the values cited in the manifest for the registered silver and gold but the actual value at point of sale will of course—"

"How much, Mister Hawthorn?"

"Four hundred thousand pesos."

Drake and I looked at each other for some moments.

"You must be wrong," Drake said.

Martin shrugged. "It is entirely possible."

"You are wrong," Drake said again. "Why would they have so much of their cargo unregistered? It is a lot to risk?"

"Does it say who the registered cargo is owned by?"

"It does. They keep meticulous records. Approximately half is owned by King Philip and the rest is divided between a number of private persons, many of whom are leading Spanish nobles as you would expect."

"Anyone you recognise from the Order of the White Dagger's books?"

"No."

Drake's head snapped up. "Any of the registered cargo for Don Martín Enríquez?"

"No."

I nodded to them both. "So, perhaps, we might assume the unregistered cargo is bound for William and his men."

"It is a fortune," Drake said. "With this much, he could fund an army and a fleet."

"He could," I said. "But we have it now." We smiled at each other but I noticed Martin gaping at us. "Why are you glaring at me like a dead fish, son?"

"This is one treasure ship," he said, jabbing a finger at his list of unregistered treasure. "How many more ships have William and Don Martín Enríquez filled with their own treasure, meant for their own private wars. How many years has William been doing this? What has he been doing with all this gold and silver? Has he amassed it or has he been spending it?"

"Christ's balls," I said, causing Drake to snap his eyes on me and glare reproachfully. I pointed a finger at his face. "Give me none of your righteousness, Francis. God will allow me to utter an oath at such dire news, I have no doubt."

"What can be done about it?"

I shook my head. "Here? With eighty men? I do not know. Likely, we can do nothing but strike at Don Martín Enríquez and run for home."

Behind the desk, Martin stood and spoke as if he were the elder and we were green boys. "That is well but we have to pass all those places we attacked and all of them will be looking for us. What if they have fortified the strait, how could we fight our way through?"

"We shall go south into the open sea," Drake replied. "But you are quite right, Mister Hawthorn. And before we may even do any of that, we have business in Panama. Have you questioned the Spanish, Richard?"

"I have."

"And what do they say of the viceroy?"

"It is just as we have heard at every port along the way. The Viceroy of New Spain continues to personally oversee the Camino Real and is residing outside of the town of Panama."

"The *Hind* is in need of repair. We must find a safe harbour, make preparations for the journey home and then we shall go to Panama. The bastard will pay for his crimes. I cannot wait to see his face as he dies."

"No," I said. "That will be too late. Even if we change our minds and do not set the *Cacafuego* free, other men will already be sending word to Panama and if we wait, the Viceroy may flee to New Spain and hide in the city of Mexico. It will be difficult to reach him there."

Drake grunted. "Impossible, more like. But Panama is well defended and we are heavily laden indeed, with a bottom in need of scraping and leaking timbers. That is to say nothing of rigging that needs resetting and sails needing repair. If the Spanish warships come out at us, I do not know that we can stand."

"The *Hind* can go north and find somewhere to wait. All I need is the pinnace and enough men to sail her well."

"Of course, but what can be achieved with so small a force?"

"All I need is for them to get me to the coast, north or south, undetected. Put into a bay, send me off in a boat to a beach. I will take a few days' worth of water and food and I shall march for the Viceroy's Palace."

"Alone?"

"Anyone who comes with me will by their weakness ruin the entire enterprise. Yes, I shall go alone. And when I find the Viceroy, I shall strike off his head."

"But you will have to escape, across miles of this pestilential forest with all the soldiers and cavalry of Panama hunting you, perhaps for days. It is madness."

"And yet it must be done. Unless you can think of a better way? I hope that you can, because I do not relish the prospect as it stands."

Drake thought for a moment before shaking his head. "If it were any other man, I would say for certain that it could not be done. But as it is Richard Ashbury that proposes it?" He shrugged. "I give you one chance in ten."

I nodded. "Let us be at it, then."

13

Viceroy

1578

THE PROW SCRAPED on the sand in the darkness and I leapt into the surf, soaking myself to the balls as I waded forward. Behind me, the men backed their oars and hissed their blessings as I ducked low and made for the black tree line ahead.

Panama was flat in those parts. Between the coast and the hills in the north was only seven or eight miles and some of that coastal plain east of the town was farmland, hacked from the dense jungle.

They had landed me at the mouth of a creek about thirteen miles east of the town and so I kept the sea to my left and headed west, keeping to the edge of fields so that I might dart into the trees if detected.

All my life, I have loved woodlands, and trees, and the animals that live in them. But that was European forest, temperate forest of the northern latitudes. That equatorial forest was a horror. The trees were all wrong, from their trunks to their leaves, which were the wrong colour, and the wrong texture. Waxy great leaves, giant fronds, wild vines, impenetrable thickets of dense bushes. And the crawling, creeping, monstrous creatures that dangled from every branch or slinked across every path were even worse. Rushing through such a place in the dark left me cursing everyone from Drake to myself, my friends, and the immortal viceroy. William I cursed the most, for he was the cause of all of it.

By going out across the fields, I made better time and I simply prayed that no farmer would see me in the moonlight. Anyway, I ran so hard that he might have mistaken me for some jungle creature rather than a man. My best hope was still that the Spanish did not yet know there was any danger and would have no more lookouts than usual.

But my hopes were soon dashed.

When I came closer to the town, I slowed and caught my breath. Panama was well illuminated by dozens of lamps, in houses, on poles, and held aloft by the men that stood or ranged about the outskirts. There were voices and the sounds of hooves. Steel flashed between the houses and every now and then clashed together.

Armed men and cavalry were abroad.

The core of the settlement lay across a stream, where the church and its square stone bell tower stood above it all. Lights were lit in that tower, perhaps serving as a beacon for Spanish shipping. The dock was further up the coast, in the mouth of a navigable river about five miles beyond. With any luck, I thought, the watching men would be focused on that approach. But that was assuming they were alerted to the rampaging Englishmen rather than trouble with the local Indians. I had no idea but either way, I had to go on.

The town itself was not my concern. All I had to do was avoid it and the soldiers that patrolled it and I would be well. I was headed for the Viceroy's Palace, about five miles north where the land just begins to rise along a track that was never patrolled at night. Or so I had been told.

Circling the town, I crossed a flimsy bridge of planks to that track and turned north, looking over my shoulder at the lights and activity of the town behind me, wary of being spotted from afar. I was in deep shadow, however, due to the growth of mature trees on either side. Indeed, I soon found myself unable to see so much as my hand in front of my face in that blackness and had to trust instead to the feel of the gritty sand under my shoes. Some assassin I was, approaching my target with both hands spread before me as I shuffled forward, like a drunkard searching for the chamber pot.

A horse approached.

I froze as the sound of hooves at a canter reached me.

Many horses, I realised, many horses approaching from ahead. And there was a glow up there, reflecting on the trees from beyond a bend. Quickly, I pushed off the path a little way before finding that the bank of the stream was closer than I had anticipated. I grabbed wildly at the branches and leaves flapping in my face and clung on lest I fall into the vile jungle ditch.

The horses approached and I ducked, turning my face away. Nothing jumps out at a man like a face in the darkness. Two or more of the horsemen held lamps aloft, and behind them came a two-wheeled cart being pulled by a single horse, with its own lamp dangling on a pole. Jangling buckles and shining helms told me that at least some of the men were soldiers. They went past about as rapidly as anyone could on horseback in the dark and as they disappeared, I wondered if they had had word of my landing and were heading to reinforce the town.

At least they were riding away from the Viceroy's Palace.

I froze.

Perhaps the Viceroy was making an escape. Was he going to the town to be amongst the companies of soldiers where he would be safe? Or was he going beyond the town to the dock along the coast, to disembark and flee for New Spain?

But surely no ship would set sail in darkness, even if the pilot knew well the waters of Panama Bay.

And were a dozen soldiers a large enough escort for the most powerful man in the New World?

It did not seem likely.

Besides, I could not very likely make my way through the town without being seen and I did not fancy my chances against a hundred or more men with pikes and firearms, plus horse, and cannon.

And so I vowed to press on for the Viceroy's estate.

The Viceroy of New Spain had always lived in the city they called Mexico and from there ruled all the New World in the name of the Spanish Crown. The viceroyalty of Peru, and the Captain-Generalship of Chile, were subordinate to him and the isthmus was in the domain of Peru.

But it was a long way between Lima and Panama - 1500 miles

-and we, Drake and I, had exposed the weakest link in the *Camino Real*. So, Don Martinez had stepped in personally to oversee the operation and to secure the isthmus. No doubt he had sold it to Philip as the best means of protecting Spain's treasure and that was certainly true. But now I believed he had moved mainly to protect William's treasure. How much was Don Martinez creaming off the top of what he sent on to Philip and to William? The amount of silver was so vast that he could probably help himself to tons of it and no one would know. No doubt the chain of silver was cut at every stage from the mines right up to the purse of King Philip but that same silver paid for the silence from hundreds or thousands of men every step of the way.

The track ended at a stone wall with a large iron gate blocking the road. The gate was closed and I was going to climb over it when I noticed the walls to either side did not extend all the way around the property. In fact, they were not more than thirty feet long and I walked around the end of the right-hand one and crouched in the shadows, watching the building. A cool breeze came down from the black hills behind, stirring the treetops.

The Viceroy's Palace was far smaller than I had expected, although it was well proportioned and built from stone foundations with thick timbers above covered with white plaster glowing in the moonlight and a tiled roof. There were two storeys, and all was dark and quiet, other than a room in the top right corner. The shutters on the front were closed but lamplight shone through the slats. And light spilled out from the right-hand side of the building onto a balcony.

If I could climb up there, and if there was a door or open window, I might get inside.

The viceroy would be served by many men who might see me first and so raise the alarm. Servants of course, and some of them might be armed as a matter of course. Soldiers would be on hand to guard him and to do his bidding. How many of them were immortals, I had no idea but if it was more than a handful, I would be in trouble.

The wind gusted and the trees rustled all around. A strange creature called, loud and insistent and utterly alien, before falling silent once more.

The easiest thing would be to slink into his chamber, quietly slit his throat and flee before anyone noticed. I could do that. But I wanted to speak to the man. To find out all he knew before I ended his life. His knowledge could lead me to William. It was more valuable even than all the treasure in the South Seas.

For a few moments, I considered abducting him and dragging him off to be questioned but I could not do such a thing quietly and I would no doubt find all Panama hunting me.

Perhaps I could assault the house directly. Break through the front doors and kill every servant and guard I found there before doing whatever I wanted to the viceroy until sunrise.

But it would be chaotic and prone to failure. While I was hunting people in the building, the Viceroy could flee, or I could miss someone who could raise the alarm down in the town.

And even if all went well, there might be women and children within. I would not murder them on purpose but with swords swinging and arquebuses firing, they would certainly be at risk. In my mind's eye, I pictured dragging screaming women into a pantry to be locked up, imagined punching one in the face to make her compliant.

I shook my head and decided to do the moral, sensible thing, and cut his throat while he slept.

Between the gate and the residence was a formal garden in the Mediterranean style with squares of low hedges. It was difficult to see what I was walking through but it was an incongruous bit of civilisation carved out of the wild jungle all around it. I stumbled against a lump of low statuary and almost fell into a hedge but caught myself at the last moment, huddling low while I caught my breath. The sound of a foot scraping against stone somewhere within the palace made my heart race but it was impossible to locate the source over the rustling wind. After a few seconds I went on toward the house, bearing right to come around the outside of the east wing.

That illuminated room on the corner did open onto a balcony and what was more the doors between the two were thrown open. All I had to do was get up there.

I had been hoping there would a tree or vines to climb but there was nothing but the plastered wall. There was a shuttered window, however, and this I used to pull myself up. It was difficult indeed to do in the dark and even harder to do quietly. My sword scraped and clattered and impeded me but I used my dagger to help, pushing it into the plaster and timbers to make a handhold. When I had both feet on the top of the shutters, I let go my dagger and leapt for the edge of the balcony.

The shutters banged against the frame as I jumped from them but my fingers found the balcony. Pulling myself up fast, I grunted and came over the balustrade, drawing my sword and stepping into the viceroy's chamber.

It was a large room but a simple one. A massive, canopied bed took up most of one side while the other, by the balcony, was appointed as a study. The desk was dark and heavy and littered with papers and ledgers.

In the centre of the room was an old man on his knees, praying with his eyes closed and his mouth moving as he muttered the words of his prayer. He was rather frail, with pale, sickly, loose skin mottled with liver spots. His clothing was plain but the cloth was thick and fabulously expensive. Gold rings covered his fingers and a massive gold chain hung about his neck.

I wondered if it was him or if it was a priest or a secretary.

He opened his eyes and his face contorted.

"Thank God!" he whispered. "Thank you, Christ. I am saved." He closed his eyes again, crossed himself and lowered his head. "I am saved."

"Who are you?" I asked in a low voice.

He snapped open his milky eyes. "I am Martín Enríquez de Almanza. You are here to kill me, yes?"

"You are the Viceroy?" I said. "And you *want* me to kill you?"

His eyes narrowed and were filled with longing. "Yes, yes. Please, I beg you."

I looked around me, suspecting a trick. Were his men lurking in the shadows? I could see no one.

"You want me to kill you?" I repeated, confused.

"With all my heart."

I stopped. "But why?"

He sneered. "I do not know how it is with you English but in the true faith it is a sin to take one's own life."

"I am no Protestant but all men know it to be a sin. You are Don Martín Enríquez de Almanza?"

"Yes."

"But why do you want to die?"

He twisted his mouth before answering. "Because I have sinned."

"We have all sinned. That is what priests are for."

He scoffed, contemptuously. "I have... I have done evil."

"If you repent..." I began before realising I was not there to save his life or his soul. "What evil have you done?"

Still on his knees, he looked sidelong at me. "You look like him, do you know?"

"William?" I asked.

Don Enríquez frowned. "Is that his true name? How strange. He does not seem like a William to me. He is an Englishman, then?"

I was not going to tell him but he would soon be dead anyway, so I did. "I suppose his ancestors are Norman French, part Burgundian, with a grandfather of some ancient and unknown race. But he was raised English, yes."

"And the same is true for you, no? You are brothers, I know it. They told me and now I see you, I know it is true."

I shrugged. "Half-brothers. My mother was as English as old King Alfred. What name does he go by now?"

"Do you swear to kill me if I tell you?"

It was everything I wanted, strange as it was. "Tell me everything I ask and then I will kill you."

He smiled, just a little, and held out a hand. "Help me up, there's a good man."

I stayed where I was. "Get yourself up."

Don Enríquez sighed and slowly got to his feet, groaning with every movement and hinging himself upright, puffing like a bellows. His spine cracked as he stood and he winced as he shuffled his feet apart.

"I shall be glad to be free of this gouty old body," he said, almost smiling again.

"You need not play the old man with me, sir. I know your true strength."

He paused, frowning, before slowly nodding to himself. "You believe me to be one of the Chosen. Yes, yes, I can see why you would think that."

"Do not seek to save your life by such a ruse. You are immortal, you can admit it to me before you die."

He pointed at his desk. "May I sit?"

I waved my sword to indicate he should do just that and he limped across the room and eased himself down into his chair, groaning again. "I do not suppose you suffer from gout, sir?"

"You cannot be gouty and immortal. Certainly, you know this."

He shrugged, rubbing one thigh. "He tells me nothing, you see. Nothing."

"William? Who is he pretending to be now? What name does he go by? Tell me, and I will make your passing swift."

Enríquez softly cleared his throat and spoke in a low voice, rasping with age. "I met your William only twice. Once when I was young and once before I came to the New World. At our first meeting, I was barely more than a boy and I was filled with such... vitality. And even more, I was filled with jealousy and with the belief that I had been wronged. I am descended from a king of Castile, did you know that? Through a royal bastard, admittedly, but I thought I should be famous, powerful, purely because of my blood, my heritage. Of course, that is true but only if I had lived up to that heritage by being a great man, a powerful man. I did not understand that yet, not until it was too late. Your William offered me riches, power, prestige, and all for the small price of being his man. Of serving him. Oh, he did not say it so brazenly, no, it was couched in obsequiousness and it did not fool me. But I allowed myself to be deceived. And so it was that I found myself with everything that I desired. Ah, vanity, sir, vanity. Do you know what vanity means?"

"Yes."

"It means emptiness and meaninglessness. That is what my obedience brought. A lie. Falseness. But I pretended to be what the world saw me as. Convinced myself, to some extent, for decades. But the lies ate away at me. I was not free to be my own man and I was loyal not to my sovereign but to the…" He looked at me. "To your brother."

"You met him twice, you said?"

"Twenty-eight years later and he had not aged a day in between." Don Enríquez shook his head. "Any doubt I had left was dispelled."

"And that was when he offered you his blood."

He jerked his eyes to mine. "No! He would not." Holding his shaking hands to his face, he leaned on his desk. "He would not."

"You expect me to believe this? I know he has a man in New Spain. I know it. Other agents I have captured have told me so. He has the man in New Spain who oversees the treasure shipments. That is you. And now you produce this story that you are mortal?"

I strode around the desk and raised my sword.

He closed his eyes and lifted his chin to expose his neck.

Instead of cutting his throat, I grasped his wrist and sliced a deep gash into his forearm. He cried out and flinched away.

"What are you doing?" he said. "You mean to torture me? You will get the same answers, the same story, I swear it to God. You hear me? I swear it!"

A hand knocked on the study door and a voice called through it. "Master? Are you well? May I enter?"

I looked at the wincing old man and slowly shook my head.

He cleared his throat and raised his voice. "I am praying with too much enthusiasm, Fernando. All is well."

The man on the other side hesitated. "You sounded hurt, master."

"It is my toe again. All is well."

"I could draw you a bowl of cold water, master, and wrap your foot with the ointment?"

Don Enríquez smiled affectionately. "Go to bed, Fernando. Rest well."

The pause was shorter this time. "I will, master. You as well."

Footsteps echoed in the hall as the man went away.

"He is a good valet," Don Enríquez said, wincing and touching his cut arm. "Better than this sinner deserves. Why did you cut me?"

"Who is William? What name does he go by?"

"If I tell you, sir, promise me in turn to make my passing swift and as painless as you can?"

"Tell me who he is."

He sighed. "When first I met him, his name was Diego de

Espinosa. He said he was Leonese and had been educated in Salamanca but he never sounded... right. Never seemed Leonese. Even before he revealed his nature to me, I always knew there was something... wrong about him. Few others saw it. Everybody knew of him but nobody knew him, do you understand?"

"I think so."

"He was a Councillor of Castile and then he was made President of the Council but no one understood how he had done it. We fear what we do not understand, of course, and no one understood how Diego de Espinosa continued to advance. He was then a chief adviser to King Philip. He became a priest in one year and in the next, Pope Pius V made him a cardinal. Just like that, a cardinal." He shook his head in wonder. "Then he was Bishop of Sigüenza, do you know where that is?"

"The place sounds familiar but it has been some time since I was in Spain. Is it near Madrid?"

"It matters not. At the same time, he had himself appointed as the Grand Inquisitor of the Inquisition. And from there is where he did most of his evil."

I stepped away, running a hand over my face. "William made himself head of the Spanish Inquisition?"

"Diego de Espinosa did, for a while, yes. But the whispers grew too loud."

"Whispers of his evil? His blood drinking?"

"Yes, yes, and of his everlasting youth. He hid himself away, emerged only at night and was otherwise hooded. But this only added fuel to the fire of rumour. A few years ago, he feigned death and went back to the shadows. Who he is now, I cannot say. Perhaps he is no one."

"Does Philip know his true nature?"

"The King?" His mouth turned down at the corners. "Perhaps not. Certainly, Cardinal Espinosa attempted to convince someone that his death was a true one, for his body was taken to be buried. They say that the embalmer cut into Espinosa's chest when the Cardinal snatched the knife from the man and killed him before fleeing. Others have said that this is nothing but a story, for how could it possibly be true? But I know. Oh yes, I know."

I sighed and pinched my nose. I felt tired. "Do you have wine?"

He was confused for a moment before gesturing at a cabinet by the door. "Wine, yes. What a fine idea, sir, yes. Please, pour us a cup of wine."

Inside the cabinet was arrayed finely cut glass bottles, filled with freshly decanted wines. I sniffed one and then another and both were delightful. I filled two huge silver goblets and took one to the viceroy. He breathed it in and took a deep drink.

"This shall be my last ever taste of wine. How curious to know such a thing. But I find it does not taste any sweeter for the knowledge."

"He told you about me?" I said. "Warned you?"

"They told me. He said he had a brother who was just like him, only evil. A brother who had betrayed Spain by pretending to be an Englishman, who had embraced the heresy of Lutheranism, and who works tirelessly to destroy all his good works."

I smiled. "That latter part is true, at least."

"Tell me, then, how did you both come to be? Did you make a pact with the Devil?"

I took a drink and looked out at the black night for a moment before turning back to him.

"Show me your arm," I said. He frowned and I gestured with my goblet. "Show me where I cut you."

He rolled up his sleeve, wincing. His flesh was pale. Deathly white, in fact, and wrinkled. He was not in good health, that much was obvious.

The cut was entirely unhealed. Blood continued to flow from it.

He was mortal.

"How is it that William has revealed himself to you and yet you are a mortal man?"

"Is this not something he ordinarily does?"

"What have you offered him?"

He bristled. "I am one of the most important men in all Spain. Which is to say, in all the world."

"But you said yourself, he helped to make you such a man. And in return, you give him... silver. Correct? Mountains of silver."

He sipped and sat back, wincing. "There are mountains of silver here. We cannot dig it out fast enough. We can barely keep up with the shipments, it pours out of the ground in such abundance and all it costs is the lives of a few thousand negroes, Indians, and poor Spaniards every year. That silver pays for Spain's armies, for her ships. Do you think Philip could keep the Low Countries under control without my silver?"

"When I left England, it seemed the Provinces were anything but under control."

"Pah! The Duke of Parma will have everything he needs to put

415

them down. What can all their Protestant anger do against Spanish silver? Nothing at all, is your answer, or you are a fool. Do you know how much armies cost, sir? Ships?"

"You are proud of your work. Why do you beg for death?"

"Ah," he said, drawing it out in a quiet wail and sloshing his wine as he waved his goblet before him. "I am proud of my service for my king. I have done my duty there."

"And what have you done for William? For Diego de Espinosa?"

"A trifle here and there, no more. Twice, I denounced *conversos* in my service and gave evidence for their tribunals."

"False evidence?"

He shrugged. "Of course, or else he would not have needed me."

"Who were they? What had they done?"

"Good Catholics, as far as I knew, but they were descended from Jews. Probably they continued to practice their doctrine in private. Many do, you know."

"And that is enough to see them executed."

He wagged a finger at me. "You are not plagued with Jews in England. Your kings had the good sense to be rid of them centuries ago and so you do not know what it is like to have them working away in secret, like a poison inside your kingdom. Rich, you know, wealthy, many of them, very wealthy. Financiers and merchants. Like ticks, they grow fat on our blood. I was pleased to denounce them. Spain will never be free until each one is expelled."

"So... bearing false witness is not the sin that troubles you?"

He glared at me. "Typical heretic nonsense. We are

commanded not to bear false witness against our neighbours. The rules are for our own people, not for others, do you understand?"

"What did you do for William?"

He put his goblet on the desk and held a hand over his mouth. I thought he was going to vomit but he swallowed and looked up.

"Not for... William. I committed no great sins for William."

I looked at him, waiting for him to continue.

"What did I do for him, you ask?" he said after a moment. "I agreed to obey his man. The world will believe you to be the Viceroy of New Spain but you will know your true place, he said. Your servants will serve you as such and your guests will honour you as such and the people of the New World will bow before you but you must not allow yourself to be fooled, Don Enríquez. For you are no more than an instrument. A tool. No, a shield. A shield, behind which your master will give your commands. And you will follow. Or I shall roast you, Don Enríquez. Not burn you, understand, but roast. I will do this slowly, so that you will live in agony for weeks, months, perhaps. When the blackness of your cracked flesh begins to overwhelm you, I shall feed you drops of my blood so that your suffering continues. Do you believe this is an idle threat, Don Enríquez, or do you believe I am speaking the truth?"

Don Enríquez broke off and when he reached for his goblet his hand was shaking so much he had to use the other to steady it.

"I do not tell you his threats to absolve myself. I had a choice. I could have chosen the suffering of my body over the suffering of my soul but I did not. And now I cannot live and so I must die. Please. Please."

"He made you serve one of his men," I said, feeling the blood rushing in my ears and recalling Catalina's words. "The one who is a giant?"

The viceroy nodded. "Lorenzo de la Vega. A giant of a man in his body and a monster in his soul. If he even has a soul. I suspect he is the Devil in human form. And I... I did things."

"You kept him in blood," I said. "Found him blood slaves."

"Blood slaves, yes. This is what Cardinal Espinosa commanded me. Find slaves and have them bled. Every day, if you can, healthy strong slaves. Negro, Indian, Spanish, all blood is the same, he said, as long as it is human. It was monstrous, perhaps, but not so bad. That is not so bad a thing, is it, sir?"

He seemed to actually want a response. "I have had servants bled for centuries. It harms them not."

"Ah," he said, smiling for a moment before his mouth turned down and his eyes looked through the far wall. "Lorenzo de la Vega was not satisfied with the slaves. Not satisfied with having them bled, he wanted to drink from their flesh. From their necks, from their wrists, from their... from their private parts. No, I said, no that was not what was agreed. For these slaves will talk and soon all New Spain will know. They will never be set free, he said. And, God help me, I had a building constructed. A fine house not far from here in the hills. From the outside it seems to be a house fit for a lord but it was a prison. He would go there, every day, many times a day, to drink and... to satiate all his desires. And there he trained his monstrous priests in the arts of killing, the men sent by his master."

I walked to the cabinet and took the cut glass bottle and refilled our cups. "One cannot keep such things secret for long."

"Yes! I thank you, sir. Precisely what I argued. Food was taken for the servants, bodies buried, word spread, of course it did. My reputation was plummeting. And then he came to me. We need more slaves for the Blood House. More! What happened to the others? They were weak, he said. I need more." He crossed himself. "He was killing one every day. More than one. And only God knows what he did with the women first. The men, too, I suspect."

"Who were these poor souls that died in the Blood House?"

"Whoever I could acquire. I purchased all the Negroes I could but it was never enough. I had Indians brought in from every direction but they are difficult to find unless they stand and fight and so few have the will any more. But Lorenzo was never satiated. The Negroes taste foul, he said. And the Indian men are weak, all their warriors have died. You will bring me only white men and the only Indians you will bring will be women and children."

"My God," I said. "You did not."

He sobbed. "I refused. Never children, I said. Not even Indian children." He leaned over with his head in his hands.

"But you did it anyway."

Don Enríquez had tears in his eyes and he raised his hands in supplication while he whispered, voice cracking. "He tortured me. Burned me. Pulled my nails from my toes. But yes, I did it. They are only Indians, I told myself. But it was just another lie. I felt the truth, here." He thumped his narrow chest.

"He was with you at San Juan de Ulúa."

"Oh," he said. "I begged him not to attack the trust of the English sailors. But he would stop at nothing, caring nothing for my word, for the reputation of Spain, by betraying my word to that English captain. When the shooting started, I prayed and prayed that he would be hit but God forsook me. Of course, the English deserved punishment for their piracy but I had given my word that we would have peace at that place. And he took some of them prisoner, questioned them, drank them. Some he sent back to his master. Some of those men said they had known you."

"Did you sail there because you knew I was there?"

"He knew someone had discovered his vile blood taverns and those disgusting whores he kept in them for the pleasure of his men. Once, I saw him drink two... women to death in one of the taverns. They let him do it, both of them. They did not struggle. Not that it would have done any good but even so."

"I heard you drank from them also."

His head shot up. "Yes. How pathetic I had become. I thought, perhaps, that I might be turned also. Or if I showed myself willing to... I do not know what I thought. It turned my stomach but I drank because I wanted... I do not know what I wanted."

He was right. He was pathetic.

I pointed my sword at his door. "Where is he? Is he here?"

Don Enríquez shook his head. "He left tonight. After sundown."

It was *him* I had seen on the track, riding into town with a handful of soldiers. "He has gone to Panama?"

"He fled to his ship, the *Sangre Santa*. We had word Drake was here. We thought you might come for us. I prayed for it, Lorenzo feared your cannons would sink his ship and destroy his treasure. So he has gone."

"He sails at first light?"

Enríquez shook his head. "I believe it was a midnight tide. The

Sangre Santa will be gone now. You cannot stop him."

A coldness crept up from my guts. "Where has he gone? Back to Spain?"

"In a manner of speaking. He would not say but I am not completely foolish. I know from the mariners that he is going to the Philippine Islands. From there, he will go home."

"The... in the Portuguese Indies? Why?"

"He has armed his ship with the best cannon and packed it with soldiers but still he doubts he can stand against yours. He will fight if he has to but he has one advantage you do not have."

"He's seven feet tall?"

"His mariners know how to cross the South Seas and how to reach the lands of China and India. That way is his best chance to deliver a hold full of treasure to his Satanic master in Spain." Don Enríquez sneered. "Your brother."

"Vega's ship has a hold full of treasure? What treasure? How much?"

"It's worth was at least a million pesos."

I stared. "A million pesos."

Enríquez waved at his palace all around him. "We had many tons here. Enough to buy a kingdom for his master."

"What kingdom? Spain? Or England?"

"Lorenzo de la Vega told me nothing about that."

"But surely you know..."

He shrugged. "I believe that they are preparing to conquer your kingdom, Englishman."

My heart raced. "How?"

Sighing, Enríquez picked at the drying blood on his arm. "I hear things, read things. Perhaps imagine things. I do not know anything for certain. But I believe they have my king in their grasp and with that power, and my treasure, they will pay for a fleet of galleons that will sail to your shores and offload an army. You know that the Duke of Parma is in the Low Countries, yes? With tens of thousands of men. Could a million pesos pay for ships enough to cross that thin strip of water the English believe protects them from Catholic kingdoms? Easily, with half a million to spare."

"The Duke of Parma is an immortal?" I asked, aghast.

"Oh, no. Not to my knowledge. But then he does not need to be, does he? He will do their bidding because he wishes to make war on Protestants and he is good at it. The best there is." The Viceroy smiled. "Your kingdom will fall. Without England, the heresy of Protestantism will be defeated. At least some good will come from all this evil."

I shook my head, thinking hard as my pulse thrummed in my ears. Every moment I tarried I risked being discovered. And it was vital above all else that this news be brought back to England and that I get after Vega with all haste. "What other immortals are there in Panama?"

"Lorenzo has half a dozen of them. All have gone with him to his ship."

"So you are free from their influence?"

"Praise God, yes. For now."

I looked at the darkness beyond the balcony. Stars were out and wisps of cloud covered the moon. "I will find him and stop him before he gets far."

Enríquez nodded slowly. "It is my dying wish that you do so. Please, sir, now is the time. You must end my days."

He dragged himself to his feet and hobbled around his desk, where he clutched the side with one hand and lowered himself to his knees, wincing. Leaning forward, he exposed the back of his neck.

It was tempting indeed. But I did not strike.

"My oath is to kill all those that William has corrupted with his blood."

"Praise God," he said with his head down, crossing himself and began muttering the paternoster.

"But you are not one who is so corrupted."

It took him a moment before he broke off and looked up, confused. "But I have served his evil. I deserve death."

"You do. I do not argue otherwise. But I have learned, for the sake of my own soul, that I cannot be the judge and the executioner of all who have done wrong in the world. If I do not resist the desire to be that judge then I truly will be evil, just as William is."

"No, no, I am guilty. I freely admit it."

"You do not understand because you are in a state of despair. But if you have sinned, repent, confess, and seek absolution. If you have committed crimes, give yourself up to the king and his men and accept their punishments. It is clear that your health is failing. These lands are pestilential and fit only for savages. You have a choice, now, on how to spend your last days. Godless and in despair, or righteously while embracing the consequences of your crimes and seeking forgiveness for your sins. Choose well, for it is the last significant choice you will face before you are judged by God."

He groaned and got to his feet, dragging himself upright.

When he looked at me, I saw he was angry. Furious, even and he took a deep breath while turning to the door.

I knew he was about to call for his guards.

Instead, I punched him in the temple.

The Viceroy fell backwards across his desk, knocking his goblet over and spilling wine across his papers. He lay there, back arched and legs hanging off the side, his toes above the floor, the wine soaking into everything.

Quietly, I let myself down off the edge of the balcony and hurried back out onto the track and headed for town. The night would be ending soon and I could not be late. I turned off the track, crossed the stream and ran through the farmlands of the plain.

I got lost. I could not find the creek mouth again and the sun was almost up when I realised I must have crossed the river in the night upstream, thinking it was no more than a drainage ditch, and I rushed back along the coast.

The boat was on its way back out through the surf when I reached it and I had to whistle when my waving did not catch their attention. When they came back, I fell into the boat, exhausted but relieved and I clapped each man on the back with such enthusiasm that more than one complained.

And it was not a moment too soon as before we were a hundred yards offshore, a company of horsemen came charging down to the beach. A few of them fired their pieces at us and then thirty soldiers marched out and took aim. We lay flat before they fired but our boat was hit from the waterline to the gunwales.

Before they could reload, our pinnace fired a cannon shot right by us that smashed into the trees near the soldiers and every one of them ran away.

"Success, Richard?" the master said when we boarded the pinnace.

"We must return to the *Hind* immediately. There is another prize. A yet greater prize that just left Panama, and we must seize it before it slips from our grasp."

He gaped. "Not that big bastard who went out last night? A greater prize than the *Fire-shitter*?"

They all stared at me, filled with wonder and expectation.

"Greater by far," I said. "The *Sangre Santa* is captained by a giant named Vega, who was the bastard who wronged us at San Juan de Ulúa. And if we can take it, we will each become as rich as a prince!"

They cheered and tripped over each other to make sail for the *Hind*.

Slumped in a seat with a piece of sausage and a cup of wine, I prayed we would not be too late.

14

The Chase

1580

"NO, NO, NO!" DRAKE CRIED. "It is not possible to make such a voyage."

"But if we catch him now, before he gets too far away—"

He turned on me. "How can you still not understand sailing, man? One cannot simply dash hither and thither on the seas going where we wish at will. The winds and the currents may push us out in such a fashion that we cannot return to this coast. And I tell you once more that the *Hind* is simply not capable of crossing that sea in her current state. She may not even make it back to the Magellan Strait, let alone heading out across half the world, into the unknown."

"We cannot cross that sea, I know it. But if we were to immediately intercept the *Sangre Santa*—"

"How do you not understand, Richard, how? We do not know the latitude he is sailing at so how can we find him in that vast nothingness? So, we try and we fail and we find ourselves out there with no land in reach. Our timbers are leaking and the action of the vast waves of that ocean will break us apart until we can bail no longer and we sink. And even if we do not, we may very likely find ourselves starving to death before we reach land again. I have no charts, no descriptions of the winds."

"So you will not do it."

He pinched his nose and took a breath before answering. "Of course I will bloody well do it, Richard! I'll not let him get away. If he truly is the cause of the betrayal at San Juan de Ulúa, then he will pay with his life. And that treasure... if there is even half so much as the viceroy claimed... you are certain he did not deceive you?"

"Certain? No, I do not have certainty. I believed him. I looked into his eyes and saw his despair and it seemed true."

"Perhaps he lied, set you off after this Lorenzo to save his own life."

"He begged me to kill him. Begged."

"You should have."

"By what authority would I have executed him?"

Drake stared. "By... moral authority. He admitted his crimes to you."

"For a time, when I was young, I would have agreed with you. I thought that because I could do great violence it gave me the right to do so. The moral right, as you suggest. I desired always to hurt anyone who stood in my way, even if they were simply doing their duty." I paused and forced myself to be honest. "In fact, I still often do feel that way but I act on the impulse less often. But in the days when I was filled with righteousness and revelled in my own power and strength, I became boorish. Rude."

Drake frowned. "You did not kill the viceroy because it would have been... ungentlemanly?"

"Yes, I suppose that's it. The times when I do not follow the law, Francis, are because there is no other way. Our oath as members of the Order of the White Dagger is to kill William de Ferrers and to kill the immortals that he has spawned. We do this because no one else can do it. These men cannot be caught by mortals, on the whole. And if they are, they cannot be hanged. Once, I even saw one partially burned at the stake and he lived. For a time. Only *we* understand what they are and only we have the power to stop them. That is what gives us the moral authority to act. To commit murder against them. And yes, there is ever the temptation to do more. We remain loyal subjects of the Crown and on occasion our duties contradict one another. But all men have many duties and struggle to fulfil each of them. Even when a mortal man is guilty, we must only execute him when there is no other choice. And even then, killing another by your own hand or by your command makes a mark upon one's soul that is difficult to wipe clean."

He nodded and breathed deeply, placing a hand on one hip and looking at the ceiling for a long moment. It was clear that the execution of Doughty yet weighed heavily on him and that helped him to understand.

"We must find a safe haven where we can restore the ship in peace. And then we will cross the South Seas, for the Philippine Islands." He looked up sharply. "What if Lorenzo's' mortal men try to protect him?"

"I am certain that they will. But do not misunderstand my intentions for those who stand in the way of our duty, whether they are mortal or not for we shall not hesitate to kill them all." I shrugged. "If we must."

We went north up the coast, past New Spain and into unknown lands where the Spanish would not follow us. Or so we hoped. Day after day, we went further north until we began to question our captain's sanity. We had passed many adequate anchorages but still he ordered us north.

"My charts say the mouth of the Northwest Passage can be found at forty-two degrees north. If we can discover it, we can find a new way back to England. Not for now but for the next voyage, and for the ones after it. Perhaps we can come at these lands from the north and the south at once and descend on New Spain and Chile to meet at Panama. Imagine it!"

"I thought our ship was falling to pieces! And this is not our primary duty."

"A few days more will matter not," he replied, happy to be exploring new lands once more. I suspected that was his greatest love, more than treasure, more than England, more than his wife.

I looked out at the cold seas and then stomped my feet. "The passage is at forty-two degrees north, you say?"

"It is not what I say but what the charts say."

"And how far north are we now?"

His smile faltered as he and the master exchanged a look. "Forty-eight degrees north."

"Forty-eight, Francis! Are you mad?"

He nodded. "The charts are incorrect, it would seem. Perhaps the passage is further north yet."

"Am I wrong to believe no man has been further north than we are in this moment?"

"Certainly, you are not wrong."

"Then your charts are a nonsense! There is no northwest passage home, there is nothing but that black shore until the top of the world! We must turn back."

"Just one more day, sir. One more day."

He might have gone all the way to the north pole but the next day, violent winds whipped up half the time and the other half, thick fogs descended. When ice formed in our rigging and the sails started to freeze, finally, we turned south again.

We had gone so far north that we had reached what would, more than two centuries later, become the border region of Canada and the United States of America. But all I knew of it then was a smudge of darkness seen through fog and driving rain and bitter winds and I prayed that we would swiftly be far, far away.

Our safe harbour was in far more pleasant lands down at 38 degrees north where Drake and his officers found a place that satisfied their various criteria, whatever they were. At first, I was too infuriated by the delay to appreciate its necessity but after a few days I saw just how exhausted were the men. Many stumbled and fell when trying to unload and convey timber, tools, and victuals up the beach.

A sheltering hook of chalky white sandstone cliffs curved around the bay for miles, protecting us from the seas beyond. The dark sands were broad and flat and the beach was protected on the landward side by those cliffs that extended right around. Here and there, low points of the cliffs allowed access up to the top where we built a fort and posted lookouts. Within the broad sweep of that protective bay was an inlet that provided further protection for the ship and for the men. In that deep haven, the men set to work on the ship. The hull had to be careened and so the ship was run up a sandbank at high tide, the men rigged up ropes and pulled her over one way and then another, spending days to hack and bash away the barnacles and scrub off the green slimy moss-like tendrils and other detritus clinging to the timbers. They were also repaired inside and out and reinforced from within. It was hard and unpleasant work but the men appeared to enjoy it, perhaps because it was something different and perhaps because they loved the *Golden Hind* and caring for her brought them great joy.

"It is like England, is it not?" Drake asked one morning as the sun rose and burned away the fog banks. "Our cliffs are so very much like the Seven Sisters. You know, on the south coast? The hills of Sussex descend to the Channel where they are cut by the waters into white chalk of a height just like these here." He took a deep breath in through his nose and let it out. "This is good land."

I looked across the wind-swept cliffs at the barren and forbidding land beneath the swirling grey sky and rising fog. "You think so?"

He seemed confused. "You do not? It is like finding another England on the other side of the world. And that is how it shall be known, from this day onward. I have already recorded it as Nova Albion. We will claim it in the name of Elizabeth and one day we shall build a town here and a port. When we have crushed the Spanish, I might take a ship up north once more and find that passage. That would be something, would it not? It is a fine land, alright, certainly you can see that. Richard?"

"All I see is scrub and stunted forest and rocks." I smiled at his bewilderment. "But you have a finer imagination than I, Francis and if you can see it and if you believe it, then that is good enough for me. Although, I would rather not live on such a—" I broke off and stood straighter, shielding my eyes from the glare of the rising sun through the fog bank. "Men standing shore watch! Arm yourselves!"

I had the men form up behind a line of pikes and arquebuses and took them forward to the edge of the slope.

There descended a native.

A single man bearing gifts.

"Put up your weapons, men!" Drake cried, pushing through the line. "Put them up, I say. Look at this, what a brave fellow coming all alone, what have you brought us, sir. Come, come, let us be friends."

I turned to the mariners on either side. "Remain vigilant. Do not trust these savages. There might be a dozen more of the bastards over that ridge yonder or five hundred for all we know."

But Drake was right. The half-naked fellow with wild black hair smiled as he handed over his presents. A bunch of remarkable large feathers tied together and a basket of strange, shrivelled black leaves that were very pungent.

"That's that tobacco leaf!" the master's mate cried upon seeing it. "The sacred leaf, it is a kind of herb that they fire and consume by their breath."

"Ah yes," I said, recalling it now. "By which they become

inebriated and benumbed and yet free of fatigue. That Portuguese physician we found off Chile had some. He said it is the means by which the savages prevent diseases."

"It is a wonder," Drake said, beaming. "A wondrous gift, sir, here, you must take this in return."

He pressed on the man a heavy golden chain worth more than a new-built mansion on the Strand but the fool would not take it. Drake tried coins, which were refused, then an ornate sword which made us all wince but still the fellow would not take it and turned to leave.

"Here!" Drake cried and took off his hat and tossed it to the man. Though it flopped into a wet depression, the Indian appeared delighted with it and went off happily. But not as happy as Drake who stood with his hands on his hips watching him go off up the hill. "He was a fine fellow, was he not? We shall have to discover his friends and, if possible, purchase this land from them."

I looked around for my valet. "Give the captain your hat, Martin. Quickly, now."

After that, I berated the watchmen and ordered our defences built higher and stationed more men on the high land. Two days later, a hundred of them came along the coast in a vast group, trailing along and singing.

"Looks like my old village going off to the harvest festival," a mariner beside me said as he loaded his arquebus.

"Do not be fooled," I said. "They are a warlike race. Remember Rob Winter and Oliver."

They drew to a stop beyond our fort and milled around, looking at us and gesturing wildly at the *Hind*. Of course, they had seen nothing like it in all their lives. Nor even heard about it or us. Drake came charging up the hill in his shirt, covered in filth from the careening work. "Look at this! My friends, you are welcome." He went marching out beyond the earthworks and our men cried out in fear and urged him to come back. Of course, he ignored us.

"Please, Mister Richard, please bring him back!" they cried.

I rushed out after him. "They have bows, Francis! Look, they are armed."

"Oh, nonsense," he said, wafting a hand at me. "Look, they have their women and children with them. They have no interest in making war, come, come."

Grudgingly, I admitted that he was right. The women at the rear were laden with children on their hips and others carried baskets filled with goodness knew what.

"My friends," Drake cried again, spreading his arms wide. "Thank you for welcoming us into your country. We welcome you into our beach and our cliff here. Listen, sirs, my friends, would you mind awfully lowering your weapons? Those, those, your bows." He mimed drawing one and then motioned placing them down on the ground.

They looked at him in astonishment and then at each other. I began to raise my arquebus and half turned to check my men were making ready.

The Indians placed their bows and their arrows on the ground, just as Drake had asked.

"How kind you all are! Wonderful, now, let us give to you some gifts that we have prepared." He turned and called out. "Bring up the hats!"

After half a day of trading items, the Indians went off back to wherever their village was, laden with clothing and whatever else we managed to press on them. And by God, if they were not a delightful, generous, peaceful people. They were tractable, free and loving in their nature and entirely without guile or treachery. There was not one hard-hearted, sour-faced old sailor who did not feel delighted in their company.

We built a fort on the shore and all the while, the natives kept arriving, a few each day. Some familiar faces, others who seemed to be saying that they had come in from miles and miles away, drawn by the tales of us strange men, no doubt. I never allowed a single one inside our fort, though they were fascinated by it and many attempted to dart through the gate before we headed them off. It was clear they meant no harm, though. I never met a more sweet-natured, admirable people.

After a few weeks, a chief came. The Indians we knew explained through gesture that he was an important man, the most important they knew, perhaps. Something like a king, we thought. The Indians came down in their full strength, proceeded by a native officer bearing a staff of state, a great sceptre of black wood adorned with crowns and chains constructed from clamshells. Behind this herald came the chief's mightiest soldiers, great broad-chested fellows with big hands and square jaws hefting war clubs. In the centre of this honour guard came the chief himself, this mighty king of the natives, wearing a magnificent headdress and a cape of the softest leather. Behind him came even more of his royal soldiers, all painted fiercely. But instead of weapons, each of these soldiers carried a gift meant for our chief, Drake. Behind them came the mass of women and their children, all beaming smiles. The herald bearing the staff drew to a stop before the gates of our fortress and the entire procession halted behind him. And then he raised his black sceptre and began a speech that lasted half an hour. When he finished, crying out something in his native tongue, his people behind cheered also.

"What was that all about?" Martin muttered at my shoulder.

"Damned if I know, son."

"What now?" he asked.

"Hopefully they will go home."

Drake stepped forward and filled his lungs before calling out in his mariner's voice. "Open the gates! Let them inside! Come on, my friends, welcome. You are welcome indeed."

"Oh, dear Christ," I said and called out to the men. "Give them room, lads. Do them no harm."

If anything went wrong, trapped together inside the fort, I knew it would be a bloodbath. For both sides.

And in they came in a great mass. Drake went to the rear and stood there while the Indians appeared to be in some sort of religious fervour and they approached Drake with astonishing reverence, asking him to be seated. At this point, certain holy men appeared and made further speeches, shaking their hands in the air and calling out to the sky above. Drake sat on a stool and took it all in with typical good grace, smiling and thanking them for their efforts. They placed garlands and necklaces around his shoulders and pushed an ornate sceptre of white wood into his hands and finally placed a wooden crown upon his head.

"They make him their king!" our men said.

"No, they think him one of their holy gods," others argued.

"What do you think, Richard?" Martin asked in a hushed

voice.

I shook my head. "I think this is the most remarkable thing that ever happened to the son of a Devon yeoman."

It was a good day.

And as much as anything else it dispelled any lingering notion that we had anything to fear from those fine people of that distant coast. They invited us to roam about their lands and this we did, heading inland into a lush country that teemed with deer and strange pale squirrels that preferred to live on the ground rather than in trees. I greatly enjoyed visiting the Indian villages, of which there were a great many all around. Their homes were timber, round with conical roofs and covered with earth and grasses grew on the top. I imagined that they would be filthy and wormy but in fact they were delightfully cool inside when the day was hot and they were warm and dry when the weather was cool and wet.

"I love it here," I finally admitted to Drake.

"Ha!" He clapped me on the back. "I told you so. Imagine how much better it would be with civilised men here. One day, Protestant Englishmen shall rule over this land in the name of the Queen and perhaps you can build a magnificent home here and be the lord of these people."

I shook my head. "As Martin is fond of saying, this land is theirs. I thought you wished only to claim uninhabited lands, Francis? Besides, I already miss England and would not live here for all the world."

"Nonsense, they made me their king! All title to the land was granted to me when they made me their king. But do not fear, we shall also purchase it from them, fair as fair. Imagine the abundance of crops that we shall grow in this pleasant climate. You can take a Sussex farmer and drop him here and once he ploughs fields into the turf and builds a real house he will know no difference at all, none! I am having Bright make up a brass plate with my name and the date upon it. We shall set it up here so that our claim to Nova Albion is made legal and enforceable."

"The ship is repaired. We must go. Already, we have tarried too long. We must find Vega and stop him. The *Sangre Santa* may be in the Philippine Islands already."

The Indians were greatly distressed by our leaving. They wailed and beat their chests. Who did they think we were? Why did they take such joy in our presence and despair at our leaving? I do not know but we civilised men were hardly less distraught to be saying goodbye ourselves and I saw more than one mariner with tears running down his weather-beaten cheeks as we sailed away.

Out into the vast unknown of the Pacific Ocean.

***

The route across the Pacific was not entirely unknown, as on one of the prizes taken we had found sailing directions and charts pointing to the best course. Also, these documents made it clear that the maps about the Pacific that Drake had brought with him from England were desperately wrong. The distances spoken of in the Spanish sailing directions were far greater. We were therefore as stocked as we could possibly be with victuals. Following the directions, the *Hind* ploughed south-west for days and then we went up above the equator again to be blown west by the prevailing winds there.

Day after day, we sailed on through that seemingly endless sea. Our prow rising and falling and breaking through countless waves under blue skies, with our wake stretching behind us like a white road to the horizon.

Sometimes there were dolphins and occasionally whales. The men who liked to try their hand at fishing from the ship every now and then hauled in strange great fishes and once we had a shark of a variety none had seen before. He was hewed into pieces and boiled well but the flesh was rather tough. The days merged one into the other and I lost track of time, often I was amazed that an event had happened that very morning, or I would believe a day had passed since a particular incident only to discover it had been weeks. The spray spattered against the decks, the timbers creaked and boomed beneath us as we struck the waves, the rigging groaned and twisted and hummed with the wind that whipped our clothes. Everything became crusted with salt despite the men's endless scrubbing.

Sixty-eight days were out of sight of land. But then we found an island and came close, finding anchorage in a delightful bay. The island itself was formed from great verdant mounds of forest like lumps arranged in curved patterns emerging from the turquoise shoals. At the base of some were white sands and from these places came streaming hundreds of natives in their long, narrow canoes made from the trunks of trees.

At first, we were delighted by them but almost at once they began stealing everything they possibly could, either from the deck or even from a mariner's purses and pockets. I found one with his hand snaking its way into my shirt and I knocked him down with a stiff blow to the belly. It did not seem to bother him much, or his friends. In fact, they were a quarrelsome people and most of them argued and grappled with each other over the belongings that they had stolen, coming to blows amongst themselves.

Forcing them away from us and then forcing them down from the ship did not appear to discourage them.

When they would not flee, we fired our arquebuses and this scattered them for a while but soon they came back, intrigued further by the weapons.

"Of course," Martin said, "they do not know what firearms can do. They must believe them to make noise alone."

"Shoot one!" a sailor called out. "That'll learn them, right?"

Drake ordered the cannon to fire a warning shot at the beach, so they understood what we could do. The blast alone scared half of them away, and they paddled their little boats like the wind back to shore.

But still the rest came for us again. It seemed to me that they were growing agitated and less than friendly. They had a taste of the wonders that we possessed and they wanted them for themselves and indeed, I do not doubt that they would happily have killed us all and divided our ship between them.

Drake hung his head and commanded the next cannon should be loaded and aimed at the approaching boats.

All of us roared and shouted and gestured that the natives should flee but they did not and they came on.

"Fire!" Drake shouted.

The cannonball ripped through three canoes, sending men and timbers spinning through the air. Native bodies were blasted to pieces and they sank into the clear blue waters. All the survivors fled and none returned.

"Bloody savages," a mariner beside me said, spitting over the side. "Why couldn't they just leave us alone?"

Our captain was deeply upset by the affair still, when we left, Drake recorded the place as "the Island of Thieves".

We reached the Philippines and found the Spanish colonies there. How astonished they were to see us and to hear from where we had journeyed. Asking after Vega's ship, they told us we were just two weeks behind the *Sangre Santa* and that the ship had headed out of the South Seas and towards the Moluccas.

The Spice Islands. Ever since the Spanish had reached them, they had become famed as the lands of nutmeg, mace and cloves. They were a byword for riches beyond counting and ever since the Spanish had relinquished their claim fifty years earlier, the Portuguese had reaped their wealth by purchasing shiploads of the produce and selling it in Europe to make their fortunes. We had reached the borders of the two great sea empires of Spain and Portugal and both would resent our presence. Likewise, the natives of those islands would be the friends of one or other and we would not be welcomed by any.

Our Spanish maps and charts and sailing directions were good only as far as the Philippines and so we had to find our own way through the maze of islands that filled the sultry and dangerous seas of the Indian Archipelago. Drake was the finest navigator who ever sailed, of that I had no doubt. But he was never so arrogant that he would not seek whatever help he could. We stopped at every likely place we could and eventually found two local fishermen who agreed to help pilot us through the Siau Passage and on into the Molucca Sea.

We had lost time and the locals told us that a Spanish ship had passed three weeks ago but that it did not seem to be in any great hurry. Why would it? Vega would not fear that we had crossed after them and no doubt they were being careful to avoid the treacherous coasts and shoals and they were doing some trading as they inched their way through. Just as we did. Often, we found ourselves waiting out tides and wind in certain bays or ports and that way our presence became known.

I thought, by that point, that I had seen everything. All Europe was familiar to me, and I had trekked to the East, crossed the Atlantic, seen the Caribbean and the Americas, seen tiny islands in the middle of endless seas. But the Moluccas were yet another wonder. Small islands with treacherous channels between, often dominated by a vast green mountain at their centre, ringed by white clouds.

It was frustrating to me to have to travel so slowly but all the officers and men were nervous and I never saw so many soundings taken. The lead was swung out and the depth called without let up every time we moved so much as an inch. Although I wanted to urge speed, I knew it would be futile. The sailors went as fast they could for they knew what prize we were chasing. A million pesos for us all and we would deny the same to the hated Catholics. There could be no further motivation provided by my fretting.

And yet we had the misfortune to be pulled into local power politics.

"Look alive!" the mate called one morning as we approached Ternate, the northernmost of the islands. Soon, we found a boat sailing out to greet us.

"It looks very fine, does it not?" Drake said.

He was not wrong; the vessel was opulent and built from exotic wood so well polished that it shone like bronze, and silk canopies fluttered over the deck.

Still, I recognised that familiar excitement in his voice.

"We want only for victuals and water," I said to Drake as the boat came alongside. "That is all."

"Of course," Drake said, frowning. "Do you think I have forgotten our prize?"

Our visitor was an ambassador from the Sultan of Ternate, a lord named Babu. In time, we understood that he wanted to keep the Portuguese out of the islands under his rule and to kick them off the places that they had already imposed themselves. There was a conflict bubbling away and the Portuguese had designs on deposing the Sultan and installing someone more welcoming. Our new friend Babu desperately wanted us to use our firepower to dislodge the Portuguese and in return, he promised to reward England with exclusive trade rights.

"We can't get involved," I said at the officer's meeting after the emissary had departed, carrying the gift of a fine velvet cloak for his master.

The officers were astonished at my short-sightedness.

"But it would mean vast riches for England! We could secure trade for us and our people that would mean England might one day rival Portugal or even Spain in terms of wealth and power."

I laughed. "Do not be absurd. Trade is not what makes a people great. Riches are meaningless if one acts without morality to get them, as the desperate and grubbing merchants do."

It seemed they took this is a great insult, which I suppose it was, and they stood and pointed fingers at me. They annoyed me and I made it worse by stating it more strongly.

"To be a merchant is to be without a soul," I said and they practically howled in protested.

Drake shouted them down. "Our friend Richard is a soldier and has a soldier's simple view of the world. Soldierly wisdom that we have all benefited from on this voyage, have we not?" He looked at them in turn and by his gaze shamed them into silence. "Now, we have a prize ahead of us that we must take, do we all agree? Good. And so we will speak to Sultan Babu for he is the most powerful king of these lands who will help us to find and pursue our enemy. If we can also at the same time extend the hand of friendship between our queen and this king then we shall do so. Perhaps we or one of our friends can one day return and wrest control from the Catholics. Now, we will sail to the Sultan's fortress."

As usual, everyone had had their say and then Drake did whatever he wanted.

The fortress was at a place named Talangam and any lingering notion I had that these were barbarous lands filled with ignorant and backward savages was dispelled. The fortress itself had been a Portuguese one and was constructed from the local stone in a European style but everything else was both foreign and yet grand beyond measure.

We were met by three enormous war galleys, each rowed by eighty oarsmen. Upon their gleaming decks stood perfect ranks of shining soldiers with lances erect over their heads and bows and arrows on their backs. These magnificent vessels rowed around and around the *Hind* while we, battered and salty from our crossing, stood and gaped at the opulence. They even fired some small Portuguese cannon in salute and we returned their greeting with a thunderous cannonade and volleys of arquebus fire. That astonished and deeply impressed the locals.

When the galleys towed us into an anchorage, the Sultan himself was rowed out. Quickly, Drake ordered us to scrub up and to bring up the silverware while he changed into his most regal outfit. The ship's musicians were plucked from their watches and commanded to play upon the command deck as the Sultan came up.

He was a fine-looking lord. Drake bowed before him, short and stocky and rough while the Sultan was tall, broad-shouldered and narrow-waisted with a regal bearing and a penetrating gaze. Drake's finery was grander than anything I owned and yet he looked like a peasant next to that eastern king. The man's waist was girded by cloth of gold and he wore bright red leather shoes and he was covered with gold jewellery embedded with precious stones. Gold rings dangled from his turban and the chain around his neck was thick enough to anchor a pinnace. The rings on his fingers were weighed down with diamonds, emeralds, and rubies each bigger than the last.

One of the Sultan's emissaries translated his lord's words into Spanish. "You shall be supplied with all that you require and from now until forever you shall be my honoured guests."

We were there for three days loading supplies and during just two more meetings, Drake charmed the sultan enough to get a trade agreement from him. The deal was that when we got home, we would have a fleet sent out to push the Portuguese from his islands and in return he would grant exclusive rights to the clove trade to the English. To seal the deal, he gave Drake a gold ring with a mighty ruby, a coat of superb mail armour and a polished helmet fit for a king, and dozens of other gifts. As further proof of his commitment, he allowed us to buy six tons of cloves for a knockdown price. Before we set off, we also loaded up sugar cane, fruits, hens, rice, sago and silk clothing. No man but Drake could have achieved so much in so short a time.

On we sailed, looking for signs of our enemy and for days we crept from anchorage to harbour while scanning the horizon.

At Celebes, we saw her.

The *Sangre Santa*.

***

We came up on Vega's ship without preparation. Though we had spent months searching for her, when we inched around a rocky headland one morning and saw her along the coast, we were somehow shocked.

She saw us and sprang into action while our men were still rousing Drake from his cabin. I stood at the rail and kept out of the way while the men jumped to obey the orders spoken by Drake and the master and relayed from stern to bow and from deck to cross trees. The *Sangre Santa* was of a size with us but she was supposedly not as well-armed and if we could close with her, we could batter her with our cannons until she surrendered.

But her crew sailed her superbly and I am certain that there were men on her who had sailed those waters before for reasons that later became apparent. The chase lasted all day. We followed her on the same tack but the *Hind* sailed a fraction closer to the wind than our prey and so wherever we could, we cut off the corners and travelled a shorter distance, inching closer. By noon, we were close enough to see the men on her deck and by the afternoon we were shouting insults at them from our bow.

Standing at the rear rail was a giant of a man.

"There he is," I said to Drake while he joined me. He was taking bites from a hunk of dried mutton the size of his fist. "Lorenzo de la Vega. The man who betrayed us at San Juan de Ulúa."

Drake was as relaxed as I had ever seen him. "We have them, Richard. We have their measure at sea and I will draw us near before darkness falls. You know these sorts of men better than anyone. Tell me, what will he do?"

"He will not surrender, if that is your meaning. No, he will fight. Without the artillery to combat ours, his only hope is to draw us to him and then to board us."

Drake chewed his mouthful of mutton. It was a hot, steamy day even over those green seas and the meat in his hand stank, as warm mutton does. "The man is a giant and possessed of immortal strength. If it comes to a fight, do you think you can beat him?"

"I have not seen him in combat but if he has had any training at all, and I do not doubt that he has, then an immortal of his stature will be a formidable opponent. And I do not like fighting on ships."

"You have done well enough so far."

"Real fighting, I mean. A true battle, between soldiers, not boarding actions between sailors."

He sniffed, put out that I thought so little of what we had achieved thus far. But it was the truth. "I assure you, our battles have been hard-fought, sir, and my men are as good as any soldiers in the world."

I nodded, looking across the frothy seas at the Lorenzo de la Vega at the back of the *Sangre Santa*. "A long time ago, I fought with King Edward III at Sluys. We had a great many ships, not like this one but grand ships for the day, though the French had more. It was not at sea but in a harbour of sorts and when their fleet began to manoeuvre, they became separated. We moved in as one, keeping together and defeated them piece by piece. All our men against a fraction of theirs, overwhelming them. Still, each ship was fought over by armoured men-at-arms fighting shoulder to shoulder across the beam and we had to break them one ship at a time. Eventually, the ships were all pressed together in a great mass. I could not even count how many. A hundred, three hundred? We crossed from deck to deck, slipping in the gallons of blood spilled across the timbers. I killed countless men that day and in all there were thousands dead, thousands. Knights and lords screaming in agony and begging for death, for their mothers, for God to save them or to take them." I looked at him. "That's a true ship battle, Francis."

He stared at me. "Not if it happened in a harbour. That's a land battle that just happened to take place on a land of wood with a sky of canvas and hemp."

I could not help but laugh. "If that giant wants to fight, we shall have a job to stop him and the six immortals he has with him. And how many of his men has he turned now? Might that be a ship half-filled with immortals?"

He squinted up at the sky from beneath the brim of his hat. "He would not be able to handle his ship so well if they were all shaded as he is. As I am."

"Even if it is just a half dozen, we shall have to prepare for them."

"Very well. How?"

I had been pondering that very thing. "We need a line of men with pikes standing upon the Command Deck but every other man will be armed with an arquebus. When the enemy gain our main deck, the rest of the men must retreat behind the line of pikemen. We shall blast the boarders and stick them."

He frowned. "Sounds complicated. As you so eloquently described, they are not soldiers and if they have not drilled this specific manoeuvre, they shall be unable to perform it."

"I drilled them well months ago and they managed similar feats then. All shall be well."

"If you say so. But what about our immortal giant?"

"Leave him to me."

The men worked as effectively as I had ever seen. Sails were pulled in or lowered with such speed that I marvelled to see it. When ropes needed to be hauled it was as though they had doubled their strength and each man had four arms. The master took us to the brink of the *Hind*'s abilities and found wind that seemed to elude our enemy.

And so we closed.

The shoals around the coast were treacherous and we had men keeping watch on them, calling out signs of reefs such as frothing eddies of white water. Every man was on edge and every man was performing at his peak.

"Let us give them a warning," Drake commanded in the afternoon.

Word was relayed to crews manning the bow chasers and soon one fired. It blasted a ball along the side of the *Sangre Santa* and threw up a splash of water twenty yards ahead of it.

"A fine shot," Drake commented.

He stood in his usual position on the Command Deck with his hands behind his back and his legs planted wide. Beside him, the helmsmen wrestled with the whipstaff that steered the ship and the master stood ready to call orders. Visibility from there was not always good, due to the sails, masts, spars, and rigging and so every now and then he would cross to the rail and look along at the enemy vessel.

I stood at that rail continuously, clinging on with white knuckles and willing the *Hind* forward.

"Aim for the rigging," Drake said and the order was conveyed to the gunners at the bow. They shot at the *Sangre Santa*, aiming to hit the mizzen mast or to whip a shot along the decks to hit the ropes that secured the sails or the spars. But those were difficult shots to take, especially when the powder was so inconsistent and the balls were of various sizes. I went to watch for a while and witnessed men mixing the powder and ensuring it was dry, and other men filling casting marks from the cannonballs to make them as spherical as possible.

The gun was hauled back from the gunport by ropes so that the mouth of the barrel was well inside the hull. Men swabbed it out with a great wad of wet rags on a pole, before the powder was poured in and the ball heaved in and rammed tight into place. When it was ready to fire, they heaved the ropes again to pull the gun tight to the hull where it was lashed into place. The master of the gun looked down the barrel, timing the shot with the rising and the falling of both ships. Beside him, a sailor took down the linstock—a staff with a lighted slow match at the end—hanging from the beam and blew on the smouldering match before standing ready.

"Fire!"

At the master's cry, the sailor standing ready with the linstock touched the match to the touch hole.

The detonation of the cannon travelled right through my body and deafened me, even with my hands clapped over my ears. A hole was ripped in their maintop sail and later, as the sun was low in the sky, another ball travelled the length of the ship and broke the spar that held the foresail, to much rejoicing.

But Drake and the officers did not cheer. In fact, they seemed glum.

"We are not going to catch them before dark, are we?" I asked.

Their silence was answer enough.

"What happens if we have not caught them by nightfall?" I asked.

The master spoke without turning. "They can change course, unseen, and slip away. We will have to guess at their heading. If we are not precise about it, they shall—"

"There!" Drake shouted. "She's luffing. There, they missed their tack. See, the wind falls from their sails! On now, on. We have them, we have them and we can take them. Change course, cut them off now."

The master began calling out orders, ropes were hauled and the ship turned until we were aimed at their bow.

Drake and the master grinned at each other. "We will come up beside them before they can catch the wind once more and we shall give them a volley into their rigging. We don't want to damage her too much as we will sail her back to—"

"She's off!" the watchman shouted. "She fills! She fills and she's off!"

"What in the world..." Drake said and rushed to the rail.

The sails of the *Sangre Santa* were stiff and she was surging ahead again, like a horse bursting through a gate.

"It was a trick," the master said beside us. "She never missed her tack, not at all. Must have loosed her lines on the larboard side so it appeared thus, right?"

Drake was appalled. "But why let us come so close?" he said. "She has given up her lead for no gain and all we have done is cut across on a different..."

The colour drained from his face and he filled his lungs to give an order when the men above cried out.

"Reef! Reef, dead ahead!"

There was a long moment of horror before the master started roaring his orders and Drake shouted at me to help him. He shoved the helmsman aside and leaned on the whipstaff with his whole body and heaved against it. When I joined him and pushed we turned the rudder to its full extent, which was a mere 15 degrees.

We had barely begun our turn when the ship struck the reef.

It was a terrific impact, throwing dozens of us off our feet as the *Hind* ground against the submerged rocks and was lifted up onto it. The sound was like an explosion and the poor *Hind* groaned like she was hurt.

Drake and I had the whipstaff to cling onto but the master had smashed his face on the navigation table and got to his feet with blood gushing from his nose. They were about to shout orders when we were thrown down once more, this time to starboard as the ship heeled over at an incredible angle. We were hung up on the reef by our larboard bow and we would have tipped fully into the frothing sea had not the stiff wind blowing from the land a few miles away kept us somewhat upright.

And yet that same stiff wind also pressed us ever more firmly aground, driving us against that reef so that our timbers ground away on it and ensuring we would not slide off.

Night was falling quickly but we saw the crew of *Sangre Santa* waving and gesturing as they sailed away into the darkness.

* * *

I was certain that I was going to die.

The crew did not panic as they set to work but I am sure they felt the same. It was dark and the waves boomed against us and with every impact the timbers were cracked and ground away further. If the wind were to drop, we knew we would keel over and be tumbled into the black sea and into death.

"Every man not at the pumps!" shouted Drake. "Will join me in prayer!"

They knelt as best they could on the sloping main deck and prayed harder than they had ever prayed before, beseeching God to deliver us from destruction. I did my duty at the pumps for longer than any other man, as my stamina was of course that much the greater. I worked until my hands, softened by the seawater, first blistered and then burst and bled. And I worked until they healed themselves and blistered and bled again. Teams rotated while I worked and drove the pistons up and down and forced the water up and out of the hold. When enough water had been ejected, Drake and the carpenter went forward and deep into the bowels to inspect the damage.

"The damage may be repaired!" the carpenter cried when they came back. "As long as we can be freed from the reef."

It was a faint hope but it was enough to give the men the strength to get through the long night at the pumps. At first light, Drake ordered a boat to be lowered and an anchor was lowered into that. He declared he would take the anchor out to a point where it could be lowered and we would pull the anchor in and so warp the ship off the rocks.

There was no ground.

That reef must have been the tip of a column of rock that rose straight up out of the terrifying depths for Drake and his men rowed around for hours taking soundings everywhere. Even as close as a boat's length from the reef there was no seabed even at 300 fathoms. The thought of such black depths beneath us made me feel sick.

"We may have to take the men off," Drake said at our conference that day.

Everyone was exhausted and they nodded wearily.

"In the ship's boat?" I asked, as ever asking obvious questions. "How many men will it hold?"

"At a push," the master answered, "twenty-five. Though we'll be overloaded at that."

"And how far is it to land?"

"Twenty miles," he answered again. "And I doubt we'll be able to land direct upon that rocky shore. Might have to go up and down the coast, looking for a spot."

"A third of the crew," I said. "We can take off just one-third of the crew at a time? And then I assume we can come back to pick up the rest?"

"A hard sail, that," the master said. "A hard sail but it's that or sit here while we break to pieces."

"I'll not abandon her while she's yet sound," Drake said but he sounded dejected. "The *Hind* is the strongest ship ever built and she holds, by God, she holds. We must lighten her as far as is possible."

We threw overboard three tons of the cloves, as well as victuals, ammunition and two of the largest cannons.

"Now what?" I asked.

"We wait to see if we slide off," Drake said as we watched the second cannon go over. "And if not, we throw more over."

"The treasure," I said. "We have tons of it."

"That, too," he allowed, "though that last of all."

"Last?" I said. "After the food and the water? We cannot eat silver, Francis."

He turned on me. "I'll not needlessly throw away all we have won thus far."

I stared at him. "Needlessly? What good is silver if we go to the bottom along with it? Throw it over!"

"No!" he said. "And that is the end of it. You are not the captain of this ship, I am! And I will not have my orders questioned."

455

The men were watching and so I bowed and said no more, though I could barely restrain myself.

Called to a service, all the crew that could be spared gathered on the main deck and prayed, led by the parson Francis Fletcher.

But as he led the prayers, he began ascribing our calamity to certain unnamed actions that we had committed. The more he spoke, the more it became apparent that he was blaming it all on something immoral that Drake had done. "By the actions of our commander did we come to this impending doom!" Fletcher roared. "And so we pray that the Lord not punish us for the crimes of that man who we were duty-bound to obey. Oh God, we beg You forgive us and if You must punish us then punish that one man alone and not us the good and loyal gentlemen and crew of this cursed vessel!"

"Martin!" I said, grabbing him up from his knees. "Run and tell Drake that he needs to shut Fletcher up. Now!"

The men stopped praying and began looking at each other and at the captain who came down calmly from the Command Deck while Fletcher continued bellowing his prayer of condemnation. "Oh Lord, you are angry at the unjust, unholy execution of your loyal servant Thomas Doughty and your righteous fury is now directed down at us but we beg you, humbly, on bended knees that the murder of the gentleman Doughty be ascribed to one man alone, just one man, oh Lord!"

When Drake reached him, he was purple with rage and I rushed over ready to stop him killing the parson.

"Francis Fletcher!" Drake roared, pointing a shaking finger, "I do here excommunicate you out of the Church of God and from the benefits and graces thereof! And I denounce you to the Devil and his angels!"

He ordered Fletcher to be seized and had him chained to a hatch in the forecastle over the part that was hung up on the reef. And he ordered a board of wood to be hung about his neck and on the board was carved the words, "Francis Fletcher, the falsest knave that lives."

Soon after that the wind suddenly slackened and then veered around into the opposite direction. While we clung on for dear life, the ship juddered and bucked and slid off the reef.

We had been delivered from destruction.

Immediately, we refitted at an island and then travelled south along the south coast of Java before refilling our water and food through trade with the locals there. We knew we had a long journey ahead of us.

All hopes for finding and catching the *Sangre Santa* were forgotten. After our near disaster, all any of us hoped for was finding our way home. If we saw her, we would try for her but otherwise the plan was to reach England without being wrecked. The *Hind* was repaired but still she had taken a significant beating and there was still a long way to go.

We crossed the vast expanse of the Indian Ocean in two months. If it had not been for the rains falling on our decks, we would have died of thirst before we reached Africa but reach it we did. When we made that landfall, we were down to less than half a pint daily for every three men. Just enough for mortal men to avoid death but not enough for wellbeing.

By God, the men were weary. Reaching the shores of Africa, finding fresh water and fresh food, restored the crew's health as much as could be expected and without much delay we continued around the southern capes into the Atlantic. The lemons and other fruit we gorged on filled us with strength but more than that, perhaps, was the growing sense that we were almost home. Strange as it was for us to think it but the sights of African trees and occasional elephants on the shore, once so profoundly alien, now brought a feeling of familiarity.

All talk was of home. Of sons and daughters and of wives and parents. Hopes they would all be found alive and well, though yearning for their men so long at sea. Talk was of fresh beer and butter, of the green hills of Devon, of our Queen and her enemies.

But at the same time, Drake and I grew pensive. Would we be welcomed for what we had achieved? Or had things changed such in our long absence so that we might be shunned or even condemned? Most of all, we thought of our failure to catch the *Sangre Santa*. Those riches would find their way to Spain and thence to William de Ferrers. With such a fortune, he could fund such mischief that we might not be strong enough to resist it.

On 26th September 1580, we worked our way into Plymouth Sound, the ship far lower in the water than when we left. A fishing boat at anchor bobbed beside the channel, the fishermen at work arranging the nets after their day's work before coming in on the tide.

I leaned over the side and cupped my hands. "Hail, fellows! Tell me. Is Queen Elizabeth still alive?"

They looked at each other, confused, before one of them stood and raised his hands to his mouth. "Aye! Alive and well!"

Behind me, the men cheered and clapped each other on the back, drawing yet more strange looks from the fishermen. I thanked them and waved as we picked our way on into Plymouth.

We had been gone almost three years. We had failed to kill the true ruler of the New World and we had let him escape with a vast fortune. In many ways, our grand voyage had been a failure.

But we were home.

15

Agents

1581

THE PEOPLE OF PLYMOUTH and Devon were overjoyed to see us and the men tumbled into the taverns and rushed home to their families, spewing forth the tales of the voyage. The very day we landed I handed off letters I had prepared and they were rushed to London. I knew we had to act fast to ensure we kept as much of the treasure as possible because soon enough everyone would come to claim their share. As soon as it could be arranged, we loaded a dozen horses with gold and silver and headed for London with scores of men to guard them, mostly crew but also men from the Order. Much of the treasure was diverted to my house in the Strand but we had to win Elizabeth's heart so we took piles of it to Whitehall. When we reached the palace, we barely had to wait a moment before we were escorted to the audience room.

Elizabeth was not there. I stood to the side while courtiers and councillors pressed at Drake from all sides with questions that came so fast that he never got to finish a single answer before starting on the next one.

William Cecil sidled over to me, looking up with a raised eyebrow. His old face had aged a great deal in the three years I had been absent. But such is the way with the aged, they seem hardly to advance in years for a decade and then do their ageing all of a sudden. It always makes me sad to see it, even in those I have little affection for.

"So," Cecil said without preamble. "You survived,"

I bowed. "I usually do."

"Come and see me after," he said. "There is much to discuss. I shall summon our friends when you are done."

"When I am done with what, my lord?" I asked.

"Come with me," he said. After extracting Drake from his encircling questioners, he led us to the Queen's private chambers. Elizabeth stood as we entered, smiling at Drake and coming halfway across the room toward him. Her ladies stood and bowed and we two men kneeled before her.

"My conquering heroes return!" she cried.

"Your Majesty," we both said in unison.

"Arise, sirs. Come, come," she said, lifting Drake by the shoulders and looking him the eye. "My heroic captain, you have returned to me."

Drake spoke earnestly. "Your Majesty, I have thought of little else these past three years than returning to stand before you, just as we are now. And though I have oft imagined this moment, no imagining can compare to the reality, as the beating of my heart will attest."

Elizabeth gasped and her ladies sighed and she placed her fingers upon his doublet over his chest for a moment before raising those fingers to her lips.

"Sir, I have not felt such joy as I feel now for as long as I can recall."

Drake grinned. "I have brought you gifts, Your Majesty, of gold and of silver. Jewels and treasures the like of which never have been seen in England."

"Oh, I cannot wait to see them, my gallant captain, though even more than your golden gifts I desire to hear your golden words. I simply must know of your adventures."

Since I entered the room, she had not so much as glanced in my direction and I resisted the urge to huff like a spurned girl.

Drake bowed again, smiling. "As well as those treasures, Your Majesty, I have brought my logs, my charts, my maps, all in my own hand so that I might illustrate the full account of my journey. Shall I show you them now?"

She smiled. "In time, my gallant captain, in time. I beg you wait in the next chamber and take some refreshments before we begin what I am certain will be a thrilling tale of your adventures."

His face fell a little. "Of course, Your Majesty, I will be delighted to do so."

She turned to her ladies. "Leave us," she commanded and they filed out through one door or another and Cecil indicated the one that we should use. As I made to follow them, Elizabeth stepped forward and placed her hand flat on my chest. When she spoke, her voice was not the high and flighty one she had used with Drake but a commanding, imperious one. "Not you, Richard. You will stay."

Drake turned, his eyes wide and his mouth open, but Cecil urged him out with the ladies until there was none left in the room but an older lady sitting by the door, focusing on her embroidery. The doors closed and Elizabeth looked at me, standing close.

The years had not been kind. Her smallpox scars seemed deeper and larger and many of her teeth were yellowed, some on their way to brown. Beneath her makeup, her wrinkled skin sagged especially at the eyes and her cheeks were becoming jowly. As close as we were, I noticed that her breath was become quite foul.

"Richard," she said, reaching out and sinking closer as she closed her eyes. "Kiss me."

What could I do? She was the Queen. I pulled her firmly against me and kissed her lips. She moaned and pushed her breasts against me and ran her hands over my back, buttocks and shoulders.

After a good while, she pushed me away, gasping for breath and filled with passion. Turning dramatically, she retreated across the room to a fine table and leaned upon it. For a moment, I wondered if she expected me to approach and lift her skirts from behind but after catching her breath she sat in a chair and invited me to sit at the other side of her table.

"If you please, Mary," she said and her servant busied herself and brought us wine and small morsels of cheese and apples, fresh and stewed. All the while, Elizabeth looked at me with her penetrating gaze.

"You have not aged a single day," she said at last, when her lady had seated herself once more across the room. "Not a single day, I swear it."

"My face may not be changed but the voyage has taken its toll, Elizabeth. At times, I felt such fear that I thought I would expire from the terror alone."

Her eyes shone. "Not you, sir. Not my brave and ever-youthful Sir Knight. Surely, you were not so afraid as all that. Not after all the lives you already have led and after all the battles waged and won. What was it that frightened you so? Can the Spanish be so terrible?"

"The Spanish?" I said, as if confused. "Not at all. The seas we sailed had waves taller even than this palace. The savages of the untamed lands ofttimes threatened to overwhelm us by their treachery. We might have died from thirst or starvation. Our ship was almost dashed to pieces in the middle of an Eastern sea by a black mountain whose jagged peak ripped at us from beneath the surface of the frothing waves."

She gasped and reached for my hand. "You must tell me all. Every moment. From England to the South Seas and to England again. Tell me, sir, whether you were successful in your missions, both secret and more secret still."

I bowed my head and did as she so ordered.

For more than six hours, I spoke of the voyage. The mutinous Doughty, the claiming of the Elizabeth Islands and Nova Albion, the natives both friendly and treacherous, the taking of prizes and the agreement we had reached with the Sultan of Ternate. Most of all, she wanted to know of the treasures and of my meeting with the Viceroy of New Spain.

"A million pesos of treasure. Eight million reals. Now in the hands of our enemies, which may be used to fund an army, a fleet, a thousand assassins, or an invasion of England."

She sat back. "So you say."

"The Viceroy told us much of William's plans."

"You trust his word so completely, this Viceroy of New Spain? Well I have the word of another who is greater and truer than your corrupt friend. I have the royal word of King Philip that he means only friendship toward us and I am minded to believe him over you or your former prisoner. In fact, I begin to doubt your competence, sir. It may well be that your wits are at fault or perhaps it is your judgement. Which would you say it is?"

She expected me to defend myself but that was a losing battle. To do so, while seeking to limit the damage I had done to her estimation of me, would be admitting that I was at fault.

"Perhaps it is your judgement that is in question, Elizabeth."

She scowled at me. "Careful, sir. I allow you great freedoms because of my love for you but do not overstep your bounds."

I sat up straighter. "If you want an agreeable fool who will cower before your royal contempt, I shall send one in for you. And if there were any courtiers present I would bow my head meekly and play the lamb. But do not mistake me for a man who will tell you only what you wish to hear in return for the royal favour. I will speak truth alone because you are our queen and also because of the love and regard I have for you."

She stared at me. "You must never think that we—"

"You do not truly believe King Philip," I said, speaking over her. "Let us dismiss that notion at once. Open war is coming and so we must prepare. The resources of the warmongers in Spain are only growing. And we must be ready or else we shall be overrun."

"You will no longer speak to me in such a fashion. It matters not whether courtiers are present or not. You are not my husband, you are not even a courtier. You are a servant and a poor one at that. I am minded to dismiss you from my presence and from my service. You will apologise at once."

"I am loyal. I will do as you command. If you wish to send me away, I will obey no matter how heavy my heart." I lowered my voice. "If you were not queen or if I was a prince, perhaps I might have been your husband. If I am overly familiar it is because I cannot help but think of the closeness we once shared, however brief. But very well, my lady, let us simply hope for peace, let us pray for it every day and publicly trust our enemies. But let us also prepare for war by building new ships and raising fortresses and by training and equipping men. The new ships must be built to exacting specifications, as advised by the lords of your navy. Sleek, swift galleons with many long-range brass cannons. They must be built at once for if war descends swiftly it shall be too late. Hope for peace, prepare for war, surely that is a sound policy for any prince?"

Elizabeth scoffed. "Always, my advisers tell me the solution to every problem is to spend more money. Tell me, how will we pay for these ships and guns and men?"

"We will use the treasure we have won to pay for part of it. But the rest must come from England."

She smiled, sadly. "There is no money. You must find another way."

"You do not understand. There is no—"

"Even my husband would know when best to close his great

flapping lips, sir. As your queen, I command you to find another way to stop this war. That is how you act is it not? Quietly and in the shadows? Well, be silent now, and leave me."

I stood and bowed. "As my queen commands."

"I suppose I shall have to listen to that little captain tell me the same stories all over again now, only he will speak to me with far greater humility."

I smiled. "Drake, speak with humility? I am sure you are quite correct, Your Majesty."

While she frowned, I turned to go and she stood.

"Richard?" she came close to me again. "Let us part as friends." She reached for me and I took my hands in hers.

"I would like that."

She looked down. "You must think me become foul indeed. The years pass and..." Her voice cracked and I pulled her close and kissed her again, softly and slowly. After kissing me back, she pushed me away and smiled. "Enough now. That is quite enough. You must go."

I caught the lady's eye as I opened the door and she raised an eyebrow but said nothing, turning back to her embroidery.

Two rooms away, I found Drake snoring in a chair with his head back and his mouth open, drool running from the side of his mouth. Kicking his feet, I woke him and told him the queen needed him now.

"Did she say how much treasure she wants?" he asked, gathering up his books.

"I will leave that business to you," I said.

"You're not coming back in?"

"Charm her with your tales and dazzle her with gold. Above

all, you must convince her to back the immediate expansion of our navy. Every lord of England must contribute and our queen must lead the way. We need a score of magnificent galleons, at least. Charm with that, also, describe how fast and manoeuvrable they will be. Delight her with images of new English ships turning rings about sluggish Catholic galleons, pounding away at them with trumpets sounding and Protestants cheering. She will like that."

"Oh? And while I am summoning a new navy from the air with my tongue, what will you be doing?"

"I must speak to Cecil about stopping this war. "Hurry now, Francis, do not leave her waiting. I am afraid I did not leave her in the best of moods."

"I am sure I can charm her just as well as you can, Richard," he said, striding out.

I watched him go and muttered to myself. "I bloody hope not."

* * *

Later that day, I sat with Stephen opposite Cecil, and Walsingham, while Dudley paced around Cecil's office, looking out of the windows and occasionally deciding to join our conversation. A light rain pattered against the glass and two gardeners were shouting jokes to each other as they worked in the grounds below us.

"Why did you have to circumnavigate the world, Richard?" Cecil asked, his tired old face grim. "Travelling to and from the

South Seas was one thing but now you have made Drake into the most famous man in Christendom. Every kingdom is ablaze with the stories and now, I fear, we have done nothing but accelerate a conflict we cannot win."

"As you well know, it was not for fame but simply an attempt to stop Lorenzo de la Vega's ship. And we almost had him."

"And you allowed him to outwit you," Dudley said from the window without turning. "Leaving us to solve a problem of your creation."

I ignored Dudley and addressed Cecil. "Do we know if Vega's ship ever reached Spain?"

Cecil turned to Walsingham who shook his head. "As far as I can determine, there has been no ship named *Sangre Santa* that reached a Spanish port this past year. I must conclude the ship was berthed under a different name or she unloaded her cargo elsewhere. A remote cove near Cadiz or run up a fisherman's beach one night on the eastern coast. How could anyone know?"

"The treasure she carried was unofficial and unrecorded," I said. "It is to be expected that it would make its way to William's purse like a smuggler landing wine."

"If such a treasure ever existed," Dudley said with his back to us. "There is no evidence that it did."

"The *Sangre Santa* was heavily laden when we found her, riding low in the water and displaying other indications that the seasoned eye of the mariners discerned as she sailed. Her hold was laden indeed."

"It could have been rocks for all you know," Dudley said, sniffing.

It was a weak response and again I ignored him. "Assuming

the treasure reaches William, and he does intend to use the wealth to raise an army and a fleet, what can be done about it?"

Again, we looked to Walsingham. "I have my men doing everything they can to discover activities all across Spain. With this new information regarding his identity as a former cardinal and bishop and once the head of the Inquisition, I will redirect certain agents to look for signs of this wealth in those places where he once worked. If we find and track the treasure, perhaps we can discover the new identity and location of the man we seek."

"Your notion of pursuing sign of the treasure is a sound one," Stephen said to Walsingham. "But we could do better to look for signs of it being spent."

Cecil frowned. "What signs?"

"Well, what do the Spanish need for an invasion? Ships, men, arms, armour, supplies. This would be a grand enterprise requiring many years of preparation. Perhaps it has already begun but I would expect to see armour being forged for thousands of men and then stored ready for use. Weapons, also. Ships take a long time to build, especially warships and many places would be building at once. What else?"

"Food and water," Dudley said. "Men always forget that supplies are the most important element of any army."

"Quite true, my lord, quite true," I said, "although these would be stockpiled closer to the date of the invasion."

"If there even is such an invasion planned," Dudley said. "It would be an enormous and irreversible step for our friends in Spain to take, would it not? And Philip is not a rash man. Far from it."

"No indeed," I said. "And yet he has certain men chewing on

his ear, day after day, pushing him to take such a step."

"Philip is a king and a great king at that. Such men cannot be exploited, cannot be manipulated, their strength of will is too strong."

Cecil and Walsingham glanced at one another.

Stephen spoke, addressing Dudley's back. "What of the Pope's mission, my lord, to Ireland last year and the year before it? Some of the soldiers were Spanish. Are we to assume that our friend Philip did not sanction it?"

"Who are you, a Catholic merchant spy, to address me in so haughty a manner, sir?" Dudley said, turning to glare at Stephen, whose face reddened.

"Will you answer me if I ask the same question?" I said.

Dudley sneered. "You are hardly the better man, Richard."

I raised my eyebrows and placed a hand on my chest, as if greatly offended. "But, my lord, I was raised the son of a knight and am the bastard son of an earl. Of course, I am not a gentleman of your standing but perhaps you would stoop to converse with me."

He rolled his eyes, knowing he was being mocked. "Son of an earl. So you say, sir. You could be the son of a yeoman, as low down as your friend Drake, and none of us would ever know it. All we know is you refuse to embrace the true faith and what does that say about your nature?"

"Come, Robert, any man can at a moment's glance perceive my aristocratic stature and bearing," I winked at Cecil and Walsingham, who scowled at me. Puritans were not known for their sense of humour and they were not impressed by mine.

"In answer to the question raised, sirs, there was indeed a

papal expedition to Ireland," Cecil said, quickly, before Dudley could respond. "Their purpose was to foment a general rising in Munster against our rule. A season later, a second group arrived and among them were Spanish soldiers, priests, and agents."

I sat up straighter. "What happened? Were there Spanish immortals amongst them?"

"If they were immortal," Walsingham said, "they are all dead now." He almost smiled, and I realised it was his attempt at a witticism. "All the invaders were pushed back into Smerwick and there they were put down."

"Put down?" I repeated.

"We butchered the Catholic filth," Dudley snapped.

"Well," I said, "that is that, then."

Walsingham shook his head. "Apart from the actions of the Jesuits that continue to undermine the true faith in England. And Stephen believes many of these men are immortals, sent to do that very thing, and worse."

"Stephen?" I prompted, as he was staring off into nothing. "Have you stopped paying attention?"

Stephen shook his head and turned to me. "You said that Cardinal Diego de Espinosa *was* William? I am astonished that he was out in the open like that for so long and yet we did not find him. There were hints of dark rumours around Espinosa but none that seemed especially credible. It is to my shame that I let him slip away into some other guise."

"Indeed," Dudley said, "it sounds as though your supposed brilliance in this secret arena are over-vaunted."

Stephen did not appear to notice that he was being insulted. "I must repeat that we did consider whether he was an immortal and the evidence was weak. Never did I imagine it could be William because, truth be told, he was described as rather fat and balding. William is far from either of these things, of course."

Cecil whipped his eyes to me. "Could you be mistaken in this?"

I shrugged. "William has posed as men from countless other races, from those of distant Tartary and China to the Turks and Bulgarians. I do not know how he has played these parts but play them he has. It would not be beyond him to shave his scalp and to wrap quilted linen about his belly beneath his priestly raiment. Or even, I suppose, allow himself to become corpulent, if it served his aims."

"What a worm he is," Dudley said, with venom.

"The vilest there ever was."

"You must go on, Stephen," Walsingham prompted. "Why are you now even more certain that our Jesuits are infested with immortals?"

"Cardinal Diego de Espinosa was the Chief Inquisitor. And the Inquisition purged the Jesuits of their *conversos*..."

Walsingham nodded. "Yes, yes, I see."

I looked between them. "Well, I do not. They purged the Jews, what of it?"

Stephen leaned toward me. "Don't you see, Richard? Such activity provided cover for William to install his own men within the Jesuits. Men supposedly vetted by the Inquisition and so above suspicion."

"God's teeth," I said, drawing hisses from the Puritans. "He first infiltrated the Inquisition and came to command it so that he could *also* infiltrate the Jesuits. It is just like William to place himself in both camps, to take both sides in what seems to be a conflict while in fact controlling everything from the shadows. We can very likely assume elements within both the Inquisition and the Jesuits are doing his bidding."

"We know the Catholic institutions for our enemies anyway, Richard!" cried Dudley. "All your clever reasoning changes nothing in that regard. We must find every last Jesuit that creeps upon our soil and we must expel him or, if he has committed a crime, execute him! Any English Catholic who has aided these men must likewise be put to death. Too long have we been lenient with them when every plot, every rebellion, every assassin we have faced since Elizabeth has been queen has had a Catholic behind it. I say no more leniency. That time is over."

I looked at Stephen and he glared at me, willing me to hold my tongue. But I knew that arguing religion with a Protestant served no purpose but to drive them to ever greater extremism.

"That is something I believe we all can agree on," Cecil said, looking at us. When we sat in silence, he continued. "But I see now we must prepare fully for the worst. I will see to it that every effort is made to expand our naval forces to the fullest extent. I have here before me the official recommendations of the Navy Board with regards to England's sea forces. We have been building ships to the new specifications but always they urge me to fund more. The Lord Admiral wants at least twenty more war galleons but we could not fund their construction. Considering the potential danger and this influx of treasure, official and otherwise, I believe it is now our duty to build as many as we can manage."

Dudley cleared his throat. "With the costs being borne by the

Crown?"

Cecil looked at Dudley through his eyebrows. "As much as can be borne but it shall require every lord in the kingdom to do his part. If he does not, he may find himself in a Spanish gaol before long, if not worse."

"We will build a galleon also," I said, drawing a look from all of them. "We have the funds, I believe, Stephen?"

He tried to control his distress. "Thanks to our profits from your voyage, we should be able to fund a single galleon. If it is not too large."

I smiled. "Wonderful."

"How very generous of you, sirs. Whatever else may happen, King Philip and the devil in his ear shall not find England unprepared," Cecil said, getting to his feet. "Now, I shall leave the spying work to you, Francis, Stephen, and Richard, but suffice to say we must win your secret war if we are to avoid the greater one."

Walsingham nodded. "Certainly, we shall combine our efforts on this more than ever and make finding the Jesuits our most urgent priority."

"If you two can find them," I said to Walsingham and Stephen when Cecil and Dudley had left, "then I will kill them."

***

Stephen and the others had been tracking suspected immortal Jesuits for years, watching their meeting places, bribing the high and the low for word of them, recruiting Protestants, Puritans, Catholics in any way they could. Over a period of months, the

Order of the White Dagger worked with Walsingham's spy network to snatch up a dozen Jesuit priests and twice as many men and women who assisted them.

We explained that we wished honest Catholics no harm. We told them that their Order had been infiltrated by evil men and a handful admitted that they suspected as much. Most of those had some faint knowledge of a shadowy leader they knew only as the Crow. He was the man with the power, who dictated who did what and where, but no one knew any more than that. All our prisoners denied ever meeting him and they certainly did not know where he was.

And yet, there was the general impression that the immortal Jesuits were panicking. We were stifling their activities and weakening them more every month.

God granted us a piece of luck. One young Catholic woman from York spoke about a fair-haired priest she met once who demanded that she and her brother bleed themselves and give the blood to him. She swore she knew not why but had done it out of a sense of duty. It was she that led us to him, a man who lived in a room in the eastern part of London.

"He's gone into the White Hart," Walt said, ducking in through the doorway where I waited and shaking the rain from his hat.

The inn was in the north of London and the man we followed to it was the secret Jesuit priest with the blond hair, of that we were certain. A former landlord of his said he was always in bed in the day and out all night and once they had argued over the price of his rooms and the blond man had threatened him, saying he would drink his blood. The landlord, a broad chested fellow with hands like hams, also said the small blond man was incredibly strong, pinning the bigger man to the wall with ease.

"Then we shall wait for him to come out again," I said, looking across the street at the White Hart Inn. We could not see much of it from where we were but we had followed him for a mile already and I did not want him to see us going into the inn after him.

Walt sighed. "Let's just go in there, drag him out and do him in."

"We must use him to lead us to the others."

"That's what I'm saying! We'll drag him back to the house, shut him in the cellar, and make him give it up. The old ways are the best ways, you know that better than anyone."

"We will continue to follow him once he leaves and he will lead us to the others." I was not certain about that idea but I had allowed myself to be persuaded. And I did not want any more immortals in our cellar.

Walt grumbled and stamped his feet. "You're starting to sound like bloody Stephen, you know that, don't you? I'm going to go in and keep an eye on him."

"Where is Goodie?" I asked.

"Down the road, by the lane in case he goes southeast between the wall and the fields."

"Tell her to go into the inn and keep an eye on him."

"Alone? In that shit pit? They'll think she's a whore."

"She used to own an inn, I think she will survive. Go on, man, why must you argue every point?"

"Alright, alright," he muttered as he went out into the rain, cursing me under his breath.

A few minutes later, Walt came back, shedding water again. He was smiling.

"What has pleased you so?"

"Oh, nothing, Richard, nothing." He chuckled and shook his head.

I looked closely at his flushed cheeks. "Are you tupping Goodie, Walter?"

"No." He sighed. "She bloody well wants it, though, I know she does."

"But she's too sensible to give it up to you? A wise woman."

"She's something, alright, the dirty old mare."

"Perhaps she wishes to be married before taking a man into her bed."

He scoffed. "She ain't the marrying type."

"But she was married before."

"Exactly."

"You love her," I said.

His mouth fell open. "Shut up!"

"You know, I think that you and Goodie should get married, Walt. After all, she is almost as shameless as you."

He stared at me, all trace of smile now gone. "She's a charming woman with a cracking pair but she's a Protestant for one thing. She ain't turning Catholic and I ain't turning heretic."

"For God's sake, Walter, I doubt you have even been to Mass in a hundred years."

"No matter what, I ain't spending eternity with her."

"Eternity? We may not age much but we are not facing *eternity*. Come now, I am surprised that either of us have lived this long as it is and I am sure that we will not survive very much longer. You especially."

"You know what I mean!" he snapped and shook his head. "Marriage. I hope you be making a jest." He frowned at me. "And you bloody well are, ain't you. Ain't you?"

I peered out across the lane. A horse was ridden from the stable yard and another followed soon after but I did not catch sight of the riders through the rain. "I was being facetious, I admit, but now I think of it, I cannot imagine why you would not want to share the rest of your days with a good woman. And she is the best you are ever likely to get."

"The best woman she is, right enough, but she ain't ever going to measure up against a score of lesser women, is she."

"A score of lesser women sounds like a typical week for you."

"Chance would be a fine thing. I have no more than a couple or three delightful ladies I frequent from time to time until they get too old or too poxed, then move on to the next."

"Sounds rather sad and devoid of meaning."

Walt scoffed. "Whores are women just like any other, some wise, some foolish. And truth be told, I like conversing with my whores almost as much as I like sticking my—"

He broke off as Goodie came hurtling through the open doorway, kicking up mud. "He's gone off on horseback, boys! Our blond lad. He met another fellow, they knocked back their ale, went out to the stable and rode off. Horses held waiting and ready."

"God's hands," I cursed and grabbed Walt. "Find Philip and bring the horses up. Goodie and I will follow on foot so find us on the road. Go!"

"Sorry Richard," Goodie said, breathlessly, as we hurried out into the lane and stomped through the mud. "I didn't want to get too close, see, and then when they was mounting I had to come back through the ale room and this big lad got in my way and I had to give him what for and then—"

"It is well, Goodie, it is well. Were it not for you, I would have missed their escape. Come now, we must follow their route as best we can."

It was a long, straight road with houses on either side. Wherever there was a gap between them, a new house was being built. That cursed city seemed to have grown in every direction every time I saw it. We were already north of the Bishop's Gate and there was nothing to slow our quarry down but the folk travelling by foot, cart or horse ahead of them. The Spital Fields were off to the east on our right and I wondered if they would cross into them and if they did they might be away across country with no hope of following them.

Or they might turn off from the road and enter a property on either side. The people on the road and the driving rain made it hard to see but it seemed the riders were yet up ahead.

"Where are those tardy-gaited, bladder-headed clotpoles with our horses?" Goodie said, breathing heavily and stomping beside me with one arm across the underside of her bosom, her sodden gown clinging to her figure so that the quivering of her flesh beneath was quite apparent. Her coif sagged atop her head and strands of loose hair clung to her red cheeks. Despite her somewhat comical appearance, she looked rather fetching. "It'll be too late soon if they don't hurry." She turned suddenly to look at me and scoffed.

"My eyes yet lay upon our prey, Goodie," I said, dragging my gaze back at the road. "They are just up ahead by the..." I broke off and slowed to a stop.

"Oh, Richard, you bawdy lout," Goodie snapped, standing with her hands on her hips and glaring at me. "Do not say you lost sight of the priest and his mate through failure to keep your ruttish eyes properly sheathed?"

"Well, I..." At the sound of horses behind I turned to spy Philip leading my horse and Walt bringing Goodie's. "Oh, thank Jesus. Here we are, let us mount and be on."

We splashed through the rain after our quarry and caught sight of them just ahead.

"Better slow, sir?" Philip asked beside me. "Best not cause them to bolt."

"Quite right," I said, looking over my shoulder at Walt and Goodie. "We shall keep the pace."

"Where you reckon they be headed, sir?" Philip asked, taking off his hat, shaking the water out and putting it back on his head.

"I pray they are headed to a meeting of yet more immortal Jesuits, where we might take the lot in one go. Stephen would wish us to follow them all if they should separate. If there are four or more at a secret meeting, you might have to follow one of them alone. Do you think yourself capable?"

"Absolutely capable, sir. You can rely on me to do my duty, sir."

"I know I can, Philip."

"Brought us fresh ale and good wine, sir," he said, leaning down to pat the heaving bags hanging behind him. "And sausages and cheese. The cheese is a bit hard at the corners, like, but it'll go down well enough with a mouthful of ale. Would you like a

481

piece, sir? Or a drink?"

"Not now, Philip, but it is well you brought it all. We may have to follow a good while yet."

"Is that right, sir? Where you thinking we might be headed then, if you don't mind me posing a question direct like that, sir?"

"This road goes all the way to Lincoln and then on to York. We know our fair-haired priest was preaching in York last year."

"York!" Philip said. "I'll have to find more food, then. Next chance we get, I'll buy enough for all of us. Wine, too. Reckon we'll have to sleep by the road? Should have brought more blankets. I'll get us some blankets, if I can, if we stop in a town on the way north."

"I don't know what I would do without you, Philip."

He beamed, happy beyond words to simply be dutiful, and to be recognised as such. We stopped speaking. The rain eased but also changed direction and began whipping into our faces.

It was growing dark when the two distant riders reached a crossroads, turned off the main road and headed down a lane to the east. We stopped where we were and I thought about what to do.

"What's even down there?" Philip asked, pointing.

"Don't point, Philip," I said. "A village or a manor house, possibly. Where are we, Walter?"

He frowned and looked around, twisting in his saddle. "Looks like... that is to say..."

"I know where we are now," Goodie said. "They are headed for a ford that crosses the River Lee."

I frowned. "It is all marsh and bog beside the Lea at the best of times. Surely, it will be flooded today?"

She shrugged. "It's a good ford, that. People use it in winter."

Walt sighed. "It might be they ain't going all the way to the ford or the marshes. You know what these sneaky shits are like. Might be wagging away in a yeoman's barn. Best not let them get away, eh? Best we snatch them up rather than that."

I agreed. "Let's be after them."

From the main road, the lane rose for a stretch and then descended into the shallow valley. Sodden hedgerows crowded on either side and wet leaves dragged themselves across our hats and cloaks and our horses tossed their heads and slowed so we had to urge them on until the lane opened out again. Ahead was a cluster of three cottages along the road. Outside the farthest one stood almost a dozen horses, watched by a couple of men who sheltered beneath the overhanging hatch against the front wall of the cottage.

One of them stood straight, peering through the drizzle in our direction and then he ran to throw open the door and ran inside.

"Bastards," Walt said.

"They spotted us, Richard," Philip said.

"Thank you, Philip," I replied as I drew my sword. "So much for spying. Goodie, stay here with Philip."

"Alright."

Philip was angry. "I can fight!"

"Yes, which is why I want you to—"

The door of the cottage burst open and ten men rushed out. Four lifted arquebuses and aimed them at us.

"Look out!" I cried and began to turn my horse when all four fired.

One shot hit my horse in the face and he tossed his head and turned and shook himself while I wrestled him under control again before jumping down. When I looked up, all the men—presumably Jesuits—had thrown themselves onto their horses and were riding hard away from us.

Walt had put himself between the men and Goodie and had been shot in the upper back but he swore he was fine.

"Goodie, I need your horse!" I shouted and jumped up even as she jumped down. "Wait here and we will return for you."

We left her standing on the road by the cottages, soaking wet and quite alone. Walt shouted at her to be careful and raced after me, along with Philip.

The three of us rode hard but our quarry were thundering down the long slope to the river and when they reached the ford they each ploughed straight into it. The river was indeed higher than usual and the horses struggled against the current so that the stragglers were still in the water while we entered the river. Though she shied away, I urged Goodie's mare forward and together, soaked and cold, we reached the far bank. The road there split off into three directions and the Jesuits divided into three groups as they rode hard for freedom.

"Philip, with me," I said.

"But they're getting away!" he cried, pointing in the opposite direction. "They always get away and we never—"

"Go, then," I snapped, pointing east, the way that three of the riders had gone. "Follow only, do not fight, do not take any prisoner. Follow and see where they go."

Philip grinned and turned his horse, holding his sword aloft.

Walt was already riding ahead north, while I turned west and Philip went east. There were five ahead of me, the largest group and I rode hard through the rain, my mare's hooves splashing through the rutted track.

We had not gone far when, upon some signal, the five of them slowed, turned and charged me together.

I slowed and looked for somewhere to flee to but they had chosen their spot well, for the river was on one side and there was a ditch and a bank on the other and then a dense hedge beyond. Goodie's mare was not trained for such things and she shied from the charging, shouting men and would not so much as stand still, let alone let me fight from her back. Moments before they reached me I slid off and ran for the nearest man's horse while he tried to run me down.

I slipped across the front of the horse, ducking beneath his head and came up on the rider's left, my blade cutting halfway through the man's body as he passed. A shower of blood poured forth as he fell and then I sliced through the next man's leg at his knee when he tried to kick me. After I killed the third, the final two changed their mind about attacking me and rode away again. Abandoning Goodie's mare, I took one of the dead men's stallions and charged after the survivors.

I gained slowly but all three of our horses were tiring and blowing hard. The closest man was trying to load a pistol as he rode but he fumbled and dropped the piece. Trying to catch it, he almost fell from his saddle and frightened his horse. That was all I needed to be on him and I smacked him off his horse and fell upon him, battering him into submission before tying him with strips of cloth.

The final man escaped but it could not be helped. I took my prisoner back to the ford where Walt was waiting for me in the gloom with a prisoner of his own lying on his side in a puddle at Walt's feet.

"Other two got away," he said and kicked his man in the belly. "This daft sod fell off his horse. Didn't you, you daft sod?" He kicked him again and the man writhed in agony.

"Let us be after Philip."

"He'll have lost them," Walt said, chuckling. "You wait and see."

We found Philip face down in a waterlogged ditch beside the road with his skull cleaved almost in two. There was no sign of the three men he was following.

"Daft bloody bastard," Walt said softly as he wrapped Philip's body in his cloak and tucked it around the cloven head.

I picked up Philip's body. "It is my fault."

He nodded. "It is. He weren't up to it. Some lads ain't all right on their own."

I found my cheeks were wet. "And he paid for my mistake."

Walt strode to our prisoners and began to kick and punch them, telling them how he was going to kill all their friends before he tortured them to death. I left him to it until the men were out cold and he tired of it.

"Come," I said. "Let us return to Goodie and take Philip home. Catalina will be heartbroken."

16

The Crow

1586

A CARRIAGE BOUNCED DOWN the trackway toward the manor house called Darley Hall and disappeared behind a row of trees.

"You reckon that's the Crow in there?" Walt asked.

"It is possible."

"How many is that?" Walt said beside me. "Twenty-two?"

I shrugged. "Depends how many men in that carriage. Could be twenty-five visitors in addition to however many were inside."

We had been watching the manor house from the surrounding hills for days while the immortals had arrived from all over the country. They were mostly Jesuit priests, at least that was what they were posing as, but their true conviction was the overthrow of our kingdom.

The two men we had captured when Philip had been killed had given up others. Walt and his men had greatly enjoyed torturing the bastards and I did not blame them. That torture had led us to more Jesuit immortals, and those men had led us to even more until we had located almost a dozen immortals throughout England. By observing these men from a distance, and snatching up a couple of them, we had learned about the great and important meeting that had been called by their leader, the most senior immortal in England, the Crow.

"You want to wait for more to come in?" Walt asked. "Might not be the Crow in that carriage, might be anyone."

"We cannot wait much longer. Even if he is not here, when we take these men, we will have smashed the hand William has reached into England's heart. Let it be now."

"You want us to capture them?" Walt asked.

"No. I have had enough of that. Time to smash them."

He grinned and turned to our men who sat waiting for the order. "Dryden, you ride to Callthorp. Twarby, go to Adams. All men are to be in place by sundown and no one attacks until we do. The battle cry is... Ashbury."

They nodded and ran for their horses.

"Ashbury," I said. "Good one."

"It'll put the fear of God into those bastards when they hear it's you come for them."

"We will lose men in this," I said, keeping my voice low so the remaining men behind would not hear.

"Not as many as they will."

I watched the distant house. It was a large place but old, still with mostly small windows and thick walls. There was a new wing built from brick but it must have been done on the cheap for the chimney was already leaning and two of the windows had been filled in. Only two on the front of the house were still large and in the modern style that could be opened on hinges.

"We are not far from Ashbury, you know," I said to Walt.

"Aye, I knew it was in Derbyshire, obviously, but it's close, is it?"

"If twenty miles or so to the south may be called close. But it is closer than I usually come to the place."

"Maybe we should go visit, Richard. You can take me around where you grew up, show me the barns where you chased the local girls." He stopped smiling. "After we murder these bastards, obviously. Assuming we're both still alive in the morning."

"It is no longer the same place. The last time I was there, the hall was gone and a new house was standing instead. A small one. Not even in the same location, it was across the yard, where the workshops used to be. Even the wood was gone, it was a pasture and the stream had been dammed to make a pond. The lord was so poor I doubt he can even pretend to be a gentleman. Of course, the priory nearby is a ruin. There is nothing of my youth left."

"Aye, well. That's England, ain't it. All the old is gone. And all that is new is worse than before." He turned and spat. "Once we kill these lads, kill William, stop Spain, we should help England become Catholic again."

I looked around to make sure none of our men were listening. "That ship may have sailed."

He snapped his eyes to me. "You going to give up on the true faith?"

"Of course not." I sighed. "But England may have."

"Never. It's all German nonsense. We'll throw it off. You'll see."

I said nothing for a while as we watched the house. Occasionally, a man or two would be seen walking the grounds, often armed with an arquebus. If one of them saw us approaching, he would shoot at us and sound the alarm at the same time. But it could not be helped. We would have no better chance of destroying William's power in England.

It had been months but still I turned to speak to Philip almost every day before recalling he was dead. I should never have let him go off by himself. Some men grow with experience and so did Philip but we all have our level and I had expected too much of him. He had always served me with the utmost diligence, I was supposed to be his master and I had failed to protect him. I had lost so many friends over the years that perhaps I should have expected to be used to it, instead I seemed to feel the loss ever more keenly. In time, I knew, the pain and the guilt would fade. Killing the men who had killed Philip would certainly help.

Turning to Walt, I nodded. "It is time."

We had already planned our approach down the hill into the dale and from there through the trees to the house. We led our horses for the most part but still went as swiftly as we were able. The sun was setting behind us and we were sure to keep a rise of land or a dense hedge or a copse between us and the house until we were in position. Nothing lay between us and the house other than a stretch of boggy pasture, the stables and a scatter of crumbling limestone outbuildings.

"Reckon the boys are ready?" Walt whispered in my ear.

I took out my wheellock pistols and began to load them. "They had better be. Even if they are not, we must kill every man inside that house."

"Stephen and Eva said to take the Crow alive."

"Easy for them to say."

Walt snorted. "Be nice to kill him slow, though, eh?"

"If we can capture him, we will," I said. "Now, I will cross to the front of the house along the fence. You lead the men around the stables and clear the courtyard."

"You going alone?"

I finished loading my weapons and looked at him. "Be sure your men stay out of my way."

Walt nodded and held his tongue as I left them, keeping low and making my way along the wattle fence surrounding the empty pasture. The sun had long gone behind the hills but there was enough light for any man on guard to see me, should he look. When I reached the corner of a building at the edge of the yard, I peered around to look at the house and ducked back behind the wall again. Two men stood outside the door with a lamp hanging over them. Their arquebuses were sitting propped against the wall of the house and they were leaning beside them to talk, each with a flagon in his hand.

Looking around at my feet, I saw a chunk of limestone the size of my fist that had fallen from the wall and snatched it up.

"Please God," I prayed. "Give me strength."

I came out running, a few strides brought me to a fence which I leapt and I crashed through a low, overgrown decorative hedge and charged across the open ground to the front of the house.

The guards jumped upright when they saw me jump the fence and they gaped in shock for a few more strides. By the time they grabbed their guns and raised them I was just a few paces away and as they aimed I threw my chunk of limestone at the nearest one and he flinched, firing his weapon off to the side. The other man panicked and fumbled his weapon so he had not yet fired when I crashed against him at a full run, knocking him into the side of the house with a wet smack. Bouncing off him, I grabbed the one I had hit with the piece of stone and lifted him off his feet, driving him to the floor, hard. Finishing with a dagger thrust through his eye into the brain, I slid to the other man and did the same to him just as the front door was thrown open from inside.

I snatched up the dropped arquebus and shot the man who came out in the centre of his forehead. He dropped into a heap and the men behind him shouted in terror and tried to shut the door, so I threw myself against it and shouldered my way in to the house while the men inside shouted in confused panic.

"Crow!" I roared, my voice filling the room inside while the men cringed away through the doorway opposite. It was a modern dining hall, with a fireplace at one end and benches and long table. Their food and drink were still on the table and stools and a bench had been thrown over as they fled. "Crow! I am come for you!"

I stood in the centre of the room while a few faces peered in. Footsteps sounded throughout the house. Upstairs, men shouted and feet banged as they ran here and there.

"He's alone!" someone cried through the chaos and one man stepped back into the hall with his sword drawn.

I pulled out a wheellock pistol and shot him in the face. The others behind him fled from me just as Walt burst in through the servants' entrance, shouting my name and began killing them.

On the far side of the house, I heard my men attacking. "Ashbury!" they cried.

Drawing my sword, I stepped over the dying man and finished him off before I went deeper into the house. My men were everywhere and Callthorp came charging out of the kitchens at the rear and pointed to a half open door.

"Down to the cellar, lads," he shouted and then followed the four that stomped down the steps.

The sound of fighting came from upstairs and then a gunshot, and another, along with cries of warning. I charged up the steps as Adams threw himself out of a room just as there was an explosion of flame within.

"Richard!" he cried, blood on his face. "The Crow. The bloody Crow is there. He's got these fire pots and he—"

I pushed by Adams into the burning room. A bed was on fire and the flames curled against the plaster ceiling. I skirted by it and jumped over the pile of bodies in the doorway to the chamber beyond. A piece of the doorframe by my head burst apart and when I straightened I saw the Crow crouching by an open window with a smoking pistol in his hand. I drew my own and fired as he jumped. My shot hit him but still he leapt from the window and I rushed across the room and looked out to him running for the stables, clutching his side. His black robes billowing in the dusk.

I squeezed my way through the window and jumped to the path below beside the guards I had killed on the way in. There was a commotion coming from the yard and I ran in to find the Crow wrestling with two of my men. He struck one hard across the face before throwing the other down and turning for the panicked horses.

493

But I was already on him and I speared my sword right into the back of his thigh.

He fell, screaming, his hat flying off and his robes falling open.

As he did so, he pulled another pistol from his belt. I rushed forward as he took the weapon and turned it against himself, placing the barrel against his forehead.

Just as he pulled the lever to release the mechanism, I swatted it aside with my sword. The blast peppered his face with burning powder and he cried out but still he reached for his dagger and tried to plunge it into his head.

I grasped his hand and used the hilt of my sword to break his nose, whereupon I took his final weapon.

"So you are the Crow," I said, holding him down. "And you must know a great deal about your masters."

"I'll tell you nothing," he said and spat a mouthful of blood down himself.

I smiled. "I have heard that before."

***

We killed twenty-six men and took three more prisoner. I lost seven of my own men, which was a severe loss but still we had done well. Callthorp and Adams were still alive and they knew of a few mortal soldiers or ruffians they could bring in to replace them. We also found piles of papers and books in the house and on the dead men. Most of them were written in code. Some we had snatched half-burned from the fire and a bundle was pulled dripping from a ditch where one man had thrown them as he ran from the house before we caught him.

Callthorp brought up a bag of fire pots from the cellar with a smile on his face. "Must be a thousand of these things down there. You know, like what they threw at Adams."

"I know them well," I said. "Very handy weapons. We shall be glad to have them."

"Not just that but cask after cask of powder, barrels of shot, and looks like well over a hundred arquebuses. Swords, and all, halberds, raw ash poles ready for spearheads. I reckon they was planning something big."

I nodded. "And I reckon you are right, Callthorp. Well done. We shall get it all out of there and take it to London. Along with the prisoners."

Walt cleared his throat. "Why don't we question the bastards here, then just blow up the rest of it?"

"As tempting as that is, we should take the papers to Stephen for deciphering. There must be a wealth of knowledge contained within. We may then use that knowledge to better question our prisoners."

Walt nodded. "Before we kill them."

"Indeed."

We trussed the prisoners up and carted them south, allowing them to develop a terrible blood sickness and giving them just enough to keep them from going mad. The Crow growled and writhed and cursed behind his gag and Walter delighted in knocking him unconscious when he got too loud. Stephen and Martin spent days working through the papers and attempting to break the codes. We left the Crow trussed up in his own cell and worked on the others one by one, breaking them and questioning them. When each one seemed to have given everything he knew, we killed him and disposed of his body.

Eventually, it was time to speak to the Crow.

He had been blindfolded for weeks and we had deprived him of sufficient food, water, sleep, and blood. We chained him to an iron chair which was fixed to the floor. I sat opposite and we put a table beside us where Stephen arranged himself to take notes. When all was ready, I nodded to Walt and he removed the Crow's bandage before taking up his place behind the prisoner. Having a man behind you is extremely unnerving.

He blinked and winced for some time, though the lamps were not bright in the cell.

"I thought it was time we had a talk," I said.

The Crow peered at me and tried to sneer. "You may as well kill me. I will tell you nothing."

"Oh? Is that so? Well, perhaps I can tell you something." I reached beside me to the table and took up a sheet of parchment. "You know, I admire your courage, I truly do. You knew I was coming for you, for your men, picking them up one by one and destroying all your work. And still you risked bringing the remainder of your men together for a final planning meeting. It did not pay off, of course, and only led more swiftly to your destruction but the fact that you took such a chance truly speaks to your character. Well done, John."

His head snapped up before he controlled himself and looked away, affecting nonchalance.

I smiled. "That's right, I know who you are, John. Well, I know who you pretend to be. Once we learned your secret codes, we found the name of Highfield Hall in Staffordshire written within and our men investigated. It seems the owner is a miserable sod who is hardly there at all, treats his servants horribly and is strongly suspected by certain men in the nearby village to be a Catholic. They say he has hair as black as pitch and a great beak of a nose. And do you know what his name is? I could hardly believe it. The locals find it amusingly apt, they could not help but tell my lads over a mug of beer." I pointed at him. "John Crowhurst."

He smiled and turned away.

I looked at Walt, who shrugged.

"Whether that is the name you were born with, I do not know," I said. "You do not look especially English but then you do not look quite like a Spaniard either. Perhaps you are a Welshman."

Walt snorted. "More like a Jew."

I nodded while the Crow glared at me. "Yes, perhaps that is it. It would explain your gift for sneaking around."

"I'm no Jew," he sat and spat at my feet. "I am a loyal servant of His Holiness."

"Oh, I think we both know you serve another master."

"You know nothing at all, Protestant."

Frowning, I leaned back on my stool and peered at him. "Do you know who I am?"

He said nothing, looking at Stephen and the piles of papers before him and failing to crane his neck around far enough to see Walt.

"I wonder who it is you think you serve," I said. "Perhaps you believe him to be Cardinal Diego de Espinosa?" Perhaps, if he had not been starving and shaking with the blood sickness, he would have controlled himself better. But I saw by the way he froze for a moment that I had shocked him by speaking that name. "No doubt Cardinal Espinosa wooed you for some time, testing your loyalty and ability. You grew close. You came to be friends, perhaps, or at least you admired him, respected him, even loved him. And you believed that he relied upon you, he needed you almost as much as you needed him. He won for you riches and position. Whatever it was you wanted, at least, he helped to provide. And then one day he asked if he could trust you with a secret. The secret of his power. The power of his blood. He told you, I imagine, that it was a gift from God and with this gift he was fighting to hold back the heretics of the new religion. Either then or later, he told you about us, here in England. He told you we were standing in the way of bringing the true religion back to England." I lowered my head and tried to catch his eye. "How close am I, John?"

He forced himself to look at me. "Not at all," he said with conviction but he could not hold my gaze for long.

"You are trying to start a war," I said. "But it will not work."

That seemed to amuse him. "War is coming, no matter what you do to me."

"Perhaps," I admitted. "But we have destroyed you and your men. Next, we will destroy your master. And then, without his corrupting influence, perhaps the Spanish will see sense."

He sneered. "Not even the king of Spain can steer us from this course now. Philip hides himself away in San Lorenzo de Escorial and prays and kisses his relics and rules through his towers of papers and correspondence. You think a king like that can resist what we have set in motion? We have now brought Portugal into his rule, which means into our power, and now the strength of their ships is added to ours. We have brought France into a madness so she tears herself apart ever more while we have paid off the most powerful faction, so now she need not be feared. One of my men shot the traitor William of Orange dead and so the rebellious Dutch provinces fall once more into their proper place. At Cadiz, our fleet grows daily, our stores grow, our immortal soldiers grow in number and power, fed by a stream of blood that will soon become a torrent and England will be brought back to God, under a king, a true king, not some Protestant bitch."

"Your soldiers are based in Cadiz?" I asked.

His sneer wavered and he hesitated. "We are everywhere. Everywhere in Spain, Portugal, France, England, Ireland, Scot—"

Sitting up straight, I peered at him. "No, no, you are not. We have scoured you from England and if there are any left we shall find them and tear them asunder, just as you will soon be."

"You are wrong. You know nothing. You have failed."

I leaned in. "I have been doing this far longer than you." I looked at Stephen. "Ask him more about Cadiz."

Stephen took up his pen and dipped it in his inkpot. "What a wonderful idea, I think I shall. Now, you say your immortals are assembled at the port of Cadiz. Please tell me how many and precisely where they are housed."

The Crow scoffed. "I know nothing. Even if I did, I would tell you nothing. No matter what you do to me."

"No matter what we do to you?" I asked. "What a remarkable boast. Tell me, do you recall a night many years ago in Epsom? You met an agent of yours at the inn and then two of my men followed you."

The Crow smirked. "That pair of fools attacked me on the lane. I saw them coming, of course, and dealt with them accordingly. I cut off their heads and left them in the woods for the dogs and the pigs." His lip curled into a snarl as he glared triumphantly.

"I see," I replied, turned to Walt and nodded once. "They were your men, were they not, Walt? Digby and Finch?"

"Aye, they was," Walt replied and took up his leather bag of butchery tools and banged them on the table. After spreading them out where the Crow could see them, he selected a cleaver and checked its edge before putting it down and lifting a boning knife and inspecting it. "So, you cut off my men's heads, did you? Tell me, Jesuit, you ever dismember an immortal while he's alive?"

The Crow shook as he replied. "You do not frighten me."

Walt chuckled. "Frighten? I don't care if you be frightened or heroic, makes no difference to me." Walt leaned in over his face and lowered his voice. "What will happen, you see, is I will take you apart piece by piece and you will tell us everything you know. And then, eventually, I will allow you to die. But you'll suffer first, you understand, more than any mortal ever has, and I'll do it for sound reasons. I'll do it so you'll tell your secrets to my mate Stephen there. But, as well as that, I'm going to do it for Digby and Finch, and for Philip, the other man you killed. Philip was our friend, you understand, and as far as I know, he never hurt no one his whole life. All he ever done was his duty. He was a good man, a decent man. And you killed him. So I'm going to make you suffer all the more. It will be days, oh certainly it shall, and most probably it'll be weeks. And you'll watch yourself shrink, piece by piece, as I slice your flesh and take your skin, your muscle, your bone, and fling them into that bucket there. You see it? The pigs in the yard will be most grateful, I assure you. You can sit here in the knowledge that those pigs up there in our yard will be eating your fingers and your toes, your ears, your cock and your balls, while we are still asking our questions, day after day. Think of that. Your cock and balls will be pig shit while you yet live. Soon, an eternity from now, you'll be in that chair looking down at yourself and you'll have no arms, no legs. You'll be nothing but a body with a head on it and both will be flayed and chopped and still we'll pour blood down your throat and you won't die, you'll just suffer and suffer until you go beyond madness and all you'll be able to do is beg me to kill you." He stood up straight and shrugged. "But I was just asking if you ever dismembered an immortal in case you had any good tips. No matter. I done this before. Now, I reckon we'll start by taking off your fingernails and then we'll take off the skin from your fingertips, alright? Peel them back like an apple, a slither at a time."

The Crow let out a gasp and then a wail that ended in a sob. Walt winked at me and bent over the man's hand.

"I will tell you about Cadiz!" he cried.

"Oh," Stephen said, putting his pen to the paper. "How kind of you."

17

Cadiz

1587

DRAKE'S FLAGSHIP, the *Elizabeth Bonaventure*, ploughed the waves hard as we came close to the Spanish coast. Behind us stretched a squadron including the *Golden Lion*, the *Dreadnought*, and the *Rainbow*. These were the Queen's ships, stout galleons of four to five hundred tons armed with great ship smashing guns. We had three tall ships funded by the London merchants which were almost as large and strong as the queen's vessels. These were the *Merchant Royal*, the *Susan* and the *Edward Bonaventure*.

Our second line was made of seven more warships of about two hundred tons and then a dozen pinnaces and smaller ships.

Drake was by then wealthy enough to fund his own ships and had brought the inventively named *Drake*, the *Thomas Drake* and the *Elizabeth Drake*. Lord Howard of Effingham, the Lord

Admiral, had supplied the *White Lion*.

All in all, we had twenty-six ships and three thousand men. It was by far the largest fleet Drake had commanded and one of the largest England had ever assembled. It had to be, for attacking the mighty port of Cadiz was close to madness. Only Drake's fame had persuaded the Privy Council and the Queen that a pre-emptive assault was necessary.

"William's great fleet may already have assembled," Martin said beside me, his eyes ceaselessly searching the horizon. "If it's at sea, we will be destroyed."

"And if we can catch it at port, perhaps we can destroy it before it can set sail. And we will burn Vega's immortal army alive in their beds."

I walked back to Drake, who stood in his usual place on the command deck, legs planted and hands behind his back. No matter how the ship rolled, pitched or shuddered, he never was unbalanced. He seemed to be affixed to the ship as much was the mainmast.

"How do you fare, Captain Francis?" I asked as I approached.

He nodded once from beneath his hat. "If God will grant us fair winds, I will bring us the victory."

I shook my head at the man's monstrous hubris but smiled at it all the same. His self-regard seemed to know no bounds but then his actions had not found their boundary yet. Looking at him from the corner of my eye, I wondered how his will would fare when confronted by the inevitable failure that meets all men eventually. Would he rise above the storm of spirit that would ensue or would he be driven onto the shores of madness, anger, and self-pity?

But he had staved off disaster in the past due to his brilliance, as well as good fortune, and so I prayed that once again he would find a way through in spite of his over-confidence, or because of it.

And he did not have the monopoly on pridefulness.

"Land me and my men at Cadiz," I said, "and I will bring us the true victory. The one that matters most, at any regard."

He glanced at me and ground his teeth. "You by land and me by sea, then. Together we will crush this invasion before it can begin."

"God willing," I said. "But speed is the key."

"I know, Richard, I know," he shook his head and rolled his eyes. "We have every square inch of sail aloft and filled with this stiff wind. If you desire more haste you should climb to the cross trees and put out your shirt. And your hose, also."

"If you truly care to increase our pace, sir," I replied, looking hard at him, "I should hoist aloft my codpiece."

Our fleet had pushed on south from England day after day for seventeen days of swift sailing and we arrived at southern Spain late in the day at the end of April. As speed was so important, Drake had not waited for the slower ships to catch up and so when we were just a few miles away, our fleet was yet spread out behind us.

But we could not wait for them to catch up. My plan for victory relied on finding Vega's immortal army in their dockside barrack rooms.

We had to go into the great harbour of Cadiz as night was falling. And Drake had brought us there just in time.

Going forward, I found Martin wringing his hands beside

Walt. "Worry not, young man, we shall be leaving you here on the ship when we assault the shore."

Martin looked between me and Walt. "Your words are supposed to reassure me, Richard? Do you know how terrible this battle will be? Do you?"

"Like all battles at sea, it shall be all banging and smoke and not much else, I expect."

"That's right, lad," Walt said. "Don't be pissing your hosen just yet."

"I am not a lad, I am a man grown and I have sailed around the very globe so do not dismiss my concerns as cowardice. You have seen the charts, I take it, and you have heard of the defences? The harbour is protected by an island that almost encloses the bay and there is but one entrance into the anchorages. That entrance is dominated by multiple batteries and there is a castle at the point of the island which we must pass. The passage in is a mere half-mile from one side to the other and we shall be blasted by mighty shore cannon as we inch our way through."

Walt shrugged. "But once we're through, we'll be alright, son."

Martin stared at him. "The reports gathered by the White Dagger agents state there are never fewer than forty ships within that harbour and the last report described sixty ships. Sixty! We shall be outnumbered three to one."

"Keep your voice down," I said. "Our reports also said most of those sixty ships were unarmed and would be carrying only supplies for the Spanish invasion fleet. Those very ships are Drake's objectives, Martin. Now, you can come with us and fight through the shore to the immortals' barracks or you can stay on the ship. What will it be?"

Martin shook his head. "I would only slow your progress on land, certainly you know this."

Walt breathed deeply. "Don't know why you ain't taken the Gift yet, son. We all know you're going to do it, so just do it. Then you wouldn't be so afraid of getting hurt all the time. If you was one of us, wouldn't matter if you got shot in the leg or if a shower of oak timbers rips into your guts."

He closed his eyes. "I should have stayed in London."

Walt grinned. "No, son, better to die on a Spanish battlefield than to live another day in the madness of London."

Martin gripped the rail tighter. "Dear God in heaven."

The defences were just as Martin had described. I had memorised the charts and descriptions when forming my own plan of attack and as for Drake, his seeming nonchalance belied the hours of planning he had done in his own mind. The castles and shore batteries cast long shadows ahead of us. Soon it would be dusk. Still, the Spanish soldiers watched us come in with a line of ships strung out behind us. As we approached the entrance to the channel that led to the inner harbour, his mariners called out asking for orders.

"Should we run out the guns now, captain?" the master asked.

"Steady as she goes," Drake said. "And keep the men's weapons out of sight, Perkins."

There were Spaniards on the shore, watching us come in. They could see our line of galleons coming slowly forward, stretching back to the horizon and yet they did nothing. The tower of the castle on the island point bristled with huge cannon but they did not fire. On the walls, men leaned against the battlements and on the batteries of the shore side the men shielded their eyes against the glare of the low sun on the water and they also did nothing.

"Why ain't they shooting us?" Walt mumbled.

"They think us Spanish," I said, half laughing. "Or Portuguese, perhaps."

"Damned fools," Walt said, shaking his head. "What's wrong with them?"

A wrinkled old mariner with his foot on a cask just aft heard us talking. "Never been hit before, have they. Can't imagine anyone would come in all calm, like. Not one captain's been brave enough to break down their gates in a hundred years. Not two hundred, nor a thousand." He shrugged his bony shoulders. "Not one captain but good Captain Drake." The mariner grinned wolfishly and spat in his hands before rubbing them together. I saw then he had his foot on the side of an open cask that was filled with axes, clubs, and swords ready for the men to grasp should we be boarded or need to board an enemy. He nodded forward and gestured with a scarred hand. "Looks like our luck's about to run out."

Two Spanish war galleys, long and lean, were coming out of the inner harbour to meet us, their banks of oars dipping and rising in unison. Galleys were ships of the Mediterranean and could manoeuvre against the wind with ease but they were low and fragile compared to our great galleons with our thick timbers and masses of guns.

"What ship are you?" A Spanish voice cried from the lead galley. "From where do you sail?"

"Shove your oars up your arse!" one of our sailors shouted in English, to much amusement on the main deck.

Walt slapped Martin on the back. "Reckon we been rumbled,

lad. Best have one last chat with the old boy upstairs before your head gets shot off your shoulders."

"Ignore him, Martin," I said. "He has always said such things to young soldiers."

"I am not a soldier," Martin said, his face white as a new sail. "And I am not young."

But the galleys both fled as quickly as they could, racing away in something close to panic while the men on decks shouted warnings to the other ships crowding the enormous harbour.

"Ain't we going to shoot our guns?" Walt asked no one in particular.

"Got to do things proper," the old sailor croaked, pointing aft now as our flags were raised. Behind us, the other galleons likewise unfurled and raised their flags while our ship turned to present a flank to the retreating galleys. Orders were shouted and loaded cannons heaved through gunports that banged open beneath us.

Walter leaned over at the sound, then gripped Martin's shoulder and cried out in joy. "This is it, son! About bloody—"

Cannons fired from the gun deck and billowing smoke poured forth across the quiet harbour. Our gunners had a clean shot, at short range across water as flat as a millpond. The first cannonball ripped longways through the nearest galley, tearing through several oarsmen and putting the thing out of use.

Eight more of Cadiz's galleys came out to intercept us. They had small cannon mounted in the bow and a couple had cannon in the stern but they were too small to do any damage to our timbers while our own shot cracked them something terrible. It was not even close to a fair fight and each galley was soon sent running as best as it could manage while we poured more shot down on them, our ship and our comrades coming in behind us.

We sailed on through the harbour at a leisurely pace while blasting at the galleys and on the merchant ships and on the shore, it was clear a panic was setting in. People fled in all directions but mostly up from the town toward the castle above it.

"Lower our boat!" I said as I climbed to the command deck.

"Soon, soon," Drake cried. "We must sow further chaos lest you be noticed."

"If we do not go now, it will be too late to achieve success."

"I must first defeat that Genoese monster there and then your party may disembark. Look at her, man, she's forty guns and a thousand tons, she'll be the ruin of us if I don't fight her proper."

I stepped closer to him. "Now, Francis. I would hate to order my company to throw you and your crew into the hold and run this ship ashore so we can step off directly onto Spanish soil."

He wagged a finger in my face. "If you are blasted to bits and sunk by cannon shot, do not complain about it to me, do you hear?" Turning to his master's mate he raised his voice. "Lower the starboard boat for Mister Ashbury and be about it most lively."

"Thank you, Francis," I said and turned to leave. "See you soon."

He caught my arm. "I will make all effort to collect you before we flee but you understand we now descend into fire and madness. I can promise nothing."

"Fire and madness is where I belong," I said and we shook hands.

Before I had taken two steps, the *Elizabeth Bonaventure* was struck in the hull by two great shots, cracking her timbers and shaking the whole vessel. It was the massive Genoese ship coming for us to do battle and while we slowed to drop my boat, our flagship was a sitting target. Still, our guns did their work on the huge enemy while me and my company of twenty men threw ourselves into the boat and rowed away using the ship to protect us while we made distance.

Coming around her stern, we rowed hard for the coast while cannon shot cracked through the air overhead. It was not yet dusk but the air was beginning to become filled with the fog of war. The other ships in our fleet were firing constantly as they manoeuvred and made their way deeper into the vast harbour. Some enemy ships darted for the refuges of the two river estuaries of St Mary's Port and Porto Reale while others were swiftly abandoned, some at anchor and others left to drift while the crews rowed desperately for shore. We looked just like such a Spanish crew, or so I hoped, as we heaved hard across the channel.

"Soldiers coming down into the town," Walt called from the bow. "Hundreds of the bastards. And coming to the shore, and all. Companies separating to guard the likely landings."

"Then we shall have to fight our way through," I said so that all my men could hear me. They were nervous. Each one was an immortal veteran and a killer but dozens of cannonballs flying overhead with every oar stroke makes cowards of men. "Every man who does his duty today will be rewarded with sixty shillings apiece, in addition to your ordinary pay."

They grinned and rowed harder while Walt looked again at the shore, where he stood taller and pointed. "If we make for that mooring, there, we shall find ourselves between one company and the—"

An arquebus shot whipped in, hitting Walt with a wet crack.

He fell into the bottom of the boat, clutching his head which bled immediately through his fingers while he writhed like a landed fish.

"Sweet Jesus!" Callthorp cried, letting go his oar to cross himself. "He's shot through the skull, sir!"

"Row, men!" I roared. "Row, row!"

More shots hit the boat and the water around us. A handful of soldiers crouched on the shore, using a low stone wall with which to rest their firearms for aiming at us, most now reloading.

"There they are," I said.

"Should we return fire?" Callthorp asked, pointing at our own weapons. "Or change course?"

"Neither," I replied. "It cannot be more than six men." I stood in the stern of the boat, planting my feet wide to brace myself and wondered if my head would be destroyed by a cannonball. Drawing my sword, I waved it over my head to get their attention and then pointed it at them. "I am coming to kill you!" I screamed. "I will kill you all!"

They fired at me and all missed and then, when I shouted again, they turned and trotted away along the wharves.

Callthorp gaped up at me. "How did you do that?"

"Walter?" I asked. "Are you alive?"

He sat up, clutching the side of his head. "How bad is it?" he asked, taking his hand away. "Am I dead?"

I squinted. "A graze, Walt. A mere graze, my friend. God is with you."

"You can't see my brains?"

"It would need a far larger wound before there was any danger of that."

"Mother of Christ, I need a drink," Walt grumbled.

"Row!" I shouted to my men over the din of the guns. "Almost there, boys, come on, heave!"

I glanced behind us to see a group of galleys forming up again in a line while more English ships came in to pour their fire against the shore batteries and the enemy vessels. The sound was incredible, a ceaseless thunder rolling across the water and filling the air.

"God's hands!" Callthorp wailed as we came up to the mooring. "It is hell upon the earth! How many cannons is this? Five hundred? A thousand?"

I grabbed hold of the mooring and jumped out, kneeling beside the boat. "Come on Adams, you first, nicely now, everyone up. Arm yourselves and move forward to that wall. Keep low, come on, that's it, take your arquebus, Wyatt. You also, Henshawe, and take your damned powder, man. On, on!"

When we were all together, I grinned at them and some returned the expression. We were gleeful because we had not been sunk and because we were in the midst of a kind of hell and facing such danger could make a man giddy.

"Now is the simple task, lads. We stroll on inland toward Porto Reale and no shooting, no fighting, no shouting unless I give the order, you understand? With any luck, they will think us friends and not foes. A mile that way, there is a river and a bridge. On this side of that bridge is a large, long building big enough to house hundreds of men. With luck, they will be gathering within. Once we reach it, we set a fire at every door and shoot them and cut them down as they come out? You all understand? Until then, let us go easy, boys, like walking through our own village field, right?"

They smiled again, taking pleasure in the mild deception. Soldiers like doing a thing that is clever, as long as it's not *too* clever.

"You would tell me true, Richard," Walt muttered as we set off, "if my brains was hanging out, would you not?"

"The wound is not so much as halfway through your thick skull, I swear it. Here, take some blood and cease your fretting."

I cut my wrist and let him suck the blood straight from my flesh. He had suffered a terrible gash, truth be told.

We made our way across the land toward the town, passing warehouses and docks and shipbuilding structures and launches, all deserted and all casting long shadows as the sun set behind us. A few groups of soldiers saw us and each time I was ready to issue orders but we were ignored. In the harbour behind us, the battle raged on and on as the sun set and I wondered how long the ships would fight in the dark. Hurrying my company, we pushed on out of the industrial area into a street of good houses where I knew from reports that Spanish soldiers and mariners lived. Those with decent incomes, at least. Again, they seemed abandoned and I assumed everyone had rushed off across the bridge to shelter behind the walls of Porto Reale.

"That it?" Walt asked, pointing at the flat walls of a large building ahead. Callthorp had the men spread out already and he nodded at it, asking the same question as Walt had.

"That must be it," I said. "You each know your parts? Nathaniel, go on to the eastern end, Adams, round the corner, the rest here. Doors barred, start the fires. Any that comes out a window or breaks in the door you shoot them and then take their heads. If they've any sense they'll come out in a rush so be ready for it. Questions?" There were none. "God be with us. Off you go, Callthorp."

We waited for them to go on ahead and moved in across the perimeter wall and across the outer yard and along the pathway to the main door.

"Shutters are closed," Walt pointed out. "No lamps lit."

I punched my fist into the wall, tearing the skin and leaving a smear of blood on the plaster. "They are not here."

"Maybe they've gone to defend the town?"

We had missed our chance to kill hundreds of immortals. My small company had no hope of finding them in a hostile town without being surrounded and killed ourselves.

I had failed.

"We must now flee for the ships and find an English captain to take us home," I said.

"Sir!" Callthorp cried, rushing around the corner.

"By Christ's balls, Callthorp!" I shouted. "We almost shot you dead, you madman."

"Sorry, sir, just thought you'd want to speak to this Negro what we found round the front. Place's empty, looks like, silent as the grave. But this slave reckons he knows where they are." He prodded the man's shoulder with the butt of his axe. "Go on, Pedro Negro, spill your guts."

The man glared at us from eyes that were freshly bruised and blood ran down from his nose over his lips. These he licked before speaking. "Yes, they are gone," he said in English. "And I am not a slave."

"Are you a blood slave?" I asked. "Do they drink from you?"

He was shocked by my question but not confused. He knew what I was asking. "No. No slave. And I am not named Pedro."

"Alright, sunshine," Walt spat, "we heard what you ain't. Now's time to tell us what you are. You one of the immortals?"

He raised his chin and said nothing. Callthorp smacked him across the back of his head. "You already told me so tell my captain or I might as well cut out your tongue, right?"

The man's mouth turned down at the corners and I could see him weighing up whether to attempt to fight his way out.

"Answer and you shall be freed," I said and when his expression signalled his doubt, I said it again. "I have no interest in you, just the men who lived here. Where did they go?"

"To the great galleon. The galleon of Santa Cruz." He gave us a nasty grin. "The largest ship in Cadiz."

I grabbed his arm and sliced it with my knife and he flinched, cursing and held it, hissing through his big teeth. "It is true!"

"When did they go?"

"Two days."

"Why?"

He shrugged.

"I am more than happy to cut off your hands if you hesitate longer."

"A messenger come to us with word of an attack. They say our men in England are destroyed. So they go, and we invade England. You Lutherans do not have long before you are crushed beneath our—"

"Yes, yes. Is Lorenzo de la Vega with them?"

He was surprised. "He is."

I sighed and nodded. "Good. And why did they leave you

515

here?"

"I am nobody. I live to serve."

Grasping his wrist, I rubbed the blood from the wound where I had cut him. It was almost entirely healed. "You are an immortal."

He lifted his chin. "I am so honoured."

"Honoured so much they left you behind."

"I guard the blood slaves. I am to bring them to the ship when it leads the fleet against England. It is a great honour."

"And yet because they left you alone, you will be dead in a few moments."

He scowled, yanking his arm back. "It is you Englishmen that are fated for death! We will drink your soldiers and take your women. Your disgusting queen will be stripped naked before crowds of her own people and my lord will take her upon her own throne and then her body will be hung from the castle of London so the crows may—"

I ripped my knife through his abdomen, slicing deep from hip to hip and I stepped back as his guts spilled out. He sank to his knees, grasping armfuls of his intestines and whimpering. We moved away from the stench and most of my men spat on him as they walked by.

"Now I seen everything," Walt said, shaking his head. "A Negro immortal? Now I seen everything. That William ain't got no standards at all, has he. He don't care about nothing. God save us."

"Do you think it will take him long to die?" Callthorp asked, looking back at the doorway where the man in his undershirt died on his knees.

"Hopefully," I said. "Adams, the other door was open, yes? Go and find those blood slaves if you can and let them go."

It was completely dark by the time they returned, carrying cups of fresh blood for the rest of them. "Some lovely Spanish girls, they was. Else, they would have been if not for all the filth and the madness. Crying shame, it is, crying shame. Still, they're free now. They'll be alright, I reckon. So, back to the boat then to the *Elizabeth*?"

The guns in the distance were still firing and shouts came from all around, along with a smattering of small arms, but it was quieting down for the night. Not that the battle would stop, far from it, but the cover of darkness would allow men to flee, and others to slip into new positions.

"Drop all this oil and kindling here, sir?" Callthorp said. "No point carrying it back to the boat."

I was struck by an idea.

"No," I said. "We will bring it with us." I looked at their shadowy faces. "We will need it to burn their galleon in the harbour."

They did not like it and I did not pretend that it would be easy or enjoyable but I did remind them of their duty and their oath. We made our way back to the boat, moving quickly and watching for enemy companies. Across the water, cannon flared and boomed, flashing and illuminating the harbour like a lightning storm. It was almost completely dark but half the sky was yet dark blue and fires burned on land and sea and it was enough to navigate by. Onshore, groups of soldiers rushed here and there but none paid us any heed. When we reached the wharf, I breathed a sigh of relief to see our boat still tied up, a pale grey shape on the black water, bumping against the posts of the wharf.

"Come on, boys, smartly does it," I said, speaking low and patting them on the shoulder as they went by, counting them back into the boat.

"God knows you're the luckiest sod there ever was," Walt muttered at my side. "But you got to know this is pushing it."

"God rewards the man who does his duty," I replied.

He scoffed. "Surely we can do our duty by getting on Drake's ship to shoot Santa Cruz's galleon with its mighty guns?"

"All our ships are outclassed by the enemy flagship and we could not sink her with guns. If we do not do this, hundreds of immortal soldiers will land on our home shores along with the Spanish armies and how will we defeat them then? It must be now, for England, or all is lost."

Walt sighed. "I've always trusted you and I'll not doubt you know. But you must know one day your luck will run out."

"Have faith, brother. Have faith. Now, get in the boat and act like the knight you are." I clapped him on the shoulder and followed him in. "Right, lads, quick and quiet. No speaking in English. I will call the strokes in Spanish. When we cross the bay, we'll get in close to the galleon and you boys take a minute to rest your arms. Then we'll be up the side, keep to your groups, we'll slip into the hold and set fires by any gunpowder you find. Start your fires and get back to the boat. No English, mind, you understand, no fuss, and no fighting... unless you have to. God is with us, boys. Let us make Him proud."

They sculled us out across the bay and through the fighting. Cannon shot crashed into the black water and blasts sounded on all sides. Men cried out in anger and in pain, the sounds strangely close over the water. Huge black shadows loomed everywhere, and forests of masts and rigging stretched into the pink-red sky. Fires burned on all sides.

Halfway across, two boats rowed by us and we shipped the oars and drifted, listening to them splashing rhythmically either side of us. Resting my hand on my sword, I strained for sign that they were friend or foe. My men reached slowly for their own weapons and one of the men nearest to me in the stern slowly started to load his firearm until I poked him in the back with my toe. The boats rowed on without stopping and perhaps without ever knowing we were there. I whispered to my men to keep rowing.

It was a long way to Santa Cruz's galleon. I knew from the charts that it was over two miles, probably closer to three and that was without considering the current and wind pushing us obliquely away from our target. The men were breathing heavily as they rowed.

"Perhaps a few minutes rest, Callthorp," I said and patted him and a couple of the others on the shoulder. "Take a breather and we shall—"

From the bow, Walt stood and roared at us. "Bloody row! Row! Row for your lives, you bastards. Row!"

A ripple of cannon fire lit up the horizon and I saw what had frightened him.

Coming up on us from the dark, a vast galleon in silhouette looming out of the fog, the rigging creaking and the sails snapping. Impossibly tall, like a sea monster from legend breathing fire and wreathed in smoke, throwing up a frothing wave that glowed white before the great blade of the prow that would hammer us down into the cold midnight waters beneath her hull.

"Row!" I roared, preparing to leap sideways from the stern into the water to get me a few feet further from the prow before it hit. "Pull! Pull!"

Men above us shouted, whether they were cries of warning or surprise or jeers of hatred, I did not know or care. We seemed to crawl across the galleon's course, inching away while she came on with unstoppable might and churning the water. Some of the men called on God through gritted teeth.

"Pull! Don't pray, you bastards. Pull! And pull!"

The bow wave lifted us and pushed us aside as the galleon sailed by our boat. I expected the crew to shoot down at us but they seemed occupied with other matters. The men kept pulling hard with every stroke and we were almost past it when a cannon on the gun deck over our heads fired, deafening us all. I clapped my hands over my ears, as did most of the men. But it was too late. My ears rang like a bell and we were engulfed in the stinking gun smoke. Another cannon fired and we rowed on until the ship was gone and the men sat slumped on their benches.

"Was that her?" one of the men asked between great sucking breaths.

"No," Walt said from his place at the prow. "She's still sitting there at anchor. But for who knows how long. We best hurry."

"Let the men catch their breath," I said.

"No thank you, sir," Callthorp said, his voice shaking. "Reckon we ought to get on."

We slowed as we approached the enemy flagship. It truly was a gigantic vessel, the biggest I had ever seen, and we inched closer until we came into contact with the hull. No one had spotted us and we crept along the waterline, looking for a place to climb up. One of the men started tying our rope to the grappling hook when Walt hissed at us to push on further. A few more yards aft we found a ladder against the hull. I could see Walt's teeth in the gloom as he grinned.

The ship was vast, filled with hundreds of immortals. Struck with fear, I was about to call it off when Walt leapt from the gunwales and he climbed the ladder as quick as a lizard. We were committed. One by one the men went up behind him, some with bundles of kindling bouncing over their shoulders, three with a small cask of oil tied to their backs, and all of us with a powder horn and slow matches.

Leaving one man in the boat, I went up last and found three of my men waiting for me. The other two groups were strolling forward and aft, casually, as if they belonged there. Spanish sailors were dotted here and there on the decks and they were working swiftly to prepare the ship for sailing. Voices called out instructions and conversations could be heard on the deck below and in the captains just aft. On the command deck above me, officers leaned over a navigation table and jabbered at each other about the probable positions of the English fleet. They seemed to think they would be ready to sail at first light and they intended to fight their way out of the harbour and into the open sea.

My men's faces were set but their eyes were wild and white all the way around.

"Stand up straight, boys," I whispered. "This is our ship, right?"

I grinned, feigning confidence, and led them across the beam amidships, looking for a hatch down into the gundeck and on into the hold. With every step, I could feel my legs shaking and I had the sudden knowledge that we would not be successful. There were too many men on the ship and they would put out the fires we started before they could overtake the ship. All the same, we had to try.

Steeling myself, I marched on to the hatch and strode down it, trusting my men to keep with me. The ladder was steep and I almost slipped in the darkness, banging against the rail as I came down. Not like a sailor at all, and the voices on the gun deck fell quiet as I stomped down into the long, low space. I could not stand up straight. A group of Spanish mariners by the open gun ports beside me frowned and peered through the gloom. Only one lamp illuminated the area by the ladder.

"Who are you?" one asked.

"I have a message for Lorenzo de la Vega. Where is he?"

They were suspicious. "With the master, on the command deck. Who are you?"

Damn.

"They said he had gone to see his men. Are you his men, friends? Are you the special soldiers for the invasion?"

Again, they hesitated but one of the four men answered. "We are the chosen—"

The first of them slapped the speaker in the gut with the back of his hand. "Go and ask the master about this." He then addressed me. "You wait here, right?"

"Oh, of course, my friends, of course, whatever you need to do, I quite understand." Forcing a smile onto my face, I bowed low as the sailor came to pass me and as I straightened I drew my sword and thrust the tip into his heart. The man fell as I withdrew my blade and rushed forward into the group. The first, I caught in the throat and he fell back across a cannon, clutching the gash as the blood poured out and his throat whistled. The next made the mistake of standing to fight and he got so far as yanking a knife from his belt before I sliced through his face with one stroke and cut through his neck with the next. The last man tried to run but my men brought him down before he had got far.

But we were not alone on the long gun deck. Spanish mariners both forward and aft cried out and began rushing about in agitation.

"Start your fires here," I shouted to my men and I strode forward with my sword up and my head down. A mass of sailors began to form and I roared at them, swishing my blade in the air before me. All I had to do was keep them away while the fire was started and caught and so I was happy enough that they were not brave enough to approach.

But then an arquebus was passed forward and then another and two sailors kneeled and took aim at me.

I was already running directly at them when they fired. One missed but the other ripped into my thigh and I stumbled and fell. Rolling, I jumped to my feet and banged my head on the ceiling just as the great mass of sailors came roaring at me with their knives and clubs. I backed away, cutting and thrusting rapidly at them. The ones before me fell, spouting blood and the men behind them slowed and edged away. But on the flanks the Spaniards flowed over the cannons on their carriages and rushed my men.

They had already started their fires and I heard the fizzing hiss of gunpowder burning so I shouted for them to flee and turned to make my own escape.

One of my men, rushing up the ladder, was thrown back. He fell with a wet smack on the deck while the rest of us fought back the swarming sailors and retreated toward the hatchway but then my men cried a warning and I glanced over my shoulder.

The giant, Lorenzo de la Vega, came stomping down the ladder. He hunched low, filling the space like a wall. Behind him, his soldiers came to block the way out with their bodies.

Vega stabbed my floored man in the chest and then bent to saw through his neck. The fire raged on one side, spreading along the spilled oil to lick the timbers from the deck to the ceiling.

Someone fired an arquebus and it hit me high on the back. I roared in pain and lashed out, catching two men who strayed too close and sending the mass of men reeling back from me. When I turned back to Vega, I saw him and his immortals killing my last two men.

I was alone and surrounded.

There were immortals forward and immortals aft and I knew I could not fight my way through either so, with a final look at Vega, who stood hunched like a beast with my men's blood on his sword and on his face, I rushed to the side. One man fell to my sword, another I smashed in the face with my fist and the rest threw themselves aside. Climbing over the massive iron barrel of the cannon, I heaved myself through the open gun port and fell, flailing, into the night.

Almost at once, the cold black water enveloped me and I was lost in darkness. I kicked my way to the surface in time to hear arquebuses fire. Struggling to swim away, I had only a vague idea of where the galleon was and I splashed with one hand while trying to unfasten my doublet with the other. Light flared and hands grabbed me and I lashed out at them until I recognised Walt's voice.

"It's me, Richard, it's me, you daft bastard!"

The hands heaved me over the side into the rocking boat just as the galleon flared into flame.

There was only twelve of my twenty men in the boat. "Callthorp?" I asked, coughing.

"The giant got him," Walt said, brimming with rage. "And his boys."

Fire surged on the ship as we rowed away and the men shooting us stopped in order to make their own escape. On the main deck, the enormous silhouette of Lorenzo de la Vega stood looking out at us, his huge sword still in his hand. Men fretted beside him and finally he turned and walked away through the flames.

The fire grew quickly and soon the entire vessel was burning from the gun deck to the cross trees in a roaring conflagration.

"What took you so long?" Walt asked. "Set the fires and run, you said."

"We were trapped."

"At least we did it," Walt said. "We bloody did it."

I shook my head. "We failed. Most of the men dead. Worse, there was time enough for the immortals to escape with their lives. All we have done is burn a ship."

Walt nodded. "It was a mad idea."

"Should have taken fire pots," Adams said.

Each of us took an oar and we rowed for the outer harbour, looking for English ships. One of the men swore that a ship ahead was the *Rainbow* and though I had no idea how he could be so certain, I trusted his word. We hailed the *Rainbow* as we approached and they let us up, corralling us at the rail until they were certain we were indeed friends.

"Are you too tired to fight on, my friends?" Captain Bellingham asked.

"Give us a draught of wine and we'll fight all night," I said, whereupon the crew growled in approval.

All the English ships, large and small, were now engaged in towing away prizes. Those that could not be taken out were set ablaze. On the *Rainbow*, casks of pitch and tar were loaded one after the other on to four captured barks and two small flyboats which we then fired as we left. Each one lit up like the devil and soon it seemed the entire harbour, great as it was, burned like a huge volcano, with smoke and fire roaring into the black void above.

"This is a rare sight," Walt said as the conflagration took hold.

There were two or three dozen ships burning from one side of the enormous harbour to the other so that it was bright enough to see the faces of the men around me on the deck of the *Rainbow*. We were tired and our faces and hands were blackened. My skin felt tight where the heat of so many flames had touched me. I would heal quickly, but surely Spain would not.

"It is a wonderful sight," I muttered.

Walt crossed himself. "It's a vision of Hell."

Just before sunrise, our fleet followed Drake's ship out through the channel back to the open sea and reached it in safety with the first light of day. We had destroyed forty Spanish ships, including Santa Cruz's great galleon, and had brought away a handful more as prizes. By destroying so many ships and provisions destined for the great Armada, we had inflicted a blow of sorts. But there were many other contingents preparing to create the invasion fleet, at Passages, and Lisbon, and into the Mediterranean at Gibraltar, Cartagena and Italy. Everywhere along the coast of Philip's European empire they continued their plans to invade England.

What was worse, I had utterly failed to even damage Lorenzo de la Vega's immortal army but had lost eight of my own.

William and Spain would still come for us.

18

Loss

1588

THE REPORTS WERE undeniable. Despite the blows we had struck, still the Spanish prepared and assembled their great war fleet, which they dubbed the *Grande y Felicísima Armada*. The Great and Fortunate Navy. It was now to be commanded by the Duke of Medina Sidonia and he would have the greatest captains of the Spanish Empire serving him. The number of galleons, mariners, and soldiers being assembled was so great that every soul in Christendom knew it was happening.

Their plan also was assumed by all. The Duke of Parma's army sat across the Channel in the Low Countries and needed only to be ferried to our shores by the Armada. And most people, whether Catholic or Protestant, doubted that England had even a slight chance of defeating either the army or the Armada.

And yet there were some convinced it could be done. Drake, of course, believed he could save England practically single handed. At a meeting of the Privy Council, we had heard from the lords of the Navy the many proposals for defeating the Armada at sea and from Dudley and other lords the plans for defending London and England generally from the Duke of Parma's army in the Low Countries.

After the many hours of talking, the Queen retired and the talking continued. Soon, I was quietly summoned to the Queen's private chambers.

She stood straight and tall with her back to the window. With the light behind her, it was difficult to see the detail of her face. It was certainly no accident that she had taken such a position. "Do you think we can beat the Spanish?" she asked, without the false tone she always adopted for audiences.

"I do."

"Why? No one else does."

"Many of us believe it. They have the advantage in the numbers of men, in ships and in money. But we are defending our kingdom. We will win because we must."

"And because of God," she said.

"Yes, we will win because God is with us."

She glanced at me, without amusement. "You are still a Catholic. You were born to it but you have still not accepted the true religion. Tell me I am wrong."

Someone told her I did not attend Protestant services. Possibly Cecil or Walsingham but more likely Dudley. "You have the right of it."

She narrowed her eyes. "So, when you say that God is with us, of whom do you speak? Catholics?"

"God will be with the English."

"English Catholics?"

"With all the English."

"How can that be true? God cannot be for one or the other and yet my kingdom is divided."

I shrugged. "I do not know other than I know God will be for the English because we are in the right and our enemies are wrong."

She flicked a glance at me. "Not much of a scholar, are you Richard? Oh, to have a soldier's simple mind. How can you know so little and yet be so certain?"

I sighed. "I just know it. In my heart. Perhaps that is God, telling me so."

She turned, the trace of a smirk on her painted lips. "You sound like a Protestant."

Shrugging, I smiled. "I have been called worse."

Laughing lightly, she touched a finger to her mouth. "Richard," the queen breathed. "It is gratifying to see you."

"You also, Elizabeth."

She sighed and stepped closer so that the light of the window no longer obscured her features. The years had continued to be hard on her face. Although her jowls had lengthened she was beginning to look gaunt at the cheekbones. Her makeup could not fully hide the degradation of her skin and the sinking of her eyes. She reached out and came so close that her hands caressed my shoulders and when she smiled, I saw how browned more of her teeth had become and I had to force my own smile onto my face.

"I have missed you terribly," she said, her fingers brushing my face.

"And I you."

"Oh," she said. "You must not lie."

"I think of little else but your safety."

"You think of England's safety. You see me as England and you see England as me and that is all you truly care about."

"No, Elizabeth. When I do think of you, I think of..." I glanced at the servant feigning obliviousness in the corner. "I think of our previous times together."

"You do not think of me as I am now, of course. Why would you? How could you?" She scowled. "I cannot bear to see you ageless. Still in your eternal youth. Still in your full health and... vitality." Sighing, she blew foulness into my face and I did not flinch though my eyes watered. "Never-ending health, what a thing it is. Sometimes, I think that I hate you, did you know that?"

I did not know what to say, so I simply bowed.

She frowned. "I wonder if you hate me, also."

"How can you think such a thing? Why would I hate you?"

"Because I am old. So terribly old, now. You must hate me for getting so old when once I was young."

"You have it wrong, Elizabeth. It is easy for me to say but I have always wished I could age. That I could grow old, with..." I was going to say grow old with a wife and to be old while I teach my grandson to fight with a sword and shield, but I did not wish to break her heart any further and took a different tack. "To age is to be as God intended all the creatures to be. Why God made me ageless, I do not know. I accept His wisdom, of course, but I know that I am an abomination. I do not hate what is natural,

531

what is Godly."

"You are right. It is easy for you to say. You call this nature and perhaps it is. But it is not good. It is decay, and it is death. Pieces of our body decay and become corrupted and it is something you shall never know. You are blessed and we are cursed. I think of you every time I look into a mirror, Richard, and that is when I hate you most."

Without thinking, I put my arms around her and held her against me. She grasped me back, her arms wrapped right around me, and squeezed me with remarkable strength. I held her against me, her body seemingly youthful and firm beneath her gown, her breasts, still somewhat firm, pushed into my chest as she breathed deeply. We stayed that way for some time, and she began running her hands over my back, my shoulders and my neck as I caressed the small of her back over her bodice. When her fingers found their way up to my head and began curling into my hair, the servant in the corner coughed once, loudly.

We pulled away from each other and Elizabeth turned away, smoothing down her dress.

"We have been too long here alone," she muttered. "You must go."

I bowed. "I would return at a more convenient time."

She smiled out of the corner of her mouth as she glanced over her shoulder at me and for a moment she looked like a young woman again. "And I would like that, Sir Knight." But then she turned away and her bearing stiffened. "How I wish that you could rescue me from my tower and take me away. Alas, it is not to be. I say it again, you must go."

I bowed and backed toward the door but she stopped me.

"Richard? Tell me truthfully now. Do you really believe that we can win?"

"Your Majesty, how can we possibly believe otherwise?"

*　*　*

"John Dee is here to see you," Martin said when I came home. "In the dining parlour. He insisted on waiting."

"Oh, God's balls," I said. "I told you to keep him away."

Martin frowned. "I am not a porter but a lawyer. And anyway, he insisted."

"If you intend to spend the rest of your days with the Order, Martin, you will have to grow a spine." He hung his head and I sighed. "Very well, I will speak to him. The dining parlour you say?"

Dee was in the corner of the room talking closely with his hunchbacked servant when I came in and called out a greeting. He turned and I was struck by how much he had aged. The man had entered his sixties and his eyes and temples were sunken and his long nose appeared even longer.

"Ah, Richard, I am so pleased you have returned. Now, I come to beg that you allow us to continue our investigations into your gifts."

"I told you long ago that we were done."

Dee's servant bowed deeply and muttered. "I'll wait in the kitchens, sir, if it please you."

"What's that? Ah, yes, yes, go on, Boote."

He bowed again and scuttled out.

"And that is why I say again I have come to beg you to reconsider. All my life I have worked tirelessly to unearth the secrets of the earth and the heavens. During your long absences I have continued to meet with Stephen Poole and even one or two of your other companions. They have assisted me most ably in my investigation and now I come close to an understanding of your true nature."

"Oh? Then you must tell me." I sat down at the table and invited him to sit across from me, which he did before launching into an excited explanation.

"Well, sir, as you must surely be aware, I am engaged also in the discovery of the language of angels and after one recent night of communing with them I was struck, inspired, I am certain, by those very angels, and I realised at once that you and your kind... are most certainly angels yourselves."

I sighed and pinched my nose. "I have had a long day at the palace. Perhaps you will forgive me if we discuss this at another time?"

"A long day? I have been waiting your return for hours and my time is more precious than yours, by our very natures. If we do not do this soon I shall grow old and die and the lessons will be unlearned!"

"I may age imperceptibly slowly, but the rest of the world continues at its own pace, John. Even now, there is a great fleet coming for us. An army across the Channel, ready to crush us. It is certain that—"

"A fleet comes, yes it most certainly does, as has been foretold. The portents are grave indeed. Signs have been noted."

I was confused by his sudden change in direction. "Signs?"

"Indeed, sir, indeed. You see, the weather is stranger than it has ever been, ever in living memory," Dee proclaimed.

I smiled. "Some of us have longer memories than others. Forgive me, please continue."

"Ah, of course, yes. Well, the mariners tell us that the wind off the coast has been as violent as was predicted. And we have had word that across the sea in Normandy, the hailstorms have ravaged fields and orchards so that there shall be no apple harvest this year, none at all. And the might of these storms has killed cattle in the fields. In Picardy, the roads have been turned to rivers and the rivers have spread everywhere, drowning the land. And so the Armada must be upon us. At any moment."

I shook my head. "We have had no word. No sight. We can assume that these winds are keeping them from England."

"Everything that is happening has been seen. *Seen*, you understand? And so I know the Spanish fleet is almost here and I also know that great death is coming with it, great and terrible death. Not just for England but also for you, Richard."

"Your communing with angels told you this?"

"Yes. During my many spells of summoning, I have communed with an angel who has told me that great suffering is in store for Richard Ashbury. Suffering and death. So much death."

I stared at him, chilled to my soul. "A moment ago you thought I was an angel. How come I did not know of this?"

"You doubt me. Mock me and you doubt. But an angel may not know he is an angel if he has *fallen*. And you are most certainly fallen."

"A truly fascinating notion, John, but I did not fall from

heaven. I was born, I was a boy, then a young man."

"Certainly, you were born, your body was born to a woman. But your spirit, your essence, that is angelic."

I smiled. "I should call Eva from the palace to hear this. Perhaps I will bring Stephen in from his study. John, if my spirit is angelic, how is my strength transmitted in my *blood*? And from the blood of my immortals into others to make revenants? Blood is tangible, essential, and the spirit is... I do not know what it is but one cannot drink a cup of it."

"Ah but one can! It is evident. A spirit needs a physical form to tie it to the earth and we know now through my investigations that the spirit resides within the blood. Drain a man of blood and he dies but why? Because you have drained his spirit. It is the same with you only your blood contains a more potent spirit whose effects are more obviously apparent and transmittable."

I did not know what to say. It sounded plausible but then logic and reason are like that. They cause clever men to believe the most absurd notions.

"What about William, then? And William's spawn. You mean to tell me that they are angels also?"

"Of that I am not certain but there are only two possibilities. One is that William is like you an angel, fallen to earth and from there has chosen a path of evil. After all, did God not grant free will to his angels also and did not one in particular and others also choose evil over good? And the only other possibility is that he is a demon."

"Now that I could believe." I frowned. "But how could he be a demon if our blood is the same?"

"Is it the same?"

"It has the same effects."

"But does it? Is it precisely the same? And if it is, might this not be because demons are in fact mirror images of angels? The precise inverse of them, in fact. As if an angel were viewed through a dark mirror."

"How then might we know which it is, angel or demon?"

"Ah," he said, holding up a finger. "This is why we must test the blood of an angel and the blood of a demon. I would like to test your blood in the precise same fashion as William's blood and observe the results."

I smiled. "John, if I had William's blood then it would mean he was dead. And then none of this would matter."

"It would matter very much indeed. But I suspected you would say as much. And that is why we would accept the blood of one of your men and the blood of one of William's men. So please would you have one of your men bled for me and also one of William's. I will wait."

"You will wait?" I said. "One of my men I can bring but as for..." I broke off and looked at him. "How would I give you the blood from one of William's men?"

"Ah, I was hoping you would prick the arm of one of the men in your cellar, Richard. I know not whether it would be best for the one named Alonso, who was the fellow you killed in my house so long ago, or if you would prefer the fellow who tried for the Queen when I was at Hatfield. And I heard you now have an awful lot more down there in your secret gaol. Choose any you think best but if I may suggest we could even, possibly, take a half a pint from each of them. These must be properly and clearly labelled immediately to ensure—"

537

My heart was racing but I held myself very still. "Who told you we are holding these men here?"

Dee stopped, confused. "Ah, well, I cannot quite recall who suggested it initially..."

"You *will* recall."

He frowned, seemingly confused. "Have I said something to anger you, Richard?"

I slid my hand down to my sword hilt while keeping my eyes on him. "You knew the Queen was coming to your house that night she was almost shot."

"Well, hardly, she comes when she will. At least, she used to. These days, sadly, she—"

"You knew, in advance. Days or hours, perhaps, but you knew to ready your astrological readings."

He shrugged, his eyes wide. "Well, of course, one must make certain preparations in order to provide an accurate—"

"And you were at Hatfield all those years later when her horse was shot and those immortals rushed her."

"A terrible business. I was deeply shocked and saddened—"

"Strange your scrying and prognosticating did not predict these attempts at murder, is it not?"

"Ah, how I wish that—"

"And ever since that day you have not been at court, nor she to your house. And there has been no further assassination attempts by immortals."

He frowned then, growing angry. "A most happy coincidence, I assure you."

I slowly pulled my sword from the sheath and laid it before me on the table, knocking over a wine cup that spilled across the tabletop, shining dark in the lamplight. Dee stared at the reflective silver blade. "Think carefully, John. Your life depends on your answer. Who told you that we have never killed our immortal prisoners but hold them in our gaol here? Stephen would not have told you, I trust him to keep all our secrets. Who was it?"

He swallowed and dragged his eyes from the steel to look at me. "I swear to you—" he began and I cut him off again.

"You will live to see dawn only by telling me who."

Dee gulped twice and licked his lips. "Boote. That is, my servant, Boote."

"The hunchback?" I stood and took up my sword. "How long has he been with you? He was there that night, I remember. Is he always with you?"

"Well, yes. He is my assistant also and helps me in my work. He is quite brilliant, in his own way and I could not do without him."

I groaned. "Does he know your codes? Your cyphers?"

"Ah, he is rather gifted at developing them, you know and in fact he taught me when I was young."

"When you were young?" I growled. "But how old is he? He does not look a day over... By Christ, John, your man is an immortal, a demonic one, and either you are working with him or you are so foolish that—"

A scream pierced the air. It came from the other side of the house and I was running even before it ended. I ran from the dining hall into the entrance hall just as my immortal prisoners came running from the back of the house.

Alonso, Brocksby, the Crow, and three of his men.

All had escaped their cells in our goal and were intent on

fleeing into the night. Nothing stood between them and their freedom. Nothing but me.

At their head was Dee's crookbacked servant, Boote.

Only, he was crookbacked no longer and stood straight as he drew to a stop and sneered. His lips and chin were bloody. "Kill him!" he shouted and together they rushed me.

There were seven of them, all immortals and all desperate to murder me. I had made those six prisoners into failures. I had caused them to be tortured and starved and imprisoned. Their hatred for me was profound and even if it had not been their duty to kill me, and they had not needed to do so in order to escape, they would have done so anyway.

Boote was armed with a sword and the Crow had a cleaver and Alonso a carving knife.

Their weapons were bloody.

The prisoners were weakened by their deprivations but Boote moved like lightning. I parried his slashes and lunging attacks as I retreated toward the front doors when the others attempted to get behind me.

The Crow swung his cleaver at my head and I slipped under it and sliced through his arm. As he began to scream I took his head clean off his shoulders and punched the man behind him to the ground.

Boote's blade cut my shoulder and I twisted away, slashing Alonso across the face and forehead and he fell back shrieking and clutching his hands to his eyes.

And then the rest of my men were there. Walt rushed out from the rear and killed Boote with three swift strokes, cutting his skull to pieces. Even Stephen killed a man and Martin rushed in, though he almost got himself slaughtered in the process.

Before I knew it, the prisoners were all dead in the entrance hall and all that could be heard was hard breathing and the sound of the fire crackling in the hall hearth.

Until the wailing started.

We rushed into the kitchens at the rear of the house and found my staff there all dead. Three women, two men and one of their lads lying dead

"Goodie!" Walt cried and ran to her where she was slumped by the side door into the yard, which was closed. When he turned her over he found her run through the chest and neck, blood soaking her. "No, Christ, no!" Walt sobbed.

Goodie coughed a spray of blood into his face and he looked at me with tears in his eyes. "Richard!"

I went forward and cut my arm so that she might drink from me and live. As I reached her, I saw the body that Goodie had been lying across.

"Catalina," I said and lifted her up so that I could give her the drink of my blood whether she wanted it or not and so save her life.

But she was dead.

One of them had stabbed her through the base of the skull and her back was dotted with wounds.

"She locked the door," Goodie said through her tears when she had been revived. "When they came and killed us here, she might have fled. But she shut the door to the yard and then grabbed the key off the wall and locked it while they rushed her. She put the key in her bodice. I did what I could." She sobbed. "I put myself across her but he stabbed his sword right through me and into her. I'm sorry. God help me, I'm so sorry."

Walt held her and told she had done everything right.

"Old Leeche is dead," Stephen said after coming up from the cellar. "That fiend Boote must have got a key from somewhere, a previous visit here I suppose, then went down and killed Leeche. Took his keys. Freed the others."

"Right under our noses," Martin said, his face white with the horror. "How could this happen, we vetted everybody?"

"Quiet, Martin," Stephen snapped. "It is my failure. I admit it. I failed. And our dear friends are dead."

"But we checked every man and woman who we know," Martin insisted, "and we check their servants, also, we—"

"No," I said. "No, that man played his part to perfection. Every day for... forty years, perhaps, he played at being a hunchbacked assistant. Dee says he did his work well. And Dee never suspected. Every day, this man hunched himself and made himself small and worked like a clerk, like an acolyte and all the while he was serving another master. A man who was willing to do that, who was capable of such depths of deceit, could not have been uncovered by your methods. Do not take guilt upon yourselves for this."

Stephen stepped close and laid a hand on my arm. "Only if you do not take it upon yourself."

"The fault is mine!" I shrugged him off. "We shall dispose of all the prisoners and then summon the authorities. Our story is that John Dee's servant went mad and slew our kitchen staff and was slain in the act."

Catalina and Leeche we gave proper Christian burials outside London. I felt bad for Leeche because he had served Eva well but he was already old when he was turned. His death was as regrettable as it was avoidable but he had lived on for decades past his natural span.

With Catalina, though, I felt nothing but despair. After her funeral, I stood staring as the gravediggers filled it in, the clods of earth drumming on her coffin. Eva came up beside me and I felt her fingers slip between mine. Holding my hand, she leaned her head on my shoulder.

"I know what you're thinking," she said softly. "But you are not to blame."

"For so many years, I have failed. Taken the wrong course, made poor decisions. Chasing across to the new world and making such a noise that Vega killed hundreds of Englishmen at San Juan de Ulúa. More of them died when we took the treasure from the isthmus and for what? I thought it was a fortune but it was nothing, not even a fraction of the wealth of the New World. And when I found Don Enríquez, I just sent Vega straight to the safety of Spain, bringing William the fortune to pay for the fleet that now comes to destroy us. Everything I did has only made the invasion more likely. I failed again at Cadiz. Turning Drake into one of us now seems nothing but folly. He no longer listens to my commands, thinking he is his own man. If it were any other man in the Order I would consider killing him but we need him for the coming fight and so I am trapped by my foolishness. Why did I ever trust Drake? Why did he ever trust me? I thought I was being so cunning but my plans have led to the death of my people, the weakening of the Order, and the strengthening of Vega and William."

Eva rubbed my arm. "I know you liked Catalina."

"All I wanted for her was…" I broke off for a moment. "She

deserved a proper life. I should have forced her out, especially when Philip died. Forced her to find a husband. Or sent her back to her own people."

"She wanted none of that or she would have asked. And you saved her from a short, miserable life in a brothel house. She had love, for a time."

"Philip?" I said, shaking my head.

She punched my arm. "You don't know. He loved her completely. It didn't matter that she was a Catholic, that she was Spanish with an African grandmother. He didn't care she had come from a brothel house. And she loved him for that. He was a good man, too. You feel too angry with yourself to think of him but you should. He was kind, thoughtful. They adored each other. They were happy."

"And both dead because of me."

"We will all die. Even me. Even you. They were happy in our house because of you."

"I promised her she would be safe with me."

"Well," Eva said. "There will only ever be one way for any of us to be safe. And you really must have faith, you know."

"I do."

"Not only in God but in yourself and in your men. You have always chosen them well. William creates immortals by the dozen and sends them off to do their evil but how many of them are equal to the men you chose? Trust your men. Trust in the choices you made when you made them. Even Francis Drake."

I took a deep breath and turned away from Catalina's grave. "We shall see."

The next day, I travelled south to Plymouth to join the English fleet.

19

The Armada

1588

"YOU KNOW WHAT I heard?" the mariner said to me, speaking softly. "I heard the King of Spain has five hundred ships and eighty thousand mariners and soldiers. That true, do you reckon?"

We stood leaning against a low wall on the heights on the west coast of Plymouth Sound, the three-mile-long bay where most of the English fleet sat ready. Behind us, further up the hill, was a powerful gun battery but the wall we leant on was not defensive. Rather, it served to keep the sheep from tumbling down the steep hill and into the bay. A soft rain drifted on us but blue skies in the south suggested it would soon dry off.

"Five hundred ships and eighty thousand men?" I repeated. "It is quite possible."

The mariner whistled and shook his head. "We're done for,

then."

"But I heard that every English ship is worth ten Spanish," I replied. "So we need not be afraid."

"If you say so, sir."

"I do."

Another man next to him cleared his throat. "You know, I heard the Spaniards called it off. Ain't coming now, so they say. Going to be next year, most likely."

On the other side of me, an older man spat. "Ireland. It's gone to Ireland, that's what I heard. And why not? Easier conquest than England, ain't it?"

"Aye but there's nought there but rain and bog. Why bother?"

The older man shrugged. "It's what I heard."

We stood in silence for a while, watching the activity below on the scores of English ships, large and small, at anchor in the bay. Our galleons and the enormous merchant ships dwarfed the pinnaces and tenders and boats streaming to and fro from all directions. To the south, beyond the mouth of the bay, the Channel stretched to the horizon showing a light swell. There were boats out there, also, watching and ready for any sign of enemy ships.

Muttering and nudging to either side drew my attention and I turned to see Drake approaching with his enormous retinue trailing behind. Even hidden beneath his big hat, all the sailors in Plymouth, in all England, recognised him in an instant and they spoke greetings and blessings and praise as he passed. Drake waved a hand without looking at any of them and came straight up to me.

"Richard, we missed you at dinner."

"I cannot eat."

"Not anxious, are you?" he said, smirking.

"Every soul in England is anxious, Francis. Anyone who is otherwise is either lying or is mad."

He frowned and plucked at my elbow. I allowed myself to be led a few steps away. "We must keep spirits up, Richard," he said quietly.

"What do you think will happen?" I asked him.

He smiled, a twinkle in his eye. "We will sail around them like hounds around a bear and we shall tear lumps from their—"

"No, no," I said, waving him to silence. "Do not top it the swaggering captain with me. Tell me straight, man."

His smile fell. "Who can say? So much to consider. The size of their fleets, of ours. The nature of the various cannons against various hulls. No man has ever seen the like of it. So much is entirely unknown, so much incalculable."

"Ah," I said. "You mean you do not know."

"No one knows." He folded his arms. "And how would I know when I am not in command?"

"Ah, I see now," I said. "You resent being made a mere *Vice*-Admiral of England."

"No! It is a great honour."

"Upon my oath, Francis, it is greater honour than a jumped-up son of a Devonshire peasant deserves, that much is for certain."

"Aye, aye, no need for mockery, I am honoured. I just pray that Lord Howard will make the correct decisions."

"The Lord Admiral will certainly not be as wild as you. He will not be dashing about like a madman."

"You do not believe that is how I command my ships."

"You have had great success with such dash but perhaps in a great and complicated battle caution is now called for."

"Ha!" Drake laughed in my face. "Richard Ashbury is the advocate for caution? Now who is the madman?"

"There is a time and a place for everything," I said.

"I agree and I will show Lord Howard how trustworthy I am. And my peers, England's mariners and indeed all England."

He could no longer even control his grandiosity for the length of a conversation.

I clapped him on the shoulder. "You must calm yourself, Francis. This high state cannot be sustained long without some ultimate collapse of strength. Let us engage in exercise of the body and not the head or the heart. What's say we draw our swords and have at each other?"

He rolled his eyes. "It would be child's play for you and no great joy for me to be toyed with. Let us play a man's game, like dice."

"Dice is a game of the stomach, you oaf. We must use our bodies in a game of skill. How about bowls? There is a game set up atop the hill."

"Fine, fine," he replied. "Let us go there."

I was excellent at games of throwing but I was distracted that day and Francis won as many rounds as I did. The admirals and captains drifted in groups up to our game until we had a hundred officers standing around, watching our game and playing their own. Despite the anxiety and tension, men soon began to laugh and wine was being drunk and certain gentlemen commanded their servants to fetch refreshments.

Lord Admiral Howard arrived and declined to play but

instead stood to one side and retained his dignity while we carried on. Soon after, there was a commotion behind us and shouts and we turned to see a group of men rushing up the hill. A cry went up from them which was answered by dozens of men at once.

"Where is the Lord Admiral?"

"Here, he is here!"

It was one Captain Fleming, commander of the senior ship of our outermost screen. He stopped, breathing hard, before the Lord Admiral and bowed low. A hush fell over the men.

"Well?" some man cried.

Captain Fleming addressed only the Admiral. "Lord Howard, sir. The enemy is sighted."

Howard nodded. "Well done, sir. Well done. My friends, it seems our wait is over. You each know your duty. Let us be about it."

The men cheered and began to all speak at once, starting to make off for their ships.

I grinned and clapped Drake on the back. He made to go with Fleming and I stopped him.

"Hold up, Francis," I said, indicating the jack and hefting my ball in hand. "We have time enough to finish the game and beat the Spaniards, too."

He laughed and he liked it so much he stole it. Drake turned to the watching crowd of officers and men and raised his voice to cry out, far louder than I had spoken. "I say, we have time enough to finish the game and beat the Spaniards, too!"

The men around us cheered and, taking aim, I tossed the ball. It struck one of Drake's and both bounced away, leaving neither of us near to the jack. We looked at each other for a moment, shrugged and marched away down the hill toward the ships.

"Remember, Francis, we must find Vega's ship above all else. No matter what else happens during the battle."

He scowled; his good mood ruined. "There is no method we can employ to do so at sea."

"We must find a way. You agreed we would find them and destroy them because no other commander in the fleet understands the danger they pose to us."

"I said so, didn't I? Now, leave me be. I must prepare my ships and my men." He sped up, pushing through the crowd who of course made way for him and his officers. I slowed and let the stream of men flow by me.

I wondered if he would make any efforts at all to stop Vega's ship. If he did not obey me, I did not know what else I would do.

Drake and his entourage marched down the hill amongst the mass of officers and sailors heading for their boats and then to their ships. Stopping where I was, I looked out into Plymouth Sound and found our ship sitting at anchor.

The Order of the White Dagger had funded the construction of a truly magnificent warship, built in the new style that the Navy Board led by our old friend John Hawkins believed would give us the best chance of victory. She was over 400-tons and carried forty guns and was crewed with veteran mariners loyal to Drake. Not to me, though it was my ship. She was hard to miss as we had painted her in a green and white harlequin pattern of diamonds.

She was not as big as the great galleons of our fleet or those of the Armada but she was built as strongly as was possible while remaining swift and manoeuvrable. We built her for a single purpose. To chase down and do battle with the ship commanded by Lorenzo de la Vega and ultimately to help me to defeat William de Ferrers.

When Drake invited me to see her when she was almost done, I knew what I had to name her.

"We will use this ship to finally redress the wrong done to English sailors by Vega at San Juan de Ulúa," I had said to Drake. "And that is what we shall call her."

Drake had frowned. "Redress?"

"*Revenge.*"

All the strength of the Order of the White Dagger was on the *Revenge* down in Plymouth Sound. I now had thirty-four immortal soldiers including Walt armed and ready onboard and I prayed that they would be enough to counter whatever we had to face in the coming battles. Many of them were newly made and I prayed they would prove trustworthy. Either way, they were all I had.

I found Walt on the main deck of the *Revenge* while the sailors made ready the ship around us.

"They've come then," Walt said. "About time."

I shook his hand and spoke to him in a low voice of Drake's lack of respect. "I thought he understood but now I fear he will not obey my orders. And now it is too late to do anything about it. How could I let this happen?"

Walt snorted. "You gave him free rein for too long."

"I did."

"He doesn't see himself as one of us, that much is clear. He never comes to the house, he never made friends with the rest of us, he acts like he's above us. He took the oath but he's not White Dagger, is he. He's just a pirate, drunk on his own legend." Walt narrowed his eyes and leaned in closer. "You always say you cannot abide an immortal who is not loyal to you, right? So..." He drew a finger across his throat.

"Not always. After all, Dracula is out there, somewhere, assuming he lives. As are the immortal monks. Priskos lives, along with his spawn and who knows how many of them there are."

He shrugged. "That's different."

"Perhaps. But do you not think it would be better to bring Drake under our control rather than murdering the man at the very moment England needs him the most?"

Walt scoffed. "Protestant England."

"It is *England*, Walt. Our people are our people, no matter what madness has gripped them. And even if that were not true, the Order needs Drake. I need him."

"Right. So how you going to control him?"

"I must find a way."

"You better be quick about it," Walt said, squinting south through the crowd of galleons toward the Channel. "This will be the fight of our lives."

* * *

The crew of the *Revenge* were excited and nervous but there was no time for them to indulge their emotions, as they had hard work to do. In the darkness, by lamplight, they warped the ship out of the Sound. There was almost no wind, as if the world was holding its breath, but the fleet had to get out before the Spanish trapped us in the Sound and so the royal galleons and the heaviest, best-armed of the merchantmen were warped out into the Channel.

We anchored in the lee of Rame Head and night wound on. I stayed up for quite some time, looking at the blackness and listening to sounds of the sea and the crew and the fleet all around us.

In the morning, the wind came up stronger from the southwest, keeping us pinned against the shore.

"We can't have this," Drake said to us at sunrise. "Howard will have to beat up into it lest the Spanish catch us on a lee shore."

"What's he on about?" Walt asked.

"The wind is blowing us against the shore. If the Spanish come up, we shall be stuck here while they have the wind behind them. The only way to get out from here is to beat back and forth at an angle against the wind, working our way slowly against the wind until we are out at sea and able to manoeuvre."

"Richard," Drake said, smiling, having overheard me. "We shall make a sailor of you yet!"

The officers laughed and I frowned. "No fear of that, Captain."

And before the sun was fully up, the Lord Admiral ordered just such a manoeuvre and I stood and watched our great galleons and the huge merchant ships beating back and forth against the wind, dozens of us being sailed by thousands of men and somehow it was done with no fuss and no panic. No ships collided, none came close to entanglement, and none of the officers or crew seemed to think anything was remarkable about it at all.

Beyond the fleet at the end of the Sound were the green hills of Rame Head where they dropped into the frothing silver seas below. Cornwall was so wild, with its grey and black rocks and deep green grass over thin turf, and the Cornish were a people half apart from the rest of the English. But that shore was England, just as much as Derbyshire or London or anywhere else. The thought of London brought thoughts of Eva and our house and of Stephen. Thinking of Eva made me think of Elizabeth. I imagined her being paraded in chains before a jeering Spanish army, with William holding the other end of that chain. I shook the unworthy thought from my mind but the stain of it remained.

The ships remained at anchor while the admirals sent pinnaces forward to keep watch of the enemy. Late in the day, there was a cry from one of our ships and then more from lookouts in every one of our galleons. When a handful of officers scrambled aloft, I followed up the ratlines to the fighting top of the mainmast, which was already crowded when I reached it. The officers were squinting at the horizon. I could see a black cloud there but nothing more and muttering curses I climbed by them up toward the cross trees where a half dozen crewmen sat along the maintop spar. Clinging to the ratlines, I looked again.

"Where are they?" I asked, speaking to no man in particular.

"There, sir," one lad by me said, his eyes wide with wonder. "Below the squall, there, do you see?"

He climbed down a few feet and held his finger out at arm's length by my head. The clouds out there were dropping rain over the horizon and I assumed they were hiding the ships. But then the lad's finger swept from the coast all the way out to seaward and then he swept his hand back again toward the coast.

When I understood, I almost fell out of the rigging. "That great black band the width of the horizon is their fleet?"

The sailors around me murmured and the young fellow

dropped his pointing finger. "Like a black wall, ain't it, sir."

"It is," I agreed. "Can you count the ships?"

"Can't see space between them to count, sir. Must be the biggest lot of warships together since the beginning of the world."

"I suppose so, yes."

Somewhere out there, in that black line of great ships, was William and his personal army of immortal soldiers and sailors. I suddenly felt like the greatest fool there ever was for not somehow making my own fleet, my own army, with me in command. How would I ever stop him otherwise? How would our mortal fleet stop theirs at all, for that matter.

"Will they reach us tonight?" I asked the sailors around me.

They all said not. It was too late in the day and then the distant squall blew up closer and obscured all sight of the Armada before the sun set beyond the dark grey sky.

"Another night of waiting," Walt said. "I could get used to war at sea. Imagine having a bunk to sleep in the night before a land battle, Richard? Warm and dry, indoors. Bloody mariners, they've got it easy, the bastards. Now, I'm off to bed."

I went to find Drake where he stood with his officers. The lanterns of the ships all around us hung here and there like a field of yellow stars and the faces on the command deck were illuminated by a lantern suspended above them. They were in the midst of a serious discussion, with much gesturing of the hands to demonstrate positions of ships to one another.

"What's happening?" I asked.

"The Spaniards have the weather-gauge. That is, they are windward of us with the wind at their backs. In the morning, if the wind stays like this, they can be on us."

"You expect them to try to close with us and board us."

He nodded. "They have the men, they have thousands of soldiers on their ships. In the morning, they will descend on us, give us a volley or two from their cannons and pin us against the shallows. We'll shoot our guns as they come up and we'll fight them as they board us but we will be overwhelmed and England will fall."

"What can be done?"

Drake smiled. "We will not be here in the morning."

In the darkness, our fleet beat out to sea, working back and forth against the wind right out into the Channel. From there, in the open water we worked west. It took all night and the men were tired.

But in the morning, when the sun came up, I was amazed. Our fleet was still together and what is more we were behind the Armada.

We had the wind at our backs, arrayed in a single rough line, and the Spanish were ahead of us.

"Do we attack?" I asked Drake.

He grimaced. "I would."

We looked up the line of ships to Lord Howard's flagship, the *Ark Royal*. "No signal."

"The Lord Admiral would rather the enemy make a mistake than make one himself, and so he is minded to do nothing at all." Drake spat and the gob of phlegm flew off toward the Spanish.

"I was thinking," I said, "to summon our pinnace to take me closer to the Spanish, to sail by their fleet. I might be able to discern Vega from a distance by his great height. Then we shall know which ship to destroy."

Drake turned his gaze to me. "You would be blasted to pieces before you got close. No one would be mad enough to take you. I certainly would not."

I frowned. "Our pinnace is commanded by young Lieutenant Bowden and he is almost as reckless as you were in the New—"

A Spanish cannon fired. We looked for the smoke and saw it was a signal gun from the Spanish flagship, the *San Martin*. It was huge, a thousand tons and fifty cannons. As soon as the gun sounded, the entire fleet began to manoeuvre into a formation none of our sailors had ever seen before. While we pointed and commented, they turned themselves into a mighty crescent that curved away from us. One point of the crescent on the landward side of the Channel and the other to seaward, with those points being closest to us and the centre further away.

It was not a perfect crescent by any means. There were a hundred and thirty massive ships; galleons, galleys, galleasses, large supply hulks called *urcas*, small *pataches*, caravels, and carracks, and they each had unique handling qualities. Despite all that, they came damned close to perfection and seeing them arrayed like that was astonishing.

"What do we do now?" I asked Drake and he shrugged. "What does the formation mean for our plan of attack?"

"Don't know," he replied. "I've never seen that before. Told you they were good sailors."

"I never doubted it. But they are not better than us."

"Might be." Drake pursed his lips. "They're certainly no worse."

"Perhaps we could assume the same formation?" I prompted and the officers muttered comments regarding my ignorance.

"We could not do it," Drake snapped. "Even if we wished to. But look, do you not see how it makes them strong? We can only attack them at the tips of the crescent, which is where they have placed their strongest galleons. And if we damage them, they could be pulled into the safety of that formation, while others take its place. Like birds flying in formation behind a leader. Worst of all, should we find ourselves to go between those horns..." he shook his head and all the officers looked uncomfortable.

"Their cannons could all shoot us at once," I said.

This appeared to rouse further contempt from the officers but Drake explained it. "Any ship that goes in there will have lost the wind to the ships on the wings, do you see? They can come up behind from both sides and catch us in such close quarters that we could not slip away. They could trap us between them and grapple and board us."

"What if we carry out a full attack?" I suggested. "Push in with all of us in a great charge and smash them."

Drake pinched his nose. "We are not mounted knights, Richard, charging on horseback. If we come close, if we drag the fleet into a general melee, then we are providing the Catholics with precisely the kind of sea battle they seek. No, we must stay back now."

"How do we harm them, then?" I asked the officers and none of them would so much as look at me. Drake looked at the *Ark Royal* but no signal was forthcoming. "No one has any notions at all?"

"We will have to come up on the horns and fire on them as best we can without getting too close," Drake said. "Fire from a distance. Be sure not to stray into the crescent. And then we shall see what occurs."

His men nodded sagely. I wanted to ask if that was the best idea the mighty Drake could come up with but their stunned silence was disturbing enough and so I held my tongue.

I was being unfair on Drake and the others. Great fleets of mighty sailing ships carrying dozens of massive cannon each was a new occurrence in the world, for them just as it was for me. Nobody knew what tactics would work best because none had been employed before on such a scale. But as Drake said, there was only one thing for it and Howard signalled for his squadrons to attack in line ahead. They followed the *Ark Royal* in a single great line as it moved to attack the northern shoreward tip of the Spanish crescent. The warships following the Lord Admiral turned just beyond their tip and attacked while heading south across the open section of the crescent.

While we in the *Revenge* turned to attack the southern tip we could look across to where the *Ark Royal* and our other leading ships were firing on the Spanish.

Our Lord Admiral was engaged with a massive Mediterranean carrack that was as big as our flagship, both firing guns as the Spanish ship turned to run beside the *Ark Royal*. Just those two ships alone firing made a tremendous sound. As each of our ships passed the enemy tip, they began firing. The next Spanish ship was surely the biggest of them all, another great carrack that engaged Howard with a vast broadside and soon they were lost in banks of white-grey smoke.

And by then we had our own battle to fight. The *Revenge* bore down on the enemy and coming up behind us was Hawkins in the *Victory* and Frobisher in the *Triumph*.

"The Portuguese Squadron!" Drake said to me as we approached, standing as was his custom with his legs planted and his hands behind his back. He had a master to sail the ship and had issued his instructions to his officers and so he had time to think and to speak and to sip a little wine as we moved up to start killing the Spaniards. "Best galleons in the fleet." He grinned. "Powerful ships, crewed by veterans. No better fighting sailors. You see that one?"

He pointed to the largest warship in the fleet, a modern galleon bristling with guns and every rail lined with men.

"I can hardly miss it."

"It is Ricalde's ship, see his flag? He is Vice-Admiral but is their most experienced mariner. A dangerous man to face."

"Sounds like you," I said.

"Here he comes," Drake said but the ship did not change course for some time.

When it did, Ricalde's galleon broke off from the other galleons and moved to sail as if to intercept us. The other ships however sailed on eastwards, leaving their vice-admiral behind.

"What is he doing?" I asked Drake and waited while he spoke to his officers.

"Seems he wants to fight."

"Alone? All of us can shoot him to pieces. Can we not?"

Drake pursed his lips, frowning. In the distance, Howard's squadron continued to do battle with the northern wing of the crescent.

"He wants to draw us into a melee," Drake said, pointing at Ricalde's galleon. "Look at the size of him, if he can get his hooks into us... he has the men to take us. *Victory* and *Triumph* will come up to rescue us. His other galleons will return to engage us." Drake shook his head and fell silent.

I looked out across the waves at the enormous galleon sailing to intercept us. "Should we not change course?"

"Perhaps there is a way..." Drake shook his head and turned to his men. "No, we shall match his course and keep to three hundred yards. We will pound him."

Orders were relayed and the guns were readied as we closed the distance with the massive galleon. And then we began to fire. The guns banged and our shot flew and the smoke filled the air and was blown away and filled it again.

"By Christ Almighty," Walt cried behind me. "The bastard's twice our size. What in God's name are we doing?" For once, he was not exaggerating and it truly was double the size of the *Revenge* with twice as many cannon.

"It is the Vice-flagship," I said, going to him and gripping the rail. "Drake believes it means to close with us and board us."

"Well let's get away from it, then!"

They began shooting at us and their shot splashed into the sea all around us. It seemed our guns were doing little damage too but as we drew ever closer, we began hitting the Spanish galleon and soon after that, we started to be hit also. The *Victory* and the *Triumph* came up and engaged Ricalde's galleon too and together we hammered the gigantic ship. It tried continually to close with one of us and we ceaselessly darted away every time, still firing, always firing, while our mariners heaved on ropes and sails to throw the *Revenge* back and forth across the seas.

"You think Vega's on it?" Walt asked, wincing as a ball flew through the rigging without hitting anything. "Or even William.

Seems like his manner to turn and fight, trusting to the strength of his men, no?"

"Perhaps." We were travelling away as we disengaged to make space for the others and yet we were close enough. I stared at the men on the railings and on the command deck of the galleon but I did not see any men I recognised. Hundreds of Spaniards, some armed, some armoured, many in steel hats, but none of them familiar. "But I do not believe he would risk everything to attack us here and now. William has always been committed to his plans, willing to throw aside his own people if necessary. And he means to land his army on English soil. What does bringing this single ship into battle against us accomplish?"

Walt narrowed his eyes. "What if he knows the *Revenge* is our ship?" I looked at Walt and he shrugged. "You said before that William don't actually want to kill you, because he never comes for you, when he could. But I don't know, I reckon he's got to be sick of you now." He glanced at me. "If I was him, I'd want to bloody kill you."

"I'm sure you would. Let us hope our mariners can keep away from that monstrous galleon, whoever is on board."

"Which one do you reckon it is then? He wouldn't be on a little ship, would he. Must be one of the monsters. Must be."

I looked at the masses of vessels crisscrossing through the swirling smoke and could not imagine how we could discover our enemy. Our ships continued sailing back and forth, firing their guns as they turned and then coming back to shoot again and again for a full hour before a squadron of Spanish galleons returned for the vice-flagship and Drake called our squadron off rather than risk one of us getting caught in a melee.

Up on the northern prong of the crescent, the ships on both sides were also disengaging and we assumed that the Spanish were content to simply sail on through the Channel in that vast crescent formation while we nipped ineffectively at their heels.

Hardly any of our ships had been damaged, other than some rigging shot away and a few dead and wounded from falling debris. Our forestay had been severed by a ball and the cable had knocked a mariner down where he cracked his head and he was apparently still half senseless. From looking at us, I doubted much of our fleet had it any worse.

We took up our positions to follow the enemy formation again and when I went to the command deck, I did not like what I saw. The officers looked confused or alarmed or concerned and they were arguing about what had happened and what they thought should be done next. Drake stood slightly apart, in silence, seeming to be only half-listening to his men. But then, he very rarely cared to hear any opinion but his own.

"Can we not hurt them, Francis?" I said, keeping my voice low.

He pursed his lips and wandered a few paces forward, inviting me with a roll of his shoulders to accompany him, so we could look down at the main deck. When he spoke, he kept his voice low.

"This is a bigger and tougher enemy than we expected. As you know, no man respects Spanish seamanship more than I but also now I see their discipline is... it is greater than ours."

"Yours, certainly."

"You jest, Richard, but you are right and I am not too proud to admit it." He managed to say this with a straight face and continued. "They must have been practising these manoeuvres for months. And perhaps I have doubted their fighting spirit in the past but these men..." He waved a hand at the Armada. "They still had as much stomach at the end of the day as at the beginning."

"But they did not harm us. You are all acting as though we have lost."

"If we can't smash them then we *have* lost, even if our ships are not damaged in the least. Look, we knew they would want to come up on us, board us. But it turns out they are far more heavily gunned than we thought. Your agents and the Queen's were full of horse shit. Turns out they have long guns enough to trade fire with us at range. And what's even worse is they have more short-range hull smashers than we have. If we go closer to them than we have thus far, in order that our guns can do damage, we'll be battered bloody or worse even if they don't catch us in boarding."

"We always knew it would be tough," I said. "We shall have to get close and fight them anyway."

"Aye," Drake said. "We shall."

* * *

As evening came, the Armada under Admiral Medina Sidonia proceeded in serene confidence, in formation, up the Channel toward its rendezvous with Parma's great army. Our Lord Admiral had initially felt confident enough to attack it with sixty-five ships but after our first feeling out commanded that none of us should engage at all until every one of our fleet could join us. We immediately began sending our pinnaces out with letters requesting reinforcements, men, ships, food, water, powder and shot.

In our cabin, I wrote a letter to Stephen in one of our codes while Martin wrote one for Walsingham, both providing a short description of events and plans. We would pass them to Lieutenant Bowden or another pinnace to run into the nearest port.

Footsteps pounded outside and the cabin door burst open. I was on my feet before Walt started speaking, scattering my letter and pen and notation papers everywhere.

"They spotted a giant," Walt said, breathing heavily.

"Who did? Where?"

"The lads come back on the pinnace from the Flagship and they run up close to the Spaniards, firing their little toy cannon they got in the bow. Fair enough, a lot of the boys have been larking about like that, sounds like, only our lads stayed to have a few more pops, coming right up close. Then one of the Spaniards breaks out of the pack and bears down at them sailing right close to the wind, scared the warm shit from their arses, so it did, and they come running back with this mighty galleon blasting away trying to kill them with the guns at the front."

"What of this giant?"

"Come speak to the lads."

I followed him out to the main deck where the two officers and six crewmen of our pinnace stood clutching their hats in their hands. They certainly looked like they had had a scare. The kind of fright that helps turn cocksure boys into men. For a while, at least.

"What did you see?" I asked and they all began speaking at once, even the crewmen. "Silence, you fools. Bowden!" I pointed to the young lieutenant. "You saw this man we have been looking for?"

Lieutenant Bowden nodded, swallowed, and half turned to glance at the Armada through the gloom of dusk. "They come up so fast they came close before we even knew they was coming for us. And by the time we started to beat back up they were almost with us."

"A hundred yards!" one of the sailors said and the others scowled at him, muttering that he was speaking nonsense.

"Not less than two hundred," Lieutenant Bowden said, correcting him. "Perhaps three hundred. Not close enough to make out faces but enough to see heads, arms, everything clear. And we saw him. We all did."

"I never," one lad muttered. He was ignored.

"Tell me very carefully what you saw."

"A line of men on the forecastle. All much of a height, some sailors, some soldiers in their steel hats. And then one man. Head, shoulders, chest above the rest."

Walt scoffed. "A normal man standing upon a barrel. You can't tell me no different, son."

Lieutenant Bowden shook his head. "His shoulders were broad. He raised a hand to point at us and turned to speak to other men. His head was huge. Begging your pardon for disagreeing, sir, but he was a giant of a man." Holding his hand flat against the lower part of his chest, he looked to his crew for confirmation. "The men beside him were yay high, correct?"

Walt and I looked at each other.

"Might not be him," Walt pointed out.

"How many seven-foot-tall men have you ever seen?"

He shrugged. "How many soldiers and sailors out there across the water? Twenty thousand?"

"Perhaps thirty."

"Got to be some big boys out of thirty thousand, eh?"

I rubbed my face and looked around before turning back to the crew of the pinnace. "You know what position in the fleet it took up?"

"I do."

"And would you recognise it again, even amongst all the other galleons?"

"I would."

"Do not lie to me, son."

Bowden was offended. "I know ships, sir."

"Very well, I shall take you at your word. What are your duties now?"

"To stand ready to take messages or men between the ships of the squadron," he replied. "But as it is near dark, I expect we shall eat our ration and stand down, sailing straight on until morning watch."

"Go eat your dinner quickly, boys but stand ready. I might want you back at your boat before full dark descends. Go on, now."

They made their way forward to go down to the galley and I hurried aft to find Drake in his cabin.

"Absolutely not!" he snapped when I suggested it to him. "There is no chance at all. If we take the *Revenge* in there, we will be rounded and destroyed, even in the dark. Especially in the dark." He crossed his arms. "And the Lord Admiral has honoured me with the responsibility of setting the watch, tonight. That means leading the fleet through the night. Our lantern is the one every English ship is to follow. If we go in to the Spanish it will start a battle. And if I extinguish our lantern first, it will scatter the fleet. Either would be a disaster."

"Well, then," I said, "perhaps we could compromise and take the pinnace in alone."

He narrowed his eyes. "What will a damned pinnace do against that monster? I saw it. A new galleon. Massive. Perhaps a thousand tons, twice our size, with two dozen great cannon at least. They won't even need those to blow my pinnace to splinters, the swivel guns alone will manage it."

"I do not wish to fight it, Francis." I leaned in. "It will be dark soon. And that is an opportunity, as long as we strike hard and then we flee."

He listened closely while I rattled through the plan, such as it was. Sighing and muttering, he agreed to lend his pinnace and its crew. We hurried to complete the transfer to the pinnace with our armour, weapons, and our explosives. Sailing beside the *Revenge*, our pinnace inched closer to the Armada with our eyes on the lantern of the ship we wanted.

"You sure about this?" Walt muttered, clutching his sword to his chest.

"Certainly."

"Don't believe you," he replied.

When full dark had descended, it was frightening indeed to be sailing with giant ships looming all around us. Terrifying, in fact, and I imagined a great prow coming up out of the ink-black sea to crush us beneath it.

"Do you think...?" Martin started to say beside me, and then stopped to lick his lips and swallow. "Do you think he will be on it?"

"We shall see."

"What if the mariners were wrong? Or they were quite correct but the giant was another man, a mortal man?"

"You are a lawyer, Martin and so you are learned. But let me tell you something you do not know. If you ask yourself too many questions about what might or might not happen, you will never take any action at all."

Martin hunched over and grumbled. I had told him that I did not want him to come but he begged and in spite of my better judgement, I allowed him to join us on the pinnace. He was a mortal, he was the least capable and most likely to die of all my men. But he had the right to risk his life for his kingdom.

The *Revenge* sailed slowly on while we drifted away on a different course. Soon, the *Revenge* fired a gun into the darkness. We prayed that would draw the eyes of all the enemy so they would not see where we came from.

To that end, our pinnace turned suddenly, heeled over and ran over the waves with the wind behind us into the rear of the Spanish galleons. We could see their aft lanterns, by which they followed each other through the darkness, and counted our way by the rearmost two and then came close to the third one. The galleon we wanted. The galleon of Lorenzo de la Vega.

I noticed that Martin now sat shivering, muttering under his breath. "Shouldn't have come. I shouldn't have come."

"You all right, son?"

"I should not have insisted on joining you, I cannot fight, I do not wish to prove myself and I—"

"Keep your voice down," I said. "And when we board, Martin, you stay in the boat."

He nodded, clutching his sword hilt to his chest.

"But listen," I added, "you make sure you come back for us, you hear me? Make sure Lieutenant Bowden comes back to take us off. We may come back in a hurry. Watch closely in case we have to jump."

"Jump?" he said, aghast.

"You may have to save us from the water."

He gaped at the black sea all around us. "How?"

"That is your duty. Can I trust you to do it?"

Martin breathed deeply, perhaps realising how unlikely it was that my plan would work all the way to the end but he nodded again. "We will. I swear it."

"God will give you strength, son," I said as I moved by him.

Going forward past the mast and the mass of men crowding the deck, I patted the shoulder of the man at the prow and whispered into his ear. "You certain?"

Without turning, he spoke softly. "Not taken my eyes from that lantern, not once, I swear it."

What could I do but believe him?

I whispered. "We strike. And we flee."

He nodded and muttered his reply. "Strike and flee."

We came up beside the ship. The light of the ship's lantern in the stern illuminated the flat tapering rear. It had stern galleys jutting from the sides and these were carved and painted red and white but when we closed to the starboard side we fell into the galleon's shadow. It was a vast wall of curving shadow like a mountain of obsidian, with white frothing as it rose and fell through the swell.

A Spanish voice hailed us from the waist of the ship while my crew were hooking us to the taut ropes at the waterline. I called back, forcing into my voice a light, slightly agitated tone. The tone of a weary messenger who was doing his duty. Or so I hoped.

I grabbed the ropes and pulled myself from the pinnace to the galleon's rope ladder and began to climb.

"Where's your light?" the man at the railing above called.

"Bah!" I said. "Went out. They'll fix it now."

There was a pause while I climbed further. Below me I heard Walt climb from the pinnace and then felt the ladder jerking to his movement. I continued climbing at a good pace but was ready to rush up, should we be challenged.

"What is it?" the man asked and I saw him hold up a shaded lantern. There was another by his side.

Was he asking me why I had come? Or had someone else warned him that something was not right?

"Message from the flagship," I called, making my voice sound as harmless as I could. "For Lorenzo de la Vega."

I kept climbing and when they did not answer my heart began to race so fast I thought I might slip from the ladder. Had we come to the wrong ship? Was Vega never on board but some other giant, if there ever was a giant at all? Was he going by another name? Or had he warned his crew to beware any who came looking for him?

I sped up, climbing harder so that the ladder, as taut as it was, swung side to side and my knees banged against the oak and I knew all it would take was a soldier to lean over and shoot me in the top of my head. All I wore was a sailor's cap and the crown of my head itched suddenly at the thought of a shot blasting into my brain.

Almost at the top, almost ready to leap over the rail, to draw my sword and to start killing, when the Spaniard replied.

"Vega? You best come up, young man."

I hurried up the final few rungs and pulled myself through the opening in the railing. "Where is he?" I asked as I did so.

One man held the lantern at head height while the other mariner answered by first gesturing aft. "All at dinner. But you best wait here while I tell him..." he trailed off as I stood fully upright, far taller than either of them. They looked me up and down, frowning at my clothing.

"Perfect," I said, happily, though my heart pounded in my ears. "Tell me, friend, where are Vega's men? You know, his special men?"

The man's eyes glanced at the nearest hatch down to the hold. "His men are... who did you say you were come from?"

I grabbed him with one hand while with the other I whipped out my dagger and thrust it under his chin and up into his brain. The second man turned to run and to cry out but Walt came surging out of the darkness to trip him and bear him down to the deck where he stabbed through the back of the poor fellow's neck. The lantern crashed down and flickered out.

"Come on, lads, come on," I hissed down to my men as they climbed the ladder.

Everywhere on the ship there were voices whispering, talking, laughing. From aft came the muffled sound of that dinner and there were officers and men.

Only four of them made it up the side before we were spotted. Thankfully, three of them carried the small sacks of fire pots that were so crucial to our mission.

"You there!" came a cry from aft. An officer looking down from the deck. "What are you doing? Who are—"

And then he spotted the bodies and opened his mouth to shout.

Walt's thrown knife hit him in the face and went down with a subdued cry of protest.

"Come up, lads, we be marked!" Adams said, growling over the side while he fished out his slow match.

I stomped aft. "Adams, clear the decks and guard the rail. Walt?"

"I know where to bloody go," he said, grabbing a sack of fire pots and heading for the hold.

"Strike and flee!" I shouted to my men and Adams repeated it.

Our men came up the side in a rush then and I snatched a fire pot and held it out so that Adams could light the long fuse jutting out of the top. When it was smoking and sparking, I ran aft with it in one hand and my sword in the other. Two of the men accompanied me, each with their own fire pots, also fizzing away in their hands.

Banging up the stairs to shouts of warning from the rigging and everywhere else, I saw a mariner open the door leading aft to the officers' cabins, stare in terror at me and my two men rushing at him before turning to run, slamming the door behind him.

I threw it open to see him fleeing aft by the two crewmen at the whipstaff. One was an officer with a sword at his hip and he barked a warning before drawing his sword. But he was unused to fighting in close confines, or he simply panicked, and his sword thumped into the beam above his head and I thrust my point under his arm deep into his chest and ran on without breaking stride.

Fizzing down in my left hand, the fuse of the fire pot was almost burnt out and I would have to throw it or be terribly burned. The wall beside me was lined with stacked boxes and piles of sacks and there were hatchways ahead leading up and down to other decks but my quarry carried on aft, threw open a pair of low double doors into a wide aft cabin. Beyond sat a room filled with dining officers.

Some were getting to their feet in alarm while the officer who had run shouted a warning at them. When I reached the doors I found two servants within, one either side of the doors. Both mariners, both burly and evidently reliable men, they tried to shut the doors against me.

I kicked it open, stabbed my sword into the back of the officer and threw my fire pot at the men seated at the head of the table.

There he was.

Lorenzo de la Vega, rising swiftly and leaping away, thrusting other men aside as if they were children as the fire exploded over them. My men came up behind me and I ducked aside as they threw their fire pots inside. After I did, I reached in to grab the door and slam it shut.

"Run!"

Those fire pots were not high explosives but were merely gunpowder inside a clay shell that would burn and blow the fingers off a man's hand if he was holding it but would not cause massive damage otherwise. Some pots were cunningly constructed of two chambers, one containing oil that would ignite when the powder went off. Others might be packed with shot that could be deadly if they stood close enough. In the main, we had brought fire pots intended to start fires.

The three that went off in the cabin would be enough to hurt, confuse, disorient and panic the officers but I did not expect them to kill many, and fewer still if the men were immortals. Even so, when Vega burst through the doors, wreathed in smoke, his face and hair blackened and fires still burning on his clothing, I was rather surprised.

He drew a pistol and fired a shot that struck me a glancing blow across my cheek, tearing a terrific gouge through my flesh down to the bone beneath. I knew nothing of the nature of it in the moment but only the flash and the impact jolting back my head and the pain had not yet registered when Vega was on me with a roar and the flashing of his sword.

I threw myself back from it by instinct and bashed the back of my head on a beam. Vega came on like a charging bullock, thrusting his blade ahead of him and I grabbed a box beside me and threw it at his face. He wielded a huge blade with a plain and sturdy basket protecting his massive fist and with this basket he punched the box apart, spraying splinters and biscuits everywhere. It gave me time to draw my own sword while backing away further so that when he came on again, losing no more than a step, I was ready to check him with a cut and a thrust of my own. He chopped at my sword and by God he was strong and seemingly unconcerned about breaking his blade on mine, his face twisted in rage as the smoke swirled around his face. The ceiling was so low that I had to duck my head and bend my knees but Vega was hunched over like an ape so that I could see the tongues of flame licking his back and shoulders. I doubted he could so much as feel it, such was his blind rage. An opponent in such a state of mindless fury is normally to be wished for because it means they have no wits with which to fight but Vega was so powerful and yet so fast that it was all I could do to fend him off while I stepped away, our blades clashing so rapidly that even to me they were little more than a blur. Though I fought mostly by instinct, that instinct was as well-honed as any there ever was and with the advantage of his size inverted by the constricted space of our arena, I knew I would get my point into his flesh before long.

Mere seconds had passed since the fire pots had exploded and through my retreat from Vega I had been aware of my men behind me fighting their own battle against Spaniards attempting to cut off our retreat.

So much for the plan to strike and flee.

My intention was to back away toward the main deck with my men and to kill Vega in the close confines along the way before fleeing to the pinnace while Walt and the others did their duty.

But crewmen had come down the hatchways from the decks above and below and though my men made short work of them, soldiers appeared and fired their arquebuses.

The first I knew of it was a cry of warning followed immediately by the terrific blasts, two almost together and then two more, each powerful enough in the low space to deafen a man and all together to resound with such terrible force it was enough to make one's legs weak. Even Vega, in his rage, flinched at the pain of it. In his moment of hesitation I forced his blade aside and pierced his chest with my own, sinking it halfway in. I missed his heart but it surely pierced a lung. A killing blow for a mortal man but Vega recoiled, howling and swiped his broad-bladed sword at my head. I ducked and whipped my blade out, fleeing once more as he came on.

One of my men was down with a shot through the front of his head and pieces of skull and brains protruding from the back, with blood flowing freely from the devastation. I had stepped on him and looked down as I passed to see what had tripped me. My horror was not only that I had lost a man but that such a fatal wound could be inflicted upon me at any moment. My other man was roaring cries of defiance as he fought his way out and I half glanced over my shoulder to see him fighting a man thrusting with a pike.

Vega fell. My wound finally making itself known and he went down on one knee, coughing out a spray of blood and cuffing his mouth, still glaring at me. I went forward to finish him off but saw two officers behind who were now clear to aim their pistols at me. As they fired, I threw myself aside into a stack of boxes. There were more of them coming up behind and more soldiers on the ladders. I turned and ran for my remaining man, crying out to warn him I was coming so that he shifted aside. I killed the pikeman with a thrust through his neck and kicked the man behind him in the chest so that he flew backward through the door. Leaping over him we came out into the night air, lit by lanterns and filled with the sounds of shouting and battle.

A score of soldiers stood waiting for us.

Armed and armoured, confident veterans and I suspected that they were immortals. When we came out, half a dozen were already aiming their arquebuses at us and the rest came forward with their swords or pikes ready.

Walt has failed, I thought. He has failed and now we will all die.

After that thought flashed into my mind, the next was the notion of fighting my way to the larboard rail and leaping into the dark sea. If I could swim to the pinnace, perhaps we could get away in the dark without being shot by their swivel guns or cannons.

I got no further than the thought for at that moment, the ship exploded.

Below the main deck, down in the depths of the ship, Walt and the men had done it. Kegs of gunpowder had been detonated in or near the soldier's berths and the blast seemed to lift the entire galleon out of the sea. The deck amidships warped, bowed up before bursting apart in an eruption of fire and smoke, throwing down every man on the ship, including me. Splinters as long as your arm came flying down even as the fire roared up from the depths as if a door to Hell had opened and a hand of flame reached up to grasp at the sails and rigging. The fire caught everywhere, the decks were burning and cables were burning and sparks filled the air.

The immortals were gaining their feet and I shook off the awe I felt to grab my man, who yet cowered face down on the deck, and pulled him up. At least, I intended to but when I turned him over I found he had two great splinters in him, one in his neck and the other through his face. He was not dead, his eyes were filled with blood but they were wide open and staring with the shock of it. Neither splinter was in his brain and I thought that with enough blood he might live. So I heaved him over my shoulder, picked up my sword and made my way toward the inferno.

One of the immortals weaved his way toward me with a shortened pike in his hands, blood running down the side of his face.

"Stop!" he shouted over the roar of the fire and his cry brought the attention of the other men who were recovering from the surprise and terror of the fire.

"Abandon ship!" I roared in Spanish at him and everyone else. "Flee for the boats! Abandon ship!"

The soldier, confused, lowered the point of his pike and I stepped forward and drove my sword through his throat.

Behind me I heard the bullock's growl that was Vega shouting at me through his wounded lung. At the rail, I turned to see him lumbering toward me, clutching his chest with one hand. Frothing pink blood clung to his lips and the light of the fire illuminated him so he glowed like a demon.

Another explosion, forward of the first, ripped another hole in the ship and the inferno raged all the hard. By then I was at the rail.

"You must swim, brother," I said and heaved Adams over the side into the blackness.

I turned and threw my sword at Vega and then jumped.

Into blackness, I fell. A long moment of terror and then I was engulfed in freezing water. Colder than I had expected, darker than I had imagined. I was under the water and I did not know which way up and which was down. The weight of my clothes dragged on me and, when they seemed to be dragging me up, I panicked. Because I knew then that I was swimming the wrong way, I was swimming down into the infinite depths. I twisted and kicked to swim up but it felt as though I was not moving anywhere. I kicked and pulled and clawed and I knew I had made a terrible mistake. I was certain I was in fact swimming down, or perhaps sideways and my lungs burned and my body ached to open my mouth to breathe in the water, just to breathe it in would be better than holding it a moment longer. But then I forced my eyes open and there was the orange of the blaze of the burning ship just there beyond a film of blurring water and I surged up, dragging my way toward the red glow. When I burst to the surface I sucked in cold air and thrashed on the surface. The waves were far larger than they had seemed from the safety of a boat and I knew I had to get away and to find the pinnace but all I could do was try to keep myself afloat. Arquebuses were going off and men were shouting in the distance. With a start, I realised that I was far from the burning galleon and was drifting further away as the ship, though it was afire, was yet sailing on and I was being carried away by the current.

"Adams!" I shouted, trying to get the water from my eyes. "Adams!" My second cry was stopped by a sudden mouthful of saltwater.

Voices, close by, shouted and then they were on me and I found myself looking up at men reaching for me. A rope splashed beside me and I reached for it but the waves washed it away and then an oar was waving over my head and I grasped on to the shaft and found myself pulled to the boat by a number of hands before falling into the bottom. It was not the pinnace but a twenty-foot ship's boat.

"Richard! Thank Christ!"

"Walt?" I managed through my chattering teeth and swiped at

the saltwater in my eyes while he helped me to a bench seat. Around us, sailors from the *Revenge* rowed us hard away from the burning ship while arquebuses and cannons sounded. Other galleons had come up all around, looming out of the darkness but illuminated by the mountain of flames. There were dozens of boats in the water, pinnaces and ship's boats, and guns firing and shouts filling the air.

I shivered and grabbed Walt. "Adams! He was in the water with me but he may have—"

Walt stopped me. "We got him. He's in a bad way but he's here. Come on."

Following him between the rowers we came to Adams' body in the deep shadows by the bow, with the splinters still through him. "Is he dead?"

"Might be," Walt said.

"Where are the rest of the men?" I said.

"Four here," he said, pointing to our men crouching in the stern, "and the rest on the pinnace."

I squinted, my eyes stinging. "Where is it?"

Walt pointed out into the darkness. "They took a few of us off and then the Spaniards shot them up with the swivels guns and they made off."

"They left us?" I growled, my rage warming me.

"Had to. Two bloody great galleons come up to evacuate the one we blew up." I looked and saw the ships looming either side of the burning hulk as Walt continued. "Luckily, your mate has come up for us and put this boat in."

"My mate?" I said and looked to where he pointed.

It was the *Revenge*.

Drake had come into the Armada for us.

20

Fire

1588

IN THE MORNING, the English fleet was in a state of disorder. The *Revenge* had doused her lantern to come and rescue us and without that guiding light our entire fleet had drifted apart in the darkness. Before the pursuit of the Armada could continue, precious hours were spent coming together again.

Drake was in a black fury. His reputation would certainly be damaged by his seemingly reckless behaviour and the Lord Admiral might grant him no further favours. Still, thanks to Drake coming close and putting his boats in the water, we lost just five men in the attack on the galleon. Scores of immortals had been killed by the explosions and the ship had been abandoned by the survivors. The smouldering hulk, with its main deck, poop deck and sterncastle blasted and burned away, was captured and towed away toward the shore to be picked over for whatever remained. The fighting strength of a great galleon had been removed from the Armada. In some ways, it had been a great success. But Vega lived, as did the immortals who had survived the blasts and our assault.

Adams was taken to the surgeon, who declared that the man should already be dead. Nevertheless, he extracted the splinters, shaking his head and cursing while he did so. When they were free, Walt dragged him from the room and I poured my blood into Adams' mouth. He coughed and almost choked on it but he swallowed enough so that when he collapsed back on the table, his wounds were already knitting together.

The surgeon returned, growling oaths at Walt and me for keeping him from his cabin and his work.

"What is this, you devils?" he muttered. "You are demons, it is true."

"Not demons, not sorcerers or witches," I said. "We are as natural as any other man. John Dee calls it a natural phenomenon."

He was bent over Adams, touching the gash on his face. "There is nothing natural about this. Please leave, sirs."

"You will care for him."

The surgeon snapped at me. "Of course I will."

I bowed and we made our way up toward the main deck. "I'm starving hungry," Walt said, wiping the corners of his mouth. "And right thirsty. What say you?"

"I will join you after I speak to Francis."

Walt nodded and lowered his voice. "Don't let him throw you overboard."

The weather was worsening and the seas growing higher and wilder. Drake was on the command deck, as he so often was, peering at the faint glow of the burning ship as the flames died down into nothing.

"The Lord Admiral will grant me no further favours after this failure," he said over the sounds of the wind and waves as I came up beside him.

"I wish to properly thank you, Francis, for coming in to save us. If you had not put a boat in and staved off enemy pursuit by your presence then—"

"Then you would have been killed, Richard, yes I know it," he snapped. "I hope it was worth it."

"We killed some of them. Men we now will not have to fight in the field. Yes, it was worth the risk."

"You failed to kill Vega."

"We will have to try again."

"Your gambit won't work a second time."

"No, it will have to be something else. Still, we destroyed a galleon, did we not?"

"And perhaps another," he said.

"What do you mean?

"The Spanish evacuated the survivors of your galleon but I believe there was a collision between rescue ships. It's hard to be certain but many of my officers believe it and I am inclined to agree. It's only a quarter moon and the clouds have blanketed it but we've had glimpses. Sounds. Another galleon is in trouble out there and they're trying to tow her. But they're struggling in this sea and making no headway. The fleet has likely left them behind."

"Good news. What will you do?"

"We stay on them, slowed to a crawl, drifting with the sea. At first light, we shall see if they are the men we want."

The man had the instincts of a wolf. When the sky began to lighten, we found ourselves just to windward of the burned galleon and another great capital ship, its bowsprit and forecastle quite ripped away, the foremast down and the rigging a total mess and the rudder was broken off.

It was still crewed and yet offered no resistance when we bore down on them. We had only the *Roebuck* in close support and the enemy galleon was one of the biggest and stoutest ships in the Armada. Even partially dismasted she would have proved a great challenge on account of her guns and soldiers. The castles were so much higher than those of our ships that we could have boarded her only with great difficulty and it would have taken hours to batter her into submission.

Indeed, they said after that they were preparing to fire all their guns when someone recognised the *Revenge* was the ship of the terrible Drake and at that their captain stood them down. Remarkable what can be accomplished by reputation alone.

The Armada was over the horizon, as was most of the English fleet but because they had scattered in disorder in the night there were enough ships to come up to take control of the Spanish galleon while we prepared to carry on. The ship we had taken was the *Nuestra Señora del Rosario*, the flagship of the Andalusian squadron and her captain was Pedro de Valde.

Before joining our fleet, we brought Captain de Valde across to the *Revenge*. Even after what must have been an exhausting and terrifying night battling his ship and the sea, he was remarkably turned out and neat in dress and manner. But that is good breeding for you. He was treated with the utmost respect and when he offered his sword to Drake, he managed to do so with dignity and good grace.

"It is my desire that you shall dine with me and my officers today, sir," Drake said after the formalities were out of the way, "and I pray you will join me on the command deck to witness the day's business. But first, I ask that you meet with my officer and friend Richard Ashbury here to discuss certain matters."

Captain de Valde bowed. "It will be my pleasure to meet with the gentleman, Captain, but I regret honour will not allow me to speak of anything that may harm the enterprise currently undertaken of my peers, my Lord Admiral, or my King."

"Of course, it is nothing of that nature. Merely... well, I shall allow Richard to explain."

They bowed again and we led him into Drake's cabin. The sun was not far up and it was dark inside, even with the lamps lit. The Spaniard was offered wine and cold pork but he asked for a cup of water instead.

"I'm going to ask you some questions, Captain de Valde."

His eyes were dark and narrow. "You are a spy?" he replied, his civility vanished like a puff of gun smoke in the wind.

"I am a soldier."

He scoffed. "I will tell you nothing. No matter what you do to me."

I smiled. "I have heard words like those more times than you could imagine, sir. But you are a gentleman and you will not be harmed."

"You are a spy, I knew it. I say again that I shall not speak of our intentions. I will never betray my admiral or my king."

I flicked my hand in the air and tutted. "I care nothing about the invasion." He frowned and I continued. "I care nothing for Parma or his army. I care nothing for your ships, for your men, your officers, or your soldiers. I care nothing for your admiral or your king."

Captain de Valde scowled, perhaps suspecting he was being mocked. "So, you care for nothing at all? Why do you bother me with such nonsense?"

"Indeed, I care very much about Lorenzo de la Vega." I watched the captain's face fall. "And I care even more about his master."

"You know Vega's master?" Captain de Valde said, his demeanour suddenly changed. "What is his name?"

I smiled. "He has gone by many names. Always, though, he hides in the shadows, never risking himself and works instead through beasts like Vega."

Valde frowned and was about to speak but he stopped himself. "The *San Salvador* was his ship, filled with his soldiers. While it burned, I was commanded to come in and rescue them but we suffered an accident." The captain shook his head. "Vega was taken off by... by another ship."

"What ship was it?"

He shook his head. "Whatever he is, I have said too much."

"Let me tell you what he is, Captain de Valde. Lorenzo de la Vega is a monster. A murderer. A blasphemer, a heretic. And he is a traitor. Oh yes, he is indeed, as you yourself know. He has no loyalty to your king. Only to his true master, who is in league with Satan. You have heard, I am certain, rumours that his soldiers drink the blood of their own sailors?" I watched the captain's face and his only response was a brief gesture of disgust. "All I wish is to know which are the galleons yet sailing with those blood-drinking soldiers. That is all I wish. No more. I know everything else. I want those men and them alone. I care nothing for the crews of the ships, just the blood drinkers and their master."

"Why would I tell you?"

"Because you know they are evil. You suspect that they are here only for their own purposes and not for those of the King. And you are quite right. It is your…" I was about to say it was his duty to God to betray them but I thought that would only antagonise a pious man and so took a different tack. "Captain Drake is the greatest captain of England. Without his brilliance in leading our fleet, we will be greatly crippled when we come to stop yours."

He smiled. "You cannot stop us, with or without Drake."

"I destroyed the *San Salvador* last night, not Drake," I said and his smile dropped. "And I will destroy every other ship in your fleet looking for Vega and his men. But if you tell me where he is, Drake and the *Revenge* will ignore every other Spaniard, and so will the rest of our squadron. Your Armada can take England, as long as I defeat Vega."

It was not true and it was an absurd assertion but he wanted to believe me and perhaps he did. Or perhaps he had other reasons.

"Their other ships are two galleons of the Portuguese Squadron, the *San Felipe* and the *San Mateo*." He smiled. "But I tell you this because you can do nothing to harm them, not even your whole squadron together. They are larger by far than this vessel. They have three or four hundred soldiers each. They have forty guns apiece."

"How will I know them?"

He found this wryly amusing and then I discovered why. "They fly the flags of the Portuguese squadron but these two alone also fly a strange coat of arms. A red chalice on a golden field. You cannot help but see the yellow flags, even if you cannot make out the cup from a distance."

"Vega's coat of arms is a cup of blood," I said, shaking my head. "I should have properly observed the enemy flags but I never imagined he would be so flagrant."

Captain de Valde shook his head. "It is not Vega's coat of arms but those of his master. Vega commands the *San Mateo*. And his master, whoever he is, commands the *San Felipe*."

"His master..." I said.

William was here.

* * *

When we caught up to the fleet, Lord Admiral Howard put out a flag calling his Vice-Admirals to a conference. I ate and rested and when Drake returned I went to his cabin and sat while he relayed how he had apologised to our commander for abandoning his post and almost bringing our fleet to ruin.

"I told him we saw sail on the horizon to the south and feared the Spanish had gone out to seaward to take the weather gauge. I put out the lantern to intercept them but found they were merely German hulks engaged in coastal trade."

"German hulks, Francis? Surely he did not believe you?"

"The Lord Admiral did not challenge me before the other captains. But I am certain I have used up the last of any remaining goodwill he had for me."

"Did you tell him our squadron must concentrate on the *San Felipe* and the *San Mateo*?"

Drake cleared his throat. "As I just said, I have done my reputation great damage already."

"Francis, I hope that—"

He snapped at me. "If I must annihilate my reputation for you then I will do so!"

Before I could answer, he strode out of his cabin and left me sitting there alone.

The rising wind and choppy seas died away throughout the day as we took up the close pursuit of the Armada once again. We did not engage for battle. Our requests for aid and reinforcements were spreading along the coast and inland and all across southern England people were sending what they could and every boat was putting out to sea. Small sails were everywhere and they came out to us with food and beer and powder and shot and the supplies were passed around as we sailed in the dying breeze.

The next day, the wind blew again and while the wind held, we drifted westward. Ships of the two fleets closed here and there, by accident in most cases, perhaps but there were often guns firing as we sailed on and on. Indeed, there was a great deal of smoke and noise, and tons of powder and shot expended but not much achieved by anyone that day. I fretted all night and worried at the notion that we could not catch William let alone destroy him in his ships.

And I was not the only one with his nerves frayed. The vice-admirals and captains agreed that although our ships were faster and nimbler and although we had more of the longer guns, our innovative tactics were not having the devastating effects that we had hoped and believed they would. The captains were stumped. What was more, we were so low on powder and shot that we could not hope to fight another battle.

The fishing boats and coastal traders still poured from ports and bays along the coast to supply. All we could do as we resupplied was follow the Armada, day after day, as it inched up the Channel in the light breeze. The weather was perfect for the Spanish as it allowed them to keep their tight formation and deprived us of the advantage of our superior mobility.

There were a handful of small engagements. Once a Spanish merchantman, enormous but an awkward sailor, tried to change position, lost the wind and fell behind. We came up swiftly in the *Revenge* and blasted the hell out of her and more of our squadron came up to see if we could take her. But the Spanish returned in force to tow her away and we retired rather than be drawn in further. We shot up that huge merchantman terribly, filling her with shot and dismasting her and certainly killing scores of men. But we retired without a prize and at the end of the day, once again, nothing had changed.

The next day, Howard reorganised the fleet into four roughly equal squadrons to be commanded by himself, Drake, Hawkins, and Frobisher. There was little that could be done with them though as the wind died away to almost nothing and we bobbed on the small waves a mile or two apart for hours, waiting for the wind to come up. There were more engagements, many hours of fighting at range and plenty of close calls when this ship or that was almost caught by a Spanish charge but we could not close with the two galleons we wanted and so we watched from afar, ready for an opportunity.

But then the wind freshened and the chase was on again. I had gathered my men in the main cabin so they could drink their ration from our handful of blood slaves and so I could discuss with them possible tactics for attack, when a sailor banged on the door and asked me to see Drake on the command deck.

"What is it?" I asked and ducked to look below the mainsail to where he was pointing. The rearmost of the Spanish ships at the tip of the seaward wing was flying a huge golden flag. "Is that...?"

He grinned. "The *San Mateo*."

"William."

"According to de Valde, William is on the *San Felipe* but we don't know for certain. Either way, one of the two ships you say we must destroy has taken its turn at the most exposed position in their formation." Drake looked at me.

I clapped him on the shoulder. "What do we do?"

Drake nodded. "It is my duty to both Lord Howard and to you that I attack."

The *Revenge* put out more sail and we gained on the *San Mateo*, coming up on her larboard quarter. Once we were in range, Drake ordered the bow chasers to begin firing. My men armed themselves and stood ready for the opportunity to board her.

"If we can engage closely," I said over the sound of the guns, "the *San Felipe* may come up to rescue her."

"Won't we be overwhelmed?" Adams asked, concerned. He

scratched at his face where the enormous splinter had spitted him.

"No, we shall defeat them, Adams." I said but it was clear the men were unconvinced. "We shall kill the head of the snake and that is all that matters."

William was so near I was sure I could feel his malevolence across the sea.

"If that Spaniard weren't lying and William really is here, you reckon he's really on the *San Felipe*?" Walt asked.

"To secure England and our Queen we must destroy them both so it does not matter," I replied, though in truth it mattered to me.

"Fifty sovereigns says it's the *Felipe*." He held out his hand. I ignored it.

We came up firing and our shot began to strike the *San Mateo*, which fired its stern chasers at us, all shots missing entirely. Even as she fired, though, she put out more sail while two other galleons fell back to take its place at the rear of their line.

I strode up to Drake. "Get after him."

Drake scowled. "We can't, Richard."

"You mean you won't."

His lip curled as he answered. "If we go in there we shall be surrounded and sunk, is that what you want?"

The *San Mateo* continued to move up into the safety of the Armada, away from us and eventually beyond our reach.

"Damn him!" I shouted as he escaped, slamming my hand on the rail so hard it cracked. "The coward runs and he runs! Always he runs from me!"

Martin hovered at my elbow. "They'll have to stop eventually. When they take Parma's army across, surely there will be a great battle."

"A battle England cannot win," I muttered.

Walt was on my other side. "We can't do anything about that. All we can do is focus on them two galleons with the golden flags, right?" He lowered his voice and sidled closer. "Reckon Drake will do it, though? Ignore the Admiral and obey you?"

I had no answer as I stared at the distant galleons as they moved away.

Our squadron dropped back once more into close pursuit along with the rest of the English fleet. The Lord Admiral was committed to forcing the Armada away from our coast lest they intended to land anywhere upon it and so we harried them all the day. And the next. Whenever elements from our two fleets came into range they fired at each other and continued to blast away at each other in fury for mile after mile.

On Friday morning Lord Howard summoned his vice-admirals to the *Ark* and he knighted Hawkins, Frobisher, and several of his own kinsman right there on the deck. All knew the decisive battle was coming.

We came to the Dover-Calais Strait and the Armada dropped anchor in their formation just off Calais and came to a stop. Our fleet's signal guns sounded and we came to anchor at extreme cannon shot range upwind of the Armada.

Unseen some way up the coast waited the Duke of Parma's great veteran army standing ready to be ferried across to invade our shores in their tens of thousands.

While the great galleons and merchantmen bobbed at anchor, the pinnaces, launches, and ship's boats darted back and forth within each fleet. Every man on every ship and boat knew that the clash could be delayed no longer.

There would soon be a great battle and victory would save England, while defeat would doom her forever.

* * *

The final conference was held on the main deck of the *Ark Royal* and once the last of the officers climbed up, our Lord Admiral raised his voice and addressed the assembled vice-admirals, captains, senior officers, and gentlemen.

"Sirs, we have come to it at last," Lord Admiral Howard said. "The Spanish ships are here at Calais and Parma is less than thirty miles away with the army ready at Dunkirk. The Dukes Medina Sidonia and Parma will certainly attempt to force a crossing. We know our duty. And we must decide how it is to be done."

What I needed was for William's galleons to be separated from the rest of the Armada and there was only one way we could think of to bring that about. I stood beside Drake and held my tongue, waiting for an opportunity to make our suggestion.

Hawkins cleared his throat. "Firstly, my lord, I would ask what of the Dutch? And the French?"

The Lord Admiral nodded. "The Dutch are doing what they can with their little boats to keep the army on the shore. But the Spanish will thrust them aside if we do not engage the fleet. And the French have been running boats to and from the Spanish ships since the moment we arrived, bringing supplies and perhaps coordinating with French shore forts. We can rest assured that the French are in all respects with the Spanish entirely."

Frobisher scoffed. "They offer themselves up as vassals to the Spanish."

"Catholics," Hawkins growled, to much agreement.

Howard raised his voice. "They must be stopped now, or there will be no other opportunity. Our guns do little damage to their vessels so what is there to be done?"

"We damage them enough," Hawkins replied. "When we are in proximity."

"Indeed," Frobisher said. "At fifty yards we hull their oak."

"There is only one thing to be done," Drake said. "We must get in amongst them and blaze at that range alone, or closer."

Hawkins pounded a fist into his palm. "But how do we engage that damned crescent formation?"

I slapped Drake on the shoulder and he cleared his throat, took half a step forward, bowed, and spoke loudly in his unmistakable accent. "We've got to break them apart! That's all there is to it, sirs, we must force them apart into smaller squadrons. And there's one tried and true way to do it." Drake looked up at the flags atop the mainmast. "The wind's right, if it stays that way, and I reckon it will. The currents and tides will be right in a few hours. Might just be time, if we work quick. What say you?"

The captains of England looked at each other, a few nodding slowly. It was not much of a discussion because there really was only one remaining tactic that we had not yet tried.

Fire ships.

Rapidly, ships were volunteered by one captain and then another. They had to be big and they had to be adaptable quickly to our purposes.

Getting in right away, Drake offered one of ours, the *Thomas* of Plymouth, the two-hundred-ton merchant ship that had been with the *Revenge* through all the fighting so far. Hawkins offered one of his and gradually six more were volunteered with the smallest at ninety tons and the rest a hundred and fifty to two hundred tons. It was a fleet of fire ships greater than any assembled before. But then it had to be in order to threaten a formation the size of the Armada.

They were stuffed with everything that would burn. Water was taken out of them, along with much of the stores, though not all because there simply was not time to unload tons of dried beef and biscuits and so on. The ships guns were loaded and double-shotted; filled with charges of powder as well as two cannonballs apiece, one atop the other. Chains and scrap iron were shoved into some guns also. These guns would go off when the fires around them grew hot enough to ignite the powder and so cause greater damage and terror when bearing down on the Spanish.

"Francis, will you make sure the *Thomas* is sent against the place where William's two galleons are anchored?" I said to him while the sun went down and a freshening wind came up. We stood at the starboard rail of the *Revenge*'s command deck with a view across to the frantic activity fifty yards away.

"Thanks to you, I don't have the authority I had a few days ago."

"Can you do it?"

He hesitated for a long time, looking out at the *Thomas* being readied. "I'll have to get the other captains to position their fire ships based on the position of mine. It won't work unless they're in line abreast. Richard, they all grow tired of my ceaseless troublemaking."

"Please, Francis. Remember your duty."

"I have other duties, Richard."

I lowered my voice. "And yet you will do as I command."

He scowled. "The glory I could have if it were not for you!"

"You would be dead of a belly wound in some New World forest if not for me."

"And how you delight in reminding me of it."

"I remind you only of this wonderful gift I bestowed upon you."

"A curse."

"That too. But you swore to obey me. I have not asked it much of you but I do demand your obedience now."

His knuckles were white on the rail. "You see me obeying, do you not? Cease your harrying of me!"

But for how long will you do so? I wondered.

"I thank you for it," I said and nodded at the fire ships, still being loaded with gunpowder, oil, and flammable material. "Will they work, do you think?"

"They will burn," he replied. "What more they will do, who can say. Whether they make contact and destroy the enemy or simply serve to break their formation, we must be on them before they can reform. Our squadron will have to be swift to isolate William's galleons from the pack and we will hammer them."

Drake nodded and turned away to send his request to the other vice-admirals to set the line of fire ships beside the *Thomas*. They complained and a couple argued but, in the end, thanks to the regard for his tactical instincts, they acquiesced.

It was midnight when the order was given. And the ships were ignited one by one as they were set off with all sails set. Eight great ships burning and growing into infernos lighting up the darkness like giant demons. They came on in a close line, each ship just two pike-lengths apart from each other.

The fire ships were not an unexpected attack and the Spanish had put out a screen of pinnaces and these moved to intercept. They attempted to throw grapples onto the burning decks to pull the vessels off their course so that the galleons did not need to cut their cables and move to safety. But throwing and fixing lines to those great infernos required extraordinary heroism and skill and worse still for the Spaniards was that our fire ships were so tightly together that only the outermost two could be attempted. And the ships were travelling fast by then, propelled by the freshening wind and the spring tide and the current of the Channel all working together to drive them on toward the galleons. And despite all that, the crews on their pinnaces swarmed the fire ships, threw out their lines and began towing as best they could.

Then the double-shotted cannons, heated into white fury, began to go off. Their shot and chains and scrap iron blasted again and again from the bows and sides of the ships, throwing out fountains of sparks and death across the water into the pinnaces. It was too much for the crews of the pinnaces and they fled the chaos, leaving the fire ships to plough on toward the anchored fleet while the guns boomed over the roar of the fires and the jets of sparks flying a hundred feet high toward the stars.

Like the pinnaces before them, the Spanish galleons also panicked. They slipped their cables and stood out to sea in all directions but most of them fleeing before the wind, which scattered them further. All the order that they had demonstrated for days was inverted. It was as if they feared becoming entangled with each other as much as they did our fire ships.

The fire ships sailed on through the abandoned anchorage, grounded near Calais and burned themselves down to the waterline without touching a Spanish vessel.

But their work was done. And our aim had been true.

When the blustery dawn came, we found the *San Felipe* and the *San Mateo* had been isolated from most of the fleet. But coming at them would be far from easy because they were close to the flagship the *San Martin*, as well two other great galleons, each enormous and powerful, the pride of the Armada.

"Now is the time," I said to Drake in the grey light. "Today is the day for our revenge."

With a grave expression but shining eyes, Drake shook my hand just as the signal gun sounded on the *Ark*. English trumpets sounded across the water and sails were put out, our flags and pennants hoisted aloft. The entire sea strength of England was with us as the sun rose. A hundred and fifty ships, all of the Royal Galleons, as many again of the heavily armed merchantmen and private men-of-war and a hundred smaller vessels, from traders to fishing boats.

We moved to attack.

21

Gravelines

1588

THE SPANISH GALLEONS fled. They risked being trapped against the shore and run aground on the maze of sandbanks and to avoid that calamity they headed for the deep water of the wide Channel instead of attempting to immediately join the Armada together again.

"We have a chase on our hands!" Drake shouted. "We must close the distance!"

While our fleet moved in to engage, our squadron made for William's ships. Hundreds of guns fired in the distance and banks of smoke began to drift across the water.

"Damn him," Drake said suddenly. "What can he be doing?"

The *San Martin*, the flagship of the Lord Admiral Medina Sidonia, moved to intercept our line of approach while William's two galleons turned away.

"We see who is truly in command here, Francis," I said. "The Spanish admiral will destroy himself and his fleet to save William!"

"Then William must be the devil himself," Drake growled.

"That he is."

Drake turned and began calling out orders. There was no way to turn right around the *San Martin* without losing the wind and beating back and forth, giving William the chance to get free. There was only one thing for it.

"We will be sunk!" his officers argued. "The whole squadron."

"The *Revenge* shall take the brunt of it," Drake said, grimly. "And then we shall be through."

The *San Martin* towered over us. A fitting flagship if ever I had seen one. A thousand tons, fifty guns and five hundred men on her and we came straight at her, leading our supporting squadron. Their guns began firing and the shot struck our hull and crashed through the rigging. A cable thrummed as a ball winged it and the foremast boomed as another clipped the edge, knocking out a gouge of splinters.

The crew were ready at our cannons and on the swivel guns and in the fighting tops and the officers were anxious indeed.

"Fire the bow chasers, sir?"

"Not yet!"

At my side, Walt crossed himself and prayed to Christ and to Mary and to a score of saints before turning to me. "Should we not go below or something?"

"No safer down there. They have great iron cannons firing shot as big as a firkin that will break through one side of the ship and take all it meets with it out the other side."

"Sweet suffering Christ," Walt said, crossing himself again. "I'll never get on a ship again. Never, you hear me?"

"When we kill William, you shall never need to."

"By God," Walt said, looking between me and the distant masts beyond the masts of William's galleons. "You don't want to go below because you want to lay your eyes upon him."

I snapped at Walt. "Go below, then, if you think it will save—"

The *San Martin* fired a dozen guns almost together, a ripple coming from the stern and starboard quarter, and half of them smashed into us, ripping into the bow and through the decks below. Men screamed in pain and terror and there were cries of men wounded in the bow and all the way to amidships. The ship shuddered, and we seemed to slow, as if she was missing a step. We were so close then that the arquebusiers on the decks and tops of the *San Martin* began firing at our crew and their swivel guns fired shot down onto us.

"Sir!" the officers shouted. "If we do not fire now, we will have no men or guns left!"

"Not yet!" Drake bellowed, standing with his hands behind his back. "Closer!"

We took no more fire from their great guns but the smaller ones fired almost continuously and their soldiers shot as fast as they could reload and fire again. Our few arquebusiers in our tops fired back but they were so few compared to those on the enemy flagship that I doubted we were having any effect. We closed from a hundred yards to fifty yards and his men were almost on their knees begging him when Drake gave the order to fire and to turn.

The trumpets sounded and our bow chasers, long brass cannons, fired one after the other. We were so close we could see the expressions of every man on the enemy decks, whether soldier or sailor, crewman or gentleman, and every face was turned on us. Our guns tore into the hull of the *San Martin*, blasting through their lower gun decks. Their small arms peppered us with shot that smashed pieces off us, throwing splinters everywhere. Men fell on the decks of both ships as the *Revenge* turned to the full extent that she could, bringing the larboard bow guns about to bear whereupon they fired in turn, again ripping through the Spanish flagship as we passed by. As each gun on our side came about, it fired and each shot smashed through the oak timbers of the enemy.

But their decks towered over ours and their men kept firing down at us. One man fell from the mizzentop to the command deck, dead with a shot through his brain before he hit the deck, spraying his blood over the officers.

Drake stood with his legs planted wide and his hands behind his back, making suggestions to the master who cried out instructions to the crew.

A shot struck Walt on the crown of his helm, knocking it to the deck. He cursed and snatched it up, banging it back on his head without inspecting the dent it had left. "Should have worn a full harness," he shouted over the guns and cries of the men.

"They shoot through plate steel at this range," I replied, which he knew already.

"Bury me somewhere pleasant, Richard," he said. "If I fall. A pleasant, quiet place."

A swivel gun shot smashed into the deck between us, throwing up a fountain of splinters as it bounced up, missing my leg by an inch and breaking the rail beside us. We both fell back just as another shot struck the broken rail and carried a section away over the side.

As we passed the enemy ship, our stern chasers fired in turn, smashing into their bow and killing the gun crews and throwing over some of their guns. And then we were by them, travelling away and bearing down on the two enormous galleons that were our true targets. Behind us, the other ships in our squadron fired at the flagship as they passed. They also took damage but nothing like we had. The great ship smashers were not reloaded by the time the last of our squadron was clear, although they had been peppered by swivel guns and every one had suffered casualties to some degree or other. Behind our squadron came that of Frobisher in the massive *Triumph*, which was the equal to the *San Martin*, if not its superior. Certainly it was larger and the *Triumph* did not follow us in our chase but instead lay close to the enemy flagship and blasted away at it, like two heavyweights standing to slug it out. Frobisher's squadron, though, swarmed the *San Martin* and raking her bow and stern, sending their shot crashing lengthways through the decks. Behind Frobisher, we saw Hawkins approaching, also no doubt determined to take or destroy the enemy flagship.

"He truly sacrifices himself," Drake said at my shoulder. "To save our quarry. By what devices does William compel a lord as great as the Duke of Medina Sidonia to do such a thing?"

"William has his ways. He might have twisted the mind of King Philip, so that the king would have ordered his admiral to do such a thing, if the situation occurred. Or William might have threatened the lives of Medina Sidonia's loved ones. Whatever it takes to be obeyed."

Drake nodded. "Just like you, eh?"

I looked at him. "You do not truly believe me to be so evil?"

He hesitated before answering. "Perhaps it is merely a matter of degrees."

"And you believe those degrees to be unimportant? Is my reminding you of your duty equal to threatening your family?"

"I wonder, on occasion, how far you would go if I did not do your bidding."

"You have no need to wonder as I made it very plain."

He nodded. "Aye, you did. Obey or die, Francis, that about the long and short of it? A matter of degrees, as I said."

I had to resist grabbing him about the neck. "You hardly—"

Walt snapped at us. "Hold your bloody tongues, the pair of you. Bickering like an old married fishmonger and fishwife, so you are. Listen Francis, Richard gets this way when William is near so you better do as he says or I don't know what he'll do. And Richard, please don't kill him just yet. We ain't even started fighting them two galleons."

Drake scowled at both of us. "We have to catch them first. That last engagement set us back. I've got fallen mariners. I need you and your immortal soldiers to haul and man the bilge pumps. With them and with God's will, we can catch our enemy before they escape or join the rest of their fleet."

It was hard to tear my gaze away from the enemy galleons and their fluttering gold and red banners but I went to help with the pumps. There was damage below decks. Holes had been blown clean through the hull and the shot had smashed timbers and caused devastation within. One group were struggling to right a cannon with a ruined carriage. Others were patching holes and shoring up decks. We had taken a single shot near to the waterline and the carpenters were working swiftly to rectify the damage but water had slopped in during our turn when we had heeled over and now had to be pumped out.

While we chased our prey, the fleets were clashing across miles either side of Calais, especially to the west offshore of the port of Gravelines where most of the Armada had run from our fire ships. Some of the bravest of them had beat their way back to come to the rescue of their admiral and so the fight descended into a chaotic brawl with English and Spanish squadrons intermingled and firing on all sides. Through it all, the Spanish discipline and seamanship allowed them to reform around their admiral, even under heavy fire, and move away in some semblance of a formation and bear him off behind a screen back toward his fleet. The English of course harried them terribly, blasting away at close range and causing considerable damage to scores of enemy ships. The *San Martin* had been badly mangled but still she sailed and still she fought, the Duke of Medina Sidonia commanding her heroically. And it seemed he felt his duty to protect William to yet be unfilled as he brought her out again to fight us as we closed with the *San Mateo* and *San Felipe*.

After heading north, they had run east, trying to reach the safety of the Armada or perhaps to reach Parma's army or to make a landing at Margate or some other part of the English coast. But we stayed on them, cutting off their lines north and west and inched closer and closer until our bow chasers could start making hopeful shots.

By that time, the urgent repairs were completed and I returned to the command deck where Drake called me over. "Go to the bow chasers, Richard, and tell them to aim for the masts and rigging. They can begin firing as soon as they are within range. If we can slow them..."

"I understand," I replied and rushed forward to speak to the crews. They were on two decks, on both larboard and starboard bows but every gun trained exactly forward.

"Can we aim for the rudders also, sir?" one of the crew asked as they were hammering in wedges to elevate the gun for a long shot.

"Drake said masts and rigging," I replied. "But just hit whatever you bloody well can, man."

Unlike the big guns at the side of the ship, the long bow chasers were not loaded and then pulled tight to the hull for firing. Instead, they were fixed loosely in place so that the recoil would send the guns back into the ship on firing, ready for reloading and running back out again. This meant they could be fired much more rapidly and the crews set to work, loading and firing. They timed their shots so that they touched the match to ignite the charge on an uproll of the ship so that the shot would arc higher and farther to its target. In this way, we came up on the *San Mateo* blasting away at her, as did the other ships in our squadron coming up beside us to fire on the *San Felipe*.

They shot back at us but their guns seemed to fire far slower and with far less accuracy so that theirs fell short or missed entirely. I willed our guns to break down William's ships and half wished one would smash through the stern into the officers' cabins and kill him. To have him ripped apart in such an ignominious fashion would have pleased me enormously but still I also hoped he would be unharmed until such time as I could face him myself. For centuries I had pictured my sword plunging into his chest, and taking off his head from his shoulders, and that was what I yearned for above all else. I prayed that the ships would be dismasted so that I could board them and cut down every one of his spawn before defeating him in single combat.

We inched closer, always firing, and then English ships came up from our fleet in support. In this way, they cut off the escape of the two galleons and we fell upon them, firing from close range on all quarters as we turned one way and then another, ripping into them. I summoned my men and ordered them to make ready in case we found a chance to board them.

"We got to be killing immortals with these shots," Walt said. "You reckon?"

"I do," I said. "By God, I do."

"Perhaps," Martin said, "we will hit their powder store and blow them up."

The men nodded.

"That would be a fine thing," Adams said. "And something to pray for."

"I have seen it happen before," I said. "But it seems to me these galleons can be blasted full of holes and yet they sail on. There are hundreds of them on each ship. Pray for a miracle if you like but ready yourselves for hard fighting."

I searched the enemy decks in vain for sight of William. Whether he was engaged in some business below decks, or if he was hiding, or if he was in fact not on the ships at all I had no idea. But there was such distance between us, even when closed

611

to a hundred yards, the smoke and chaos of the fighting and the close press of men and officers, that it was possible I had looked right at him many times without seeing him. With each hour, though, I feared ever more that William was on neither ship, and never had been, and that he was on some other vessel or had never been with the Armada at all. Such thoughts caused me to feel nauseated, sickened with frustration and anger.

But Lorenzo de la Vega was there on the deck of the *San Mateo*, I could see his bulk standing at the stern. We closed with Vega's galleon and our guns blasted it ever more into pieces. We swarmed that ship and surrounded it while keeping to windward of the *San Felipe* as it fired on us. The men around Vega were dying or wounded and their guns fell ever quieter. The immortal soldiers on the deck fought on, though, shooting their arquebuses tirelessly at us, even though they were covered in blood and suffering terrific wounds. Though they fought on, we kept shooting their hull until she was leaking like a sieve and sat lower in the water.

"We are going to kill them all!" I shouted to Walt. The noise was deafening and we could scarcely hear each other speak. Indeed, it seemed as though I would hear nothing ever again.

In reply, he nodded, hands clapped over his ears.

Smoke clouded the view but I noticed it was also growing dark. We had been fighting for hours and the weariness hit me with the realisation. Where had the day gone? I prayed we could finish them before dark.

Martin pounded me on the shoulder and I followed his outstretched hand. The Spanish flagship was once again ploughing into the fray to protect the *San Mateo*, which limped away shooting with small arms at everyone who came near.

"We must get after Vega!" I said, rushing up to Drake.

"Can't you see what has happened?" he snapped. "The Duke has saved them."

"Let us go around. He is getting away and we are losing the light of the day."

"Go around? This is not a horse and carriage, Richard, we cannot go where we will and disregard the winds. We must fight our way out of this."

"But those pinnaces in our squadron go around the Spanish flagship even now!"

"The *Revenge* is no pinnace, Richard. They may go where we cannot."

"Then I will take my men in pursuit by pinnace. You must call ours in and let me take my men off." I stared at him. "You can do that much, I know."

"You want to assault a galleon with a pinnace?" Drake shook his head. "He will blast you to pieces before you close."

"Most of their great guns must have been thrown over by our shot, for they have not fired in an hour or more. Look how battered they are, half his men must be killed. Come, Francis, we must stay on them or we may never get another chance. Signal Lieutenant Bowden, we will do what we can to stay on them and then you will come up as soon as you are able."

"We are outgunned and outmanned by the Duke's flagship," Drake replied. "We may not survive to rescue you and even if we do you will be alone in the dark until morning. Stay with the *Revenge* and we'll hunt them again tomorrow."

"They could land anywhere before then. Hundreds of

immortals on land, causing untold devastation, and William could escape me again. See, the *San Felipe* escapes, let us take the *San Mateo* at least. I will not pass up this chance. I will not let him get away. Summon the pinnace, now!"

Looking at his expression, I wondered if he was secretly glad to be rid of me and my men. Perhaps he was already thinking how much better his life would be with me dead. Whatever his reasons, he did as I said and the *Revenge* fell back a few cable lengths and I transferred my immortal company to the waiting pinnace.

"Mister Richard, sir!" Lieutenant Bowden cried as I climbed in. "Whatever is happening?"

"The great galleons are fleeing from our squadron. You will take us after them and, God willing, when opportunity presents itself, we shall board them."

"By God!" Bowden said, his eyes popping from his head. "This seems to be another impossible task, sir."

"It is a difficult business, to be sure. Yet the task falls to you, Lieutenant Bowden. The safety of England depends on our success."

He looked at the massive galleons ahead of us and then up at his pennants and bowed his head. "Then we must do it."

We eased out of the fray heading northward while the *Revenge* moved into range to begin blasting the Duke's flagship, drawing in ever more ships of all sizes from both sides. The formations of the squadrons were broken up as ships became separated and reformed in swirling confusion, all the endless sound of guns firing. The whole mass drifted east and south toward the shoals and sandbanks of Flanders while the Spanish fleet tried and failed to break free against the mass of English ships and the wind and tides.

"This is madness," Martin said as our small ship chopped and skimmed across the waves, heeled over and throwing spray over all of us.

"Don't you start again," Walt snapped. "You never should have come."

"I know my duty as an Englishman," Martin replied, holding his head up to look Walt in the eyes. "And I mean to do it."

"Good man," I said. "But stay back as much as you can."

"You can trust me," he said.

There was a commotion amongst the crew and I went aft to where the officers stood looking west, back down the Channel.

"What is the..." I trailed off as I saw the low black clouds approaching. Beneath them dark grey rain fell. "Looks like a bad one."

"That is does, sir," Bowden said. "That it does."

It was worse than bad. It came up so fast that we barely had time to prepare before it was on us, driving rain slashing into us and whipping up the sea and scattering both fleets. Water fell so thickly it ran into our eyes even beneath our hats and hoods and even when we dashed our eyes clear, it was impossible to see much farther than the bowsprit. We hung on while we were blown before the gale, riding the thrashing of the waves. In the middle of the storm the torrent falling across us died down and we found a great galleon bearing down on us out of the gloom and we hauled and steered and shouted uselessly until we passed by each other close enough to spit. Soon, though, the terrible squall passed over us and we found the ships scattered everywhere across the sea as the sun fell.

"We nearly had the bastards," Bowden said. "Why did God send the tempest?"

"Can you see the *San Mateo* and the *San Felipe*?" I asked.

"Aye, they're out there beyond the galleasses, sir. Surprised they didn't sink in that. Half drifting now, see?"

"I see them."

"Do you want to go on, sir?" Bowden asked. "There's a way through, though not an hour of light left."

"Where is the *Revenge*?"

"Can't see her, sir. Not mixed in with the Spanish, at any rate. Must be away upwind of us now. Looks like the Spaniards are going on up the coast."

"Then so shall we."

The Spanish ahead of us were in a bad way following the battle, that much was obvious even at a distance in the dusk. Most of the great galleons were low and leaking and all had lost spars and their rigging was in a terrible state, hanging in tangles and they had certainly suffered heavy casualties. The sea was covered with detritus and once or twice we saw bodies floating at the surface, rising and falling in and out of view.

"Should we not recover him for burial?" Martin said when the first was sighted.

"Catholics," a sailor said and turned to spit downwind.

I glanced at Walt but he simply grimaced and held his tongue.

Toward the coast, a massive Spanish merchantman was going down slowly, boats taking off the crew though she listed drastically. It had been mauled terribly in the battle and no doubt the weather had finished her off. And then, just as the light was failing, our commander ran the length of the small ship down to the starboard bow and pointed.

"There," Bowden said. "There, there!"

As we sailed beyond the sinking merchantman, we sighted both galleons making for the shore. They were badly damaged and low in the water but they might have sailed on with the others, if they had wished to.

"William would not risk his life and his men on the water when he might live to fight another day. He will make for Parma's army and seek to cross with them, no doubt."

"Or he'll flee again," Walt said. He turned to Martin. "He always bloody runs. You'll see."

"It is just one galleon which has run aground on a sandbank," Bowden said suddenly as we closed. "Look, the other is still afloat but it has sailed on."

"Can it beat back upwind?" I asked.

Bowden pursed his lips and blew while he looked at his men, who all shook their heads. "Stiff breeze tonight and it's stiffening still. He'll have to anchor, come back for the other on the tide. Assuming the wind drops."

I grabbed his arm. "One is isolated from the other? That is why He sent the tempest, men. God has served them up for us. Unless the other can warp back in support?"

Bowden and the crew shook their heads again. "Against this tide? Not a chance."

Walt and I grinned at each other.

"Let us go in fast," I said to Bowden. "We shall board and you anchor, if you can."

Bowden made a face. "Treacherous waters, these. Sandbanks everywhere, vast tides, terrible current. Don't know if we'll be able to avoid grounding, here or elsewhere."

"Can you go back to the *Revenge* and bring them here, Bowden?"

He almost laughed. "Beat against this wind, in the dark, and find our ship amongst a hundred others? I'm a right good mariner, sir, but—"

"Yes, yes, I know." I felt nauseated. I knew in my bones I had been reckless and that without the *Revenge*, I had doomed us. But I was committed now. "Come then, let us board them."

Adams cleared his throat while scratching his cheek and raised his voice over the terrible wind. "How shall it be done, sir?"

"Up the sides and kill them all," I said. "Any questions?"

22

Revenge

1588

FULL NIGHT HAD fallen by the time we reached the stern and the howling wind that drove us onto the sandbank also covered the sounds of our approach. The galleon was heeling over to larboard, tilted by the wind and tide.

The surviving crew of the *San Mateo* worked frantically to cut at the tangled rigging with the help of the immortal soldiers. Many shouted orders or advice from all along the ship as scores of jobs were being undertaken by lantern light. Hammering came from within the hull as the carpenters and volunteers repaired the holes below the waterline, axes chopped at spars and shattered timbers to clear the way. Casks and sacks were being tossed over the sides to lighten the ship. Signal trumpets sounded, calling to the *San Felipe* which was still being dragged away along the coast as it struggled to anchor in the silty sandbanks against the force of tide and wind.

All this activity covered our rapid approach out of the darkness and even the sound of our bow banging and scraping against their stern did not alert them. I thanked God for sending the howling wind and waved at my men to throw their grapples.

We had three and these were swung expertly up onto the stern gallery again, without notice. My heart raced and Walt's eyes were bulging so much I could see them even in the shadow of the massive stern. If we were both in such a high state, I knew my men were on the edge of panic. If we ran into serious trouble, I thought they might break quickly.

Speed was the key to it. If we could start killing them quickly and keep killing them before they knew what was happening, we might have a chance.

With our satchels and sacks slung, we climbed the ropes, hand over hand. Mine twisted and swayed in the wind, even though the pinnace crew held the ropes taught. I climbed over the broken railing of the gallery just as Walt did the same on his rope and Adams came over a moment later. The rest of the men climbed behind us. The gallery had taken the damage and it wobbled under the weight of our men. I prayed it would hold until we were all on board. The full width cabin at the stern—probably the captain's, or perhaps for multiple officers—was dark. I peeked through a cannonball hole and could see nothing. I had half hoped to find Vega alone within but darkness and emptiness was almost as good.

Adams crouched and unslung his satchel to pull out his fire pots. They were damned fine things for creating confusion and panic, and for killing and maiming, and making fires. They also tended to attract attention.

"Wait until the alarm is given, or until I say," I hissed in his ear.

"I know. So do the boys."

Voices shouted from amidships as a boat was lowered over the larboard side. I thought for a moment we had been seen but I heard them over the wind shouting about an anchor and a cable so I knew they were intending to tow one out to pull themselves off the sandbank. Three more of my men came up and the gallery lurched under the weight. I moved to the low door into the cabin and lifted the latch. The door rattled but did not budge.

I glanced at Walt and he shrugged. Bracing myself against him, I kicked the door, hard. It gave in, shattering the frame in a terrible splintering sound that could surely have been heard across half the ship. It also broke my foot, or at least badly damaged my heel. I shouldered my way into the darkness and limped forward as my men came in behind me.

Feeling my way across the cabin, I drew my sword and reached blindly for the door.

Voices and footsteps approached. "If that's you, Diego, you lazy shit, I swear I'll give you such a slap that you'll die of—"

The cabin door burst open, the Spaniard still shouting rapidly and shaking his fist.

I stabbed him in the throat and forced him out into a space with small cabins on either side. Limping on my hurt foot, I rushed forward though it with my men coming up behind me.

A cabin door opened beside me and a small, tired looking man with a mallet in one hand and a lamp in the other stepped out and froze in surprise. Behind him, another man stood gaping at me, cradling a box filled with nails. Carpenters who had done nothing to me and who likely did not deserve to die but I killed them both before they could cry a warning. Some of my men got in front of me and I came up after them as they cut down four soldiers who sat slumped exhausted on a pile of sacks, stripped to the waist and soaking wet. One man, run through three times, stood and drew his dagger while blood gushed from his chest and out of his mouth. I stepped forward and kicked him to the deck.

"Take off their heads," I growled to my men, "or at least hack through their skulls. They're immortals!"

Taking my advice, Adams sawed through the wounded man's neck just as a group of soldiers rushed down the open hatchway forward of us, in a line one after the other. I charged as they raised their weapons and opened their mouths to shout at me, at my men coming up behind me, and then I was on them and cut them down, killing one with a swift cut to the side of his neck that sliced his spine right through and the next I punched hard enough to cave in his face and throw him back and down to the deck. The next man I kicked in the knee and shouldered him aside while I thrust into the eyes of the man behind him before he could raise his arquebus. My men fell upon the ones I had not killed and finished them off in seconds.

A shout echoed in the space and then another. A face at the hatchway appeared and then another.

"Fire pots!" I snapped to Adams and to the rest. Half of them flapped open their satchels and passed the fire pots out while matches were passed around. Footsteps hammered as Spanish ran toward the growing cries of alarm from the men on the poop deck above. "Quickly!"

A group of soldiers rushed up the ladder from the deck below but we cut and thrust and kicked them down as a half dozen fire pots were thrown down behind them. They burst into roaring flame and the men below screamed as they were engulfed while others fled shouting from the fire.

Other Spaniards shot down at us from the deck above. One of my men was hit in the chest and he went down, crying out in pain and frustration.

"Blood!" Walt shouted as he dragged our wounded man back and Martin ran forward to offer his own. He had elected to come with us after all. My heart sank, for I knew he would not survive the assault. Already we had become pinned at the stern and the entire ship needed to be cleared.

"With me!" I shouted and swung myself onto the ladder and took the steps two at a time with my sword over my head. Blades flashed down, clashing on my sword, but I was faster than any of them and I leapt up and out into the open air where a score of mariners and soldiers clustered around the hatchway. I slashed left and right at the soldiers before me, forcing their swords aside and the men behind thrust pikes at my chest and face. I grasped a pike behind the head and thrust it aside as I rushed in to slice off the pikeman's head. But my blade caught under the back of his steel hat and he jerked back suddenly as he died, ripping my sword from my hands. The other pikeman shortened his grip and whipped the spearhead around at me. I shifted forward and grabbed the shaft with both hands and swept it back toward him, forcing the pole against his body and propelled him so hard across the deck he went spinning over the rail and into the sea with nary a sound and I kept moving, ducking an attack and whipping the pike into two more men, snapping the shaft.

My men were up behind me, laying into the Spanish at the stern and tossing their fire pots down at the next deck forward and below ours. I found my sword and joined them, killing two men before the others retreated and we chased them down the ladders to the command deck.

Arquebuses fired as we reached it and some of my men went down. I cursed but all I could do was push forward all the harder and so I jumped the six feet down from the stern deck to the command deck and began to kill the line of men who had fired. There was confusion everywhere, with men shouting in Spanish and English, arquebuses firing and fire pots sailing overhead to smash on the command deck or down onto the main deck beyond. Fires here and there cast everything in flickering light and shadow.

The *San Mateo* listed further to larboard and men lost their footing, sliding as the deck tilted. I slid with them but stayed on my feet and killed the ones who came skidding under them.

"Ashbury!"

The voice roared my name like the bellowing of a bull.

Vega had come.

He was forward, down on the main deck with sword in hand, standing in his sodden white shirt. Perhaps he had been low in the bow, helping to shore up the damage, but he was challenging me now and I smiled to see it. Soon, I thought, I would have him under the edge of my sword. I came forward, ready to jump down to the main deck when I heard a Spanish officer shouting at his men.

"Fire!"

There was perhaps half a second between an arquebusier pulling the lever to release his matchlock spring and the shot leaving the barrel. The match whips down on its spring-loaded arm to ignite the powder in the flash pan which fires the ignition of the main charge in the barrel that explodes and thrusts the shot forth at its target. Half a second to throw myself down as a score of shot smashed into the timbers where I had been standing.

Sliding down the sodden deck toward the rail, I grasped at a coil of rope only to find it unravelling as I slid into the bodies of the men I had just killed, arresting my descent. A fire pot exploded beside me throwing up a fountain of flame. Blades clashed, men shouted and weapons fired all around. My men fought for their lives.

Footsteps pounded and there was a bull's roar rising above me as Vega stomped from the ladder with his huge sword raised, reflecting the fire from the wall of flames beside us. I jumped to my feet and leaped aside but my injured foot slipped in the blood and I fell. Rolling to my back I got my sword up to cover me as Vega swung his own like an axe to end my life.

Walt was there, charging out of the flames to throw himself bodily at Vega with a guttural cry of rage and his sword stabbed into the giant's chest and forced him back. Vega grabbed Walt and they grappled for just a moment before Vega lifted him off his feet, turned him in the air like he was a child, and smashed Walt's face on the rail with a wet crunch. Gripping Walt's head he rammed his face again on the rail, caving the side of his face in and then a third time, spraying blood across the timber before hurling him down to the main deck.

By then I was up and charging Vega, thrusting at him just as he threw Walt. I knew I had him, for Walt's sword was stuck in Vega's chest and even an immortal is slowed by such a wound. And yet he twisted, ducked and snatched up his sword as he darted away from me and in the same movement aimed a nimble cut at my head, then a back cut and a thrust and I avoided the first two only to feel the thrust cut along the side of my skull. I fell back with my sword up and watched Vega yank Walt's sword from his chest. He winced and gasped but he did it in a single swift movement before coming at me again, now with a sword in each hand, one dripping with his own blood.

A fire pot smashed into the deck in front of Vega and he cried out and flinched as the flame burst up over him. I glanced up and behind me at the stern deck and was shocked to see Martin, grinning and lighting another fire pot.

Before he could throw it, he was shot in the leg.

Martin's knee exploded in a shower of blood and bone and he fell, dropping the fire pot beside him. It rolled away down the deck and exploded. Even through the cacophony of the battle, I heard Martin's scream.

Vega was on me again, charging through the fire and thrusting and cutting with both swords, one after the other and I stepped back, blocking and parrying and ducking his attacks as I retreated up the slanting deck, slipping in blood and tripping over cables, bodies, and detritus.

He slipped, too, and I darted in to cut his face but he knocked my sword aside. Before his second sword sliced through my cheek, I understood the bastard had only feigned his slip. In a rage, I rushed forward into him, punching his ox-sized head with my first and cutting his belly, then his chest and I pushed him back and cut at his throat. He twisted away and I cut his chest again but his great bulk was opened up now and blood gushed forth to soak his white shirt. Then it was he who was retreating and tripping over rigging ropes and bodies. The deck was slick everywhere with blood and oil and seawater and when his heel shot out from under him I was ready with a thrust at his neck. But he was not just a giant, not just powerful and fast, he was also cunning and instead of trying to save himself, he allowed himself to fall. He crashed down onto the deck and rolled away before throwing himself down the ladder to the main deck where his men still fought mine.

Fires were everywhere, from bow to stern, and men roared and the fighting was by then thickest forward of amidships on the main deck. My men fought shoulder to shoulder from rail to rail. We had pushed them back across half the ship and they were still dying in our flames and under our blades. I allowed myself a moment's hope that we were doing it, winning the ship, killing the immortal soldiers.

At the forwardmost hatch, a stream of Spaniards emerged, their steel helms reflecting the firelight, a dozen, a score, and more poured forth with arquebuses, pikes, and swords ready and they took up position on the forecastle and began firing as they emerged. My shouted warning to my men was lost in the clamour and then Vega was on his feet again, down on the main deck behind my men. Clutching his chest he turned to me, scowling and then hurled himself into the rear of my soldiers.

Ignoring the ladder, I jumped down to the main deck and slipped to my hands and knees before rushing Vega. Before I could reach him, he grabbed Adams from behind and half fell upon him, crushing him against the deck before lifting his stunned body and hurling him over the rail into the sea.

I stabbed Vega though the back of his thigh just as I was shot in the chest.

It was like being kicked by a horse and I was on my back before I knew what had hit me. Vega hobbled through my men's line to the safety of his soldiers and I looked around frantically for a mortal to drink from. Just five feet away a Spanish mariner crawling aft through the pools of blood. I scrambled to him, bashed his skull in with my fist and sank my teeth into his neck, ripping the skin and flesh away. I spat it out and sucked down his warm blood. It gave me strength immediately, the moment it reached my stomach.

There was a growl of agony beside me.

Black Walter groped for me, his one visible eye glaring. One side of his face was caved in and one eye was gone. Pushed into his shattered skull or perhaps pulped. His nose and cheekbones were a mass of bloody tissue and shards of bone and when he opened his mouth to speak his teeth were a jumble inside his shattered jaw.

"Christ almighty," I said and dragged the mariner to him. I held up the bloody neck for Walt to drink and he did so, whimpering and choking as the blood went down.

"Drink him dry and find another, drink and drink, Walt!"

I left him hugging the dead body while the fires burned closer all around him.

"Vega!" I roared, taking up my sword and charging forward into the Spanish soldiers battling my men. Vega was in the bow, jabbing his finger and ordering them to stop me.

I would have to kill them all to reach him.

Few of my men were left alive to keep them busy and twenty of the soldiers closed on me. Behind them, a dozen stood over their arquebuses, reloading them frantically. Three pikemen came on first with their weapons levelled, trying to contain me and box me in. I forced the spearheads aside and cut two down, hacking off the arm of one man at the elbow before crushing his face with my handguard. Swordsmen came behind them, thrusting to keep me back while they tried to circle around me. Pulling the dagger from another man's belt, I sliced it across his throat and stabbed it into the next man's eye, while I cut through the neck of another.

They were afraid of me and their fear made them hesitate. And I killed them, one after another, blood flying and men screaming and the survivors flinched away. Vega shouted curses and hobbled down the forward hatchway while the arquebusiers took aim. I charged at the man at the far left of the line and shouldered him over the side. He screamed out as he spun like a cartwheel down into the darkness. The next man aimed his weapon and I lifted it aside before cutting his throat. My sword was horribly twisted and bent and so blunted I had to saw back and forth while the blood spurted up to properly cut through his spine. I ducked aside just as men to starboard fired and the shots smacked all around me.

One sliced through my arm and hit me in the chest.

Throwing my bent sword at the nearest soldier, I ran bodily into them and threw them down, or flung them off the side of the ship. One man squirmed away on his back and I stamped down on his neck until his bones cracked and another crawled for the hatch before I kicked off his helm, knelt on his back and used the steel hat to pound his skull in.

It was quieter on the main deck. The fighting was dying down, though the fires were spreading along the rigging and licked at the furled sails. Flames still leapt from the aft hatches behind the men still fighting. So few, now. A dozen immortal Spaniards and just three of my men fighting for their lives. All of them were drenched in blood. Groans came from the dying men everywhere.

I looked for a sword on the deck with which to save what remained of my company when a shot banged. I was knocked forward onto my front. Terrible pain came just after and I reached behind me to feel a wet hole in my lower back. I rolled over to see Lorenzo de la Vega, grinning from the hatchway. He stood on the ladder so that only his massive upper body was above deck. Smoke drifted from the mouth of the barrel of the arquebus in his hands.

Rage alone drove me to my feet. Rage forced me forward while blood poured from my back and down my legs.

Vega, his savage grin turning to a snarl, threw his arquebus at me and I swatted it aside and rushed forward. He retreated down the ladder and I had enough sense to look for a weapon. A pike lay at my feet. I broke it in two a foot behind the head and jumped down the hatch.

The galleon was tilted so drastically that it was impossible to keep my footing and I slipped as I landed.

Vega was there aiming a cut at me even as I hit the deck, so I went with my fall and rolled aside. Vega's blade hacked into the wood where I had been moments before and I came up, lashing out with my shortened pike.

He was bleeding from wounds all over his body but it did not seem to slow him much. The monster had spent his immortal years guzzling the blood of strong men and young girls, filling him with power. He ducked sideways from my thrust and slashed a backhand cut at me while he twisted away and I rushed up the sloping deck to cut at him again, catching him on the shoulder before he threw himself down to the deck below. He fell heavily and he groaned where he lay, clutching his leg.

Fire burned aft and smoke rolled forward along the deck I was on and the heavy gun deck below was also burning some way aft. The fires might burn themselves out or they might ignite the powder store. I had to kill Vega quickly, find Walt and my men, if any survived, and get off the galleon. There should be a ship's boat in the water that we would have to take to get clear before it exploded.

The thoughts flashed through my mind in a fraction of a second and I jumped down to Vega before he could get up. I landed heavily but I was ready for the slanting deck that time and did not slip far.

Out of the corner of my eye, I saw two men standing ready and I knew at once I had been tricked. Vega had laid a trap for me and I had blundered right into it. Shoulder to shoulder with their backs against the hull, they took aim with their arquebuses and, before I could do more than flinch, they fired. In the close confines of the deck, the sound was like a thunderclap.

Both shots hit me in the chest.

I fell back, sliding away from them and Vega, clutching at the agony in my chest. Blood poured through my fingers and it hurt to breathe. I could barely suck in an ounce of air before I was coughing out mouthfuls of blood, drowning in the stuff. Vega got to his feet, grinning and stepped back to watch me suffering. I lifted my pike in a shaking hand, ready to defend myself, but he was not taking any chances.

"Again!" he shouted at his men, which I could just hear over the ringing in my ears.

They were already pouring powder down the barrels of their guns. My head whirled and the pain was a vice about my chest but if I did not move, I would be dead.

At the bow, two enormous cannons pointed forward, run back for reloading and not yet run back out again through the open gun ports. There was enough space between the ends of the barrels and the hull for a man to stand. I charged forward and up the slanting deck in front of the mouths of the guns around to the other side of the ship and rushed the two soldiers who were still reloading. Vega shouted at them to flee but they were focused on their weapons. I was on them as they turned to run away and I sliced the pike blade sideways through the neck of the first man and speared the spine of the second, bearing him to the ground. My pike blade ran him right through as he fell and buried itself in the boards of the deck.

Vega, cursing, slashed at my arm as I jumped back but I hit the carriage of the nearest cannon and before I could get over it or change direction he thrust his blade into my belly and ran me through.

Christ save me, I thought. The pain was terrible. He cried out in triumph but before he could withdraw his blade and strike off my head, I grabbed his wrist with both hands and held on.

Frustrated, he punched me in the face, and then again, breaking my nose and cracking the back of my head against the cannon so that I was knocked almost senseless and my vision clouded with bright stars. Still, I held on to his wrist and he roared, lifting me up to slam me into the boards of the deck above.

Kicking him in the body, I scrabbled for something to brace myself against, reaching for the joists but he was too strong and he smacked my head into the oak once, twice, a third time. Through my daze, I saw what I thought was a pike or a sheathed sword hanging from a hook on the joist and I snatched it, believing I now had a weapon.

Yet it was nothing but a linstock.

Vega threw me down and yanked his blade from my guts, my blood gushing forth with it.

Filling the space above me, he sneered and lifted his sword. "You should have—"

Getting my feet under me, I forced everything I had into my fist and launched myself upwards at him. My blow caught him clean just under the ear and snapped his head back. His arms flew wide and he staggered away toward the bow. I hit him again and shoved him, pushed him back against the hull where the gun port was. Not thinking straight and without a weapon, I stupidly thought I could force him out through the open port.

But of course, he was far too big. He braced himself against the gun port with both hands spread wide and his head and shoulders against the hull.

I was about to whip him in the face with the linstock in my hand when, purely by instinct, I leapt forward and laid the slow match on the end against the cannon's touch hole.

The massive iron gun fired.

It had been loaded but it was never meant to fire while run in and was untethered. The carriage and the gun itself flew back from the enormous recoil and crashed into the deck above before bouncing away. I was thrown back across the deck into the starboard hull while the cannon came to a rest against the other one. Smoke filled the deck and my head rang with the sound.

I got to my feet and peered through the smoke, afraid that Vega had jumped aside before the shot hit him.

He had not.

His legs lay beneath the gun port, both ripped off at the upper thigh. Movement in the shadows caught my eye and I picked up a lantern that had been knocked to the floor and the guttering flame lit up the rest of Vega's body.

His head, shoulders, chest and arms were all that was left of him and, astonishingly, he was still moving.

Vega pulled himself along the deck, inching forward and dragging a trail of stinking intestines behind him. His arms reached forward and clung to the gaps between the boards and the hideous thing seemed set on getting somewhere. I stood on one of the hands and the head turned slowly to peer sidelong up at me. His mouth opened and closed but no sound other than a gargle came out.

"I must tell Doctor Dee about this," I muttered, before coughing up a handful of congealing blood.

Fire exploded aft, roaring halfway along the gun deck sending inky black smoke boiling along the underside of the ceiling toward me. I flinched, ready to dive through a gun port, but the fire curled back again as the smoke filled the deck.

Knowing that if I did not get blood quickly, I would soon be dead, I left the remains of Vega to die slowly in agony and climbed up the first ladder and then the next, coming out into the cold night air and the gusting wind. The fires were burning down and there was less light than before. It reeked of smoke and blood and bodies filled the decks from bow to stern.

All the Spaniards were dead, yet none of my men were in sight. Not even Walt.

I pulled myself up and found a sailor to drink from. He was whole from the waist up but his legs were smashed, perhaps falling to his death from the foretop. His blood was going cold and congealed and I almost vomited it back up but I needed it and so forced it down. The pain in my chest eased and I was no longer dying.

"Lorenzo!" A voice roared from across the water. "Lorenzo, you there?"

My heart skipped a beat.

I recognised the voice.

"William," I growled and got to my feet.

The *San Felipe* had returned.

It was just thirty yards from the stern of the *San Mateo*, having warped back as the tide ebbed and the wind died down. I found a sword on a dying immortal Spaniard and cut the man's head off. It was sharp.

I went aft to the main deck and there found Walt and two of my men crouching low.

"Richard!" Walt managed. "Jesus Christ and all His saints, I thought you were dead."

His face was a bloody mess and his left eye was gone but his mouth and skull at least appeared partly healed beneath the caked red-brown filth covering his skin.

"It is William," I said, nodding at the ship standing off behind ours.

"Thought so," Walt said. "You owe me fifty sovereigns."

"Are you well?" I asked.

He nodded, though he looked terrible. "Me and the boys been finishing off the Spaniards. There's a lot of them. Tough bastards."

"There's three hundred more on William's ship."

My men slumped and Walt shook his head. "We're buggered then."

"It appears so."

"You killed Vega at least?" Walt asked and I nodded. "Ah, that's something, anyway. What do we do?"

I looked around. "William can't see us here, he's the other side of the sterncastle."

"You mean we should hide?" Walt said, and the other two men looked half hopeful before Walt continued and dashed their hopes. "No point, is there. When they search the ship, they'll find us and I don't fancy dying like a rat being dragged from a hidey hole. Right boys?"

They stared, wild-eyed, and nodded.

"Very well," I said. "We shall lie in wait for the boarding parties and kill them until we are overwhelmed."

Walt grinned, his face like a hideous mask, and he clapped the shoulder of the man beside him. "What do you say, boys?"

"Aye," the older of them said. "Aye, we'll kill them."

"You'll send my pay to my mother?" the other asked. "When you and Richard don't come back either, she'll still get the—"

"Don't worry, son," Walt said, smiling. "My mate Stephen will take care of her. All will be done proper."

"Oh," he said, smiling. "That's alright, then."

"Good lad."

There were still wounded men here and there, groaning and I thought we should finish them off first. Otherwise, with a bellyful of blood they would be back to strength again. We spread out to cut the throats of every soldier we could find. Walt went below to find any who were half burned and I, keeping low, went up to the command deck which was littered with corpses.

Martin lay on his side, half curled up and covered in blood and soot from a fire. The hair on the side of his head was burned off and the skin on half of his face was red and shiny. His knee was ruined, shattered and bleeding.

He was still alive.

"Martin!" I hissed, sliding over to him.

He breathed rapidly and his face was grey. His eyes met mine but they were unfocused.

"Here, lad, drink this." I slit my wrist and held it to his mouth.

Clamping his lips together, he jerked his head back. "No," he managed.

"Come on, you fool," I whispered, "you'll die."

"No, no," he said. "Don't want it."

"You would rather die than be one of us?" I asked, astonished.

"Take my chances," he replied, almost panting.

"You will not live," I said.

A cry came from the *San Felipe* astern of us and Martin smiled. "You neither."

"No," I said and patted his face. "You have been a good man, Martin. I wish... I wish things had been different for you. Rest now, son. Rest easy."

He nodded and closed his eyes.

I stood and walked aft. Though I had planned to kill them when they came on board, I could not resist. William was there and I had to face him one last time before I died. Voices called out from the other ship and I went to meet them.

The *San Felipe* was as enormous as the *San Mateo* and was also severely damaged from the battle. We had blasted the hell out of them, killing many of the crew and severely limiting their sailing ability. But still it thronged with sailors and soldiers and they crowded the decks and rigging, heaving on the cables that shifted them into place and calling for survivors. It inched closer, pulling themselves astern of our ship and our galleon shifted on the bank, coming more upright. There were two boats in the water ahead of the galleon, helping to tow it against the wind and to keep it from grounding.

William called for Vega again just as I stepped up to the taffrail. "Lorenzo, come out now, if you are—"

He stood at the larboard forecastle rail with men either side of him. He was dressed in a red doublet with billowing, quilted sleeves and a large black hat with great feathers on one side fluttering wildly in the wind. A powerful lord in gold and silver, with a magnificent sword at his side. Even with the lamps on their ship and the smouldering fires on ours, it was hard to see his face in the darkness but I fancied I could just about make out the furrowed confusion upon it, quickly replaced by an expression of fury.

"Richard!"

I smiled and raised my voice over the wind and waves. "Hello, William."

Some of William's men muttered, agitated by my use of English. A soldier raised his arquebus and William snapped at him to lower it.

"You are alone, Richard?"

"Vega is dead. So are all your other men."

They cursed and shouted but William forced them into silence with a look. "How many men do you have?"

I smiled. "Come over and find out."

By way of an answer, he turned and spoke to his crew. Lanterns were lit or brought forward to help them see onto my ship. At the same time, others threw grapples across the gap and three of the hooks clung to the taffrail. The cables were pulled tight and the San Felipe inched closer while men with lead lines sounded the depth below. The deck shifted beneath my feet as the force of their ship pulled us back a couple of feet and righted further upon the sandbank. With the tide turning, we might find ourselves floated off. But I doubted whether I would live long enough to see the high tide.

"It was you on that galleon, leading the squadron that attacked us," William called.

"I defeated you," I said and then repeated it in Spanish.

He scowled, holding his arms out. "Look again, Richard. You will soon be under my boot."

I inspected my borrowed sword. It should serve well enough. "Fight me," I replied. "Come across and fight me, you coward."

For a moment, perhaps, he was tempted and his hand drifted to the ornate hilt of his sword. But he shook his head.

"Why should I fight you?" he said. "When I can have my soldiers shoot you down from here." He indicated the arquebusiers lining the rails.

I switched to Spanish to answer him. "If you have any honour, you will fight me yourself! Decline and you shall forever be a coward, a dog, a craven, spineless worm!"

He laughed and answered in English. "You mean to shame me? How can you not know I care nothing for such nonsense? No matter what you say now, soon you will die while I will live on."

"I would rather die with honour than live with shame!"

William nodded. "And that is why you have lost."

"You are the one who has lost!" I shouted. "Your invasion is defeated. Your great fleet flees, leaving your broken ships behind. You have failed!"

"Yet I live. And will return. And without you, England shall be mine."

I pounded a fist on the taffrail. "Fight me, you damned coward!"

"Before I kill you, Richard, know that I will now hunt down and destroy every one of your men, wherever they may be."

I scoffed and spat. "You have attempted it and failed these many centuries. You always will."

"I never made it my duty to destroy you or your pathetic little brood. I could have killed them whenever I wished. Now I shall!"

I forced a laugh. "The depth of your self-delusion is matched only by your evil, William. I have bested you for centuries!"

He was close now and I saw his smile turn to dead eyed hatred. "No more than a thorn in my side, brother. But it is time to remove you."

Turning to his soldiers, he barked an order and they raised their arquebuses. I dived flat to the deck as they fired and the taffrail was hammered to bits and I crawled away just as their swivel guns blasted the deck with fist sized shot.

The firing stopped as abruptly as it had begun. Shouts of warning rose from the other ship.

In the distance, a gun fired. A cannonball smashed into William's *San Felipe*.

I got to one knee and saw the panic on the galleon astern of us. Sailors hacked at the cables tying their ship to mine, the gunners swivelled their weapons forward and William's soldiers rushed to assemble on her decks.

Another gun sounded and I peered into the darkness where a galleon bore down on us in the moonlight.

The *Revenge* had come.

"Drake!" I roared, shouting to my men, shouting to the enemy, to William, to God. "Drake has come!"

The *Revenge* came on hard, heeling over and firing the bow chasers from close range, smashing into the already-damaged *San Felipe*.

William stood at the rail, glaring at me with pure hatred for a moment before roaring at his men. As they came to him, he snatched an arquebus from one and aimed it at me across the water. Before he could fire, a cannonball ripped through the ship where he and his men were standing and there was a cloud of splinters and blood flying through the air.

My heart raced. Had he been killed? Had he avoided the shot? The galleon was floating off, the bow turning out to sea away from me and the *Revenge* slowed and turned with it, bringing the forward guns to bear and firing directly abeam into the flank of the ship, ripping through her lower decks. It twisted and made off, sails coming down and the men in the boats pulling frantically to get away from the devastation. By then the swivel guns and arquebuses on the *Revenge* were also firing, killing the soldiers and crew on the decks of the *San Felipe*. They were taking such a pounding I saw men leaping into the cold water and striking out for unseen shore or for the boats, the choppy waves throwing them up and down.

Walt and the others came up behind me, grinning like madmen and we waved at the *Revenge* as it passed us, roaring our thanks and praise. The pinnace came behind, with Lieutenant Bowden standing beside the lantern, raising a hand to us.

"Bowden found Drake," I said to Walt over the din of the guns. "God save that man."

"But William's getting away again," Walt said. "Just like I said he—"

The *San Felipe* exploded.

Her powder ignited and half the ship was blown apart, while the other half turned into an inferno.

The immortals were killed outright, or burned, or drowned in the ocean. I could scarcely believe my eyes but it was undeniable.

William was dead.

23

Death

1588 - 1603

THE WIND KEPT UP and blew the Armada east, beyond the Dover-Calais Strait and away from Parma's army in the Low Countries. The Spanish fleet turned into the North Sea and ran before the relentless winds up the east coast of England. Most of our fleet followed them closely all the way while one squadron stayed to block Parma's army from crossing.

The Armada looked for ports along our coast they might take but with our fleet at their heels they would find themselves battered to pieces if they attempted it. No doubt they prayed for the wind to change direction but day after day it held and they could do nothing but run on up to Scotland and then travel west around the British Isles. From there, they would sail down the west coast of Ireland and back home to Spain. Many would be lost along the way.

Our fleet, having protected the entire south and east coasts of England, put in at the Firth of Forth and let them go.

And thanks to God we had defeated them at sea so thoroughly, for our armies had not managed to fully assemble in time to meet an invasion. When the Armada was spotted, Dudley had summoned the yeomen from across Southern England to Tilbury to form into a great army that would fight off Parma's and Medina Sidonia's veterans outside London.

They were slow about it. Not even the men of Essex, where Tilbury was located, arrived for four days and then it was just four thousand foot and a few hundred horse to add to a thousand arquebusiers sent from London. William's immortals alone could have taken them in the field, let alone the might of the Spanish veterans. Gradually, thousands more came in and London itself was protected by ten thousand militia who could have managed a stout defence of the walls. But all in all, it was a closer run thing than I had ever imagined.

"The whole city was up in arms," Stephen said when we met him outside Whitehall Palace two days later. "It was not safe to be out on the streets. Goodie has foolishly taken to wearing Catalina's cross around her neck and a gang of lads saw it and accused her of being not only a Catholic but a Spaniard. Goodie thrashed the bastards and has been armed with a cudgel ever since, just in case."

Walt's head whipped up. "Goodie's all right, is she?"

"She's fine, Walter, but the oafs who attacked her are not. Bloody fools. I swear, it is easier to find flocks of white crows than one Englishman who loves a foreigner."

"And quite right we are, too," Walt snapped, "for if we were not so disposed, we would have today found ourselves overrun by those bloody foreigners, would we not?"

Stephen rolled his eyes. "Anyway, Richard, you must go to see the Queen. The vice-admirals and sea captains are quite sucking up all the royal attention. She will not know it was we who gave her this victory if you are not there."

"William is dead, Stephen," I replied. "What does it matter who the Queen favours? But I shall go, if only to retrieve Eva. Poor woman has suffered long enough."

"I'll come with you," Walt said, grinning.

"Not until you get a patch to cover that missing eye."

Walt frowned, touching his face. "It's that bad, is it?"

The Palace was in uproar and we could get nowhere near the audience rooms or even to the inner palace and it took an age even to find a servant to bribe to carry a message to Eva. Eventually, she came out to meet us.

"I shall be glad to be gone from this place," Eva muttered. "And I will, the moment the Queen gives me leave to do so."

"Why not come home now?" I suggested. "We have no further need for her favour."

"How can you say that," she tutted. "The court is hellish but she... she is magnificent."

"Oh?" I said. "I would have thought you ready to throttle her by now."

Eva shook her head. "You should have seen her at Tilbury, where the army assembled. She rode down there where the soldiers were arrayed in ranks, thousands upon thousands of them with their pikes and arquebuses raised. Dudley and the rest were frantic with worry that one of the soldiers would try to kill her."

"Because they might be secret Catholics?"

"Precisely so. Also, that they may be agents who had infiltrated the regiments."

"A fair concern."

"Certainly, and so I said my piece. But she would listen to none of us. All I could do was remain as close as possible when she went amongst them. Dudley on one side, Devereaux on the other, Ormonde bearing the Sword of State before her and Sir John Norris behind. I was behind him and watching everywhere for danger. And yet... the soldiers were cheering her. You should have heard it, Richard. Thousands cheering, roaring, and weeping to see her riding through them on a great white gelding in her white velvet and silver cuirass, beautifully embossed. She bore in her hand a silver truncheon chased in gold and she was bareheaded but her hair decorated with great white plumes and pearls and diamonds."

"Sounds magnificent."

"It is difficult to convey to you the emotion that was in the air, Richard. They cried out blessings, their everlasting devotion, their willingness to die for her. Then there was a review, the men marching past a platform where we stood above them, and then the cavalry paraded, and all assembled again to salute her. She gave a short speech and there was not a man among them I am sure who was not deeply moved. Deeply indeed."

"What did she say?"

"Oh, I am sure I cannot recall."

"You have a faultless memory, Eva."

She sighed. "I don't recall precisely but my loving people, she said, we have been urged to keep away from armed multitudes, for fear of treachery. And that was certainly true, Richard, we had urged her not to expose herself to danger. She continued to say to the soldiers that she would never distrust her faithful and loving people. They cheered that. Let *tyrants* fear, she said. I have always put my trust in the loyal hearts and good will of my subjects. So I am come here to live or die amongst you all and to lay down for my God and for my kingdom and for my people, my honour and my blood, even in the dust."

I smiled. "She would, too. I bet they cheered for that."

"For some time, they cheered," Eva said. "And she carried on when they fell once more to a hush. I know I have the body of a weak and feeble woman, but I have the heart and stomach of a king, and of a king of England too. And think foul scorn that Parma or Spain, or any prince of Europe should dare to invade the borders of my realm. Rather than submit, I myself will take up arms, I myself will be your general in the field." Eva's eyes had taken on a faraway look. "It went on like that. There was ever such a roar."

"Not a bad speech. Shame there was no battle to follow it."

Eva smiled. "I am overjoyed to hear you defeated them at sea. And... I was unsure that I decoded Stephen's letter properly. Did..." She smiled and lowered her voice. "Did you truly kill him?"

I did not return her smile. "I never found his body."

"But he is dead?"

"Thanks to Drake, William's galleon was destroyed. The burned wreck ran aground and we searched it. Bodies were pulled from the waves and a few immortals yet lived. Until we killed them. William was not one of them. Bodies washed up on the beaches. We took a boat along the shore and looked for him. He was not there. Adams was, thank Christ, and we revived him in time. But no William."

"So his body sank beneath the waves? Or was broken to pieces?"

"Perhaps."

Her face fell. "Stephen conveyed no doubt." She sighed. "I understand that you wanted him to die by your own hand. And so you are unsatisfied by such a victory."

"If he is truly dead, I shall be satisfied." I smiled. "In time."

She patted my knee. "Shall I take you to Elizabeth? I am sure she will find time for you shortly."

"No, no. I must go and see to Martin. He may be dead already but the physician has been summoned so there is yet hope."

"Why have you not turned him?"

"He refused."

"How is Walt? His injury was severe?"

"And permanent. He is now missing an eye."

"God's bones, poor Walt. Is he very angry?"

"It does not seem to bother him in the least."

"Oh dear, he must be heartbroken. Poor Walter. He will need you to take care of him."

"I just said he was fine, woman."

She sighed, shaking her head. "I must come home soon."

I took her hand. "You must."

Leaving Eva at the Palace, Walt and I made our way back to the house off the Strand. The city was in a state of uproarious cheer and it was a delight to see men grinning everywhere we went. It seemed the whole city was drunk and they would stay that way for days yet.

"I'll leave you here, Richard," Walt said, looking up the road at the city.

"You are not coming into the house?" I asked. "You have not been home at all so far, where can you be going?"

He shrugged. "You know how it is after a battle. Got a hankering for a piece in Pie-corner. If the whores have any strength left, that is. Lot of lusty sailors about this day, I'll warrant, but I'll find a strumpet somewhere."

"Goodie was asking after you. Don't you want to see her?"

Walt laughed, shaking his head, scuffing his feet on the dirt. "She ain't like to want to see me, is she. Not like this."

"I am sure Goodie will not mind about your eye, Walt," I said.

He hesitated and then forced a laugh. "I'm sure she'll prefer looking at your face, not this wreckage. But worry not. Worry not for me, Richard."

I smiled. "If she wanted you for your looks, she never would have been interested in the first place. Look, you almost died a couple days ago, what are you waiting for?"

He grunted and nodded, looking at the floor. "Might be I'll just go for a stroll before I come home. Got to fetch something from someone." With that, he made off through the crowds toward the city.

When I reached the house, the physician was just taking his leave but I stopped him in the parlour before he could get his hat on.

"Sir, how fares Martin?"

His expression was grave indeed. "The corruption has

returned. I am fetching my assistant and my instruments and I shall return directly. His leg shall have to come off." He peered at me. "It should have come off already, sir."

"And that will save him?"

The physician grunted. "The corruption is already above the knee. That corruption may now be in his blood and if so, it is already too late."

"What can I do?"

"You should pray. All his friends must pray. But have faith, sir, we shall do everything that may be done." He put on his hat, patted my arm and made his way out to the street.

I took the stairs two at a time up to Martin's bedchamber. It was dim, the curtains closed. Stephen was there at the foot of the bed, his forehead furrowed, and hands clasped. Martin writhed beneath the sheets, drenched in sweat and the room reeked of fetid air and pus and death.

"Thank God you have returned," Stephen said. "The physician—"

"I saw him downstairs."

"Then you know it is time. Come, he was brave to refuse you before but now it is time. Give him your blood."

I sat on the bed and stroked Martin's hair. It was drenched. Goodie came in carrying fresh water and clean linen and I moved aside while she washed Martin's face, neck and chest and spoke kind, gentle words as she did so. Her ministrations soothed him and he slept more soundly.

"What are you waiting for?" Stephen said. "You can cure him. So cure him."

"He was very clear about his wishes," I said.

"But he will die."

"It is his choice."

Stephen pounded a fist into his palm. "But there is no reason to it. No reason at all."

Goodie tutted. "Keep your voice down, Stephen. And certainly there's no *reason* to it. He made a moral choice. Richard is right. We must honour it."

"But *you* chose eternal life, Goodie!" Stephen said to her. "Why deny it to him?"

Goodie sighed, patting Martin's forehead with a cool, damp cloth. "If he dies, he goes on to eternal life with God."

Stephen threw up his hands. "It is not the same thing!"

I put my arm around Stephen's shoulder and pulled him to me and then I wrapped both my hands around him and held him tight. He resisted for a moment before giving in. "The physician shall take his leg," I said, releasing Stephen. "And we shall pray for him."

He nodded, wiping his eyes. "He is the best physician in London," Stephen muttered. "Which is to say the best in England."

I joined Goodie at the sideboard where she wrung out cloths in a bowl and I poured in more water from the ewer. "Walter is avoiding you."

She raised her eyebrows. "Something I done?"

"It is my belief that he is ashamed of his disfigurement."

"Just his eye that he lost, was it?" She squeezed a cloth and laid it on the table with the others.

"Missing a few teeth on one side, too."

"Very deformed, is he?"

"Hardly more than he already was," I quipped.

"Oh!" Goodie said and thumped me on the arm. "He was the handsomest man in England." She thumped me once again for good measure. "But why should he care what I think?"

"I think he cares very much indeed," I said.

She said nothing but I saw her smiling as she worked.

The door banged downstairs and Goodie and I went down to meet the physician only to find that it was in fact Walt who had come rushing back, slightly out of breath. He saw us descending the stair and flinched, turned to flee but then stood his ground as we came down to the hall.

"Has something happened?" I asked him.

"Ah, no. No, all's well," Walt said, looking at the floor and turning his bad eye away from Goodie. It was then I noticed he clutched a small wooden box to his chest so tightly that his knuckles were white. "Just thought I might come have a word with Goodie. Well, not a word as such. That is to say, I would like to speak but that ain't what I..."

"What in the world you blathering about, Walter?" Goodie asked, her hands on her hips.

He shuffled his feet and then thrust the box at her. "Got you a gift, Edith."

She stared at him for a moment before slowly taking the box. "What's the special occasion?" she asked as she opened it.

"I know it's foolish, it's foolish, what with Martin how he is but I had it made so long ago and I kept almost giving it you but it ain't ever the right time as there's always something bad happening and then the other day I almost died and I thought, well, I thought..."

"Oh!" Goodie said, her voice catching as she lifted from the box a large and beautiful gold pendant sparkling with purple and transparent precious stones. "What's this for?"

Walt scuffed his feet. "Just a gift, Edith. Not for anything."

She peered at him, eyes twinkling. "Amethysts, is it, Walter? These guard against drunkenness, do they not? You trying to tell me I'm a sot?"

Walt gaped, horrified. "Christ, no! The goldsmith said they promote harmony and good understanding."

"Oh, that what we need, is it?" Goodie said. "And what are the diamonds for?"

Walt sniffed. "It's... it's the stone of love, ain't it?"

She threw her arms about his neck and pulled him down to plant a kiss upon his lips. "Let me look at you," she said, turning his head and touching his face. "Oh, it is nothing at all." She kissed his eye and turned to me. "And what are you staring at, you ruttish lout?"

I started and heading back upstairs. "Ah, yes. Pardon me."

Walter and Goodie were married that spring. It was a gay affair indeed, with an enormous number of friends in attendance and much feasting, dancing, and drinking. I had never seen Walt look so happy.

And thanks be to God, one of the honoured wedding guests was a tall, thin, one-legged London lawyer named Martin Hawthorn. Not whole and never quite in full health again but mortal and contented. That very year he married a pious young woman and later fathered four sons and three daughters. The Hawthorn line continued to thrive.

***

Francis Drake was the greatest living Englishman and was famous across the world. As far as Christendom was concerned, Drake had defeated the Armada single-handedly. The year after the Armada, Drake led our fleet to attack Spain. It did not go well and thousands of men were lost to disease.

I took my own men into the Low Countries to look for William or any of his surviving men. We could find no sign of him, though we looked for many months. There was an air of chaos across that land due to the years of battles and sieges and thousands of soldiers marching and camping. We found tales of people who had been mysteriously murdered or gone missing but they could just as well have been victims of deserting soldiers or mortal sailors. A young Frisian woman had gone missing the day after the battle after she went to pick whelks and dig clams from the shore but her family guessed she had been caught by the tide or had run off with a man. Her trail, like all the others, led nowhere and I took the men home, beginning to hope William was truly dead after all.

Drake and I grew apart while he continued his war against Spain. I declined to join him. It was my fight no longer and neither did I have a use for Drake so I said nothing as he launched a new campaign against New Spain but the New World was wise to him now and they had invested in massive forts and fleets that could defend against his methods of attack. The next generation had caught up with his methods and had neutralised the threat that he had once posed.

Years later, we sat in our parlour together and discussed Order business. We knew there had to be stray immortals to catch in England and elsewhere and Eva and Stephen continued their work, though without the urgency they once had.

"You must deal with Drake," Stephen said. "He cannot go on as he is, running wild, waging a private war against Spain."

"He is doing no harm to England," I replied.

Eva cleared her throat and leaned forward. "He is failing. His failures embarrass us."

"You know that containing him will prove impossible. He must be at sea and I have no desire to be with him."

Eva and Stephen exchanged a look and Eva spoke. "I'm sorry to say it aloud but we expected that he would be killed in New Spain. Instead, he goes on, coming back and forth to England every season with a handful of small prizes and lists of dead English mariners."

"He causes the White Dagger no trouble. I'm in no hurry to take action against him."

"He is gone rogue and uncontrolled," Stephen snapped. "And that should be reason enough."

I sighed and sat back. "Do I still need loyalty?" I asked them. "From any of you?" They looked steadily back at me and I knew they had considered that very thing. "Now that William may be dead... is there any need for the Order of the White Dagger?"

"We did not get them all, we could not have done," Stephen said.

"I agree with Stephen," Eva said quickly. "William is dead but there may be dozens more out there. We need the Order to continue until we are sure."

"And then there is Priskos," Stephen said. "We must build our strength to assault him and his sons. Vlad Dracula is out there somewhere with his monks and we must ensure they are not doing evil. And so the Order must continue to find rogue immortals. Well, we know where one rogue immortal is. We must do what we are sworn to do."

"Yes, yes," I said. "It all sounds well reasoned."

Stephen spoke quickly. "You do not wish to harm Drake because you feel you owe him for saving you. And for killing William."

I sighed. "Do you know, I turned Drake into an immortal after we ambushed that great treasure with the help of those *cimarrones*, the escaped slaves. We had to set sail for England with haste before the Spanish galleons caught our little ships but Drake invited the leader of the *cimarrones* and two more of the senior Negroes into our hold before we went and he told them to choose anything they wished for themselves as a reward. These men were chiefs of mud and straw, you understand, with not more than a hundred souls in their village. Drake was pulling out bolts of bright silks and crying that they should take as many colours as they had wives." I laughed to recall it. "Yards and yards of the finest silk, it was absurdly generous. But the chief was not paying attention. We looked at him and he held aloft Drake's golden scimitar. We took it off a Spanish captain who was transporting it for a noble governor. You should have seen it. The entire scabbard was gold and encrusted with such jewels that even in the gloom it shone. Drake had fallen in love with it on sight. I should have seen then his boundless ambition for he had meant to wear it at Elizabeth's court where even there it would be the most wondrous object in the room, or even in the whole palace. I was stunned that Pedro had even dared to touch it but then he drew its perfect, shining blade."

"I'm surprised you didn't run him through in fear!" Stephen said.

I smiled. "Pedro was our comrade. Drake had befriended him and his people and we had won the gold together. Still, though, it was absurd for him to ask for such a thing as his reward. It was worth more than his village. More than a hundred of his villages. And do you know what Drake said? He said, ah, a worthy gift for a valuable friend."

Stephen gaped. "He gave it to him? Why?"

I laughed. "Precisely what I asked him. He shrugged and said that generosity was good for the soul."

Stephen frowned. "I don't understand your point. What are you saying?"

"I'm saying... I don't know."

Eva smiled. "You're saying he's your friend."

"But for how long?" Stephen said. "How can we trust him to keep our secrets? How long before he turns on us in some way? You know it is probable."

Eva leaned across the table. "However you feel, something must be done with him, Richard."

I rubbed my face. "And I was having ever such a nice dinner."

They shifted in their seats and cleared their throats and I knew they had more bad news for me.

"There is something else I must say," Stephen said, pulling at his collar and glancing at the doorway as if making ready to run. "And I ask for your forgiveness in advance."

"Dear God," I replied, putting my eating knife down. "What the hell have you done?"

He shook as he spoke and addressed a plate of boiled eels between us on the table. "It has been a slow development and not without considerable thought and no little prayer on my part and much reading. Very much reading. And prayer, as I have said. But after many years of deliberation I must now admit to you openly that I have... embraced the new faith."

I leaned back and let out the breath I had been holding. "Christ Almighty, Stephen, is that all? Jesus wept, you villain, the way you were speaking I thought you were about to admit to something terrible." I shook my head and scooped up a few rounds of eels. "It is not so surprising, truth be told."

"You mean... you're not angry?"

I chewed my eels, crunching the soft spines. "All that matters, Stephen, is that we are Englishmen and we are brothers of the White Dagger."

He smiled broadly and glanced at Eva.

"Richard," she began.

"Oh, not you, too!"

By the time I organised a ship, a crew, and set out for New Spain in search of Drake it was a little late in the year for the crossing. But we weathered it well enough and soon followed Drake's trail from port to port around the West Indies. After three weeks we found his fleet anchored off the island of Escudo, not far from Nombre de Dios. The crew ran up a flag warning that they were diseased and shouted the same news across the waters to us.

"None may come across to their fleet with me," I said to my

own crew when we found them. "I shall row myself across."

Taking the boat from my ship to Drake's flagship, the *Defiance*, I found his crew dysenteric and in a deep depression. They told me how Drake had made yet another assault by land on Panama itself, charging out of the forest to attack the outer forts of the city with hundreds of veteran Englishmen. But this time the men had found the Spanish prepared behind strong walls and they had failed, returning with seventy men lost to enemy fire in the assault and the survivors riddled with a ghastly jungle disease.

"Where is the admiral?" I asked and they nodded aft.

"Where he always is."

I knocked and, finding no answer, let myself in. It was dark and fetid in his cabin. Drake lay on his bunk, an empty cup rolling back and forth in the swaying of the ship in the swell.

"Francis," I said.

He sat up, wiping his mouth. "Richard? Am I gone mad, is it truly you? How are you here? Why are you come?"

"Are you ill of your body, Francis? Is it the blood sickness?"

He scoffed, snatched up his cup from the deck and dragged himself to his feet. At his desk he poured more wine. "The sickness of failure, that is all. The illness is of the soul."

"You speak of your failure to conquer the Americas with this small squadron?"

"I see you came all the way from England to mock me."

Stepping closer to his desk, I looked at his charts and writings. "Why are you here, Francis?"

Drake stared. "Why? How can you ask me that? I am making war on our enemy. It seems hardly any Englishman but me is doing his duty."

"Indeed, it seems this war is being waged by you alone."

"If you mean to criticise me, Richard, then do it openly."

"Francis, you may live another century or even more. For how long do you intend to wage this war?"

"As long as it takes."

"For what?"

Drake scoffed and stomped away across his cabin. "I know how you love the Spanish, I know. You're a Catholic to your core. You would like me to leave your dear friends alone but I shall not."

"My regard for them is not dependant on the form of their faith, it never was. They are an admirable people and I know you agree with that much. And I do admit I never wished to fight them and only did so to get at my true enemy and to defend England. Both reasons no longer stand and they have not done since that night when you saved my life. Francis, don't you also wish to stop fighting them?"

He ignored me.

I crossed to the aft door to the gallery and opened it up, throwing light and fresh air into the cabin. "You are living in a state of putrefaction."

He flinched and I saw his untended beard and red-rimmed eyes. "Close the door, I cannot bear the light. This cursed sun, it never ceases to burn my eyes, my skin."

"I never thought to see you so changed."

He sneered. "Aye, and you are the one who changed me. Once, I was a man. Now, I am this thing." He slapped his chest." I should have died. After we smashed the Armada, I should have died then, in my glory. That was the peak of my life, a lofty mountain and all has been running downhill since. Down into defeat and ignominy."

"It is merely that the Indies have changed since your youth."

"Changed!" he cried, waving his cup in the air. "Changed is right, I never thought any place could be so changed. As it were from a pleasant arbour into a desert wilderness. Even the wind and weather is now stormy and blusterous as never it was before."

"The world changes, Francis. I have learned that, if I have learned nothing else. It changes with the years so that the world you once knew is lost and then it is lost again. Kings are born, they rule, they die. Even the Church. A Church of England, governed by an English queen." I shook my head. "But that is the nature of life. Chaos is ever at the edge of our civilisation, like a rabid dog gnawing away and threatening to tear everything loose, so that order is lost and the law unmade. It is like the forests here, the wild green life and the pestilential airs that consume everything if it is not kept at bay. It is our greatest duty to preserve our people and our kingdom, even if they are the ones trying to tear it apart. We must uphold and to conserve everything that we can because no matter how hard we fight, we *always* shall lose this battle or that. Civilisation is a precious and delicate thing and no matter what changes beneath us we must hold fast to that which is most dear."

He frowned. "God?"

"England, Francis! Our people. Their safety, their prosperity, their happiness is all that matters. Above all, their preservation in the face of those that would destroy us, whoever they are."

"But that is just it, Richard! That is the truth of it! England has no more need of me. No matter how hard I try, I find I can win her no more battles. I am of no use." He eyed the sword at my side, nodding. "That is why you have come. I knew I would see this day. You warned me. Loyalty above all to the Order of the White Dagger. Obedience or death. And I have ignored you utterly these last... five years, is it?"

"Seven, since last we spoke."

He nodded to himself. "Will you murder my men, also? They still love me, you know, even now."

I stepped closer. "All England loves you. And they always will. But it is time for Francis Drake to die."

He turned to look at the light streaming in from the open door. The blue-green sea flickered and shone. "Bury me here, will you. In deep water." He drank off his cup. "You will let me pray, won't you?"

Two days later, the fleet anchored nearby at Puerto Bello. There was a sermon on the Defiance, delivered before the captains, the senior offices, and some of the longest serving crew, and the lead coffin of Admiral Sir Francis Drake was gently lowered into the sea to the doleful notes of trumpets and the thunder of scores of guns.

I stood on the deck of my ship, watching from a distance. "A fine send-off," I said.

"It doesn't seem right," Francis said beside me, scowling. "And someone will speak the truth. Sailors can't keep their mouths shut, you know."

"It matters not," I replied. "Men will say Francis Drake was a demon, or a sorcerer of blood magic, or a witch. Men will say you yet live and perhaps even that one day you will return. But it matters not. Stay away from England, from New Spain and from the ports of Europe for just twenty or thirty years and you may return to the sea once more. You know, there is much talk of creating English colonies in the north of the Americas, can you imagine that? Perhaps you could help to keep them safe, or even help to rule them. Plenty of work for a man of your ability."

"What about your work? What about the White Dagger? You'll need a captain, perhaps?"

"Indeed we will. Especially with the world growing so large. If there are immortals still to hunt, we shall do so together. And if not, you can be a pirate again. If you like."

"Twenty or thirty years in hiding first," he said, almost wailing. "A lifetime."

"Indeed, and it can be a very pleasant lifetime, if you are willing to make it so. You can find some pretty Protestant wife and live happily."

"But Geneva of all places, Richard. Why must it be Geneva? So far from the sea."

I smiled. "Well, that is precisely the point. God willing, few will recognise you there. And, you know, Francis, Geneva has a very large lake to sail on."

***

"The Queen has sent you a letter," Eva said one morning a few years later, coming into my chamber.

"To me directly? What does it say?"

Eva held it out to me. In a spidery, shaking hand was written only this.

Sir Knight.

"What do you think she wants?" I asked Eva as my servant dressed me.

"She is dying."

I nodded and went there at once and found the palace thronged with lords, gentlemen, and their servants. When I saw the crowds, I wondered if she had already died but that was not it. Everyone knew she was suffering and they all knew they stood at the edge of the end of an era. What would come next, who would be crowned her successor? Would it be her nearest royal relative, King James of Scotland? Everyone thought so but nothing was certain.

A servant appeared at my elbow. "Mister Ashbury?"

I followed him to the Queen's private chambers and was eventually shown in. She reclined on a low chair, surrounded by pillows, breathing heavily. Her resplendent corset had been replaced by a plainer, wider one and the plumes and collars and pearls removed. Still, her mask of white remained and she gazed out at me with heavily lidded eyes.

"Your Majesty," I said and bowed low and long.

"Get out," she said and her servants left us but for one or two at the edges of her chamber. The Queen looked me up and down. "It sickens me to see you. Eternally beautiful. It sickens me. But not as much, I do not doubt, as the sight of me sickens you, sir."

"Elizabeth, I am happy to see—"

"Do not speak it, I hear such courtly deceit that I need no more as long as I live. Which, thanks to God, shall not be too long."

"Surely, you are well, my lady, for you have strength enough to rule."

"My rule is all but over. Still, my work is done. England is well."

"Better than she ever was in all my days."

"Flattery."

"It is true."

"Well, then," she said, a smile on her thin, painted lips. "And I am told that your work is done also. Your great enemy defeated. Your secret society rendered useless."

"He is dead, yes indeed. And yet there are some of his progeny remaining, we feel. Here and there. We shall find them and end them also."

She closed her eyes for a moment and I thought she had fallen asleep. But then she spoke. "All my friends are dead and soon I shall be also. I feel it inside me and I know it, as well as I know anything. Do you know Cecil died? Of course you do. His son serves me now. He is not the father, you know. But then I am not the Queen. Not the one his father served, at the least. I am alone."

"I am here, Elizabeth."

"Yes, you are here before my eyes with your ageless vitality to break my heart. But this is the last time I shall see you. I am commanding you now to not return. I could not bear you to see me in my deathbed, withered and raving and consumed. Give me your word."

"You have it. And anything else in my power."

She licked her wrinkled lips. "I hear you went to my Robert before he died. Did you argue with him again?"

I smiled. "I apologised to him. He had gone to take the waters at Buxton in the hope that they would restore him. I knelt by his bed and told him that I understood now what he had meant, so many years ago and asked him to forgive my pridefulness."

Narrowing her eyes, I caught a glimpse of her old shrewdness. "What is it you now understood?"

"He told me once that we must have faith in our friends. And that trust is earned due to a man's actions. I know now that being a Catholic or a Protestant does not make a man, or a woman. But their actions alone. For so long I was terrified for the prospect of a Protestant England but now I see the truth. They are English first and foremost, just as they always were, whatever else they are. And so I have faith in England again, just as he was trying to tell me."

"A lesson I learned long ago." She smiled. "And what did he say to that?"

"He asked me to look after you for the rest of your days. And to look after England always."

"My dear one," she muttered. There were tears in her eyes. It was clear that she had never loved anyone as much as she had loved Robert Dudley. When she spoke, her voice was soft and breaking. "Now, Sir Knight, kiss me for the last time." She held out her hand. I took it, the bones small beneath her papery skin, and kissed her.

"Elizabeth," I said, releasing her.

"Say no more, sir. Leave me be. Go and live. Live forever."

The Queen faded over many months before dying in her sleep, surrounded by her ladies with the rain pattering on the window, at three o'clock in the morning on the 24th of March 1603.

Her funeral was as grand and heartfelt as any there ever was. The procession to Westminster Abbey was solemn indeed, following her hearse were a thousand black-clad lords, councillors, gentlemen, courtiers and servants, as well as hundreds of the poor. Along the route fluttered bright banners while trumpeters played to herald her passing. Thousands upon thousands lined the way, multitudes in the streets, windows, leads and gutters, and when her coffin passed the crowds groaned and cried out and wept. The people mourned her more than any sovereign I had seen before or was to see since.

So ended the last of the Tudors.

Her successor was indeed James VI of Scotland, who became James I of England. I never knew him but I did not like him. The successes of his reign were due to the trajectory that Elizabeth's had set it on, and the failures of it were all his own.

I spent the following years finding hidden immortals here and there, relics of William's plots. One I found hiding amongst a company of London players called the King's Men. Another rumour I chased all the way across Christendom to Hungary where a countess was rumoured to bathe in a bath of virgin's blood. A few years after that I pursued a Barbary pirate who raided our shores and sold thousands of English men and women into barbaric slavery.

Soon, all that remained was the final task of killing my immortal grandfather who, as far as I knew, yet resided in the Black Forest. But I found myself unwilling to take up that task. If anything, I wished to travel there again to speak to him, and to ask him about his past and his origins but I did not do that either. Not yet.

Gradually I began to accept the truth that William truly was dead and gone. I accepted also that I would never have the satisfaction of killing him by my own hand but the fact was he had been blasted to pieces that night years before and the world was free of him. Finally, my oath had been fulfilled.

Then, he struck.

After the Armada, William had been washed up far along the coast close to death and when a young Frisian woman had come to scavenge his corpse, he had consumed her and fled into Europe. As he ever did, he bided his time as he grew in strength before returning to deliver the hammer blow.

This time, his intention was to destroy the English crown itself. His actions would throw England into a devastating and bloody civil war which would see hundreds of thousands dead, a king beheaded, and our glorious nation brought to its knees.

But just as he had threatened that night on the deck of his galleon, he meant above all to destroy the Order of the White Dagger and to kill me once and for all.

After centuries of being the hunter, I was to become the prey.

AUTHOR'S NOTE

Richard's story continues in *Vampire Cavalier: the Immortal Knight Chronicles Book 8*

If you enjoyed *Vampire Armada* please leave a review online! Even a couple of lines saying what you liked about the story would be an enormous help and would make the series more visible to new readers.

You can find out more and get in touch with me at dandavisauthor.com

BOOKS BY DAN DAVIS

The GALACTIC ARENA Series
Science fiction

Inhuman Contact
Onca's Duty
Orb Station Zero
Earth Colony Sentinel
Outpost Omega

The IMMORTAL KNIGHT Chronicles
Historical Fantasy

Vampire Crusader
Vampire Outlaw
Vampire Khan
Vampire Knight
Vampire Heretic
Vampire Impaler
Vampire Armada

For a complete and up-to-date list of Dan's available books, visit: **http://dandavisauthor.com/books/**

Made in the USA
Las Vegas, NV
18 December 2020